LOOKING ON THE BRIGHT SIDE

"You could go out looking to hook up," Fay said.

"I'd rather sit in a bath of acid and drown myself."

"There are still some nice blokes about, you know. What about Friday . . ."

"Shut up about Friday. I'm not interested in nice blokes. I'm not interested in Friday!"

Fay gives me a strange look. "I *meant*, what about going out on Friday? Friday night? Not for guys if you're not up for it, just for a drink. You and me. We haven't had a night out in ages."

No. We look at each other quickly, and I know what she's thinking. Not since Daniel walked out. I haven't exactly been in the mood for going out. I haven't exactly had the money to spare, either.

"We don't have to spend much . . ." she adds quickly.

"It's all right. Louise gave me a bit extra last week for doing the garden."

"We can forget about being grown-up," she urges me. "Just for once."

"Will it be okay with Simon?"

"Of course it will. You know Simon. He just sits in front of the TV every night. It doesn't matter to him whether I'm there or not. Or how many kids are asleep upstairs."

So that's all right then.

And the shopping only comes to fifty dollars.

And it's stopped raining.

So that's all right, too.

Life's not too bad, is it?

Books by Sheila Norton

WOULD I LIE TO YOU?

WILL SHE OR WON'T SHE?

Published by Kensington Publishing Corporation

Would I Lie To You?

Sheila Norton

KENSINGTON BOOKS
KENSINGTON PUBLISHING CORP.
http://www.kensingtonbooks.com

KENSINGTON BOOKS are published by

Kensington Publishing Corp.
850 Third Avenue
New York, NY 10022

All Kensington titles, imprints and distributed lines are available at special quantity discounts for bulk purchases for sales promotion, premiums, fund-raising, educational or institutional use.

Special book excerpts or customized printings can also be created to fit specific needs. For details, write or phone the office of the Kensington Special Sales Manager: Kensington Publishing Corp., 850 Third Avenue, New York, NY 10022. Attn. Special Sales Department. Phone: 1-800-221-2647.

First Trade Paperback Printing: December 2005
First Mass Market Paperback Printing: November 2006
10 9 8 7 6 5 4 3 2 1

Printed in the United States of America

For all my "girl" friends, including Sue, Gwen, and Jen (from school); Lesley (from way back!); drinking mates Geraldine, Marilyn, Rebecca, Sally, Janet, and Brenda; and all the girls at work especially "The Blondes": Louise, Pat, Sandra, Lorraine, Rachel, and Carol. And so many others . . . with thanks for all the emotional support!

Acknowledgments

Thanks to Gillian and everyone at Piatkus for taking me "on board" and being so helpful and supportive.

Special thanks to Jenny, my own real-life "Beth," whose hard work on my housework has given me an extra few hours a week to write my novels!

Monday

Monday is Park Farm Close.

Every day, a different road; every day, a different type of mess. Mondays aren't bad—not as bad as Fridays, for all sorts of reasons (mostly to do with a man with too much testosterone and not enough clothes, but more about that later). Park Farm Close, on the other hand, isn't a bad place to spend a Monday morning—or any other morning, really, if you're lucky enough to live there instead of (like me) just work there.

I don't mind getting up on Monday mornings.

I don't mind it today, even though it's pouring down with rain and the sky's so black outside it looks like it's still the middle of the night instead of quarter past eight.

Quarter past eight?!

I leap out of bed with the grace of a startled young gazelle. Well, I'd like to think so, anyway, but probably more like a gorilla with gout.

"Why are you running to the bathroom? Are you going to be sick? Are you going to wet yourself?"

That's Ellie, my four-year-old daughter—obsessed

with bodily functions. Perhaps she's going to be a doctor when she grows up.

"I'm running because I've overslept!" I shout, peeling off my pajamas and throwing them on the floor as I turn on the faucet in the bathroom. "Quickly, Ellie, get dressed. We're late."

"Why are you cross, Mummy?" she asks without much interest, watching me from the bathroom door. "Why is your clock ringing? Why don't you turn it off?"

"Bloody thing!" I mutter, returning to my own room to hit the alarm clock hard on its OFF switch. "Set it for seven fifteen and it rings at eight fifteen!"

"Can I have Weetabix? Can I wear my red teddy-bear jumper? When will it stop raining, Mummy? Why does it keep raining?"

Yes, No, and I Don't Know. Let's look up the answers together, shall we?

"I don't know!" I admit, glancing at the rain pouring down the window of Ellie's bedroom, where she's now climbed onto a chair to pull back one of the yellow stripy curtains. "Perhaps the trees and flowers need a lot to drink!"

"Trees and flowers don't drink!" she retorts, giggling. "They can't hold a cup!"

"They drink through their roots," I try to explain patiently. "I'll show you how it works some time."

"Now!" she squeals, climbing off the chair. "Show me now!"

"There isn't time. Later."

There's never time. I pull on jeans, shirt, socks, shoes. Brush my hair, frown at myself in the mirror, and shrug. No time for makeup. Is there ever?

"Weetabix, Ellie. If you're quick . . . !"

* * *

She appears in the kitchen with her trousers on back to front and no socks on.

"I want Shreddies."

"You said Weetabix! Come on, I've warmed it up!"

"Shreddies. Don't like warm. Don't like Weetabix."

"Oh, Ellie, please don't be difficult. Please! And where are your socks? I put them on the bed. What are you taking to Fay's?"

I run from the kitchen to the living room, gathering up books and toys, stuffing them into Ellie's red teddy-bear backpack. She watches me, glaring, arms folded across her chest.

"Don't want to go to Fay's."

Don't start this again. Please, God, please just let it all go smoothly. Warm Weetabix, socks, a bag of toys, and off to Fay's. Without a scene—please!

"Don't *want* to go to Fay's!" she repeats, louder, fixing me with a warning grimace and stamping one bare foot. "Don't want Weetabix. *Don't want socks on!*"

Thanks, God. Thanks a bundle.

Ignoring the shrieks of Ellie's tantrum, I force her feet, minus socks, into her boots, force her rigid arms into her coat, throw the no-longer-warm Weetabix in the trash, and march her, yelling, to the car, where I strap her into her harness and start the engine, turning up the radio to equal the volume of her noise.

"I'm not listening to you, Ellie!" I shout above Westlife's crooning, and wish I could silence the voice in my head telling me that's half the problem.

"She hasn't had any breakfast," I apologize to Fay. "And she's in a horrible mood."

"*Not* in a horrible mood," sniffs Ellie, spurting fresh tears. "*You* are in a horrible mood, Mummy, horrible Mummy."

"Her socks are in her bag . . ."

"Don't want socks!"

"Go on," says Fay with a smile, taking Ellie's unwilling hand and leading her into the house. "Go on, Beth, you'll be late. See you later. Don't worry, she'll be fine when you're gone."

She'll be fine when I'm gone. Back in the car, I take a few deep breaths to control my own anger. Anger with a four-year-old for not wanting her socks on? For not wanting warm Weetabix? What's the matter with me? It was never going to be like this. When I was pregnant, when I was breast-feeding, stroking those tiny pink soft hands in the middle of the night and planning our life together, me and my child, me and my perfect little girl—this wasn't part of the dream, was it, pushing feet into boots and arms into coat sleeves, turning up the radio to drown out her screams, dumping her with a babysitter, and what for? What the hell for?

So I can go and clean someone else's house.

The houses in Park Farm Close are all big, and all different. Detached, Georgian windows, some with porches, some with double garages, some with satellite dishes. Neat front lawns trimmed by gardeners, shiny BMWs and Mercedes on the drives, washed by the car wash, polished by hand.

The Range Rover is backing off the drive of number 16 ("Park Cottage") as I pull up outside. Park Cottage? Does a cottage have five bedrooms and three bathrooms? Does a cottage have a spiral wrought-iron staircase and a state-of-the-art kitchen, in forest green, with ceramic stove and two ovens?

"Morning, Beth!" calls Louise Perkins, lowering the Range Rover window as I get out of my Polo and slam the door. Have to slam it or it won't shut, result of a glancing blow to the offside by a milk float last winter.

"Sorry I'm late . . ."

"Don't worry. Can you do the girls' rooms this morning? Jodie spilt lemonade over the duvet and I've *told* Annie to clean up her mess, but you know what they're like. Oh, and Solomon's left his football stuff in the kitchen and one of the cats has been sick. Sorry! And can you clean the big oven? I did a roast last night."

"OK."

The Range Rover window slides up and the three Perkins children wave dutifully to me from the backseat. Off to school, no doubt with uniform intact (including socks), homework done, lunch boxes packed, and breakfasts, warm or otherwise, eaten without fuss and tantrums.

Or maybe not. The interior of Park Cottage never fails to take me by surprise. Pinkly perfect in its outward presentation to the world, with heavy oak front door and brass nameplate, redbrick doorstep complete with black iron bootscraper and rack for the milk delivery, hanging baskets on either side of the doorway trailing pink and yellow spring blooms, but once you're inside the house drops all its pretense and grabs you by the throat like a mugger in a monastery.

First, you fall over the shoes. Children's shoes of all descriptions and all sizes—boots, sneakers, slippers, football boots, ballet shoes, school shoes, party shoes, and shoes out of the dressing-up box. Louise's shoes. Ben's shoes. Shoes that don't look as though they belong to anyone who ever lived here. Every Monday, the first thing I do is pick up all the shoes and put them away, and by Thursday, the next time I'm there, they're all there on the floor again, just inside the front door, waiting for me to fall over them. The whole family must spend the entire week climbing over them, or else they never use the front door. Then, when you've negotiated the shoes, you come to the toys. If I ever thought Ellie had too many toys—if I ever hollered at her to tidy them up and keep them in the cupboard, put them away, not leave them all over the floor, for God's sake, for someone to fall over and break their neck or I'll put them all in a black sack and leave them outside for the dustmen!—I changed my tune when I came to Park Cottage. Jodie, Annie, and Solomon have so many toys they'd need to be at home all day everyday for the rest of their lives just to get around to playing with each of them. The girls have dolls of every size and description: baby dolls, teenage dolls, crying dolls, talking dolls, boy dolls, girl dolls, dolls with babies of their own, and dolls with houses, cars, horses, and wardrobes full of clothes. They have cuddly toys to match every mood and every outfit—pink pigs, blue monkeys, cats, rabbits, and teddies dressed as ballet dancers or pop stars. Solomon has cars ranging from small enough to hold in his hand to big enough to sit in and drive down the street in. He could go out, drive to Tesco, and get his mother's shopping. He has a racecourse that stretches from the dining room to the kitchen, toy soldiers in combat gear who ride around the house in tanks, firemen and policemen with moving parts and push-button vocabularies.

And, of course, they have educational toys. They have computers that teach them their times tables, how to spell, how to recognize maps of England, Wales, Australia, and the Isle of Wight, and how to say "please" and "thank you" in four different languages even if they never say it in English. They have telescopes and microscopes. They have PlayStations and workstations. In the summer, the garden's littered with bikes, skates, slides, trampolines, inflatable bouncing toys, goalposts, nets, and things that rock, roll, ride, and rust. The clutter and mess is unbelievable. No one in this family ever puts anything away. In the kitchen, cups and plates and saucepans from last night's dinner are heaped in the sink or piled on work surfaces. Socks and knickers litter bedroom floors—expensive suits and blouses thrown on the bed where Louise has tried to choose her outfit for the day, children's clothes from the best shops piled on chairs with the two cats curled up on top of them, or stuffed carelessly half in and half out of drawers and cupboards. Papers and magazines are left open on tables, sofas, the floor. A radio's left on in the kitchen; a light's left on in a bedroom.

Park Cottage is a lived-in house.

It makes me feel needed.

By half past ten, when I stop for a cup of coffee, order is beginning to emerge from chaos. It gives me some sort of satisfaction to see clean surfaces, clean floors, space and tidiness, even though I know everything'll be back to normal as soon as they all come home, when Louise leaves her smart office and picks up the kids from their smart school again in the Range Rover, when Ben comes home from his smart city bank in his smart suit, and they all slop around and throw their toys and papers everywhere again.

It doesn't matter. I won't be here to see it. I'll have done my job, written my note to tell Louise that I've cleaned the oven, that the lemonade came out of the duvet cover all right but the cat sick has stained one of the cushions in the living room. I'll have collected my money from where Louise leaves it in the envelope in the kitchen drawer, and I'll be off down the road in my old white Polo to pick up Ellie and have lunch with Fay.

Fay isn't really a babysitter. She has two small children of her own and she minds Ellie for me during the play-group's holidays. Fay's my best friend. She doesn't need to go out to work—her husband Simon earns enough money to support them all and keep them in the relative luxury of a three-bedroomed semidetached house on a new estate just outside the town, midway between Asda and the leisure center. She doesn't take any money from me for looking after Ellie.

"We enjoy having her," she says. "It's company for Lauren and Jack. What would be the point," she goes on, "in you going out cleaning, if you had to pay me to look after Ellie?"

"I have to pay the playgroup," I point out, "during the term-time."

"Not for much longer."

Ellie and Lauren will be starting school in September. They'll both be four and a half. Fay says she'll still look after Ellie during the school holidays.

"You'll be able to get a proper job," she says. "A decent job, in an office."

"You might want to get a decent job in an office your-self."

"I'll still have Jack at home."

Jack's not two yet, and he wears her out. He hardly ever sleeps, hardly ever eats, hardly ever stops yelling. She says she's aged twenty years since she had him.

"Look at me," she says. "A human wreck. Barely even human. I function like a robot. Get up, load machines, cook, empty machines, clean things, fold things, put things away. I do it in my sleep. Sometimes I don't even remember doing things, don't even remember feeding the children or dressing them. It's scary. See these rings under my eyes! I look like a zombie."

Actually she looks lovely. She's small and slim with shoulder-length blond hair. Men always eye her up when we go out together with the children. She flirts with them without knowing she's doing it. I watch her, wondering how she does it, how she doesn't know she's doing it, and why I can't do it. Then I remember I don't want to anyway 'cos I'm finished with men, aren't I.

"It's still raining," says Ellie, looking up at me from her painting at Fay's kitchen table. She's wearing a big apron with red paint splashes on it. Her hair's in her eyes and she's flushed and excited and I love her so much it hurts. I've forgotten about how angry she made me this morning when I was late and she wouldn't eat the warm Weetabix or put her socks on.

"Me and Ellie went out in our boots and splashed in the puddles," says Lauren.

"We splashed Jack and made him cry," adds Ellie.

"That wasn't very nice!" I admonish.

"Jack asked for it," says Fay, smiling, from the kitchen doorway. She's holding Jack on her hip and stroking his head, trying to quiet him down. "He tipped all their puzzles upside down this morning before I could stop him . . ."

"Boys are a pain!" declares Lauren in a very practiced, very grown-up voice.

Fay and I exchange a glance and raise our eyebrows.

Ellie nods agreement, sighs, and states while stirring her paintbrush in a jar of red water, "Girls are better than boys. Boys are *useless*!"

* * *

You see, our daughters won't be falling for the same old game, the same old tricks of their hormones. Oh no, not our little girls. We'll bring them up differently. They'll be strong, they'll be free, they'll be independent. They'll never need to rely on a man. They'll never want to.

"As soon as they're about eleven or twelve," says Fay, leaning back in her chair and sipping her coffee, "as soon as the old hormones start doing their stuff, that'll be it. You might as well forget it. Everything you've tried to tell them will be out the window. They'll be smiling and fluttering their eyelashes at the boys in their class. The boys won't know what's hit them. Look at the pair of them!"

Ellie's dark head and Lauren's blond one are almost touching as they lie together on a giant cushion, watching TV. Four years old, innocent and beautiful. A huge lump comes to my throat, the way it always does when I think about Ellie growing up. I want to hold her tight in my arms and never let her go, never let her out into the world to face the unknown future, to face hormones and spotty teenage boys, and love, and pain.

"Cheer up!" laughs Fay, looking at my face. "It'll soon be Friday!"

"Very funny!" I smile.

Actually it's not very funny at all. I know exactly what she's getting at, about Friday, and I'm trying not to think about it.

"I'm not going to think about it," I say primly. "It's ridiculous!"

"If you say so," says Fay.

Sometimes, now, I can think about Daniel calmly. I can take out my feeling for him, like taking a letter out of an envelope, examining it, turning it over and over, and then putting it neatly back again. Before, I couldn't have done that—couldn't have borne to look at it or think about it. I had to keep it pushed into a dark corner of my heart where it lay still and quiet without troubling me too much while I got on with my life, my life without him. Now, to my surprise, I can sometimes stare it in the face. I can take a deep breath and say, inside my head, the words: *I loved him, and now he's gone*. And the ground doesn't shake, the sky doesn't darken and fall in. Perhaps this is acceptance, then—the state of grace my doctor, my mother, and my friends used to talk about when he first left—accepting that which we cannot change. He's not coming back, get on with your life, you and your child; you're better off without him. Acceptance first; then, maybe, even enjoyment of a new lifestyle. New friends, new job, new life. New man? Oh, I think not.

Not even on Fridays.

Fay gets Jack into his stroller so we can go out to the shops. He's kicking his shoes off as fast as she puts them on.

"All right, then," she says matter-of-factly. "Don't wear your bloody shoes, I don't care if you have cold feet."

"Mummy said bloody," announces Lauren to Ellie.

"*My* mummy says bloody all the time," retorts Ellie.

It's obviously a matter of personal pride to her that I swear worse than her friends' parents. How have I managed to corrupt the mind of my child to such an extent in four short years?

"I suppose he'll want his bloody shoes on as soon as we get out the door," mutters Fay, doing up the safety straps on Jack's stroller. "Bloody kids!"

"Does Simon swear at the children?" I ask her as we push our carts round Asda. Jack's leaning out of the toddler seat in Fay's cart, throwing items of her shopping onto the floor at regular intervals. Lauren and Ellie walk hand in hand, noses in the air, well-behaved little ladies sighing and tutting with exasperation at the antics of the delinquent male.

"Not really. He says 'For Christ's sake' a lot, though. The other day Lauren told him, 'Hurry up, Daddy, for Christ's sake!' and he didn't find it very funny."

"Don't you think it's hard? Having to be careful what you say all the time?"

Not saying, "Oh, shit!" when you drop a bottle of milk. Not shouting, "Shut the fuck up!" when a baby won't stop screaming. Not yelling, "Just piss off out of my life, you bastard, you wanker!" when your boyfriend tells you he's been seeing another woman. Just for instance.

"I suppose it's part of growing up," says Fay gloomily. "It's what you have to do when you have kids. Learn to control yourself." She stoops to pick up a packet of cookies Jack has just thrown out of the cart. "They'll all be broken now, Jack! Will you just *stop it*!"

Shut the fuck up, Jack! For Christ's sake!

"I don't want to be grown-up," I find myself saying.

I thought I did. I thought it would be great, moving in with Daniel, having our own place, having a baby, being a family. Being the adults, the older generation, the ones who made the rules. But now I've changed my mind. I want to rebel. I want to go back to the days when I could stay out all night, go to clubs, drink myself silly, smoke pot, and lie in bed all day on Sundays. I want to be a teenager again. I want to go back to university and do the whole thing over again, and this time . . .

This time not fall in love with Daniel?

This time not have Ellie?

My heart constricts and I shut out the thoughts, smack down the lid on them and close the suitcase, sit on it, zip it up, and padlock it. Can't think things like that. Can't, can't, can't. Got to get on with it. Shopping, cooking, cleaning other people's houses. Paying the bills, keeping the car on the road. It's not so bad. Lots of people worse off. When Ellie goes to school I'll get a job in an office. Use my degree. Make my mother proud.

"We can always pretend," suggests Fay. "We can pretend not to be grown-up, when it suits us. It wouldn't hurt, would it?"

"When? How?"

"Let Ellie stay over one night. Let Simon babysit. We can go out clubbing if you want. Get totally rat-arsed! It won't cost us much, we're so out of practice—one vodka and I'm anybody's . . . see who we can attract . . ."

"You're married," I remind her.

"I know."

I don't like the way she says it.

I like Simon, but in a funny sort of way I'm a bit wary of him. He's ten years older than Fay. She met him when she was working for an insurance company, temping, during our final year at college, and he was her boss. When they first started seeing each other I didn't think she was very keen, but I was spending all my time with Daniel and I think she was just glad to have a boyfriend. Sometimes they came out with us, to clubs or the Student Union—but he didn't fit in. He wore suits. He didn't talk like us. He liked different music and different politics. In some ways the ten years separating him from our student crowd was a tangible barrier, as if he spoke a completely different language.

"When *I* was a student . . ." he'd say, and we all used to groan and hold our heads. He sounded like our parents.

But he was good to Fay. He obviously loved her and, in

the end, two years after we graduated, two years after Daniel and I had moved into our flat together, she married him. Big white wedding, big fuss, all the families wearing hats, honeymoon in Antigua—the works. Nice house, nice furniture, nice car. She seemed happy.

She *is* happy. She tells me all the time how happy she is.

So what's all this about going out to flirt with guys?

"Just joking," she says with a shrug.

"Good."

I don't like jokes like that. I don't like the way she's looking, the way she's shrugging, as if it's nothing important we're discussing here. As if it wouldn't matter much either way, whether she was joking or not, whether she was really thinking seriously about leaving the kids with her husband and going out to find herself a bit on the side.

"*You* could go out looking to hook up."

"I'd rather sit in a bath of acid and drown myself."

"There are still some nice blokes about, you know. What about Friday . . ."

"Shut up about Friday. I'm not interested in nice blokes. I'm not interested in Friday!"

She gives me a strange look. "I *meant*, what about going out on Friday? Friday night? Not for guys, not if you're not up for it, just for a drink. You and me. We haven't had a night out for ages."

No. We look at each other quickly, and I know what she's thinking. Not since Daniel walked out. I haven't exactly been in the mood for going out. I haven't exactly had the money to spare, either.

"We don't have to spend much . . ." she adds quickly.

"It's all right. Louise gave me a bit extra last week for doing the garden."

"We can forget about being grown-up," she urges me. "Just for once."

"Will it be OK with Simon?"

"Of course it will. You know Simon. He just sits in front of the TV every night. It doesn't matter to him whether I'm there or not. Or how many kids are asleep upstairs."

So that's all right then.

And the shopping only comes to £54.29.

And it's stopped raining.

So that's all right, too.

Life's not too bad, is it?

Tuesday

Tuesday is Oakleigh Court.

It's just around the corner from Park Farm Close and it's a new development, two blocks of luxury apartments, tastefully decorated and thoughtfully planned to reflect the lifestyle of the Single Young Executive. If I were a Single Young Executive, this is where I'd live. The apartments have one nice-sized bedroom and another tiny room that you *could* use as a spare bedroom but it's much better as a study. There's a small kitchen (tastefully fitted), and everything centers around the living accommodation. As a Single Young Executive, you wouldn't need another bedroom and you wouldn't want a big kitchen—you wouldn't do any cooking, you'd live on expense-account business lunches and takeout. The living room is where you'd spend your time, when you came home from your executive position and you'd finished your takeout; and the living room is very nice. The carpet's deep enough to lose a small animal in. There are French doors leading out to the patio, or a little balcony if you're upstairs. You could have your Single Executive friends round here for cocktail parties in the summer and have the

French doors open. You could have your Single Executive girlfriend over to watch a video on winter evenings and pull the curtains and be nice and cozy. A bit like living in a student flat but without the peeling wallpaper and the mice, without the squabbles over the phone bill and whose turn it is to wash up. And with furniture instead of boxes.

I don't know the Single Young Executive who lives in 4a Oakleigh Court. I do know his name's Alex Chapman and I do know his mother. His mother lives next door to Louise and Ben in Park Farm Close, and that's how I got the job of cleaning Alex's new apartment. This is only my third week here. I've never met Alex, but if he's anything like his mother I don't think I want to. The way she looked at me when she was asking me what my hourly rate was, I thought I must have farted. When she gave me her son's front-door key and a piece of paper with his address on it, she tried not to touch my hand, like cleaning houses for a living might be a disease, a virus she might catch and have to put on rubber gloves and an overall and go out scrubbing herself. I pulled a face at her behind her back. Stuck-up old cow.

Still, the son must have a good job.

It's hard to actually tell anything about him from this apartment. Apparently he's been living here for some time, but it doesn't look like it. Not that there are packing cases around the place waiting to be unpacked, or pictures waiting to be hung, or shelves waiting to go up, no, nothing like that—everything's in its place. Too much so. You wouldn't think anyone lived here at all; it's just a show home.

And what sort of young executive wants to live in the same town as his mother anyway? Wouldn't you think he'd want to have his luxury apartment in central London, where he can go to the best clubs and restaurants and get the tube home at four o'clock in the morning, fall into his luxury bed for a couple of hours, and then be up and out to his city office without all the hassle of suburban buses and trains to worry about? What's the matter with him?

He irritates the life out of me and I don't even know him.

Why doesn't he make any mess? Where are the toast crumbs, the butter smears, the rings from the coffee mug? Doesn't he eat?

Why is his bed always perfectly made, with the duvet straight and the pillows plumped up? Doesn't he sleep? Doesn't he ever go to bed? You can't tell me it's normal for a man to make a bed like that. Every man I've ever slept with has left the bed looking like a heap of rags in the middle of a war zone. If you ask them to tidy it up, they tweak a corner of the duvet and say, "That'll do." What's the point of making it, they ask, when you're going to be getting back into it in a few hours' time and messing it up again? One of the greatest gifts a woman brings into a man's life is the gift of clean sheets. Oh, lovely, clean sheets! they cry, all of them. Nothing like them! They purr and stretch like giant pussycats, relishing the feel of the fresh bedlinen washed and dried and aired and put onto the bed by their thoughtful partner. Leave them to their own devices and the sheets stay unchanged for six months. Clean sheets? What for? I haven't wet the bed, have I, ha ha ha, these'll do, they've only been on the bed for a couple of weeks, for God's sake.

What sort of man puts his socks away in pairs?

What sort of man changes the toilet roll and buys spare ones before they even run out?

What sort of man has ornaments?

I mean, nice ornaments. Probably expensive, but not

flashy. You know? The sort of ornaments couples usually buy together, for their first home, but then stop bothering. He's got vases and crystal animals and those little silver clocks people give you as anniversary presents. He's got china plates propped up on the top of the dresser on plate stands. Plate stands, for Christ's sake! I've never even seen a plate stand before. I can't make head or tail of Alex Chapman. I don't think he's normal. And more to the point, his mother has employed me to do four hours of cleaning once a week and, even going slowly, it only takes me half an hour to hoover up the fluff (no dirt, no crumbs) and half an hour to clean the already clean bathroom and kitchen.

So I've got time on my hands.

The first week I felt guilty. I hoovered all over again. I dusted invisible dust off spotless shining surfaces. I walked around the apartment with a feather duster, waving it at clean light fittings. I ached with boredom. I looked at my watch, looked out of the window, wondered about leaving early but had a horror of the mother coming round to check up on me.

Last week, I half expected it to be different. Perhaps he'd tidied up for me the first time, to make a good impression. No man could keep up a good impression for more than one week. This time it would all be back to normal—kitchen in a tip, clothes on the bed, stains of unknown origin all over the floors. I was almost disappointed when I let myself in and found everything as spotless as the first week. What's the point of paying a cleaner if you never make anything dirty? But who am I to argue? It must be the easiest money in the world.

Today I come to a decision. If this is how it's going to be, I'll make the most of it. I'll do something with the time, his time, the time he's buying and doesn't really need. I'm not going to waste it. I'm going to use it myself, for myself. I'm going to do something I've always wanted to do. I give the apartment its unnecessary half-hour hoover and its unnecessary half-hour polish, put the cleaning things away, make myself a coffee, and take a deep breath. Alex Chapman need never know, his snotty mother need never know, his apartment will be clean and tidy and what do they care? As from now, I'm starting a new career for myself.

"Have you ever done anything dishonest?" I ask Fay over lunch in her kitchen.

"What? Like cheating? I once wrote some math equations on my hand before an exam. Still failed."

"No, come on, we've all done that. Not kids' stuff."

"I had it off with Nicola Davidson's boyfriend in her back garden while she was passed out in the bedroom at her twenty-first birthday party."

"*Did* you? I never knew about that!"

"Neither did she!" She laughs.

"But—have you ever—you know . . . done anything seriously dishonest. Like with money?"

"Stealing?"

"I suppose."

She thinks for a while, chewing on her tuna sandwich.

"Traveled on the buses and tubes without paying. Loads of times."

"That all?"

"What is this? Dare, Command, Truth or Promise? When is it your turn?"

"Come on. I want to know."

"Well . . . I did take something from a market stall once. I was only about ten."

"Listen. If you got paid for doing a job, and you didn't do it, and no one found out, would you feel guilty? Would you tell them—tell your boss—you weren't doing it? Or not?"

Her eyes widen. "Why?"

"Just wondered."

"Come on, why? What's up?"

"Nothing. Just wondered. Shall I make another coffee?"

The whole point of cleaning, instead of doing a proper job, is that I'm still in charge of my own time. Up to a point. My priority is still being there for Ellie. Up to a point. If I had a proper job, an office job, I wouldn't be home at lunchtime to pick her up from playgroup or collect her from Fay's. I'd have to pay someone, properly, a real nanny, to look after her for the whole day and so what would be the point of all the extra money I'd probably be earning for doing the proper job if it just went straight to the nanny? And Ellie might not like the nanny. God knows she makes enough fuss about going to Fay's sometimes; and then I'd be in a state of guilt and panic all day everyday about leaving her, so what would be the point of that?

And to be honest, also, I can't be bothered to start looking for a proper job yet.

I will, of course I will, when Ellie starts school. Then she'll be out all day instead of just half days, and the holidays—well, I'll start paying Fay, insisting I pay her properly, to have Ellie all day, while I'm out at my proper job. The job I always intended to get, the one that's going to make my mother glad I went to university.

"Don't you think it's time you started looking?" says my mother when I phone her this evening.

"Looking for what?" Like I don't know. Like we don't have this same conversation at least twice a week.

"Jobs. I've sent you the supplement from the paper again. You were going to start looking."

"Mum, it's still six months till Ellie starts school."

"It doesn't hurt to start looking, Beth. You know. You know how long it took, *before*." She says the "before" in a pointed, accusing tone of voice that makes me wince.

Before was my other life. My life when I first left university, with the world at my feet and my dreams stretching out in front of me like an unplowed field, the city and its bright lights beckoning, my degree the glittering prize that would carry me forth into wonderful employment prospects. Jobs with huge salaries and amazing benefit packages. Bosses who would fall at my feet, begging me to please, please, work for their company, give them the chance to employ me, if only for a day!

Several dozen interviews later, I stopped sending out my résumé and signed on as a temp.

"Why?" cried my mother.

"Because it's demoralizing. It's disheartening. Because nobody warned me it would be like this. Because I'm pissed off with it. And because I don't really care anymore if I have a career or not. I want a baby."

A baby? screamed my mother.

A baby? screamed my friends.

A baby? screamed Daniel.

What was the point of all that work, all that studying, all that sacrifice? If all you wanted was a baby you could have left school at sixteen and joined the stroller army down at the benefits agency.

What was the point of women chaining themselves to railings to get equal rights for people like you, what was the point of your mother force-feeding you education from the time you could recite your alphabet, forcing you to school, forcing you to do your homework when you wanted to be out on your bike or out behind the bike sheds? If all you were going to do, in the end, was give in to your hormones like some peasant woman in an African tribal village, your parents might as well have sold you to a rich husband at puberty and have done with it.

"But, Mum, you told me education is never wasted. You told me if I wanted to have children, they'd benefit from my education, too. You told me a degree was a passport to life, that it never expired, that I could have a career break and always be welcomed back into the workplace . . ."

"You can't have a career break," said my mother crisply, "until you get a career."

That was the *before* that she spoke of so chillingly. *Before* I gave up, became a professional temp, drifted from typing job to filing job, signing my time sheets, collecting my pay checks, stopping my Pill. *Before* I got my own way, convinced my friends I knew what I was doing, convinced my mother it was a valid graduate decision to consciously choose parenthood first and career later . . . convinced Daniel that he wanted to be a father at the age of twenty-five.

Before Ellie.

Now, even more now, I have to look after Ellie first and me second.

"I'm not applying for any jobs until Ellie starts school," I tell my mother firmly, more firmly than usual because I suddenly feel stronger, and do you know why? Because I've just remembered my decision, the decision I made today in Alex Chapman's apartment, my plan for my new career.

"I have something else up my sleeve," I tell her casually. "I have other plans."

"My God," says my mother in a quick gasp. "You're not having another baby?"

* * *

I don't know how people cope, how Fay copes, or how my mother, for instance, did, having more than one child. One child wears me out, drains the life out of me, so I feel sometimes that there's nothing left, not a scrap of energy or time or substance remaining of my life that doesn't belong to her. She takes me over. Even when she's asleep, even when she's at playgroup or at Fay's, I feel like she's in control of my life, dictating the choices and decisions I have to make, dictating what I can or can't do, where I can or can't go, who I meet, what I eat, when I sleep. What I think. Mostly, I think about her. I worry about leaving her with Fay, whether she'll grow up resentful that she didn't spend more of her formative years with her mother. I worry about her not seeing her father. I worry about the effect on her of spending so much time with Jack and starting to hate him. I worry about whether the other kids at playgroup like her, whether she's too bossy or too shy or too big or too small for her age, whether she'll like school, and whether she'll ever go to university. Will she get a career, or will she give up and be a temp? Will she meet someone who loves her and wants her to have his babies? Will she be able to get a mortgage? Christ! She's only four and I've worried her into middle age.

"You're only twenty-nine," says my mother. "You have plenty of childbearing years ahead of you."

"Mum I don't *want* any more children. And even if I did, I don't want a man, OK? I don't want to have sex with anyone. It's usually a prerequisite."

"You hear of all sorts of things these days. *In vitro* fertilization. Surrogate mothers. All sorts. There's plenty of time. Women of fifty are still having children."

Why are we having this conversation? Do I sound like I'm even remotely interested in it?

"I'd rather boil my head than have another baby. I don't know why anyone in their right mind would want more than one. Apart from you and Dad, of course," I add quickly.

The third child of the marriage: *We already had a boy and a girl, so we decided to try for another one.*

In the hope of what? A dog? A rabbit? They got me. And here we all are: my brother's a lawyer, my sister's a doctor, and I'm a cleaning lady.

Perhaps you never stop worrying about your kids.

Fay phones me just before I go to bed.

"It's all sorted," she says.

"What is?"

My mind's fuddled from studying my credit card statement. I'm going to get through this month, definitely, without using the plastic. At all. Even if those shoes, the ones with the little straps and the open toes I liked in Faith, are reduced next time I pass the shop, I'm not going to be tempted. What's the point? I never go anywhere to wear open-toe shoes, they'd just sit in my wardrobe mocking me and forcing me to pay huge amounts of interest on the credit card. Ellie needs new shoes—that's different, she has to have them. But I'm still not using the plastic. I'll find the cash. Definitely.

"Friday," says Fay impatiently. "It's all on, for Friday. Simon's having the kids. We can go out, like we said. For a drink. Or whatever."

Cash for Ellie's shoes. Not for a drink. I'm a mother, I have responsibilities. I can't just go throwing away my hard-earned cash, can I, and let my daughter go barefoot. I'll have Social Services round here before I know it. There'll be headlines in the local papers: GIRL OF FOUR WEARS OLD SHOES WHILE MOTHER DRINKS IN PUB.

"I can't come. I can't afford it."

"But you said! Come on, Beth, just a couple of beers! You said Louise had given you some extra."

"I need it for Ellie. She needs shoes. I forgot."

"Put the shoes on the credit card. What's the matter? Have you gone over your limit?"

"No, that's the trouble. They've put my limit up again."

"They always do, if you pay on time. Good! You can get the shoes *and* get some cash for a drink."

"No, I can't. I won't be able to pay it back. I can't afford to pay anymore, Fay." I suddenly feel furiously ir-ritated by her. What does she know? What does she understand about my position? She's got Simon handing her whatever money she needs. She doesn't have to sit up at night checking her credit card statements and her bank statements, doing little sums in the margins, working out when the electricity bill will be due and whether she can afford soap or not. "You don't understand," I say flatly.

I'd say more but I don't want a row.

"I do," she says quietly. "I know you think I don't, and it's a fair assumption. But I do."

"You don't have the same problems."

"No, but that doesn't mean I don't see yours."

My annoyance vanishes as quickly as it came. "Sorry."

This is my friend, my best friend in the whole world, who looks after my child, day in and day out, without tak-ing a penny from me, who never complains, who never says, "Sorry, it's not a good day today, I've been awake all night with my own fractious toddler, I've got a migraine, my house is a mess, and I just can't face one more child to contend with today." Who was at my side within minutes, holding me together, when I phoned her in a state of hys-teria the day Daniel finally left for good. We went through university together, we went through our first pregnancies together. We've seen each other at our best and our worst.

We don't need a lot of words to tell each other the stuff we feel.

"Sorry," I say again. "I've just spent ages looking at my statements. It's depressing."

"Can you get any more work? Afternoons? Evenings? I could have Ellie."

"No." I'd never see her at all. She'd start thinking Fay was her mother. "No, it's not long till she starts school. I'll manage. I'm probably just sulking 'cos I can't buy myself those shoes from Faith."

"The ones with the open toes?"

"I'd never get to wear them, anyway, so what's the point?"

"The point is being able to treat yourself. We all deserve a treat now and then. Life gets grim and gray without treats."

"Yeah, well. OK, let's have a drink on Friday night."

"I'll pay . . ."

"No, you won't. You're right, I'm being ridiculous—a couple of beers won't break the bank. Remember that time in the first year at college?"

"When we only had enough for a half of lager between us?"

"When we couldn't even rake up enough cash for a packet of chips?"

"And that old guy at the bar felt sorry for us and gave us some money for another pint!"

"That old guy was probably about thirty!" I point out, and we both burst out laughing, and then, suddenly, both fall quiet.

We're both nearly thirty ourselves now, aren't we.

What was I going to do by the time I was thirty? Where did I think I was going to be? When I sat in those sociology lectures, staring out of the window, dreaming my dreams—what did I imagine, if I ever let myself imagine myself as a graduate, a proper grown-up member of society?

I was going to Be Someone. I always knew what I really wanted to Be, but if I couldn't be that, I would at least be Someone—not just Anybody. I didn't ever expect to be ordinary. Even with Daniel, even when we became an item, we were never going to be an ordinary couple. We were destined for something great, us two. We wouldn't ever become boring. We wouldn't ever live in suburbia or have a mortgage. We wouldn't work nine to five, clean our car on a Sunday, and mow the lawn in the same direction as the neighbors. We wouldn't have arguments—we were different. We were special. We were soul mates.

"We were never going to become boring, were we?" I whisper to Fay over the phone, a horrible lump somewhere in my chest suddenly making me ache all over.

"We're not!" she retorts sharply. "What are you going on about? We're not boring! We're in our prime!"

"You reckon?"

"Definitely! Come on, cheer up! Friday night, girl, we'll hit the town and we'll leave it reeling . . ."

"I'm not sure I'm up for it . . ."

"Of course you are," she replies firmly. "Get your arse into gear. Get a couple of beers inside you and you'll be fine."

"If you say so."

I have the definite feeling I'm only going along with this to keep Fay happy.

Friday

———◦◦◦◦———

It hasn't been a bad week really. I wanted it to be good, for Ellie's sake. It's half term so she hasn't been to play-group all week. I always promise myself that when she's on holiday from playgroup we'll have quality time to-gether, mother and daughter, going out for walks in the fresh air and counting flowers and things. Looking at books together, playing I-Spy in the supermarket to teach her the alphabet. In reality, she gets bundled into the car, usually showing off about something she didn't have for breakfast or couldn't wear, dumped at Fay's until I've fin-ished work, and then is expected to carry on playing qui-etly with Lauren and not murdering Jack, while Fay and I relieve our tensions over a couple of coffees and a sand-wich.

This week, I've made a supreme effort. On Wednesday, after I finished at Dottie's (Hillside Avenue), I borrowed Dottie's dog and brought him back to Fay's so that Ellie and Lauren could come with me to take him for a walk. You'd need to know Tosser to understand what an act of great personal sacrifice this was. Tosser's the dog, and he's an absolute bastard. Dottie acquired him as a puppy from the widow of a drunken Scotsman who never referred to the dog as anything other than "ye wee tosser" before he took off on a bender one night and ended up drowned in the canal. The wife had wanted the puppy even less than she'd wanted her husband around, so she was pleased to see the back of him when Dottie expressed an interest in having a dog as a companion. I normally take Tosser for a walk every Wednesday morning anyway, 'cos Dottie's got such bad arthritis she can't walk him anymore and she worries about him not getting his exercise. She needn't, actually, worry at all as he gets more than enough exercise throwing himself at my legs and jumping at my throat to last him all week. Anyway, for some obscure reason the children think he's cute and enjoy taking him out for walks, so he got a double exercise ration this Wednesday. Not only does this mean I have to put up with being savaged by the little tyke in my own time, as well as while Dottie's paying me for the privilege, but it also means I get subjected to a conversation something like this for the rest of the day:

"Mummy, why can't *we* have a doggy?"

"Because they cost too much money."

"If I give you all my money out of my piggy bank can we have a doggy?"

"No, you haven't got enough in your piggy bank. There isn't enough money in all the piggy banks in the world to make me buy a doggy."

"Why can't we keep Tosser?"

"Because he belongs to Dottie." And he's a ferocious, vicious, sadistic brute who's given me scars on both shins and I wouldn't give him shelter even if you paid me.

"But you *said* Dottie couldn't walk him anymore because her legs hurt . . ."

"He's still Dottie's dog."

"I'm going to ask Dottie if we can have him . . ."

"No, you're not. We're not having a dog."

"But I *want* a dog! I love Tosser, Mummy! I want a dog like Tosser! I want a dog . . ."

"That's enough about wanting a dog! I don't want to hear any more about it! I don't want to hear any more about bloody Tosser!"

"I hate you, Mummy!"

Me and my great ideas.

On Thursday, after Park Cottage, I took Ellie and Lauren swimming. This was my treat, my way of thanking Fay just a little bit and letting her get some rest if only she could persuade Jack to sleep for an hour or so.

"Jack go swimming!" growled Jack thunderously as he watched me picking up the girls' bags with their towels and costumes.

"No, Jack," soothed Fay.

"Another time, perhaps, Jack," I offered a little half-heartedly.

"You're too much of a pain!" Lauren told him dismissively. "You scream."

Jack promptly started to scream.

"See!" said Lauren reasonably.

"I wish he'd stop screaming," said Ellie. "If he did, we'd take him, wouldn't we, Mummy?"

"Mm."

Maybe.

Going to the swimming pool with two four-year-olds doesn't rank as one of life's all-time highs. Trust me. We go in the baby pool. Ellie can swim with armbands on, Lauren's just learnt to swim without them 'cos her dad takes her to the swimming pool every Saturday morning. Ellie is jealous, so she takes her armbands off even though

she can't swim without them and keeps going under.
Every time she goes under she comes up crying and gets
crosser with Lauren, who's swimming round her and
showing off. I divide my time between snapping at Lauren for showing off and snapping at Ellie for taking off
her armbands and trying to drown herself.

If you can't swim without armbands, keep them on, for
God's sake.

I can. I can swim without armbands. Stupid armbands.
I'm not a baby.

Nobody's saying you're a baby. You just can't swim.
Yet. Almost. But not quite.

Can. I can swim. Look at me, I can swim like Lauren.
(Glug, glug, gurgle, choke, scream.)

No, you can't! Now will you be told! Stop crying! It's
your own fault! Lauren, will you *stop* swimming around
with that look on your face! I *know* you don't need armbands anymore, and yes, I think you're very clever but
you're getting on my last nerve at this very moment . . .

We ended up going home early, the girls sitting in the
back of the car in stony silence, not talking to me and not
talking to each other.

"Let's get a video and some chips to take home!" I said
cheerily, feeling guilty about taking Lauren back in a foul
mood from her afternoon out.

"Don't like videos," said Lauren sulkily.

"Don't like chips," said Ellie, glaring.

I might take Jack next time.

And now it's Friday, the last day of the half-term holiday,
and Fridays are Canal Street. I don't look forward to
going to work on Fridays. The houses in Canal Street are
all the same: two-bedroomed, terraced, probably built in
the 1940s, tiny back garden, no front garden—door

straight on to the street. But don't be fooled—I've seen Canal Street houses in estate agents' windows and the prices would make you look twice. Canal Street is very convenient for the station, you see, and for the town center, with resident-only parking. Number 73 Canal Street is a rented property and the tenants are Oliver and Nathan, two young men with no interest in their housework whatsoever, who let me get on with the job without any instruction or input from them. The job would be all right if it wasn't for Oliver. Nathan's no problem—he's never there. Apparently he works for a recording company in London, which I'd find quite interesting if it wasn't for Oliver telling me about it. Oliver, you see, works from home most days. And he makes a point of working from home on Fridays.

When I first met them, I presumed they were in a relationship together. So it came as a bit of a shock, to put it mildly, when Oliver started making passes at me. At first I dismissed it as my imagination. Reading too much into a silly bit of banter. Haven't had sex for so long, I'm starting to fantasize about every good-looking young man I meet! But the next week, he was rather more direct. Like—Hey, don't bother making the bed; I was rather hoping we might get into it in a minute.

Now, quite apart from the shock of being propositioned (a) by my employer, during working hours; (b) by someone I'd been pretty sure was gay; and (c) well, really, by anyone at all, now that my confidence has been shredded to pieces by the only love of my life walking out on me—as if all these factors aren't shocking enough, he's also quite a few years younger than me, with a body to die for and the sort of looks you normally only see in films and hospital sitcoms.

You see? Anyone with those sort of looks, in my experience, usually turns out to be gay, quite apart from sharing a flat with his best friend. There's no way I want any part of a *ménage à trois*. Don't get me wrong, but if I'd wanted to share a man with someone else, be it a male or a female, I might as well have asked Daniel to please stay with me and please, feel free to bring his new girlfriend to stay as well, and sleep in our bed whenever she wants.

I told Oliver I'd prefer to get on with the housework, thank you very much for asking, and perhaps he wouldn't mind leaving me to it?

"What a shame." He smiled. "Never mind. Perhaps next week."

And every week since then, it's been the same.

"How about a quick one before you start the hoovering?"

"Bit warm today, isn't it? Why don't you take a few clothes off? We could have a shower together . . ."

"You look tired today, Beth. Why don't you come and lie down for a little while?"

"You look lovely today, Beth. I'd really like to kiss you . . ."

"There's only the two of us here. No one to disturb us. Nobody need ever know . . ."

I tell him to get on with his work, let me get on with mine. He goes into the kitchen, spreads books and papers out on the table, makes a coffee, puts on the radio. For a little while he gets on with his work, but it's never very long before he comes looking for me again "to see how I'm getting on." And guess what he does for a living? He's a garden designer, a landscaper. Did a degree in horticulture and works for himself. Don't you think that's unusual for a man of twenty-three who lives in a house without a proper garden? I made the mistake of expressing interest when he told me about his work. Now he keeps buying me plants. Every Friday, there's another unusual plant waiting for me. My backyard ought to look like Kew Gardens by now, but I'm useless at looking after them, and half of them are dead already. I'm careful not to sound too excited when he talks to me about Nathan's job, in case he starts asking him to bring CDs home for me. And what would Nathan think?

"What would Nathan think?" I asked him eventually, one week when I was finding it particularly difficult to rebuff his demands politely.

"Why should Nathan think anything?" he replied, giving me a curious look.

I hesitated. I couldn't ask him outright, could I? It's a bit odd to ask someone who continually pesters you for sex whether he's gay.

"Nathan and I are friends," he said eventually, with a knowing smile. "Friends and flatmates, that's all. Do I *look* gay?"

Well, actually . . .

"Of course not," I said hurriedly.

And the mistake I made, several weeks ago, was admitting to Fay that I fancied him.

"*Do* you?" she squealed. "*Beth!* Oh my *God*!"

"You don't have to sound so shocked," I said peevishly. "I do still have all my hormones intact. He's absolutely gorgeous."

She raised her eyebrows at me and smiled suggestively. "So . . ."

"So, nothing. I'm not going to do anything about it. I don't want anything to do with men ever again, gorgeous or not."

"But there he is . . . gagging for it."

"Thanks!"

"And you could spend every Friday morning having fantastic, wild, uncomplicated sex . . ."

"And when am I supposed to get the cleaning done?"

"Beth! Cleaning? For God's sake!"

"I'm *not* getting paid for sex, Fay. It'd be demeaning."

"Clean first, then. Sex afterward."

"I'm not having sex with him! God! I wish I hadn't told you!"

"I just don't understand how you can keep refusing. If you find him so attractive, and he's so . . . demanding."

And, of course, she's quite right. It gets more difficult every week. He's wearing me down, and he knows it. I dread going there because I know how it's going to be, but I've started thinking about it, too—imagining actually doing it with him. In the shower. On the carpet I spend so many hours hoovering. On the sofa. On the kitchen floor. On the stairs. And in the bed. The bed I make every week—quite often with him watching me.

No way. It's just not going to happen. If necessary, I'll just have to give him my notice, which I can't really afford to do until I find a new client for Fridays.

So I go there every Friday, keep my eyes on the work and strictly averted from Oliver's naked chest (he's recently decided he can work on his garden plans more effectively when stripped to the waist), and pretend not to notice when he passes me a little more closely than necessary in the hallway, or touches my hand as he gives me a cup of coffee. And never look into his eyes.

This week's no different.

"Hello, Beth, darling," he croons as he lets me in. "You're looking particularly gorgeous today."

I'm not. I'm wearing my oldest jeans and a brown sweatshirt with stains on the sleeves. I do this on purpose, to try to give out the message to him that I am not a sexual person, not someone with warm blood and warm feelings at all but just a cleaning machine, a robot holding a duster who moves from room to room, hearing nothing and seeing nothing and certainly feeling no lust whatsoever at the sight of his very pert backside in their tight shorts this morning.

He seems to be wearing fewer and fewer clothes every week. And it's February.

"How about a kiss before you start work?" he says softly, leaning toward me.

I duck out of the way and march purposefully toward the kitchen.

"Lots to do," I say without looking at him. "The state of this floor! I don't know what you get up to!"

He's laughing at me as I blush violently like a schoolgirl.

"I mean, all this dirt, all this sticky . . ."

"That's probably where I was rolling naked on the floor covered in molasses," he says, and I can feel his eyes on me, watching for my reaction.

I shrug and run some hot water into a bucket. "Oh, well. Should be easy enough to clean up, then," I say.

"Have you ever tried it?" he persists.

"What? Washing sticky floors—all the time. I make a living out of it!"

"The molasses. Or honey. Or chocolate spread's lovely . . ."

"On toast, yes. Lovely."

I know I sound like Felicity Kendall reading an Enid Blyton story. I fix my eyes and my mind on the soapy water in the bucket. Mop in, squeeze, mop out, wash floor. Mop in, squeeze, mop out . . .

"You don't fool me, Beth," says Oliver very quietly. "You can go on pretending as long as you like, but I know you're turned on by the idea, really, and I know you're turned on by me, too. We could have a great time in bed, you and me, if you'd just let go and give into what your body's saying to you."

My body, at this point, is actually saying it's quite warm and quite damp. I mop furiously at the floor, trying to ignore it, and ignore him, and the pictures going on in my mind.

"When you're ready, just let me know," he says, sauntering out of the room.

"The arrogant little sod!" exclaims Fay with disgust at lunchtime. "I hope you told him where to get off!"

"I didn't tell him anything," I admit. "I just went on with doing the floor."

"So you're considering it!"

"No! No way!" I drop my eyes from her stare.

"You are, aren't you!" she insists. "I know you, Beth Marston, and I know that look on your face!"

"What look?" I ask, trying to sound innocent.

"That . . . disgusting . . . *lusty* look. You can't hide it! No wonder you've got him climbing up the walls!"

"Fay, that is so unfair! I'm doing absolutely everything I can to put him off! I'm going round there in dirty old clothes . . ."

"Probably turns him on!"

". . . ignoring him, pushing him away, telling him to get on with his work and leave me alone. . . ."

"But all the time, you're secretly fantasizing about screwing him."

"I can't help what goes on in my mind, can I?"

"And he knows."

"I don't see how he could."

"I've told you. It's written all over your face."

Jesus. If every thought we have shows in our faces, what hope is there for any of us?

Every time we look at someone and wonder what they'd be like in bed; every time we talk to someone we can't stand, but smile and make polite conversation; every time we congratulate someone on their success while secretly hating them for it—just imagine how the social fabric of our community would fall apart, if we could read each other's thoughts. It doesn't bear thinking about.

"He can't," I say firmly. "And anyway, I don't really want to do it with him. It's just a fantasy. He's got a nice body. And I haven't had sex for a long time."

And I don't want to, either. It just complicates things. I don't want anything to do with men, remember. It'd be all right if you could just kind of unzip your body, let your body get on with it without involving your mind or your feelings, then just get back into your body again and go on with your life. Yeah, that'd be cool.

"That's how men do it, anyway," comments Fay when I tell her. "So why shouldn't we?"

"I don't want a man in my life again," I say. "I don't want someone in my flat, cluttering up my space, smelling and leaving dirty washing lying around."

"You don't have to," she points out. "You just do it at his place. Then you just get dressed and come home. You don't even have to speak to him if you don't want to."

Sounds quite appealing in a way.

Ellie's going to stay the night with Lauren. She's been excited all day. She starts packing her bag before she's even had her tea.

Teddy, toothbrush, blue pajamas, dressing gown. Bottle of Ribena, two packets of chips, a pack of Kit-Kats . . .

"Hey, what's all this?" I ask, looking in the bag. "Fay has got food in her cupboards, you know!"

"Midnight feash," she says importantly.

"Says who?"

"Lauren. We're going to have a midnight feash, when we go to bed. In her room."

"Feast. It's called a feast. And you're not."

"What *is* a midnight feast?"

"It means eating a lot of food in the middle of the night. You won't. You'll be asleep."

"But Lauren said!"

"Lauren will be asleep, too. There's no way Simon's going to let you sit up in the middle of the night eating chips and KitKats."

She starts to cry as I take the food out of her bag. "Lauren *said*! I hate you, Mummy! You're horrible!"

I'd *like* her to be able to have a midnight feast, to be honest. Where's the fun in life? Where's the joy, the excitement, if you can't sit up in bed with your best friend at the age of four and have Ribena and chocolate and chips? What's it all about?

"Look, I'll leave two KitKats in the bag, and you and Lauren can have them before you go to sleep, if Simon says it's OK. But you clean your teeth afterward. OK?"

She puts her little soft arms round my neck and kisses me wetly on the cheek. "Yes, Mummy. Lovely, Mummy! Thank you, Mummy!"

She skips around the room singing about midnight feasts and I wonder whether she'll make herself sick with excitement before she even gets there. She's still young enough to get so much pleasure from such a simple thing, and I suddenly ache with envy. Why does life become so complicated when we get older?

"I wish I could get excited at the idea of having a sleepover and eating KitKats in bed," I remark to Fay. We're on the bus going into town. "We lose that, don't we, when we grow up. That capacity for excitement."

"No, not necessarily. I still get excited about going on vacation. Or buying new clothes. Don't you?"

"No, not now, now that I have to worry about what I'm spending all the time."

"But even little things like having takeout instead of cooking dinner. Christmas presents. Watching a new episode of a program you like on TV." She paused. "I've been excited about coming out tonight."

"Have you?" I look at her in surprise. "But you and Simon go out all the time. You have babysitters and go out for nice meals, and see shows."

"I know. But this is different."

I feel a bit humble at this. I hardly ever have evenings out anywhere now, but I haven't really given tonight much thought at all. And yet Fay's been looking forward to it, actually getting excited about it, despite her regular social life with her husband.

"I'm touched," I tell her. "And yes, it is nice to be going out, just the two of us. I'm glad. We should do it more often."

"We will!" says Fay, her eyes shining.

How surprising.

We go to a bar in the High Street, one of those erstwhile comfortable pubs that now rejoice in names like the Slug & Lettuce or the Newt & Tomato, and have vast areas of empty floor with poles supporting small round tables, where people stand propped up as if they were on a tube train.

"I'll get us a drink," says Fay, making for the bar.

I stand against one of the round tables, feeling awkward and conspicuous.

Most people are either in groups or in couples. The couples occupy the few dimly lit bays of seating around the walls, holding hands across the tables or sitting closely together, heads touching, sneaking the odd kiss between drinks. I think, involuntarily, of Daniel—but only briefly, like a short sharp stab of indigestion that goes away again leaving me a little bit breathless, a little bit nauseous. The groups of friends, mostly very young, call out to each other loudly across the bar.

"Kaz! Ice in your Tia Maria and Coke or not?"

"Want any chips, Shazza? Plain or salt and vinegar? Does Wills want any nuts?"

"Taz! Is Jez coming tonight or not?"

"We going on to Oscar's after this or what, Gaz?"

Gaz, Kaz, Taz, Shaz. I wonder idly what their real names are, watch with mild interest as they nudge and shuffle their way from bar to group and back to bar, with bottles of beer and vodka pops, packets of chips and cigarettes balanced on top of each other, laughing and stuffing their bundles of money back in purses and pockets. The new young rich. Good jobs, good clothes, good prospects, plenty to laugh about. Bet they're not temping, or settling down to have babies.

"Do you ever wish we were like them?" I ask Fay as she returns from the bar with our beers, nodding at the nearest group of young drinkers.

"We had our turn, when we were in college," she points out. "We had some laughs, didn't we."

"But no money."

"It isn't everything."

I don't bother to contradict her with the obvious statement: That's easy to say when you've got enough of it.

"You can be comfortable," she goes on, "or even well-off, and still be miserable."

"Of course! Of course that's true, but it must be nice to

just have enough to go out and enjoy yourself, like this lot here, and not have to worry."

She shrugs. "You can't go by appearances. People can be unhappy, or just bored with their lives, and cover up by getting dressed up and going out, spending money, looking as if they're having a good time . . ."

"I'd never do that," I declare, taking a good swig of my beer. "Why cover up? Why pretend? If you're unhappy, you should do something to change your life."

She doesn't reply. I glance at her and see her looking at the door.

"What?" I ask her. "What's wrong?"

"Nothing. You're probably right, but it's not always that easy. Probably. If people aren't happy. Not easy to change things. If other people are involved."

"I haven't got the slightest idea what you're going on about." I frown.

"Sorry." She puts down her bottle with a thump and asks, "Want another beer?"

"Christ, Fay, I've hardly started this one. And it's my turn."

"Don't worry. You can get the next one. I'll get these. You can line 'em up."

I watch her make her way back to the bar. I'm a bit bemused by her; by the speed she's drinking and the way she's talking. Is she not happy with Simon? Have they had a row? She normally tells me when they do, and she hasn't said anything lately.

She's a long time at the bar, and when I catch sight of her through the crowd she's talking to someone, a man. She comes back, finally, looking a bit flushed, and puts down the beers without saying anything.

"Who was that?" I ask.

"Who?"

"The guy you were talking to at the bar."

"Oh . . ." She waves dismissively. "Just someone started chatting to me while we were waiting to be served."

She changes the subject. We talk about the kids. About playgroup. About the forthcoming meeting with the girls' reception class teacher at their new school. About Jack and his tantrums.

We finish our second beers and I go to the bar for the next one. I'm beginning to feel a bit drunk already. I'm not used to it. I can see the guy who was chatting to Fay more clearly now. He's on a stool at the end of the bar, with another bloke. They're both smartly dressed, about our own age, drinking shots. The one who was talking to Fay turns to look at me as I order our drinks. He's tall and dark with very short hair and designer stubble. He looks from me, back across the bar toward Fay. I turn round in time to see her smile at him.

"You *were* joking, weren't you," I say when I return with the beers. "About coming out to meet guys?"

"Of course! Why?"

"Giving that bloke the eye! I saw. And he's looking at you now."

"Oh, come on, Beth! Only looking! Only chatting!"

She's smiling across at him even as she's saying this. I can't believe it.

"Does he know you're married?" I snap.

"For God's sake! I haven't offered to sleep with him! What the hell's eating you?"

So perhaps I'm overreacting. Perhaps the drink's making me aggressive.

"They're coming over here," I hiss, watching as these two guys slide off their bar stools and make their way toward us.

"So what do you want to do? Leave? You think I shouldn't even enjoy a little harmless chat with a couple of perfectly harmless, friendly—"

"No, sorry. You're right. No harm, I suppose."

"Hi. You girls want another drink?"

I look at Fay. She's still smiling at the same one, the dark one. No harm, of course.

"Well, OK!" she says, as if she's had to think about it. "Thanks very much."

"Neil," he introduces himself.

"Martin," says the shorter guy, smiling straight at me. "What would you like?"

"A Becks," I say, "please."

I watch Fay and Neil talking as Martin goes back to the bar for our drinks. They have to lean closer to hear each other above the music and the noise of the crowd. He says something that makes her laugh and she holds her head back, neck stretched, smile stretched, eyes wide, sparkling, and I suddenly know with absolute certainty that this was why she was so excited about coming out tonight.

Whatever she says, Fay is looking to meet men.

And her husband's at home looking after our children.

Great.

Saturday

After Daniel left, the weekends were the worst. We always stayed in bed late on weekends. Ellie, once she was past the baby stage and old enough to get out of bed on her own, used to come into our room in the morning, thumb in her mouth, teddy under her chin, and snuggle into bed with us, warm soft little limbs curled around our arms, and we'd doze contentedly, the three of us, while the sun climbed higher in the sky and the day warmed its toes on the edge of breakfast time.

After he left, we found it harder to lie in bed. I welcomed her warmth and company into my solitary sleeplessness, but neither of us seemed to take any comfort from each other's fidgeting, and eventually, having kicked the duvet onto the floor and the last crumbs of patience out of the window, I'd sigh and heave myself out of bed, heavy of heart and limb, and start the day as tired and grumpy as if it were a weekday.

It's a little easier now, like my life in general.

Strange how resilient the human heart can be. Once I thought I'd die from the pain his leaving caused me; now I have to concentrate hard to remember how it felt to hurt so much. Ellie cried, too, at the very start, and asked for her daddy—but now she hardly ever mentions him. Is that bad? I have terrible moments of panic about her psychological deprivation. Daniel thought it would be best for her if he stayed right out of her life.

"She's young enough," he said, "to forget about me quickly. It wouldn't be fair to come in and out of her life, bringing her sweets and outings on weekends and confusing her."

The charitable side of my nature wants to believe that this was noble of him. Hard for him, too, because he loved her. Perhaps not the way I love her, like an organ of my own body, a fragment of my soul, my heartbeat, my pulse—who can ever feel like that except a mother?—but I know he loved her, I could see it in his eyes, his smile, the way he touched her head and held her hand.

But the bitter, resentful half of me thinks it was an easy option for him. A clean cut heals more easily than an open wound.

This Saturday morning, I wake up on my own. No sweet little warm scented body in the bed next to me, no soft little song being sung about currant buns in a baker's shop or wheels on the bus going round and round. No teddy bashing me on the head to wake me up. I lie for a while staring at the ceiling, watching the light through the gap in the curtains.

It's not raining. Well, that's one improvement.

Ellie stayed at Fay and Simon's for the night.

I slide out of bed, needing a pee, needing a glass of water. It's been a long time since I had a hangover.

Sitting on the toilet, I remember the argument with Fay

and I groan and hold my head to stop it falling off and rolling between my legs and down the toilet. I think I'll just sit here for a while. Not sure if I feel ready to stand up again. The floor looks kind of strange and floaty.

No, I'm not going to be sick. I'll definitely be fine if I just sit here for a few more minutes.

I prop my head on my elbow, lean my elbow on my knee, and close my eyes, but open them again quickly because closing them makes me feel more nauseous.

Fuck it, I can't sit here on the toilet all day.

Why did I have that stupid argument with Fay?

We were both drunk. If I hadn't been drunk I'd never have gone off on my own, got a taxi home on my own, and left her . . .

Oh, yes.

I remember now.

Sobering up suddenly, I get off the toilet and go into the kitchen to make some tea. Of course. That was the whole problem. I left Fay with Neil, and got a taxi home on my own because he was the source of the argument. We left the bar with Neil and Martin. They wanted to go on to a club.

"Come on, Beth!" Fay had pleaded with me in the ladies' room when we were leaving. "Come on, just for a little while! Why not?"

"Because I'm drunk enough already. I just want to go home. And *you* said . . ." I glared at her. "You said we were just going out for a little drink, just the two of us."

"Yes, that's what I thought, but look, what harm is there in just another hour or so, since we're already out, and Neil and Martin are good company, aren't they?"

"We don't even know them," I said primly, sounding like my mother. "And what would Simon say?"

"Simon doesn't need to know," she replied curtly.

I raised my eyebrows at her.

"I mean, there isn't anything he *needs* to know," she amended. "It's just another drink, at another venue . . ."

"And then?"

"And then home," she said. "Of course."

"Sorry," I said, "but I think we should go home. Now. Not later."

"You're being boring," she pouted.

"And you're behaving dangerously."

I was quite surprised I managed to say that, as I was really quite drunk, but also because it was quite a challenging statement in the circumstances.

We looked at each other for a few minutes; she seemed to be considering saying something but thought better of it. I was just concentrating on not swaying.

"Well, then," she said eventually. "Suit your bloody self." And walked out.

I followed her, trying but failing to grab her by the arm. "Wait! Where're you going?"

"Where do you think? To the club. With Neil."

"Well, thanks very much! And I'm supposed to just make my own way home?"

"Your choice."

I think, now, resentfully, crossly, about her lack of concern, not even asking if I had enough money for a taxi, not even caring that I was going home drunk on my own. I sit in my kitchen, gradually feeling better as the hot tea hits my stomach, and I wonder whether to phone her before I go and pick up Ellie. Despite my resentment I feel anxious about her—whether she got home all right, whether Simon was angry that she was late. Not that she didn't deserve it. As I put my cup in the sink the doorbell rings.

"Mummy! We had crussongs! With jam!"

"*Croissants*. Hello, darling!" I hoist Ellie up into my arms and hug her tight. "Did you have a lovely time?"

I look at Fay over the top of Ellie's head. "You didn't have to bring her back. I was coming to pick her up."

"Yes, Mummy, and we had a Night-night Feasht!"

"*Midnight . . .*"

"No! *Night-night!*" She struggles out of my arms while she corrects me very importantly. "Simon said midnight was too late for feasts but we could have one at bedtime and he called it a Night-night Feast 'cos all the time we was having it, we was shouting 'Night-night, Simon!' "

"*Were.* We *were* shouting . . ."

Poor Simon.

"Can I have a drink of milk, Mummy? Can I watch TV? Can I do painting?"

"Sorry," says Fay as Ellie runs off to turn on the TV. "She's very hyped up. She'll be tired out by lunchtime."

She meets my eyes and we look at each other for a bit without saying anything.

"I've brought her back," she says at length, "so I could talk to you."

"So talk."

"I mean, without Simon. Without Simon hearing."

I wait.

"I told Simon you came with me. To the club."

"Why? If it was so harmless, why lie about it?"

"Just so . . . you know. Just so he doesn't worry. Unnecessarily."

"And you don't think he should be worried?"

She fiddles with her hair. "Why are you being so . . . so moralistic about this?" she asks finally.

"I don't understand. I'm not sure what you're playing at. Is everything all right between you and Simon? Come on, don't just sigh and look the other way!" I hiss at her, exasperated. "What's going on, Fay?"

She pulls out a chair and sits down.

"Nothing. All right, OK, I suppose I'm just bored. It sounds bad, I know, but if you want me to be totally honest—there's nothing wrong between me and Simon, except that he's older than me and—"

"He's always been older than you! It hasn't just happened!"

"But it's got more apparent. He's got more . . ." She shrugs helplessly. "Well, more boring. I just want to have some fun. I don't want to hurt him. But he wouldn't come out drinking or clubbing, and I miss it, Beth! I miss getting dressed up and going out, having a good time . . ."

"Chatting up other guys?"

"Only for fun. I don't understand you, Beth. You'd have had a laugh if you came with us last night. Martin would have liked you to be there."

"Sod Martin!" I snap. "I don't even know him! I only spoke to him at all because you were so busy with Neil. And then you left me to come home on my own. Great!"

She looks down at the table sadly. How does she manage to make me feel like it's me being unreasonable?

"OK," she says. "If you feel like that, I promise next week we'll stay together. OK?"

"Next week? Who said anything about next week?"

"You did. Last night. We agreed we should do it every Friday night as we were having such a good time."

"Well, perhaps I agreed when I'd had a few drinks, but that was before . . ."

"And Ellie and Lauren will stay with Simon again. He's up for it!"

Dead on cue, Ellie comes charging back into the room asking for cookies. "When can me and Lauren have another sleepover, Mummy? When can we have another Night-night Feast? Fay said we could! When can we, Mummy?"

I stare at Fay. "This is emotional blackmail," I point out.

"No, Beth. It's called getting a life again. Let's just enjoy it."

So perhaps it is me being unreasonable. Unreasonable and moralistic. Perhaps it's not really so serious that Fay wants to go out and have a bit of fun, have a drink, have a dance, flirt with a few guys and lie to her husband about it. What he doesn't know won't hurt him? Perhaps I shouldn't be judging her. It's her life, not mine.

Except that she's my best friend. Except that, by default, I'm involved in her deception. Even my child's indirectly involved in it. Except that I know what it feels like to find out that you've been cheated on. And I don't want Simon to find that out about Fay. I'm too fond of them, both of them. It scares me.

And other people's mess doesn't just stay there, in their lives, keeping itself neatly to itself—it overflows, trickles into the lives of everyone around them, becoming our business whether we like it or not. And I don't.

Ellie goes to bed early tonight and I turn off the TV and get out a pad of paper and a pen. I sit at the kitchen table and stare at this blank paper. I doodle some lines, turn the lines into boxes, put lids on the boxes and turn them into houses, put chimneys on the houses and smoke coming out of the chimneys, and then I stop and stare at this page completely covered with a smoking housing estate and wonder what it says about me. I rip out the page and stare at another blank one. What to write? Where to start?

This, you see, is my ambition, the great plan, the thread running through the tatty fabric of my life. Most of the time, my ambition is buried under the dust and fluff of everyday life. It lies there, somewhere beneath the surface, and I just can't put everyday life on hold for long enough to lift up the surface and let it out. If I do get half an hour to myself occasionally, like now, I sometimes think about it. This is it, I tell myself sternly. This is the time that you say you never have. In thirty minutes you could write at least a hundred words, and that would be a start. How are you ever going to become a famous scriptwriter if you don't start somewhere? You'll end up sad and bitter when you're too old to hold a pen.

"I was going to write something amazing," you'll say, sadly and bitterly, "but I never got the time."

And I answer myself: "Shut the fuck up. I want to watch TV. I want to sit with my feet up and enjoy a cup of tea and half an hour of peace before I go to bed. I want to read the paper. I even want to go through my bank statement. There'll be another time. Next week. Or next year. When life gets a bit easier."

And, of course, life doesn't get any easier. I've put it off now so often, for so long, that I've stopped even bothering to make excuses to myself. I've even stopped nagging myself because I've realized I don't listen.

But now I've got an idea. I know how I'm going to do it. I just need to make a start, get into the right frame of mind, make some notes, jot down some ideas, and then it's going to be easy. I'll really do it this time.

If I could just get beyond the doodling phase and into actual words, I'll be away.

Or maybe if I make a cup of tea and put the TV back on, an idea might come to me more easily.

When I go to bed (the paper still blank), I can't sleep. It's not raining tonight and I don't really know what it is that's keeping me awake. I'm thinking about a lot of different things—about Fay and Simon, and whether it matters that she's bored with him and wants to go clubbing, about Ellie and all the millions of tiny and huge worries I have about her, about my life in general and why it's so crap and why I can't even manage to write a measly hundred words when I've got half an hour to spare, a blank pad of paper, and a brilliant idea for how to become a famous scriptwriter.

After I've tried both sides of the bed, both sides of the pillow, light on, light off, eyes open, eyes closed, counting sheep and trying to think about the most boring thing I can imagine (probably cleaning Alex Chapman's flat), I give up and get out of bed. I put on my dressing gown and head for the kitchen to get myself a drink, but as I pass Ellie's room I can hear her talking. She's talking in her sleep—she does it occasionally when she's been overtired or had too much excitement. I stand in her doorway listening to her little grunty mutterings. I won't wake her or disturb her; she usually stops after a while, shuffles around a bit in bed, and then settles into a deeper sleep again.

They say eavesdroppers never hear anything good. Not even mothers eavesdropping on their own children's dreams, apparently.

"Ask your daddy," says Ellie in a little whisper to her dream companion. She sighs and mutters and frowns in her sleep. "Ask . . . Daddy. I'll ask my daddy. Ask *my* daddy . . . Daddy?"

A tiny hiccup of a sob stops the dream abruptly and she turns over to sleep silently again. I hurry away to the kitchen, wishing I hadn't listened. What you don't know can't hurt you. How is it that she dreams about him? She hasn't seen him, hasn't asked for him, hasn't even mentioned him for so long. It's my fault. I should talk to her about him. I knew this would happen. She's psychologically disturbed. Should I talk to her teacher? The doctor? My mum? Panic makes me feel weak. I pour out a glass of milk and drink it in great gulps.

This is all because of you, Daniel, you bastard.

Where are you now? Why did you leave me with all the responsibility, all the problems, all the worries? You pay money into my account every month and you think that makes it OK, while you live with your new girlfriend in your new home and pretend we don't exist, that you never had a child, never held her, newborn and slippery, in your arms and cried with emotion. And now it's Ellie who cries in her sleep, and you don't even know. You don't even care.

And I want to cry, too, but I find I can't. I've got past the crying stage, long past it. Instead, I sit here in the kitchen with my empty milk glass, and I make a decision. I'm going to show you something, Daniel Potter. I'm going to show you something about me that you didn't know, something that'll shock you. I'm going to become something, I am. I'm not just a cleaning lady, not just your ex-girlfriend to be tossed aside, thrown away when someone new comes along.

I'm going to write this TV script, and it's going to make me famous. I'm going to start right now, tonight, and I'm not stopping till I've done a hundred words.

And this time I mean it!

Wednesday

Dottie Anderson's eighty-three but thinks she's about twenty-five. She can't understand why she's got arthritis at her age, or why she's a bit deaf; she tells me no one else in her family had these sort of problems at such a young age. She won't take medication of any sort.

"Bad enough having to take pills and potions when you start getting on a bit," she explains. "I'm not starting yet, while I've still got me youth and me health, thank God."

She keeps an eye on the two "old ladies" (both younger than her) who live next door, and regularly takes them hot dinners or fruit pies she's made herself.

"They can't get out much, poor old dears," she says, shaking her head, and completely overlooking the fact that she can't get out much herself. "They can't get to the shops, you see."

In fact I see them regularly in Tesco when I do Dottie's shopping for her. They have one small wire basket between them and load its contents carefully into a wicker basket on wheels, which they both hold on to to walk home. I push a cart around the shop for Dottie, and on her list is written:

Biscuits for next door
Half a pound of mince for next door
Six bananas for next door
Small granary loaf for next door

"They can't manage it all, you see," she explains when I question the length of the list. "They're getting on a bit."

I like Dottie. I like going to her bungalow, making tea in her little blue kitchen, polishing her old brass and silver ornaments, tidying her garden, kicking Tosser when he goes for my ankles.

She's got some stories to tell, has Dottie. She talks to me the whole time, even while I've got the Hoover going and can't hear a word she's saying. I keep telling her I can't hear her but it doesn't bother her in the slightest, she just goes on and on. She tells me about her husband and what a complete bastard he was and how much happier she's been since he died in 1962 from a dog bite.

"A dog bite?" I asked in amazement the first time she told me, looking at Tosser with fresh distrust.

"Went septic. Whole arm went poisonous. Gangrene set in. Killed him in a week. Nothing they could do." She shrugged philosophically. "That's life."

She tells me about her children, who've gone to live abroad—the son to Australia, the daughter to the States.

I feel sorry for her. She hasn't any family left alive in this country except for a sister who's in a home ("completely barmy").

"That's life," she says, slurping her tea. "Isn't it? I just get on with it. No good complaining."

She tells me how the two "old ladies" next door come in for tea every Monday afternoon and spend the whole time complaining.

"But they can't help it. They've got so many ailments, poor old dears. Pills for this, medicines for that, doctors

and hospitals . . . not that they do any good, if you ask
me. I'm just grateful for me youth and me health, I am."

And she struggles painfully to her feet and hobbles
into the kitchen.

"I'll wash up!" I protest as she starts to run the hot
water.

"No, you won't! You've got enough to do, with the
shopping, and taking Tosser for his walk."

She looks at me sadly. "I'll be better next week, love.
I'll be able to take him out meself. Just a bit of damp got
into me knees, I think. If I just rest up for today, I'll get
back to normal by next week."

She hasn't been able to take him for walks for about
five years.

"Don't worry, Dottie," I tell her with a smile. "I like
walking him," I lie, shaking his jaws off from around my
wrist as I try to put on his lead.

"He's only being friendly," she says, reaching down to
pat him with a knobbly brown old hand. "Aren't you,
boy!"

He bares his teeth and growls.

Nice doggy.

Two days a week, a couple of teenage girls from the local
school come to see her. It's part of their Community Service. I met them once when they called back on a
Wednesday because one of them had left her mobile
phone behind on the Tuesday evening. They both had
dyed black hair cut very short and silver nose rings. She
says they're nice children. They take Tosser for a walk,
make Dottie a cup of tea, and ask if she needs anything.
They ask her a lot of questions about what it was like living in the old days before television.

"They have to do a project." She smiles. "They write down everything I tell them."

I have a mental picture of school notebooks crammed with pages and pages of stories about the bastard husband.

"They love Tosser," she says. "Don't they, boy? They bring him biscuits."

So he gets walked on Tuesdays, Wednesdays, and Thursdays, and the rest of the week, as far as I know, he has to make do with prowling about in her little back garden.

Perhaps that's what makes him vicious.

Today, while I'm dusting the ornaments on her fireplace, Dottie's talking to me about her grandson, the youngest child of the son in Australia.

"Wants to be an artist," she says.

I look at her with interest.

"Stupid child," she adds dismissively.

"Why?"

"I don't know. Thinks he'll be famous, I suppose," she says with a toss of her white head.

"No, I mean, why do you think he's stupid? It's good to have an ambition, don't you think?"

"Ambition? He wants to get a decent job if you ask me, never mind about ambition. Hasn't brought home a penny since he left school!"

"But I thought you said he was at university?"

"University!" she sniffs.

It's a favorite topic for her, one of the greatest ills of modern society, the tendency of too many stupid children to go to university, which are, as everyone knows (because it says so in the papers)—

"Hotbeds of politicians. And sexual liberties."

"Liberation." I smile.

"I don't see how he can bring money home, if he's at university," I add quickly, before she can steam into her other favorite topic of sexual immorality. Not that she complains about it. She just thinks it's unfair that she's not able to get out and get any of it herself.

"He's finished university," she says without any pride. "For what it's worth."

"What degree did he get?"

"Art with English."

"That's great!" I say warmly. "Good for him."

"You think so? Art? That's not a proper subject, is it—it's a hobby. Drawing and painting! And why's it so great to get a degree in English? He speaks it already, doesn't he? If he'd done French or Latin that would have been worth something."

"But it's . . ." I sometimes wonder if she's winding me up. She's not stupid. "You have to study literature, for an English degree. A lot of literature. It's very hard work."

"We all read books, love," she says patiently. "Nothing hard about that."

"Anyway, he's done it. He's graduated."

"Yes. And now, my son says, he's moping around, talking about modern art and expressing himself. Lot of nonsense. How can a boy that age hope to express himself, and who'd give a damn if he did anyway? You need experience of life before you have anything to express yourself about. You need to have lived a bit, loved a bit, suffered a bit. Seen things that amazed you and things that frightened you."

I stare at her. I'm so often taken aback by the simplicity of her wisdom. "You're quite right, of course," I say humbly. "But perhaps he wants to get started—practicing."

"Then he should damn well get out and get a job while he's practicing," she says firmly. "Shall we have another tea?"

I think about this while I'm taking Tosser for his walk. If it's true that young people shouldn't presume to express themselves, how do some of them get novels published? Occasionally, the arts review columns in the papers carry the name of a completely unknown "new talent" whose first novel is feted by the critics for its freshness, its originality, its vision. So how do they cover up their lack of experience? I read those reviews with an envy bordering on morbid resentment. How can these fresh young talents get to the stage of having novels published when they're barely out of their teens, while I'm still doodling on blank pieces of paper at the age of twenty-nine?

Except that I'm not just doodling now. Not anymore.

I take a deep breath to steady the tremor of nervous excitement that suddenly bubbles into my brain.

Yesterday, I started writing. I stopped making promises to myself about it, stopped playing at the idea, and I sat down, with the notes I'd made when I sat up late into Saturday night, and started writing. Sat down, to be exact, in Alex Chapman's flat, in Alex Chapman's time, at Alex Chapman's computer, and started writing.

Well—can you blame me?

No, honestly—can you?

Look, his mother wants me to clean the flat, and I do, don't I? You couldn't fault the cleanness of the flat. If he doesn't make it dirty, can I help it?

I know it's not strictly honest. I suppose in a perfect world, if I were a perfectly honest, decent person, I'd tell the old bat that I don't need four hours to clean the place because her son's some sort of cleanliness freak who never lets so much as a crumb fall on the carpet. I'd refuse to take the money she puts in a brown envelope and gives Louise every Thursday to give to me, probably afraid of touching my hands herself because of the germs I might be carrying.

If I were a decent, honest person, it wouldn't even cross my mind to turn on someone's computer while I'm only supposed to be dusting it. I know it's wrong. I have been brought up properly, you know. I went to Sunday School.

But come on, give me a break.

It's sitting there, doing nothing, and it could be earning me a fortune. It could be my route to becoming a famous TV scriptwriter, achieving my lifetime's ambition, allowing me to afford lovely holidays abroad in hot countries with soft white beaches, making my mother proud of me. And making Daniel curse the day he ever left me. I'm sorry, God, but there just wasn't any decision to make. I had to do it. When I'm famous, I'll pay Alex Chapman back for the electricity.

"How was Dottie?" asks Fay.

I've brought Ellie and Lauren back from playgroup. Normally Fay collects them and takes them to her place till I finish work at one or two o'clock, but on Wednesdays it's my turn, because I'm always finished at Dottie's by half past twelve and I collect the girls on my way home. I get Dottie's lunch ready for her, and then I go while she's eating it, while she's stopped talking.

"Off you go, love," she said before she took her first mouthful. "See you next week—I'll be a bit better on me feet by then."

"She'll never be any better on her feet," I sigh to Fay, "unless she sees her doctor and gets something for her arthritis."

"Obstinate old bugger," remarks Fay.

"But she doesn't want to be old," I retort, understanding her completely. "She doesn't want to be ill, or incapacitated. She wants to pretend to herself . . ."

"And what about when she gets completely housebound? Bedridden? Too sick to take care of herself?"

"We'll have to think about that when it happens."

"*We? We*, Beth?"

I color slightly. "I mean, I'll have to contact Social Services and see what they can do."

"*You'll* have to?"

"All right!" I say tetchily. "You don't have to keep repeating me like a parrot. Yes, I suppose I'll have to, 'cos—"

"You're her *cleaning* lady, not—"

"But she hasn't got anyone. No family, not even any friends really unless you count the two old ladies next door."

"She's got a son and daughter abroad, hasn't she?"

"Yes. OK, so I'll contact them. If things get bad, I'll contact them. But it's hardly likely they'll come rushing back over here to arrange her nursing care or whatever, is it. They've got their own lives, they've got families and jobs and so on."

"And they're her children," says Fay, looking at me with her eyebrows up in her hairline. "And you're her cleaning lady."

"OK, OK, I know."

I stand in her kitchen, staring out of the window, screwing up the papers I'm holding in my hands. I don't know why I'm so annoyed.

"That's my *finger painting*!" squeals Ellie, rescuing

the ball of scrunchy yellow paper covered in red and blue smears. "Mummy, you've ruined it!"

"Sorry, darling!" I look in mortification at my child's precious artwork. What the hell's the matter with me? What was I thinking of?

"Look, Ellie," says Fay quickly. "It's modern art!" She smoothes out the paper on the kitchen table. "We can make it into a collage! Spread glue over the creases and stick on some leaves from the garden . . ."

Lauren, watching, rushes to get her own painting and turn hers into a collage, too, and I smile my thanks at Fay as the two girls, kneeling on their chairs, lean over the glue pot together, frowning with the studious concentration of artistic creation.

"You're good at it," I remark to Fay. "Being a mum."

"So are you," she says, putting her arm round me affectionately. "You daft cow."

Louise Perkins phones me when I get home. Her voice is shaky. "Beth, I need to tell you . . . I don't know how to tell you this . . ."

"What's the matter?" I ask, alarmed.

Louise is usually so calm and happy. She sounds terribly upset. "We're going to be moving. I'm sorry."

"When? Why? Is it Ben's job?"

They love Park Cottage. She's always told me how much they love the house, how comfortable it is, what a lovely family home for the children.

"Ben's job?" She gives a kind of snort, like I'm being purposely sarcastic. "In a way. Yes, in a way."

I wait, not knowing what to say.

"He's only just told me," she says suddenly, and it all comes out in a rush. "We've got the most horrendous debts, Beth. We've been living outside our means, big time, like you've no idea . . . like *I* had no idea. I knew the mortgage was massive but he told me he was on top of it, he was earning overtime, getting bonuses. All my salary was going on the food and the kids, so I let him get on with it . . . the mortgage, the bills, the credit cards, the finance agreements, the loans, the overdrafts . . ." She starts to cry.

"You don't have to tell me," I say weakly.

"It's all hit the fan now," she sobs, ignoring me. "We're in arrears with the mortgage, the finance companies are going to repossess the cars, the TV, the stereo, and the living room furniture. We're being sued for the repayments for the double glazing and the fitted kitchen, and . . . and we can't pay the children's school fees. We'll have to take them out."

"God," I say. "You poor things."

Poor things. I thought *I* had problems. Perhaps it's better not to have anything, after all, than have it all and not be able to keep it.

"We've got to sell the house," she concludes, "as quickly as possible."

"Where will you go?"

"I don't know. We'll have to rent something. Something very small."

She sniffs and adds, "I'm so sorry, Beth. I know you need the money, but . . ."

Not as much as she does, now.

"It doesn't matter," I lie. "I just wish I could help."

"You can, actually," she says. She sighs. "We've got so much stuff in this house."

You can say that again.

"You'd like some help packing up?"

"No, we'll have to get rid of most of it. Come round and take what you want."

I feel very embarrassed now. I mean, I want to help

her, I really do, she's so nice and she doesn't deserve this. But I can't afford any of her family's stuff. Even if she sent it to a rummage sale I wouldn't be able to afford it.

"I . . . don't know," I mumble. "I . . . might be able to take a couple of things. If I can pay you over a few weeks . . . I feel awful but . . ."

"Beth!" she exclaims, her voice suddenly firmer. "For God's sake! I don't want any money from you! You're my friend!"

"But . . ."

"You've looked after us, cleaned up our mess, for all this time, and the last thing I ever wanted was to have to let you down. None of this mess is your fault. The least we can do is let you have a few bits and pieces for Ellie; things the girls have grown out of. We'd have been chucking them out anyway. I'm just asking you to do me a favor, come round and help me get rid of them."

"But you could sell them. Seriously, your kids' things are so good—all their lovely clothes—you've spent a fortune on them. You could get a lot of money back—put ads in the paper . . ."

"I haven't got time," she says. "And I haven't got room to store stuff. Please, Beth. It would help me so much. I can't face having to do all that, on top of everything else."

I hesitate, wanting to help her, not wanting to take advantage of her own disaster.

"Come round tomorrow at your usual time," she goes on decisively. "I'm taking some time off work to try to sort things out. You can help me to start . . . No, not tomorrow." Her voice wavers a little. "We've got a meeting with the bank manager tomorrow. Come on Monday, Beth. Please! I'll be desperate for some help, by then—and someone to talk to."

I decide on a compromise. "All right. Look, I'll come round and help you sort stuff out. I'll help pack up what you need to keep and what you want to get rid of. Then I'll take it all to a boot sale for you."

"No! Just keep it! Keep whatever you want."

"I'll keep a couple of things for Ellie, if you really insist. But I'll do the boot sale. I'll get you a lot of money back, Louise. I promise."

"Well, we'll share it, if you do."

"Don't be silly. I'm OK. I'll get another job."

I switch on the kettle and stare wearily, through the rising steam, out of my little kitchen window into the tiny paved yard I laughingly refer to as my patio garden. Ellie's little pink bike with its stabilizers is pushed up against the wall and there are half a dozen pots of plants, most of them from Oliver, most of them half dead. I haven't got much, here, but, thank God, I've got all I need. Who would ever have thought that Louise Perkins, with her lovely house, her smart job and executive husband, would be in a worse state than me?

I can't even allow myself to dwell on the fact that I'm losing two days' work per week. That would be just too selfish for words.

Friday

"The playgroup is looking for new staff," says Fay.

"Yeah, but the pay's rubbish."

"Of course. But whichever mornings you worked there, you wouldn't pay for Ellie. It could work out better for you than doing the cleaning and paying for her five mornings a week. Have you ever considered it?"

"Not really," I say gloomily, opening a packet of chips and picking out the biggest one. "I don't think it'd be very good for Ellie, having me there. Anyway . . ." I shrug and take another chip.

"What?"

"Well, I expect I'll manage."

"Beth, you're always saying you can barely pay the bills. Losing two days' work . . ."

"It's not Louise's fault!"

"Nobody's saying it is. But at least they can move downmarket. And take their kids out of that snobby school."

"It'll be hard for them. They're in real trouble. I feel really sorry for her—she didn't even know . . ."

Fay snorts. "Great marriage, isn't it, if the husband doesn't even tell the wife what's going on financially."

"Perhaps he thought it would get better. And then it just got worse and worse and he was too frightened."

Fay snorts again and I feel like I don't want to discuss it anymore.

We eat in silence. The children are watching TV and eating their lunch.

"How was Oliver today?" asks Fay with a wicked grin.

"Same as ever." I give an involuntary shiver.

"Not given in to his demands yet, then?"

"You'd be the first to know!" I laugh.

She smiles. "It must be quite exciting to be wanted so badly."

"By Oliver? I think he probably lusts after everyone he meets. It's no great compliment. I just happen to be there."

"Probably it's a challenge. The fact that you keep turning him down. Perhaps it doesn't happen to him very often—if he's as good-looking as you say."

"Oh, he certainly is!" I agree.

"I wouldn't mind half a chance myself," she jokes.

I look at her thoughtfully. "You'd run a mile, wouldn't you. If someone actually came on to you, they wouldn't see you for dust. It's all talk."

"Of course." She smiles. "You know me. All talk, talk, talk." She swallows a mouthful of sandwich and adds, "Still up for going out again tonight?"

And that's the funny thing about Fay. She knows me inside out, she knows and understands how hard up I am, she's just heard me telling her how I'm going to lose two days' work a week, and that I'll try to manage somehow, and she's told me I ought to take a job at the playgroup. Then in the next breath she asks me if I still want to go out to the pub tonight.

"No," I snap crossly. "Can't afford it, can I. You know I can't!"

"Just one beer? I'll pay."

"Fay, you said last time we were just going to have a couple of beers, and look how it ended up."

She looks down at the floor, doing a very good impression of shamefaced apology. "I know. I was out of order. I'm sorry. Look, I've promised it won't happen this time. Let me buy you a beer tonight, Beth—please. To make amends. Please?" She makes it sound like she's doing me a favor. I don't know how she does this.

"I've told you," I say, getting up and getting ready to leave. "I can't afford it. Subject closed."

So here we are again, at nine o'clock this evening, back in the Cress & Lettuce or whatever this stupid bar's stupid name is. This time we've got seats in one of the cosy corners where all the couples sit. I feel slightly resentful about how easy it was to talk me into something I didn't really want to do. What's the matter with me? I'm a pushover. As soon as I had Ellie and Lauren ganging up on me, crying and whining about how I was ruining their lives by not letting them have their sleepover and their Night-night Feast, I caved in like an igloo in a heat wave. Fay didn't have to say a word. In fact, she put on a good show of taking my side against the children.

No, children. If Mummy says no, Ellie, then I'm sorry, it's no.

But, Mummy! You said! You promised! I hate you!

Now come on, Ellie, don't sulk, don't cry. Lauren, stop crying. Beth said no.

But it's not fair! You said we could! Beth said we could!

Well, it's different now. Beth says no.

Boo, hiss, the wicked old witch Beth says no and makes little children cry.

"I could still bring Ellie round to sleep," I suggested. "If it's OK with you. Or Lauren could come and stay with us. Even if we don't go out."

"Simon's coming home early," said Fay, "because he's expecting to babysit. So if you bring Ellie round to sleep, we could always just have that one beer while you're already out. It seems such a waste of him offering to babysit, otherwise, doesn't it? Almost ungrateful, really. But of course, I quite understand if you'd rather not . . ."

Like I say, a pushover.

And here we are, already on the second beer. Now Fay's bought me two, I'm going to look like a real tightwad if I don't offer to buy her one, and I know she won't refuse, and before you know it, we'll end up just the same as last week.

And just to prove the point, look who's coming in the door—Starsky and bloody Hutch themselves.

"Hello, Neil. Hello, Martin," croons Fay, but she's only looking at Neil. "This is a surprise!" She says it in a silly voice that irritates the life out of me.

"Want another drink, girls?" asks Neil, smiling at Fay.

"We'll be making a move in a minute actually," I say pointedly.

"Perhaps just one, then," says Fay. "A quick one!" She pretends to find this hilariously funny and laughs an absurd, tinkling, little-girl laugh while doing some unnatural twiddling stuff with her hair. Neil hasn't taken his eyes off her.

"Becks?" Martin asks me. He raises his eyebrows toward the other two and gives me a slight twist of a smile, and I suddenly think perhaps I could like him. If I was to bother to get to know him, which I'm definitely not, because we're going after this one drink.

"Please." I nod. "But we can't stay long. Sorry."

He brings the beers over and sits down next to me. "So what's the hurry to get home?" he asks.

"Well, I wasn't going to come out at all. Fay talked me into it," I admit grudgingly.

"I can imagine how that could happen." He smiles.

I force myself to smile back. "I didn't mean it to sound like that," I say. "Like she's some sort of control freak and I'm a wimp who can't say no. Well, anyway—she's not a control freak!"

"But you can't say no?" he says with a lazy grin.

"I can when I want to. I should have, tonight. But you know how it is. She's my best friend. She does me the most enormous favor, almost everyday of my life. It's hard to refuse her when all she wants is a night out."

"And you don't? You don't want a night out?"

I shrug. "Couldn't afford it, to be perfectly honest. She's just bought me two beers, and you've bought me another! Don't worry, I'll stand my round in a minute."

"It doesn't matter. For God's sake!" He brushes this aside impatiently and offers me a chip. "So what's this enormous favor that Fay does for you everyday?"

"Looks after my daughter while I'm working."

He nods. "Where do you work?"

Of course, I knew that was coming. I shouldn't be embarrassed about this. There's nothing demeaning or degrading about cleaning houses. It's fine, honest labor. It's people like me who keep the wheels of industry and commerce running, by freeing other people to spend their time at their careers, doing what they do best, instead of doing their own housework. It's not menial or subservient. There's glorious satisfaction in it.

"I'm a scriptwriter," I say.

Now, where did that come from? I wasn't going to say that.

I put my fingers up to my lips as if I can't believe the words came out of them. "I write TV scripts," I add.

Jesus! If I sit here much longer, I'll be introducing myself as someone famous.

"Wow!" he says, and adds with a little chuckle, "Are you famous?"

"Not yet," I say enigmatically.

For God's sake!

"I'm working on it. Of course, it's a very competitive business, but I'm pretty hopeful about my current work."

"Really! Where are you hoping to sell it?"

"Oh . . . I . . . er . . . leave all that sort of thing to my agent."

"Of course. That's really interesting. Makes me feel quite boring."

"What do you do?" I ask, trying not to sound condescending.

"I'm a heart surgeon."

He's only a *junior* heart surgeon, of course, but it still makes me feel pretty ridiculous the way I've been posing and posturing about my TV script (which in reality is of course only the first few pages of a TV script and probably never even likely to see the inside of an agent's office). But how the fuck can I tell him, now, that I'm really a cleaning lady? OK, I'm not actually ashamed of it, but it's kind of difficult to slip into a conversation between a heart surgeon and a TV scriptwriter.

In fact we're quite a long way into the conversation, and it's moved on from heart surgery and scriptwriting, and we've covered a lot of things including films, books, politics, the weather, holidays, favorite restaurants, take-out places, how long I've known Fay, how long he's known Neil, where we went to university, whether we've been married or had children (he hasn't), and the state of the world in general, before I've realized that it seems to matter. I mean, it matters, now, about being a cleaning lady and him not finding out.

And that's bad news, isn't it?

It's bad news because it shouldn't matter, in the least, because I hardly know this guy with his floppy dark blond hair and easy lopsided smile. I had no intention of getting to know him, even an hour ago; in fact, my only intention was to drink that beer and make a quick exit, and here I am with yet another beer, laughing and enjoying his company as if the whole thing was a great idea all along.

And it's bad news because I've told him a string of lies about being a scriptwriter, and I don't tell lies, normally, and I hate myself for it, for being too embarrassed to tell him the truth and too scared to admit it now.

And . . . it's bad news because I forgot about Fay.

I forgot, all the time I've been sitting here chatting to Martin as if he were my long-lost friend, I forgot that I wanted to keep an eye on her and Neil. I wanted to watch her and make sure the flirting wasn't over the top. All right, all right, I know she's over the age of consent and I'm not her mother, but I am her best friend and I do care about her marriage. And her making a fool of herself. So where was I when things moved on a stage? How did I fail to notice when things, for instance, progressed from sitting together to sitting *together*? I'm sure I don't have to spell out the difference to you. Here they are now, sitting with thighs touching, shoulders touching, and hands brushing at every opportunity. Feet on feet, arms resting on arms. Faces closer than the conversational volume necessitates.

I stop talking to Martin in mid-sentence. He follows my gaze and we look at Fay and Neil, both knowing what we're looking at here.

Neil notices our silence before she does. He turns and looks back at us, eyes wide, inviting comment. She, in full flow, doesn't see, doesn't stop. I only catch the end of her sentence, which falls into our sudden pool of quietness like a brick: "... when you sent me that Christmas card."

Christmas card. *Christmas* fucking card?

She stops, finally aware that we're watching, listening, waiting.

"Christmas card?" I repeat softly. The silence is horrible now, like life all around us has suddenly been suspended. "I thought you two had only just met?"

She exchanges a glance with Neil, and I see it then, see it as clearly as if she'd stood up and announced it to the world. Even now, I'm hoping she'll say something to prove me wrong, to make it all OK. An innocent explanation. A Christmas card sent to the wrong address. Sent by mistake to the wrong person. But would I really be able to believe it, when the evidence is sitting there staring me in the eyes across the pub table?

She looks at me now, and the honesty of our relationship, the gut-wrenching, soul-searching, know-everything-about-you love that exists ... *existed* between us as best friends in the whole world, is reflected there for one split second in her eyes, and makes her drop her gaze from mine, and I feel that probably from this minute it's gone forever. I don't know her anymore.

Neil gets to his feet. "Anyone want another beer?"

Everyone ignores him.

"Why didn't you tell me?" I ask her.

"I was going to."

"Were you? When?"

"Soon . . ."

"How soon?" I persist, hearing my voice beginning to rise. "How soon did you think would be soon enough to tell me, Fay? Or were you ever going to tell me?"

"Of course!"

"No, you were just going to carry on like this, weren't you! Using me as a cover—covering up for you meeting your boyfriend, pretending you'd only just met him, when all the time . . . !"

"I didn't want to compromise you . . . make you tell any lies for me."

"So *you* lied to *me* instead? After all we've been through, all this time, all the secrets we've told each other! I can't believe you'd do this to me!"

I'm almost beside myself with self-pity. How could she?

"We need to talk," she says, finally looking up at me, misery in her eyes where just a minute ago there was that bright spark of excited lust. "I need to explain. You need to understand."

"Understand?" I repeat scathingly. "I don't think so. I don't think I *need* to understand anything. I just need to go home." I get to my feet, dropping my purse, picking it up and dropping my jacket. Martin picks up the jacket for me and hands it to me silently. I'm shaking slightly.

"Don't be like this," says Fay.

I ignore her. "I'll be round in the morning to collect Ellie," I say, putting on my jacket.

She watches me. "You're not going to say anything? To Simon?"

I stop, turn to her, stare at her, shaking my head. "I can't believe you just said that."

"Sorry," she says as I walk away.

I'm walking toward the bus stop when Martin catches up to me.

"I suppose they sent you after me," I say morosely as he falls into step beside me.

"No."

"I suppose you were a part of all this farce? Brought along to make up the numbers? Keep me quiet?"

"No."

"I don't believe you."

"I can understand that. But for what it's worth, I didn't know Fay hadn't told you about her and Neil. I didn't know they were pretending they'd only just met. Christ, Beth, do they *look* like a couple who've only just met?"

No. Of course they don't, in retrospect. That's what makes me feel so stupid. Why didn't I see it? They were practically all over each other.

"Well, anyway, you've done your bit, haven't you. I won't be coming out with them anymore to provide their cover story, so you don't need to tag along either." We're at the bus stop. I turn to face him. "So—see you!"

"Do we need to fall out over it—you and me?" he asks with a shrug.

"We don't even know each other, really, do we? We both just got used."

"I don't feel used, but I'm sorry you do. Neil asked me

to come out for a drink with him and his girlfriend, to meet her friend Beth. If I hadn't liked you, I wouldn't have come out a second time."

Oh, please.

My bus is coming.

"Fay is not Neil's girlfriend," I say crisply. "She's Simon's wife."

"I know. But I'm not Neil's priest, I'm only his friend."

"Perhaps you should redefine what a friend is, then," I say haughtily as I get on the bus. I sit down and don't look back as the bus pulls away.

I'm so angry, so angry and upset, I can't even remember walking home from the bus. I go around the flat opening doors and slamming them. What good is this doing? How is it helping, to slam things around and stamp and kick things in my own flat, on my own, when probably what I should be doing is having it out with Fay properly? I should phone her up now and demand an explanation, an apology for lying to me and taking advantage of our friendship, a promise that she's going to stop seeing Neil and that our relationship can go back to how it was before.

But I can't, because she's out somewhere with Neil, her *boyfriend,* the boyfriend she's been seeing since some time before Christmas—that's for at least two months and who knows how much longer? Six months? A year?— without telling me about it. And Simon will be there and she won't be able to talk to me, much less argue with me about it because he'll hear and he'll want to know what's going on, and whatever else I might feel like doing I'll never let him find out that Fay's been unfaithful to him.

And I can't because, anyway, our relationship *can't* ever go back to how it was. That's the thing—no matter what I say to her, no matter what she says to me, it can't go back now. I don't even want it to. I don't feel like I can ever trust her again. I don't want to see her, I don't want to speak to her. I don't want her looking after my daughter.

For just a few minutes, in between kicking the bedroom door open and throwing my shoes across the bed, I contemplate going round to her house, getting Ellie out of bed, and bringing her back now. But quite apart from the battle I'd have with Ellie and the fact that she'd probably never forgive me for ruining her sleepover, I know I wouldn't be able to explain it to Simon and I know I'm probably also being childish.

I can't do anything.

I feel helpless, frustrated, and just so, so angry.

I can't kick anything else or throw anything else.

I can't tell anyone and I can't stop thinking about it.

I put on my sneakers, put my jacket back on, and go for a jog around the block. Still not tired enough, I go around a second time, running harder. I'm not particularly fit and by halfway the second time I'm gasping for breath and holding my sides, but I don't stop until I'm back at my doorstep. I let myself in, drink a couple of pints of water, undress, take a hot shower, and go straight to bed.

At about one o'clock in the morning, the phone rings.

I lie awake counting. It rings twenty-five times. After it stops ringing, I dial *69 and it's Fay's number. I have a sudden fear that perhaps they're phoning me to tell me that something's wrong with Ellie. She's been taken ill, she's had an accident, she's fallen out of bed or choked on some chips during her Night-night Feast, and all the time they're trying to contact me I'm just lying here counting how many times the phone rings.

If she's ill they'll bring her home.

If she's had an accident they'll phone me again from the hospital.

I lie awake for another hour, wanting to call back, wanting the phone to ring again.

When it does, it makes me jump. But I still let it ring twenty-five times, and I still don't answer it. And it doesn't ring again.

Monday

⬥━━━◆◈◆━━━⬥

I take Ellie to playgroup early so I can get away without seeing Fay.

"Where's Lauren?" she says, pulling at her hair anxiously as she looks around the room.

"She'll be here in a minute. Go and play. Go and play in the house corner. Look, Katie and Cara are over there."

"Don't want to." She puts a thumb in her mouth and holds on to my sleeve with her other hand.

"Don't be a baby," I hiss at her. "You're a big girl now. You'll be going to school soon. You can't always have Lauren around."

"Lauren *is* coming to school, too!" Her eyes fill up with tears and I immediately feel guilty and irritated at the same time. It's been a mistake to let her get so attached to just one friend. A mistake for her, a mistake for me. It's been too easy, too convenient, and I haven't stopped to think about the possible problems.

"Of course Lauren will be at school," I try to soothe her, quietly, in a corner so the playgroup leaders can't see me being a bad mother who destroys her child's confidence. "But so will all the other children. Try to make some other friends, too, in case one day Lauren . . . doesn't come to school."

"If Lauren doesn't come, I'm not going!" declares Ellie through a mouthful of thumb.

"Come along, Ellie!" calls Pat the playgroup leader in that peculiar sing-song voice used by all infant and kindergarten teachers, nannies, Sunday-School teachers, Brownie and Cub leaders, and mothers of hordes of children. She approaches us purposefully, hand held out to take Ellie's and lead her away from her useless mother into the care of the professionals, "Come along now, you don't usually make a fuss like this, do you!" (smiling sympathetically at me—never mind, you can't help it if you're not a very good mother—she never cries with *us*). "Now, come and play with the dough and let Mummy go off to her work, there's a good girl, that's right. See you later, Mummy!"

Dismissed, I leave hurriedly and gratefully, get into the car, and drive away just as Fay's car pulls up. In the mirror, I see her park, get out of the car, and stare after me. I drive on.

I haven't spoken to Fay since Friday night.

I know, I know, it's not very satisfactory and it's not very adult, and it's going to have to be dealt with eventually, but how? And when? And why should I make the first move?

When I went to her house on Saturday morning to collect Ellie she was still in bed, and Simon was whispering and making the girls tiptoe around the place so as not to wake her up. He was carrying Jack in his arms, giving him drinks and cookies to keep him quiet, so Fay could have a nice lie-in because she was tired from looking after him and she deserved it.

Normally I wouldn't have argued with that. She does work hard, looking after my kid, as well as her own two, and still managing to keep her house and garden nice, especially with Jack being such a little sod who never lets her get any sleep. But I knew that she wasn't having a lie-in because she was exhausted by her virtuous maternal duties. She was tired from boogying in the nightclub and making out with her boyfriend. And from being up till all hours trying to phone me and not getting an answer.

So I thanked Simon profusely for the babysitting and the Night-night Feast and everything that went with it, took Ellie and left. And every time the phone rang later in the day, I left it ringing until it stopped and then dialed *69. Once it was my mum, and I had to call her back and pretend I'd been in the toilet. The other three times it was Fay's number, and I didn't call her back. She didn't try anymore after the third time.

When I arrive at Park Cottage, I suddenly forget my own problems. Louise opens the door in jeans and a sweatshirt with her hair tied up on top in a scarf. I've only ever seen her when she's been dressed for work, in full makeup and smart business suits. She's got rings under her eyes and worry lines I haven't noticed before.

"Come in, Beth," she says, and her voice is a sigh of distress.

On an impulse, I give her a hug, and she hugs back for a full minute. I can feel her swallowing hard, like she's struggling for control.

"Thanks for coming," she says, attempting a smile as she pushes some strands of hair back under the scarf. "Sorry about the mess."

I step into the hall. I'm used to stepping over things in this house, but this time it's different—different in a way that would make you want to cry. Boxes are piled everywhere; boxes, bags, and crates of toys, clothes, crockery, ornaments, books—the contents of five people's lives hastily packed up, and not packed up with cheerful excitement the way you do when you're moving to a new house, going somewhere different because you want to, because of an exciting new job or a bigger, better home or even a smaller, neater home—but with sudden desperate need because there's no alternative.

"In the living room," says Louise, stepping carefully over a line of bulging black trash bags, "I've dumped all the stuff we won't be taking. So far. There'll be more, I know, once we've got up into the loft, and sorted out the spare bedroom, and the tops of the wardrobes . . ."

For the first time, I can see what a nightmare it can be to have too much of everything. If I ever get to be rich, I'm going to throw things out on a regular basis. Take stuff to charity shops or bring and buy sales, anything, anything, rather than accumulate mountains of material possessions that take over your home and strangle the life out of it.

"Just go in there, Beth!" Louise flings open the living room door and steers me into the space just inside. It's the only bit of space in the room. "Go in, grab an armful of black sacks, and take what you want."

I stand there for a minute with my mouth open. I feel like a contestant on a game show where they have to watch all the articles going by on a conveyor belt and memorize as many as they can. *And a toaster, and an electric drill, and a set of encyclopedias, and a cuddly toy . . .*

"Is that OK?" asks Louise anxiously and I realize I'm rooted to the spot gawping like a tourist, which isn't only horribly rude, but also pretty unhelpful in the circumstances.

"Of course," I say firmly, picking my way carefully through the piles of stuff until I find a spot in the center of the carpet where I can push things aside enough to make a clearing. I squat down on the floor and prepare to sort through a heap of girls' clothes. "Go on, carry on with what you're doing and leave this lot to me," I add with more confidence than I feel.

Louise retreats into another room, looking relieved, as I sit back on my haunches and take a deep breath. OK. Two black trash bags to start with. This bag on the right for anything that might be good for Ellie. The bag on the left for anything going to the boot sale. I'd like to say I'll have a third bag for rubbish, but none of this family's stuff is rubbish.

You can get strangled by too much stuff whether it's rubbish or designer gear. The only difference is you don't want to send designer gear to the dump.

Two hours go by without me even noticing. Louise brings me a mug of coffee and looks around her in surprise. "You've cleared a lot of it!"

To my right and to my left are neat lines of trash bags. In front of me and behind me are still piles of clothes, toys, and books.

"Louise, you must let me pay you for some of this stuff I'm taking. The girls' clothes! Some of these things have hardly been worn! The books are as good as new!"

She shrugs. "Jodie and Annie have outgrown them. They're no good to us. I should have gotten rid of them years ago."

I hold up a little navy-blue coat, age five to six, which will fit Ellie perfectly next winter when she'll need it for school. "This is saving me so much money, and look at the quality of the clothes my daughter will be wearing!"

"But I'm letting you down, aren't I," says Louise with a sigh. "You needed this job."

"That can't be helped. It's nothing, compared with your own situation," I say, folding the coat carefully and putting it on top of another bag. "Are you *sure* you won't let me give you something for these?"

"No, just get rid of it all, Beth. Please."

She goes back to her packing, and I start on a pile of toys and games. Some of these are so perfect, the boxes hardly ever opened. I could give them to Ellie as extra birthday presents. I could give some to Fay for Lauren . . .

But not now.

I sit back against the wall and rub my hand over my eyes.

Not now—none of this will go to Lauren, because I'm not going anywhere near Fay.

I'm not seeing her.

I'm not talking to her.

I'm not phoning her.

She can bloody well sweat.

I don't care if I never see her again, I'll manage without her, because who needs a friend who takes advantage of you like she has?

I'd keep all this lot here for myself rather than let her have any of it.

Cow.

Fucking cow.

I don't know why I'm crying.

At quarter past twelve I load as many sacks into the car as I can.

"I've got to go," I tell Louise. "But I'll be back on Thursday to do some more. I'll use my key if you're at work—just leave everything in the living room like today. Then I'll sort out the boot sale."

She hugs me again. "You're a treasure."

"No, I'm not. I'm more grateful than you can ever imagine—all these lovely things for Ellie."

"I'm glad it's all going to a good home."

I get to the playgroup before the children have got their coats on. Ellie stares at me through the window.

"Why are you here?" she demands when she comes out. "Where's Fay? Are you taking us home today?"

"You. I'm taking you home."

"What about Lauren?"

Lauren is standing behind her, looking uncertain.

"Your mummy will be here soon, Lauren," I tell her.

She looks puzzled. Ellie looks furious.

"Come on, Ellie." I want to get away before Fay arrives. "Come *on*!"

"Why? *WHY*, Mummy?" Her voice reaches an angry crescendo. "Why can't Lauren come? Why does she have to wait for her mummy? Why can't I go home with Lauren? Where are we going? Why aren't you at work?"

I should have gone through all this before, shouldn't I, but you know how it is—there's never time. You just hope that when it comes to it, there isn't going to be a scene. And, of course, there *is* a scene, because basically children aren't stupid. We bring them up not to be stupid. We spend everyday of their lives trying to educate them, make them brighter, quicker, more inquiring, more reasoning, more intelligent. Then, when it suits us, we want them to meekly accept what we tell them without arguing. And we don't like it when they won't.

"Just get in the car! Just get a move on and stop asking questions! Just do as you're told!"

"No! I'm not coming!" shouts Ellie, stamping her feet.

"I want to come!" says Lauren, starting to cry.

"Not coming!"

"Want to come!"

"Not coming!"

"Want to . . ."

"What the hell's going on here?"

Great. It's Fay.

Just to make me feel even worse, if anything could, both the children run toward her and throw themselves at her legs as if she's the only safe and reassuring thing in their lives.

"Come on, Ellie," I say. "In the car."

She ignores me, burying her face into Fay's thighs.

"Beth . . ." starts Fay, trying to walk toward me, dragging a child clinging onto each leg. "Lauren! Ellie! Get off! What *is* the matter with you both?"

"Beth says—!"

"Mummy said—!"

"I'm taking Ellie home," I interrupt before I can be accused of all manner of child abuse. "Say good-bye to Lauren, Ellie."

"None of this is the kids' fault," says Fay softly over their heads.

I stand, waiting, hearing but not listening.

"Don't you think we should be more . . . adult?"

I raise my eyebrows at her. More adult? What, like in a screwing-around kind of adult way? Or in a taking-advantage-of-your-best-friend kind of adult way?

"No," I say shortly.

"You're upsetting the kids," she hisses at me, looking angry.

Angry? How does *she* get to be the one looking angry?

"It's your fault," I hiss back.

The two girls have stopped yelling and have lifted their

heads from Fay's skirt. They look from one of us to the other, eyes wide.

"Are you fighting?" says Ellie in surprise.

"No," I snap. "I'm just cross because you won't do as you're told. Come on, get in the car!"

"You are!" says Lauren, watching Fay's reaction. "You're fighting! You tell *us* not to fight!"

"Are we all right out here?" calls the sing-song voice of Pat the playgroup leader, pushing her way through the crowds of mothers and children struggling into coats and boots in the cloakroom and heading in our direction. "Have we got a problem? Do we need any help at all?"

That's another funny thing about women who work with little children. Have you noticed? They call everyone "we." Are we drinking our milk? Can we tie our shoelaces? Do we need to go to the toilet? Have we wet our pants?

"No!" I shout back across the cloakroom, to stop her advancing any nearer. "We haven't got a problem, thank you, Pat."

"We're fine," adds Fay.

We'll let you know if we wet our pants, thanks very much.

We wait until she's gone back into the classroom. Most of the other children and parents are drifting out of the door. Bye-bye, James, bye-bye, Tamsin. See you tomorrow. Don't forget my paintings, Mummy! And my Play-Doh model of Bob the Builder! Can Katie come to our house to play, Mummy? Oh please, Mummy, can I ride my bike, can I watch TV, can I have some sweets, can I have spaghetti for lunch, can I fly to the moon, Mummy?

It's very quiet.

"You get cross when *we* fight," says Lauren again, looking accusingly from Fay to me.

"We're not fighting," I tell her gently. "We just . . .

don't need to see each other in the afternoons at the moment."

"Don't we?" says Fay, looking at me stonily.

"No, I don't . . ." I look her straight in the eyes. "I don't need Ellie to be looked after . . . at the moment."

"Is that right? You can manage, can you, Beth?" Her voice is tight.

I feel the hurt, as if it were an elastic band stretching between us, between our two hearts, stretching tighter, tighter, tighter, until I imagine any minute I'm going to hear it "twang" and feel it snap.

"Yes, I can manage."

"I see."

She takes hold of Lauren's hand. "Come on, then, Lauren. Jack's probably screaming blue murder in his car seat."

"But, Mummy! Why can't Ellie come?"

"Mummy! I want to!" starts up Ellie again.

"No!" I tell her sharply. "That's enough! You've had all morning playing together, and you'll see each other again tomorrow morning. Now just stop it, both of you!"

They both burst into a fresh burst of howling.

"Well done," comments Fay drily as she leads Lauren out of the door. "Punishing the kids . . ."

"Whose fault is that?"

"Mine, evidently. I seem to have become the bogeyman." She ushers Lauren, sobbing, into the backseat of her car beside Jack, who wakes up and starts to yell an accompaniment.

Ellie, who's quieted down but has a face like thunder, gets into the back of my own car and glares at me out of the window. I go to open the driver's door but Fay puts a hand on my arm to stop me.

"It wasn't intentional," she says. "I didn't plan any of this."

"It 'just happened,' I suppose," I retort with contempt.

"Yes, it did."

"And you 'can't help it'?"

"I wish I could."

"Oh, please! Spare me this *crap*, would you?" I look at her with disgust. I can't believe this is the sane, sensible woman I've known since we were both nineteen. "Just tell me one thing," I demand. "How long? Eh? How long has it been going on, without me knowing, without you telling me?"

"Three and a half months."

Unbelievably, where there should be a look of apology, of regret for having cheated and lied to her best friend in the whole world, of shutting me out of the one thing she should have shared with me—unbelievably, there comes over her face this look of pure, unadulterated *yuckiness*. It's all the sloppy Valentine's Day cards, all the blurry-edged candlelit soft-music chocolate and underwear ads, all the lovey-dovey mopey-dopey pathetic love song ballads in the world, all rolled into one silly, irritating, inappropriate grin, and I want to smack her for it.

"I met him in the doctors' waiting room," she says, eyes misting over at the memory.

I want to throw up.

"I was there for my smear test, he was there for a hepatitis vaccination."

Very romantic.

"And . . . we just got talking. And we just kind of . . . hit it off. We had such a lot to say to each other, we just knew we had to see each other again."

She smiles at me, and I hate her for this smile. It's a smile of pity, like she knows I don't understand, but how can I hope to?

"It was like . . ." She pauses for effect. "Like it was our destiny."

I shake her hand off my arm and open the car door. "I never thought," I tell her quietly, "that I'd ever hear you talk such absolute bollocks."

"That's a rude word," sniffs Ellie, "that is."

Tuesday

———◦◦◦◦———

Ellie greets Lauren at playgroup this morning like a long-lost friend. They run off together to the cutting-and-pasting table, holding hands, chatting in excited whispers as if they were going off for some adventure or other, yesterday's tears and tantrums forgotten as if they never happened. As always, I feel envious of their ability to pick themselves up from emotional upheavals and just carry on with their lives. When does life start to become more complicated? At what age do we start making it difficult? Seven? Ten? Thirteen? Does it have to happen at all?

"So you don't need me to collect Ellie?" asks Fay coldly as she passes me in the doorway.

Looks like the soft melting smiles and the misty eyes went out of the window when I called it all bollocks.

"No, thank you. I'll be here for her."

I've worked out the logistics of this. It isn't going to be easy. I'll leave Oakleigh Court at twelve-fifteen, drive over here, pick up Ellie, drive back to Oakleigh Court with her, and she'll have to sit quietly in front of Alex Chapman's TV and eat the sandwiches I've already made and packed in her lunch box while I do the last hour of the time he pays me for. I can't skimp on his time. Especially as I'm spending most of it writing my TV script. What I'll do is, I'll save the actual housework till the last hour, when Ellie's there. That way, I'll still have most of the time to concentrate on the writing while I'm on my own.

I let myself into 4a Oakleigh Court, kick off my shoes in the entrance hall (the floors are cleaner than the soles of my shoes, believe me), go to the kitchen to make myself a cup of coffee, and then straight to the computer.

The computer is in Alex's spare bedroom—the little room he uses as a study. Even though this is a spare room, it's as neat and tidy as the rest of the flat. Nothing out of place, no boxes of junk, spare duvets or pillows piled up in the corners, old lampshades or bags of books waiting to go to the Oxfam shop but never quite making it there, like most people have in their spare rooms, if they're lucky enough to have spare rooms. No. Just a computer desk with the computer, in pristine condition, looking as if it's never used. No computer games lying around—just the essentials, neatly stacked in their correct places on the desk: a couple of spare ink cartridges for the printer, a box of floppy disks, a packet of white A4 paper. The packet's always got the same amount of paper in it, every week, so I know he never uses any. Why have a computer if you never use it? But I'm not complaining. I'm making use of the situation. I don't use any of his stuff—I bring my own disk and I don't use the printer. I'm doing it. I'm finally doing what I've always wanted, and if he were here now, I'd thank Alex Chapman from the bottom of my heart. Except that I couldn't, because then he'd know what I'm doing in his flat when I'm supposed to be cleaning it.

* * *

I've always wanted to do this. It was what we used to talk about all the time—Daniel and I—when we were at university. He was going to write novels, I was going to write TV scripts. We were both going to be famous, rich, and live somewhere abroad where it's always hot and we wouldn't have to pay tax on our enormous wealth. We'd be interviewed on chat shows and photographed for *Hello!* magazine. We used to joke about it, trying to outdo each other with our elaborate plans for what we'd do when we were rich and famous.

"We'll have parties every night and invite all the celebrities," I'd say.

"No, banquets. We'll have banquets every night," he'd say.

"We'll have two cars each. A sports car and a jeep."

"Why only two each? Are you joking? And what about the yacht?"

"And a helicopter!"

We'd be lying there in one of our single rooms at university, on one of our single beds, smoking pot, listening to music, dreaming these ridiculous dreams about being famous writers, and yet not thinking it ridiculous at all. Even when we first moved into the flat together we used to do it, like it was a game. We'd be out doing the shopping in Tesco and he'd start off.

"When we're famous we'll buy some of that pâté and that champagne for our parties."

"Of course we won't! We won't have to buy anything at all—the kitchen staff will do all that! We'll just come down to dinner in the evenings and everything will be brought to us."

"Yeah—we'll have waiters and butlers and cooks and footmen . . ."

"What are footmen?"

"Men that look after your feet?"

"Or are they men that foot the bill?"

"Or do they stand at the foot of the table?"

And we'd end up collapsing with laughter over our shopping cart, the cart that was full of economy burgers, cheap white sliced loaves, packets of frozen food that were on their eat-by date and reduced to sell quickly, and special-offer biscuits. We didn't care, because this was only temporary. This was only till we got famous.

We used to laugh a lot, then. We laughed about everything. We laughed when we ran out of money, we laughed when the car broke down and we had to walk home in the rain, we even laughed when the key broke in the lock and we couldn't get into the flat at two o'clock in the morning and we were both desperate for the toilet. Being together made everything fun. It was how life was supposed to be, what I'd always imagined it would be like to be really, properly happy. But apparently it wasn't enough for Daniel.

At twenty to twelve, I save my work to the disk, turn off the computer, and make myself another coffee. I've got the beginning of a headache and I need to stop now before I lose my concentration. It's been a long time since I've worked on a computer and I'm finding it hard—my eyes ache and the back of my neck feels tight with tension.

I carry my coffee into the living room and sit down by the French doors, enjoying the weak wintery sunshine. I love this room. It's so light and spacious and uncluttered. I love Alex Chapman's taste in furniture, the pale beige soft leather sofas and low coffee tables, the terracotta walls and the deep, stone-colored carpet. I could live here, I think for the hundredth time, I could live here and be really happy even if I had to be on my own for the rest of my life. I could live here like a Single Young Executive, and microwave my frozen dinners-for-one in the neat little kitchen where nobody's expected to do any cooking, and work everyday on the computer in his brightly lit study with its blue carpet and navy and white curtains. I could tend the plants on the patio and sit outside on summer evenings with a bottle of wine and a book and nobody to worry me.

Except that it's not really a place for a child.

There's not enough room for a bike or a dollhouse. There's nowhere to roll out pastry or do finger painting or make homemade perfume out of crushed rose petals, lemon juice, cloves, and lavender polish. Nowhere to have your friends round for a tea party or a sleepover. Or a Night-night Feast.

Ellie!

I jump up, almost spilling the last drop of coffee, grab my keys, and rush out of the door, down the steps and into the street, into my car, praying it'll start the first time, and put my foot down almost to the floor to get it warmed up as I head, with a jerk and a splutter, out to the main road back to the playgroup building.

The kids are only just getting their coats on. Fay's waiting for Lauren at the cloakroom door. She pretends she hasn't seen me.

"Mummy! Have you got my video?"

This is part of the deal. I've promised Ellie a new video to watch while I finish off at Oakleigh Court. It is, of course, one of the box of children's videos I brought from Louise's place yesterday. Thank you, Louise.

"Yes—it's in the car. Have you had a nice morning?"

She's smiling, bubbly, no whining today about going back with Lauren. Amazing how quickly kids get over things.

"We sang 'The Wheels on the Bus,' " she says, giving a little skip of pleasure. "And we had the insteraments out."

"Instruments."

"And I had a tambourine! And then I had a drum, but George snatched it off me, and he got told off and had to give it back to me."

"Good." She's holding my hand, pulling me toward the door. "Aren't you going to say good-bye to Lauren?"

I know I don't want a repeat of yesterday's scene, but I feel horribly guilty seeing Lauren's sad little face watching us leaving.

"Bye, Lauren!" calls Ellie without even looking at her. "Come on, Mummy! I want to see the video!"

Amazing.

I put the video on and sit her on the floor with her lunch box on a tray in case she makes a mess.

"Here's your drink. Don't spill it. Be very careful, Ellie!"

"Who lives here?" she asks, looking around the lounge with interest. "Are there any children?"

"No, just a man."

"A man on his *own*?"

I smile at her surprise. Is this possible? Can a man live on his own and look after himself?

"Yes, and he keeps this flat really, really, clean and tidy, Ellie, so please—be careful."

She picks up her drink with exaggerated care, holding the little cup with both hands, setting it down again on the tray very slowly. "All right, Mummy," she says obediently. "I will be careful. Can I watch the video now?"

* * *

I start cleaning the kitchen. I can hear Ellie laughing at the cartoon, and I smile to myself as I wipe over the stove, the microwave, the surfaces that are already sparkling clean. This job is a joke. I can't believe I'm getting paid to do this. And then I remember that when Louise moves, I'll have to have a new arrangement for collecting my pay from Alex Chapman's snotty mother. Thinking about Louise moving stops me smiling for a while. Perhaps I should advertise for a couple of new clients. Or should I leave it, and see if I can manage till Ellie starts school and I look for a proper job? And if I do, what's going to happen about Ellie in the school holidays if I haven't made up with Fay?

This thought wipes the smile off my face completely.

Of course I'll make up with Fay, won't I?

We've been best friends all these years, for God's sake—she'll have to back down soon and apologize. She must realize what a bitch she's been to me, using our friendship, taking advantage of it, using me as a cover for her lies, her affair, and not even telling me about it. She'll come crawling to me with an apology, she's sure to.

"Mummy!" calls Ellie from the living room. "Mummy, I've only spilt a *little* bit of orange juice . . ."

I'm doing the ironing at about half past eight this evening when Martin phones.

"Who?" I ask ungraciously. I've forgotten all about him.

"Martin. Neil's friend."

"Oh yes."

I don't know what to say. "What do you want?" is perhaps a bit too direct.

"I just wondered how you were," he says, sounding embarrassed.

"Fine."

Why shouldn't I be? What's his problem?

"Only I heard you and Fay have . . . well . . . fallen out."

"How? How have you heard?"

"From Neil. Sorry. That probably sounds like we've been gossiping about you."

"Yes, it does."

"Sorry," he says again.

There's an awkward silence. I feel like saying goodbye and hanging up.

"I was concerned about you," he says, suddenly loud as if he's decided to speak his mind. "I know you were upset the other night . . ."

"Can you blame me?"

"No. No, I don't blame you at all. I'd have felt the same if someone had done that to me. But I think Fay probably didn't mean to . . . I think she probably never thought it through."

I don't want to listen to this.

I don't want to hear someone I hardly even know making pathetic excuses for Fay's behavior. Why should I care what he thinks?

"I don't care what you think," I tell him, bluntly. "It's between me and Fay."

"Yes," he says.

"Sorry," he says again, sounding totally miserable.

I suddenly realize what it must have taken for him to make this phone call. He's almost certainly regretting it now. I was in a foul mood when we last parted company, and I'm being a bitch to him now he's trying to be nice to me. I suppose this whole thing isn't really his fault, and the truth is—before I found out about Fay and Neil, I was actually enjoying Martin's company and starting to quite like him.

I don't particularly want anything to do with men in general, and I certainly don't feel as though I want much to do with someone who's a friend of Neil's.

But, on the other hand, when you've only got a four-year-old to talk to, when you spend your mornings on your own cleaning other people's homes and your evenings on your own cleaning your own home, well—I could use a bit of adult company.

"It's not your fault," I say.

"I hoped you'd see it that way," he replies, and I can hear him relaxing. "At least let's talk about it?"

"No, let's talk about cars. Or football. Or the news. Or anything, other than Fay and Neil. Please?"

"OK. You're on."

He hesitates. "I suppose you can't come out for a drink?"

"No, my little girl's asleep in bed. But you could come round, if you like."

I put the ironing board away, turn off the TV, and put some music on. I think about changing out of my jeans, but then decide I don't want to look as if I care. It's strange having someone come to the flat—anyone, but especially a man.

He taps on the front door. "Didn't want to ring the bell in case it woke your daughter," he says quietly, and I find myself smiling at this thoughtfulness.

He's brought a bottle of wine. I get two glasses from the kitchen, and open some chips from the multipack I keep for Ellie's lunches. I feel embarrassed about the odd glasses, the cheap snacks, the tatty furniture.

"Sorry everything's a bit . . . well . . ." I begin, waving a hand vaguely around the room.

"Don't apologize." He smiles. "It's fine. It must be difficult, waiting for the royalties."

Oh, shit. I forgot about that.

"Where does it all happen?" he asks, looking around with interest.

"What?"

"Where do you do your writing? I suppose you've got the computer in another room?"

A computer would be nice. Another room would be even nicer.

A picture of Alex Chapman's neat little study flashes into my mind, and before I can stop myself I'm gushing, "Oh, I don't write here. I like to keep my work separate from my home."

"Good idea." He nods approvingly, pouring the wine. "So where . . . ?"

"I rent a little place," I say lightly. "A little studio apartment, nothing too grand, just keep the computer there, you know, and use it as an office."

"Wow. No wonder you're finding it a struggle, renting two places at once."

"Well, it won't be for long, hopefully," I backtrack quickly. What on earth am I thinking of?

"No, once you become famous I suppose you'll be moving upmarket!" he says, smiling at me happily.

"Yes, cheers!" I raise my glass to my lips and take a large gulp. Christ. How am I ever going to extricate myself from this now? "Anyway, that's enough about me," I say quickly. "Let's talk some more about heart surgery!"

* * *

As we progress fairly swiftly through the bottle of wine, he tells me a couple of stories about his colleagues at the hospital.

"I can't tell you about the patients," he explains. "Confidentiality." And he moves the conversation on, instead, to our previous relationships. I feel uncomfortable with this, but I'm reluctant to give him any opportunity to go back to scriptwriting.

"How long since you split with your little girl's father?" he asks matter-of-factly.

"Eighteen months," I say. "He walked out on us," I add. "For another woman."

Actually to be totally honest, I threw him out when I found out about the other woman, but this is purely academic.

Martin shakes his head sympathetically. "My ex finished with me last summer," he says. "It knocks your confidence, doesn't it."

I think about this for a minute. Has it knocked my confidence? It did a lot of things to me—broke my heart, sank me into a black bog of despair, made me cry, rage, yell, throw things around, and go off the male species in a big way. But it also made me learn how to get on with life when things seemed impossible, how to stand on my own feet, how to support myself and my child and how to be happy again.

"I think, if anything," I say thoughtfully, "I'm more confident now than I was before."

He raises his eyebrows in surprise.

"I'm better off without that bastard," I say firmly, finishing off my glass of wine with relish.

"I'm sure you are." He smiles. "But he obviously wasn't the right person for you in the first place."

Oh, wasn't he?

The familiar sharp little spike of pain to my heart makes me take a quick breath.

Daniel and I were so right for each other.

We were so perfect together.

We fit, like two halves of a whole, like two shoes of a pair. We thought the same, laughed at the same things, talked the same language.

Do you know what he said, when I told him I knew about his bit on the side? When I told him that bitch had phoned, asking for him, telling me brazenly he was supposed to be meeting her that night? When I screamed at him, sobbed at him my accusations and my unbelievable, unbelieving hurt?

"I thought you'd understand," he said. "I thought we were bigger than this."

Yeah, right.

"Can a relationship survive it?" I ask Martin now. I'm a bit the worse for the wine. Not so much the quantity as the speed with which I've demolished it. "Can a couple survive an affair? Do people really get over it, accept it, and carry on?"

"They do," he says. "Apparently, they do, all the time."

"What about Fay? What about Simon, if he finds out? Eh? Do you think she's thought about that? Will he just turn a blind eye, or forgive her?"

"Probably she hasn't thought about it. Probably she's just carried away by the whole thing and doesn't believe he'll find out."

"Well, let's hope he doesn't," I say fervently. "He doesn't deserve that."

He looks at me solemnly. "I agree," he says.

"Do you want a coffee?" I ask, suddenly deciding I need to sober up a bit.

"Great. I'll help."

I go to stand up, but stumble slightly and fall against

him. He catches my arm and I suddenly feel a fit of the giggles coming on.

Oh dear, this isn't really funny. I shouldn't be drunk and giggling like this when I've just invited the poor guy to my flat for the first time.

But the more I think I should control myself, the more I giggle. And when I look at him, he's laughing, too, and that just makes me worse.

"I'm . . . sorry . . . I don't know . . . what I'm laughing at," I splutter.

"It's all right!" he responds, still holding on to me as if he expects me to topple over at any moment, which actually feels pretty likely. "Don't worry . . . it's funny."

And the next thing I know, he's kissing me.

Well, that sobered me up.

More quickly than a coffee would have done, too.

We step back from each other, wiping our mouths in that very awkward way you do when you've just had a long sloppy kiss with someone you still don't really know that well. Not well enough to want them to see the dribble running down your chin.

Now neither of us knows what to say.

"Er . . ."

"Um . . ."

"Coffee, then?"

We go to the kitchen together, not looking at each other. I fill the kettle and switch it on, and point to the mugs, which he gets off the shelf. I pick up the jar of coffee and rummage in the drawer for a spoon, and then I feel his arms come around me from behind, turning me to face him, and I put down the coffee jar and my arms go around his neck and this time it's not a surprise, and it doesn't feel awkward anymore. It feels nice. And I know,

I *know* what I've been saying, that I never wanted another man in my life as long as I lived. But this is reminding me of all sorts of things I thought I'd forgotten. And what the hell? It's been a long time, and I'm only human.

I just wish the last thought I had before I came wasn't: Daniel!

Wednesday

I can hear Tosser barking before I even get to Dottie's front door this morning.

"Shut up!" I hear her shouting as I ring the doorbell. I've never had my own key here. Never been necessary—Dottie's always home. "Shut up, you moron dog! It's only Beth! Put a sock in it, will you!"

"What's up with him?" I start as the door opens, but I stop in surprise, the words half out of my mouth.

The door's being held open by one of the Old Dears Next Door. She's wearing one of Dottie's aprons and she's got one of Dottie's tea towels hanging over her arm, and Tosser's growling around her ankles baring his teeth.

"Come in, Beth, dear," she says cheerfully, leaving me to close the door after me as she turns back down the hall-way.

She shakes Tosser off her ankle as she walks. "Get off, there's a good doggy. Go through to the sitting room, Beth, and I'll bring you a nice cup of tea."

I stare after her, bewildered. Have I come here to work or am I invited to a coffee morning?

"Is that you, Beth?" hollers Dottie from the sitting

room. "Get yer arse in here, girl, hurry up! I need some young company—all these old ladies fussing around over me!"

She's propped up on the sofa in her pink nylon quilted dressing gown, with a blanket over her legs. There's a meager-looking bunch of tulips wilting in a vase on the fireplace, with the Tesco label still intact on their sad bent stems, and a lurid floral Get Well card leaning against them. The gas fire is on full blast so that the heat nearly knocks you over as you walk in, and, most disconcerting of all, there's a bottle of pills on the table next to her.

"What happened?" I ask her through the huge lump that's suddenly materialized in my throat. "Are you ill?"

"Course I'm not ill, girl—what do you think I am, a sad old case like these two old dears here? No, thank God I've still got me youth and me health, otherwise it'd be a different story, wouldn't it? It'd be a bloody heap of bones lying here instead of what you see—a woman in the prime of life . . ." She falters slightly.

"So what's wrong?" I ask again, gently, sitting down on the other end of the sofa and taking hold of the dry old hand that's plucking anxiously at the edge of the blanket.

"She had a nasty fall, she did!" exclaims the Old Dear from Next Door happily, kicking open the sitting-room door with a fur-slippered foot and depositing a tray of tea mugs precariously on the edge of the table. "Come on, Dot! Sit up! Drink up! Take your tablets! Do as the doctor says!"

"Doctor, doctor, bloody old fool," mutters Dottie, scowling to herself. "I don't know why you had to go and call him out in the first place, Edie."

"Doctor knows best," says Edie primly. "Warmth and rest, he said, and take the tablets."

"I don't *want* the sodding tablets!" shouts Dottie, picking up the bottle of pills and throwing it over the back of the sofa. Tosser immediately grabs it in his drooling jaws and runs off with it, shaking it from side to side like a rat, and then stopping dead in his tracks, eyes glowing red and evil, at the rattling sound of the pills inside.

"Drop it, boy!" I call without much hope.

He fixes me with a stare of pure hatred, a low warning rumble emanating from deep down in his chest like the sound of a volcano building up slowly to its wholesale and indiscriminate destruction of vast areas of population.

"Nice doggy," I murmur apologetically. I'll get the bottle later. When he's asleep, or when I've ceased to have need of my right arm.

"Got to do as the doctor says," repeats Edie sniffily, going back out to the kitchen. "Me and Nora always take all *our* tablets."

"You and Nora are a pair of sad old bats," counters Dottie viciously. "I don't mean it," she adds as the door closes behind Edie's stiff offended back. "They've been very good, they have, the pair of them—poor old dears. It's not as if they've got their own youth and health, without having me to look after." And to my distress, a single tear rolls down her plump red cheek. I push the blanket out of the way and put my arms round her, holding her tight.

"Don't! Don't cry! Come on, this isn't like you!" I urge, close to tears myself. "You'll soon be back on your feet, you know you will. You're a fighter, you are, Dottie!"

"That's right, dear. That's right," she nods, gripping my hands tight.

She doesn't seem to be able to say anything else.

"What happened, exactly?" I ask Edie, out in the kitchen. I've sat her down with a chocolate Hobnob while I finish the dishes, trying to make amends for Dottie's bad temper.

"She was outside, putting her trash out. Me and Nora saw it all, from the front window," says Edie importantly. "Tosser ran out of the front door and she made a grab for his collar to stop him running out in the road."

Pity.

"And he pulled her over. He's too strong for her, if you want my opinion," she added, looking very satisfied with herself for having given her opinion whether I wanted it or not.

He's too bloody strong for the entire British Army, never mind Dottie.

"Has she broken anything? Did you call an ambulance?"

"No, we called nice Dr. Ali-Khan from the health center. He was very kind," she told me sternly, as if suspecting that I was about to launch into a criticism of his credentials.

"Good. And he sent for an ambulance?"

"Yes, he asked to use the phone."

I try to arrange my face to look suitably impressed with his politeness.

"And me and Nora went with her to the hospital." She folds her arms, now, really getting into it. "They took her *straight through*. You can say what you like about the NHS!"

I nod sagely.

"But all I can say to you is this: They took one look at us, and we were *straight through*."

"Good. I'm pleased to hear it."

"After all, we've paid our stamp, haven't we? We've lived through a World War, and when it comes to the crunch, we might be getting on a bit, but after all—"

"So what happened then?" I interrupt, suspecting Edie's lost the plot a bit.

"They took us *straight* to X-ray, and . . . nothing broken," she finishes abruptly, suddenly looking tired. "Any more Hobnobs, Beth, dear?"

I pass her the packet.

"Why don't you go back home now and have a bit of a rest?" I suggest. "While I'm here with Dottie? You and Nora must have been very busy looking after her."

"Busy? Me and Nora are used to being busy, dear. Some people might think, just because we're getting on a bit, we sit around doing nothing, but let me tell you . . ."

I shepherd her gently by the elbow as she's telling me, vociferously, about the pattern of their busy days next door, and finally help her over the doorstep and close the front door behind her with a sigh of relief.

"Has she gone?" calls Dottie loudly.

"Yes."

"Thank God."

I look into the sitting room and smile at her. "She means well, though, doesn't she?"

"Fussing. Bloody fussing around me like a pair of demented old hens. They get on my bloody nerves."

Glad to hear her talking like her old self.

I turn the gas fire down and open the window a fraction to let some fresh air in. "Aren't you hot? It's like an oven in here."

"They keep on squawking about warmth and rest. Bloody doctor! Get enough warmth and rest when I'm dead, won't I? All I want to do is get back on me feet and take Tosser for a good long walk again. Eh, boy? Soon be back to normal, Tosser, old boy. Soon be taking you out for a good long walk over the common, eh, boy?"

Even Tosser doesn't look as if he believes her anymore.

When she falls asleep later on, I phone the health center and ask to talk to Dr. Ali-Khan.

"No, I'm not a relative. I'm . . . a friend. She hasn't got any relatives in this country. I'm worried about her."

"I can't talk to you about her medical condition," he begins quite apologetically.

"I realize that," I put in quickly. "Confidentiality—I know. I've got a friend who's—" I stop myself just in time from starting to talk to this complete stranger about Martin.

"Who works for the Health Service. But there isn't anything I need to know, really, about her medical condition. I understand she hasn't broken any bones. I presume she's just a bit bruised and shaken. And I know she suffers badly with arthritis, although she won't take the tablets you prescribe her."

He laughs a rueful acknowledgment at this.

"I just wonder what . . ." I hesitate for a second, and then go on quickly, "What's going to become of her, doctor? She hasn't got anyone to take care of her, only these two old sisters next door, and sooner or later I suppose there's going to come a time when she won't be able to manage."

"Her family overseas will need to be aware of the situation," he says, "if she's not able to make arrangements for herself."

"Like selling up her bungalow? Going into a home?" I ask, lowering my voice. "She's *able*, but she'll never agree to it. That's what bothers me. She thinks any day now she's going to be back on her feet, running the London Marathon."

"Then her family will need to talk to her. It'll be their responsibility. Or they'll need to appoint someone over here who can handle things on their behalf."

"Mm. I bet she hasn't even told them about the fall. She's a stubborn, independent old thing."

"Most old things are!" he says lightly. "That's how they got to be."

"Got to be what?"

"Old things."

I take her another cup of tea when she wakes up, and sit down on the sofa next to her.

"I'll take Tosser for his walk in a minute," I say, looking at his malevolent expression with resignation. "Is there anything else in particular you need me to do?"

"A few bits of shopping?" she asks with a weak smile. "Those two old dears keep saying they'll do it, but I know they don't get out much. I'll be back to normal myself by next week, you know, but . . ."

"You might not," I say gently.

She ignores me pointedly by picking up the newspaper and looking for her glasses.

"Have you phoned your son? Or your daughter?" I persist.

"Not lately." She glares at me. I feel as if she's one step ahead of me, knowing exactly where I'm leading, daring me to go on.

"You should let them know about your fall. They'd want to know."

"No, they wouldn't. What's the point of worrying them? They're too far away to do anything. They'll only start nagging away over the phone, do this, do that, see the sodding doctor, take the sodding tablets." She looks up at me. "I don't need them worrying over me, Beth. I've got you, haven't I . . ."

"But I can't be here everyday, Dottie!"

". . . and I've got those two little girls from the school coming in tomorrow. They've been ever so good, too. They brought me things the other day. Sweets, and magazines."

"Good."

"And I've got the two old dears next door if all else fails," she adds. "I'm all right."

I give up. "So what shopping do you need?"

"Only need a couple of packets of crackers, a loaf, and some butter. And some dog food. And tea bags."

"Are you eating properly?" I ask her sternly. "Shall I get you some mince, or chicken? And some greens?"

"I'll eat what I want, thank you very much!" she retorts. "I'm not so old and bloody stupid that I need nannying—it's bad enough with those two next door!"

"All right. I know," I soothe her. "Come on, Tosser. Let's get your lead on. Try to keep your teeth to yourself, there's a good dog."

Dottie pretends to be reading her paper while I put on my coat and get Tosser ready. But when I look in the room again to say good-bye, she's gone back to sleep.

She's still dozing when I return. It's not like her. I wonder if it's still the effect of the shock, or whether the ministrations of Edie and Nora are wearing her out. Very quietly, I get the battered old notebook she keeps by the phone and take it into the kitchen, where I copy down two phone numbers—the son in Sydney and the daughter in Chicago. Then I get on with some housework till it's time to make her lunch.

"I'll call in and see you on Friday," I promise her. "I'll bring Ellie."

"Lovely," she says, brightening up. "Your money's in the drawer, Beth, dear."

It sometimes feels like taking money for visiting a friend.

I phone the Chicago number during the afternoon.

"I'm sorry for interfering," I tell Dottie's daughter. "But I know if it were my mother . . ."

"Of course," she says, quite warmly. "It's very good of you. Mum talks about you all the time, Beth."

"She does?" I say in surprise.

"Yes, I think she needs the companionship more than the cleaning, doesn't she? It's such a relief for us to know she has you calling in, keeping an eye on her like this."

"But I enjoy it! She's such a lovely lady, your mum— so full of life . . ." I hesitate, then continue, "I just hope this shock doesn't knock the spirit out of her too much. She seems . . . very tired."

"If only she'd listen to her doctor!"

I laugh, thinking: *sodding doctor.*

"David and I," she goes on. "That's my brother, David—he lives in Sydney—we've been trying to persuade her to go out there to live. She went out to stay with him and his family a few years ago."

"Yes, she often talks about it."

Tells me she hated the place.

"She won't admit she liked Australia, you know. She pretends she hated it out there, so we won't keep trying to persuade her to move. But it would be so much better for her!"

For her? Or for the family?

"So much more convenient, to have her close to one of us. I'd have her here in Chicago, but the winters are dreadful. It'd be lovely for her in Australia, and David's got a beautiful house, with plenty of room for her, and Julie—that's his wife—would look after her." She sighs.

"I do wish she'd change her mind. It would save all this worry. Talk to her about it, won't you, Beth dear?"

"I don't know if she'll listen to me," I say awkwardly.

Why the hell should she?

"Well, listen, thank you again so much for phoning—and I'll ring my brother and talk to him about it."

I hang up, not really feeling any less anxious about the situation. Perhaps I should have been more direct: *Look, you and your brother need to make arrangements for your mum. She's going to need care. One of you needs to get your arse over here and sort something out for her.*

But perhaps that's what they're going to do.

It isn't really my business, is it?

I just get paid for cleaning her bungalow, that's all.

I spend the evening watching the TV and listening for the phone. Not that I'm expecting Martin to ring. It just might be nice if he did.

After all, don't you think when you have sex with someone for the first time, it's kind of nice if they call you the next night? I mean, don't you think that's a normal kind of thing to do? If they don't, let's be honest, it leaves you feeling a bit insecure. Wondering did they think you were crap at it? Were they glad to get out of the door, jump in their car, and as soon as they were around the corner did they wind down the window, rip out the page of their Filofax with your phone number on it, and chuck it out, hoping never to see you again? Not that I'm paranoid in any way at all, but my last partner cheated on me and I haven't had sex with anybody during the intervening eighteen months so it's quite possible, even though I enjoyed it, in fact I'd go so far as to say it was absolutely great—it's quite possible that he thought I was crap. Who's to say? Especially if he doesn't phone me.

When the phone finally rings, at nearly ten o'clock, it makes me jump. "Hello?" I say, a bit breathless.

I probably picked it up too quick. Should have made him wait.

"Hello, Beth. It's Louise."

Oh.

"Hi. Are you all right?"

"Yes, Beth, Ben and I have just been talking, and I wanted to let you know. We've decided to have a party."

"What?!"

I want to say: *Have you both gone fucking mad?*

A party! A *party*? They're broke, they're bankrupt, they're being forced to sell their lovely home and nearly all their belongings, their lives are in an absolute shambles, and they want to celebrate?

"I know it sounds like a strange idea. But so many people have been so good to us since all this happened. We've got so many lovely friends, and they're all standing by us."

"But of course they're standing by you!" I exclaim. "What did you expect? That's what friends do! It isn't as if you've both been arrested for some terrible crime."

"Well, we just thought it would be nice . . . to say good-bye to all the neighbors, and thank everyone."

"But how on earth can you afford to throw a party?" I ask her bluntly.

"We've got bottles and bottles of wine," she says, and I can hear a sort of chuckle in her voice. "You know, Beth—the cupboard under the stairs!"

Oh, yes. Ben's "wine cupboard." I know now why Louise is enjoying this. She always complained about it.

"Why does he have to keep all that wine stacked away in there like some old miser?" she'd grumble. "Why can't we just get it all out and bloody well drink it? He buys cheap stuff for us to drink at home, and hoards all this 'good stuff' for some special occasion. When are we going to have the special occasion, I keep asking him?"

"You've got your special occasion, at last," I say to Louise now, smiling.

"Yes, he's agreed—we can't take it all with us, and our friends deserve to help us drink it. What do you think, Beth? You're invited, of course!" she adds quickly.

"Oh! Thanks—I think it's a great idea—but perhaps you should ask everyone to contribute . . . bring a bottle . . ."

"No," she says firmly. "There's enough in there for everyone! I want to ask you something, though. Will you help with the food? I'll pay you, of course," she says tentatively.

"Pay me? Don't be ridiculous. Are you inviting me as a friend?"

"You know I am. I wouldn't insult you by suggesting I only want you to come to the party to do the work!"

"Well, friends don't charge for helping the hostess with the food, do they? For God's sake!"

"Thanks, Beth. I'll see you tomorrow morning, anyway—if you're still OK to come round? I've sorted out a lot more of the stuff. There isn't too much more to do now."

"Of course I'm coming. But I might not be there till after you've gone out, Louise. I've got to take Ellie to playgroup first."

"Problem with the babysitter?"

"Sort of."

I put down the phone, feeling a mixture of pleasure and sadness. I've worked for Louise for over a year, but it's only now she's in trouble and she's going to be moving that we've begun to think of each other as friends.

And I could use another friend right now, what with not having Fay to talk to.

Perhaps I should phone her back and tell her the whole story about Fay. It'd be nice to be able to tell someone, someone who'd sympathize.

Or perhaps I should phone her back and talk to her about Martin.

The bastard still hasn't rung.

Friday

Despite my life being not exactly what you could call great, and my career path at the moment being absolutely bloody terminally *crap*, there are very few mornings that I actually wake up and think: *Oh, no. Another day*.

But the mornings I do think it are always Fridays. And the reason I think it is always Oliver.

I never want to rush to get ready for work on a Friday morning. I always think, every week, that I should stop working at Canal Street. But now, with losing two mornings' work a week for Louise, there's no way I can keep thinking along those lines. Canal Street is necessary to my existence. I have to keep on putting up with Oliver, ignoring him, and hope eventually he'll get bored with me and look for a new challenge. And I have to keep ignoring my sexual fantasies and tell myself he's not really a gorgeous-looking man with a gorgeous body but just a little twat who fancies himself.

Actually today it's not at all difficult to tell myself this, because my sexual fantasies, since Tuesday night, have all been about Martin (the bastard who still hasn't phoned), not Oliver. And I'm so totally pissed off with Martin for not phoning, and with his shit of a friend Neil for carrying on with Fay behind my back and behind her husband's back, and with the whole male race in general for being such a load of unreliable, lying, cheating, disappointing, useless jerks, that I really can't imagine ever getting turned on by a single one of them, ever again.

Who needs it?

I ask you, who needs it, when you turn up for work, prepared to slave away for four hours cleaning up after two pathetic specimens who haven't got a clue how to clean up after themselves, to be greeted by one of them posing half naked and obviously considering himself God's gift to the female population, grinning at you like a gorilla in heat and making lewd suggestions about the wardrobe?

The *wardrobe*, for God's sake.

"What's the matter with you?" I ask scathingly. "Are you stuck somewhere in mid-puberty? Wardrobes? Nobody over the age of fifteen has sex in wardrobes." Nobody over the age of fifteen is normally small enough.

"Did you do it in a wardrobe? When you were fifteen?" he asks with renewed interest.

I think it'd probably be unwise to relate the story of me and Christopher Collins, playing Sardines at his sister's sixteenth birthday party. It'll probably only encourage him.

"Never," I say dismissively, trying to get past him in the narrow hallway to get to the kitchen. As always, the closeness of him, his smell—clean and soapy but somehow slightly *bedsoiled*—the heat from his body, the look in his eyes that I try to avoid—assail my senses as I pass, trying to breathe in and not touch him.

But this morning I'm not letting my hormones get the better of me.

I'm not affected by it.

He's not sexy, he's not desirable, he's just a sad, pathetic little wanker.

"Come on, Beth," he drawls, moving in closer and laying a warm hand on my arm. "Come on, what are you waiting for? Let's do it."

I don't know why. I don't know what comes over me. But I look straight at him and the words just jump straight from my thoughts and out of my mouth, sort of bypassing my brain.

"You're not sexy," I tell him calmly, watching the smile fade slightly from his face. "You're not desirable."

Stop now. Stop now, for fuck's sake, while you've said just enough to make him drop his hand from your arm and step back to let you pass. While he's looking surprised and disgruntled but not actually completely shocked. Quit while you're ahead, yeah?

"You," goes on my mouth, speaking without my permission, bypassing not only my brain but my common sense and my instinct for survival, "are just a sad, pathetic little wanker."

His eyes and mouth both fly open wide. I wonder if he's going to shout abuse at me. But he just says, deadly quiet, "Is that so?"

"Yes," I say, standing my ground. "So go on, get in the wardrobe and fuck yourself."

I'm cleaning the cooker when I hear the front door slam. I wait for a few minutes, and then I go to the front room and see him getting into his car and driving off. I don't feel particularly bothered about this. It's what men do, isn't it, when they're upset. *We* might throw things around a bit, have a cry, tear something up, or even get it out of our systems by doing something constructive like digging the garden or cleaning the windows really energetically. Men do like to take it out on their cars, don't they. They stamp on the accelerator and the brake like they're kicking someone's head in. They slam it into gear like they want to wrench the lever out of its socket. Wham! Take that! Into first, thump down on the pedals, screech out into the traffic, jump on the brake just in the nick of time, back up the gears with a succession of impressive noisy jerks, lean on the horn—out of the way, you stupid bastards! I was here first, it's my road, piss off out of it, let me through, I'm in a bad mood!

Well, fine, let him drive around the place taking out his temper on innocent road users, no skin off my nose, I'll just get on with my cleaning in peace and perhaps when he comes back we can have a coffee, put the whole thing behind us, and now he knows *exactly* what I think of him he'll stop all that stuff and leave me alone to do the job he's paying me for.

I feel an enormous sense of relief. Thank God I let my mouth take over from my brain and my common sense. Perhaps, every now and again, it's what we need to do. Just say what you think, no holds barred, spare no feelings, tell it how it is. I can probably afford to be quite nice to Oliver now, now that's all out of the way. We might even get to be friends.

So here I am, happily scrubbing the toilet—well, as happily as it's possible to scrub a toilet that's been used by two men for a week since its last clean—and imagining this new friendship accord, this state of understanding that's about to develop between Oliver and myself, when the front door slams again and Oliver comes back in. I hear his footsteps as he walks to the bathroom door. I turn, still in my position on my knees by his toilet bowl with the brush in one hand and a bottle of cleaning liquid in the other.

"Hello, Oliver," I say in my new tone of friendship and understanding.

"You're fired," he says. "I've been to the agency in town to hire a new woman." I drop the brush in the toilet and struggle to my feet, dribbling green cleaning liquid over the floor. "So you can get out. Now."

"Wait!"

In a situation like this, there's dignity, or there's desperation.

Dignity would have been standing up straight, taking off my apron and my rubber gloves, putting down the bottle of green stuff, and calmly walking out of the house without a word or a backward glance.

Desperation is running after him, dropping the bottle of green stuff, tripping over it and skidding on the mess of it on the bathroom floor, running to catch up to him, catching hold of his arm, pulling him back as he tries to walk away, begging him, "Wait, Oliver! You can't! You can't sack me!"

Begging.

There's no dignity left. I need this job. I bloody need it. He can't do this to me.

"I can," he replies, coldly, shaking me off. "And I have. And I asked you to leave."

"You've got no grounds! I've done nothing wrong!"

"Your work is unsatisfactory," he says. "Look at that mess on the bathroom floor."

"That's *crap*! We both know what this is about . . ."

"Do we?" He turns to face me. Just an hour ago, there was white-hot lust in his eyes. Now they're as cold as ice. They make me shiver.

"Yes, I insulted you. I know, and I'm sorry, but you pushed me to it—for God's sake, Oliver, you know you did, you've been on and on, pestering me, for weeks . . ."

"I tried to be friendly, a little harmless joke . . ."

"Friendly? Harmless?" I gasp. "It was harassment."

"Harassment!" he snorts. "Don't kid yourself."

"I'm sorry if you can't take rejection," I say, beginning to shake with anger and distress. "But, yes, as far as I'm concerned it was harassment, and I could fucking take you to court for it!"

I don't know whether or not I could, but I'm angry enough to try.

"Do you seriously think anyone would believe," he says smoothly, "that *I*"—he says the *I* as if he's the best thing since sliced bread, the Prince of Wales at the very least, a film star, a member of the newest and most popular boy band—"that *I* would even *look* at someone who comes to clean my house? Someone in dirty old sweatshirts and an apron, who can't get a decent job and who's at least ten years older than me? In your dreams, Beth. In your fucking dreams. Go on, get out of here."

He turns his back on me.

I'm crying.

I've lost the battle, as soon as I started to cry.

I creep out of his house, a sad huddle of a person in a dirty old sweatshirt and an apron. A sad and crying state of a person who can't get a decent job. Who thinks she's being harassed by someone who can't stand the sight of her.

And you know what hurts the most?

He thinks I'm at least ten years older than him.

It's only six.

Ellie wants to know why we're not going to the Nice Man's house after playgroup like I said we were.

Why are we not going, with her lunch box and her

thermos, and another cartoon video from Louise's bag, to the house where the Plant Man does his drawings of gardens, like I said we would, so that she could see him doing his drawings?

Because he's a pervert, darling, who tried to talk Mummy into having sex in a wardrobe, and then sacked me for telling him to go screw himself.

Because he's turned out to be just about the nastiest slimiest toad of all the nasty slimy toads on the surface of the planet, and I thought I'd already met quite a few.

"Because we're not," I fall back on, daring her to ask another why not.

"But why not?"

"Because I said not!" I snap, hating myself for it.

"It's not fair!" she whines, and I know it's not, I agree with her completely. It's not fair, and I want to shout and cry and scream about it, and kick my feet, and shake my fists, and show off till I'm sick. But I'm a grown-up. Unfortunately.

I take her to the park, and let her play on the swings, and eat her lunch out of her lunch box sitting on the park bench by the pond, watching the ducks, and then I buy her an ice cream even though it's only the middle of March and there's a wind howling around us that feels like it's blowing out of the frozen wastes of Alaska.

And at least one of us is in a better mood now.

We call on Dottie in the afternoon. The prospect of seeing Tosser has cheered Ellie up so immensely, you'd think she'd never been let down by her heartless mother about the man who does the garden drawings, never been stopped from having daily lunches with her best friend and, in fact, never had anything unfair happen to her in the whole of her four-and-a-quarter years. She talks nonstop in the car all the way to Dottie's house, about how much she would love to have a doggy like Tosser, how she would love him, how she would give him his dinner and take him out for walks and play with him and he would be her best friend. She's in a state of high excitement as we ring Dottie's doorbell.

Tosser immediately starts barking his head off and a roar goes up: "Shut up! Stop your stupid noise! Idiot canine fool!"

Ellie looks at me, wide-eyed. "*I* don't shout at doggies, do I, Mummy?" she says self-righteously.

"No, but you don't live with one," I take the opportunity to explain. "They can get on your nerves with their barking."

To say nothing of their aggressive displays of teeth and their regular savaging of your limbs.

Dottie opens the door and holds it open for us to enter. Ellie looks at her a little nervously and goes shy, hiding behind my legs and clutching at my trousers.

"Nothing to be frightened of, sweetheart," says Dottie cheerfully. "He's not a bad dog really, just noisy."

"I'm not frightened of him," retorts Ellie. "I'm frightened of you."

"Kids!" I say ruefully to Dottie. "They can be relied upon to embarrass you at every turn."

But Dottie's laughing out loud and patting Ellie gently on the head. "She's only being honest, bless her heart! I must be the most frightening thing she's seen for a long time, isn't that right, my lovely?"

"Well," says Ellie, getting a little braver and studying Dottie more closely, considering this. "Well, I don't think you're *quite* as scary as the Wicked Queen."

"She's just been watching *Snow White*," I explain to Dottie apologetically as she goes off into fresh howls of laughter.

Ellie starts to laugh, too, and, aware that she's now the center of attention, adds, "Or the Big Bad Wolf!"

Dottie wipes the laughter from her eyes and takes Ellie by the hand, leading her toward the cookie tin.

"Or Captain Hook," Ellie goes on, giggling, obviously thinking her way frantically through her new video collection.

"That's enough, Ellie," I warn sternly.

"Or—"

"I said that's enough!" I snap.

Tosser growls at me warningly. Ellie gives me a look that's only slightly less menacing.

"Or Cruella," she finishes under her breath.

"Do you like that story?" Dottie asks her calmly. "The one about the dalmations?"

"Yes! I love doggies, I do!" She sits down on the sofa, next to not-so-frightening Dottie, and sucks happily on a custard cream.

"I love *your* doggy," she adds, holding out her sucked-upon, soggy cookie to Tosser, who, to my amazement, sidles up to her, wagging his tail, sits at her feet, and takes the offering with the utmost gentleness from her soft little fingers. "Ooh, Tosser, your tongue *tickles*!" she giggles as he gobbles the cookie messily on the carpet.

Tickle? He'd normally chew your hand off up to the elbow.

"He likes you, my sweetheart," says Dottie appreciatively. "Dogs know. They know when someone's their friend, I always say."

Doesn't say much for me, then.

"Mummy won't let me have a doggy, though," confides Ellie sadly. "She says we can't afford one. I said I would use my piggy bank but she *still* says no."

Boo, hiss, boo—the wicked queen strikes again.

"Never mind," Dottie says consolingly. "Tosser can be your special friend, can't he?"

Ellie's eyes light up. "Can he? Can he really? Can I take him out for walks? Can I give him his dinner? Can I play with him?" She looks at me hopefully. "Can I, Mummy?"

"Whenever we come to see Dottie, yes," I compromise. "Now, Ellie, just be quiet for five minutes, can you, please? I want to talk to Dottie."

Ellie gets down on her hands and knees on the floor and starts a conversation with Tosser, telling him how she's going to be his special friend and play with him and give him his dinners. Every time she says "dinner" his ears spring up like two little antennae and he looks all around, bewildered, wondering where the dinner is and why no one's doing anything about producing it.

"So how's it going?" I ask Dottie quietly. "How are you feeling?"

"Oh, you know," she says vaguely. "Not so bad."

The bruises have all come out on her knees and shins, black and purple, and she had to hold on to the furniture to hobble to the door and back.

"Are Edie and Nora still coming in to help you?"

"I think it's worn them out!" she chuckles. "Poor old dears! They haven't got the best of health, you know . . ."

"So how are you managing?"

"I'm not completely helpless," she retorts with a sudden return of her usual spirit. "I can still boil an egg and do meself a bit of toast, and open a tin for Tosser's dinner."

The antennae go up again and he looks at her expectantly.

"And did the girls from the school come yesterday?"

"No, exam week, apparently. They'll be round next week, I expect."

"And . . ." I hesitate. "And have you heard from your daughter? Or your son?"

"Yes, they've both been on the phone," she says, waving her hand dismissively. "Nagging away as usual."

"About what?" I ask innocently.

"Oh, they're always on about it. They want me to move out to Australia. Silly bloody idea. What would I want to go out there for? They're all raving mad out there, I'm telling you, Beth. I went for Christmas, didn't I, a few years back, and they had Christmas dinner on the beach. Can you imagine? Raving mad. I couldn't stand the place."

I smile to myself. "But perhaps they'd feel happier, you know, if you were near to your son. They could look after you."

She gives me a scathing look. "D'you think I need looking after?"

"Well. Not normally perhaps." I pause. "Did you tell them about your fall?"

"What would be the point of that? Have them fussing and worrying all the more. I told them, both of them—stop fussing about me and start sorting out those kids of yours. No bloody sense in any of them, if you ask me. They either drop out of school and train horses, or they waste their time learning English at university. Wouldn't mind if the Australians could speak proper English in the first place!"

I laugh, but add gently, "Perhaps you shouldn't dismiss the idea, though. Just think about it."

"I have," she says firmly. "And what I think about it is that I don't want to go there. I don't want to live on the other side of the world. I want to stay here." She clamps her mouth shut defiantly and stares straight ahead of her. Subject closed.

"OK," I say.

"You want to take Tosser for a walk?" she asks now, directing this at Ellie, who's getting restless.

Ellie jumps to her feet, nodding excitedly. "Come on, Mummy! Where shall we go? Can we take him to the park and show him the ducks?"

I put on my coat and get the dog's lead on. "Any shopping?" I ask Dottie.

"No, I'll be fine," she tells me a bit curtly. "I'll be going out myself in another day or so."

I don't try to argue with her.

My mum phones while I'm cooking dinner. I let Ellie talk to her.

"I ate my lunch in the park! We watched the ducks! *And* I had an ice cream!" I hear her rambling in excitement.

"Wasn't it a bit cold for that?" asks my mother in tones of disapproval when I take the phone.

"No, it was a lovely day here," I reply wearily. "You must have had a cold spell in Surrey."

"And how's the work situation?" she asks.

I shudder, wondering how to change the subject. There aren't any words in which to tell your mother that you've just lost one-third of your remaining earning potential by calling your employer a wanker.

"Oh, it's all much the same," I say non-committally.

"Applied for any proper jobs? Been looking at the ads in those supplements I sent you?"

"Well . . ."

"Phoned any of the agencies? Done your résumé?"

"Mum! I keep telling you, I'm not looking until Ellie starts school."

And as I listen to her, going through the usual bit about how long it'll probably take me to get a decent job, remember what happened before, remember how easily I gave up, think how difficult it's going to be now, with a child to look after, and it's never too soon to start, got to get my name down with some agencies, got to get my résumé ready . . . I suddenly feel so unutterably depressed I want to just put the phone down, quietly put it down without interrupting her, without saying a word, and just walk away from the conversation, walk away from even thinking about it.

Because the truth is that not only have I not got a proper job, but I've barely even got a cleaning job anymore, and if I don't want to live on crusts of bread or be thrown out of my flat, I'm going to have to get my arse in gear just to find myself some more clients for this abysmal career choice, never mind worrying about doing anything "decent." And talking of which, how am I going to get myself a decent job when Ellie starts school, if I haven't got a babysitter? And how am I going to afford one, if it isn't Fay?

"Mum, please don't worry about me," I say, right in the middle of her telling me about a Web site she's heard of where you can get your résumé professionally written in five different languages. "Please just leave me to sort my life out the best way I can."

Which is precisely how?

"But I do worry about you, Beth," she continues relentlessly. "Your brother's doing well, your sister's doing well . . ."

Rub it in, why don't you?

"Whereas you . . ."

Are not.

"We worry about you, Beth. All of us worry about you."

How wonderfully reassuring. I can now picture the entire extended family sitting around their respective tables, in their respective lovely homes, discussing their various successes in their various careers, all looking at each other sadly and saying how worried they are about Beth.

You are the weakest link . . .

"Well, don't," I say. "Don't worry. Trust me. I've got something worked out, Mum. I've got plans."

You'll be proud of me, one day. You will, if it kills me.

"I'm going to be a scriptwriter," I say out loud—but I don't say it until I've hung up the phone. "That's what I'm going to be. A TV scriptwriter."

Ellie looks up at me without much interest. "What's a skipwriter?" she asks. "Are my fries ready yet?"

Saturday

It's raining again today. It's gray, and cold, and dreary, and the rain's pouring off the guttering over the window, which is probably blocked by leaves and shit that the birds drop, not that there are any birds around at the moment and who could blame them? Might as well stay put in their nice warm nests, like me and Ellie, snuggled up on the sofa watching rubbish on TV.

There's a cartoon on, American of course, in which a fat, bald, little man is yelling at his thin, pale, sad-looking wife—and their child (who turns out, surprisingly enough, to be a Superhero merely disguised as a normal mortal child wearing spectacles and short trousers) obligingly intervenes and turns him into a hamster. It's great. Ellie is bouncing on the sofa in delight as the hamster squeaks its fury at the Superhero child, when she suddenly turns to me and says, as if there'd been a lead-up to it, "Will my daddy come back one day?"

I ponder, briefly, whether it would serve any purpose to tell her that he's been turned into a hamster, but there's only so far a mother can go to bend the truth.

"No, Ellie," I say, trying to keep my voice level.

"We've talked about this before, haven't we? You know he won't come back."

"But why?" she says, pouting, still looking at the TV. "I want a daddy. Why can't I have a daddy?"

I don't feel very proud of this—but the fact is that I'm pleased she's saying she wants *a* daddy, and not *her* daddy. You see? She just looks at the kid on the TV, and wants to be like him, with a daddy to turn into a hamster. Not Daniel. Just any old daddy.

"Daddies don't really get turned into hamsters," I say, pretending to laugh, cuddling up with her a bit tighter. "That's just pretend."

She turns away from the TV and gives me a look that makes me feel like something so unbelievably stupid I shouldn't ever be allowed to open my mouth. "I don't want a daddy to turn into a *hamster*," she says scathingly. "I want a daddy to take me *swimming* and stuff. Daddies do things like that," she adds for my information, obviously aware that I'm too thick to have noticed this.

"Well, so do mummies," I try. "I took you swimming, didn't I, with Lauren . . ."

Whoops. Bad move.

She screws up her face in concentration. I can see her trying to puzzle this out. "Yes, *and . . .*" she begins slowly.

Wait for it. *And* another thing!

"Why can't I go to Lauren's house anymore? Why can't we go swimming? Why can't we have another Night-night Feasht?"

"Feast."

She ignores this, looking at me, challenge in her eyes. Well? Eh?

"It's just . . . difficult at the moment," I say. "Mummy's very busy right now, Ellie, because Dottie isn't well."

"Yes, I like taking Tosser for walks."

OK, let's not get started on the whole "Mummy Wouldn't Buy Me a Bow-Wow" scenario.

"Yes, and because of Louise. You know, Louise is moving houses and I'm helping her to sort out all her things."

"Videos and toys and lovely lovely dresses for Ellie!" She smiles happily, bouncing on the sofa.

"Yes, but it's very sad for Louise because she doesn't really want to move houses. They have to live in a smaller house because Ben hasn't got so much money anymore, so that's why she has to get rid of a lot of her things."

Ellie stops bouncing and thinks about this solemnly for a while. "Are those children sad, too?" she asks.

She's never met Louise and Ben's children but I often quote them to her.

Jodie and Annie and Solomon are always dressed and ready for school without any fuss.

Jodie and Annie and Solomon never scribble on their books.

Jodie and Annie and Solomon put all their toys away tidily everyday.

That last one is a direct and outrageous lie, but I prefer to think of it as maternal license.

"I expect they're very sad," I tell her. "They've got to leave their school and go to a new one."

"Like me going to big school instead of playgroup?"

"Yes, but they'll be living somewhere different. So they'll have to make all new friends."

And they'll be the only kids in the class who've been to private schools. They'll be ahead in math and English, and behind in street wisdom. They'll be picked on for the way they speak, their manners, their lack of cheek and lack of swearing. My heart bleeds for them, but within a few weeks they'll have conformed, to survive. It's a jungle out there.

"I wouldn't like to leave *my* friends," says Ellie sadly.

She's only four but she's sympathizing with these children she doesn't even know. I give her another hug. "And they've given me all their nice toys," she remembers, looking at me with a stricken expression.

"They've got lots of toys," I reassure her. Understatement of the year. "Those are things they've grown out of. Like we gave your baby toys to Jack. Remember?"

"Yes, he broke them," she says, shaking her head in such an adult way that I have to laugh.

We turn our attention back to the television program, where the Superhero Kid has just saved his hamster—father from the family cat and is about to magic the contrite hamster back to his original shape and form.

"I still *wish* I had a daddy," says Ellie wistfully, lying back in my arms and putting her thumb in her mouth. "I might ask for one for my birthday, when I'm five."

She's been invited to a birthday party this afternoon. It's a little girl at playgroup named Janine, whose family have only just moved to the area.

"She hasn't really got any friends yet," Janine's mother told me the other day. "But she wants a party and she's asked for Ellie to come. We'll just be taking them all to McDonald's, and then back to our house for a video," she adds almost apologetically. "Will that be all right?"

All right? Bloody marvellous. Ellie's beside herself with excitement.

"McDonald's, McDonald's," she keeps singing around the house now, dressed in a red velour party dress that used to be Jodie's or Annie's. "Will we have fries, Mummy? Will we have burgers in a bun?"

"I expect so," I say, smiling.

She looks so pretty.

Thank you, thank you, Jodie or Annie, for having been exactly the right size and exactly the right coloring when you were the same age as Ellie.

"Have a lovely time, darling," I say, dropping her off at Janine's house.

For a minute she looks around her a bit hesitantly and I wonder if there's going to be a problem. Lauren doesn't seem to be coming. But Janine's mother comes and takes her by the hand.

"Come in and see Janine's birthday presents, Ellie," she says. "She's got a hamster in a cage!"

Ellie looks round at me, her eyes huge. I put my hand to my mouth to stop myself laughing, and she grins back at me, sharing the joke.

"Not a daddy!" she whispers, and goes off happily holding Janine's mother's hand. Janine's daddy, who definitely doesn't look like a hamster, is pouring out glasses of orange juice in the kitchen.

"Good luck!" I say to him as I pass, and he smiles and gives me a resigned shrug.

Something hurts, very briefly, somewhere inside, and I try to ignore it. Yes, it must be nice, having a daddy there to help with the orange juice at a child's birthday party. But it's not essential, is it? It's definitely not essential.

At home, on my own, I start to unpack some more of the black sacks full of clothes and things from Louise's house, sorting them out—clothes that can hang up in Ellie's wardrobe ready for her to grow into, clothes that will be too big for a couple more years and need to be folded and stored in the suitcase on top of my wardrobe, videos and toys she can have now, some that I'm going to keep till her birthday, or Christmas, or for when she's a bit older. The sacks of things I'm going to sell for Louise at the boot sale next week are still at Park Cottage. I haven't got room for them here. I sit down on Ellie's bed and look at all the new things she's got in her room now, things she's got because someone else has had some really bad luck. Why does that happen in life? The old saying is that "It's an ill wind that blows nobody any good," but that's not fair or sensible, because you feel guilty benefiting from someone's misfortune. You don't feel as if you should be enjoying it. But, on the other hand, there are Louise and Ben, still together, still married, despite everything, and still with their three lovely children who are all healthy and intelligent and charming. At least their children don't suck their thumbs, when they watch cartoons on the TV, and ask why they haven't got a daddy. Do they?

I want to talk to Fay.

I miss her.

I want to tell her about Martin, and what it was like having sex with someone new after all this time, but I can't, because what if she then tells me the same thing about her and Neil?

It would be the normal thing to do. It's what girlfriends are for, isn't it—you always discuss that kind of stuff.

So why? Why didn't she tell me when she first met Neil, when she met him in that poxy doctor's waiting room and decided it was destiny? Why didn't she tell me, when he first phoned her, or when he sent her that Christmas card, or when he first kissed her, or when she first made that decision: *I'm going to do it. I'm going to cheat on my husband. I'm going to have sex with another man.*

She cheated on *me*, too. She did all that stuff without telling me. We had lunch together, we went shopping together, we talked for endless hours about the children, about playgroup and school and money and the weather, and what was on TV, and what we were cooking for dinner—and, all the time, she was hiding the biggest secret possible inside her heart, away from me, locked away from me.

How can you do that, and still be a friend?

How can I ever go back to how it was? How could I phone her, now, to discuss Martin, and what it was like to kiss him, and how one thing led to another, and how the bastard hasn't called me since, and how that makes me feel—to get some sympathy and understanding from her—when *she* hasn't confided in *me*?

I need another friend.

I pick up the phone, suddenly and resolutely, and dial Louise's number.

"I just called for a chat," I admit. "But only if you've got time."

"Time?" she sighs. "It's good to have a break from this endless sorting and packing, Beth. How are you?"

"I'm OK."

No, I'm not. That's the whole point, isn't it?

"No, I'm not," I amend quickly. "I feel a bit low, to be honest. Ellie's been asking why she can't have a daddy. And I slept with someone a few days ago, the first time since Daniel left, and he hasn't phoned me since. And I've fallen out with my best friend."

And I've lost a day's work per week—another day on top of the two I've lost with you—because I told my client to go and fuck himself. But I don't mention this, because Louise feels bad enough as it is about her two days.

"Poor you," she says sympathetically. "Is Ellie OK?"

"Yes, yes, she's fine. She's at a party. She's wearing the little red velour dress from one of your girls—she looks lovely in it! She's so thrilled with all her new things."

It occurs to me, as I'm saying this, that I should get Ellie to thank Louise and the children herself. She could talk to her on the phone, or even come with me to meet them.

"And what about this man, then?" asks Louise. "Come on—tell all! Who is he?"

So I tell her about Martin, and as I'm telling her I realize I'm not even sure how much I like him. He was pleasant, and friendly, and we got on really well together, and had a laugh, but would I have slept with him if I hadn't had quite a lot of wine and been quite a long time on my own?

"So what?" says Louise. "You don't have to make excuses for yourself. You're a grown-up. You wanted to, so you did."

"And I suppose that's the end of it?"

"Do you want to see him again?"

"Not if *he's* not interested. Perhaps he just thought of it as a one-night stand."

"No, he's met you three times now. Why don't you phone *him?*"

"I didn't get his phone number."

Oh, pathetic.

"Have you tried the directory?"

"OK, no, I haven't. Because I want *him* to phone *me*. I feel rejected."

"We're living in the twenty-first century, Beth. Girls can use the phone too, you know."

"I suppose so," I say gloomily. Do I like him enough to make the effort? Or do I just want to be wanted?

"And make it up with Fay," adds Louise gently. "Life's too short . . ."

"It's up to her," I say sharply. "I suppose she's so involved with her new lover, she doesn't even care. Doesn't even miss me."

"I bet she does. She's probably just waiting for you to forgive her."

"Well, perhaps she should think about apologizing."

"Would it make any difference?"

I think about this after I put the phone down. Would I forgive Fay if she phoned, right this minute, and said she was sorry? Am I such a bitter and unforgiving person?

Daniel asked me, when I found out about his new girlfriend, if I would ever forgive him.

"Why should I?" I retorted.

"Because I've admitted I'm the one in the wrong," he replied. "I know it, you know it, and I'm throwing myself at your feet, saying I'm sorry. Because you're in a position to forgive."

"But I don't want to," I said.

I didn't want to grant him that luxury of being forgiven. I didn't want to make him feel better, to feel absolved of guilt. I wanted him to go on suffering, to pay him back for hurting me.

"Everybody makes mistakes," he said.

"And everybody has to pay for them," I told him.

That's my philosophy.

Make 'em pay.

When I bring Ellie home from the birthday party, the red velour dress has something sticky all down the front, the pristine white lacy tights are in wrinkles around her ankles, Norah Batty-style, her hair looks as though someone had held her upside down and shaken her, and she's exhausted. She won't put down her McDonald's hat and her party bag to get undressed, and I end up letting her take them to bed with her. She falls asleep almost as soon as she lies down.

I'm in the kitchen, trying to sponge the sticky stuff off the party dress before putting it in the wash, when the phone rings.

It's Martin.

I bite back the urge to say something sarcastic about presuming he'd left the country.

"Sorry—I just haven't had a chance to phone," he says. He sounds genuinely apologetic. Perhaps I've just been a bit paranoid. After all, I suppose it's only been a few days.

"That's OK," I say, like I haven't been waiting, and wondering what was wrong with me and whether he didn't like the smell of me or the color of my underwear or something.

"It isn't OK," he insists. "I didn't want you to think I wasn't going to call you . . . especially after the other night . . . it was great."

Oh. I start to relax. No problem with the underwear, then.

"It's just that we've been so busy—at work—I've been on nights, and . . ."

"On call?" I say. "I understand."

Selfish of me, not to appreciate the demands of his job. There he is, tending to sick patients, putting new hearts into people, saving lives, performing miracles everyday of his life, and all I can think of is whether he's going to phone me up to congratulate me on my sexual technique.

"On a night shift," he corrects me.

There's a silence.

Shift? Surely heart surgeons don't work shifts? Do they?

"And that's the other reason I've put off phoning you," he adds.

I wait.

"I've lied to you," he says. "And I need to stop lying now, because I want to go on seeing you. And I feel like such a prick for lying to you, and I didn't know how to tell you."

"So tell me," I say stonily.

Does everyone make it their life's business to lie to me? Is there something about me?

Something that makes people avoid telling me the truth?

"It's my job," he says. "I'm not really a heart surgeon, Beth. I'm a nurse."

Tuesday

———◆◇◆———

And—well, the thing is, of course, I've lied to him, too, haven't I?

I'm back at Oakleigh Court this morning, in the Single Young Executive apartment, my employer's apartment that I've pretended is mine, working on the computer I've pretended to own, on the TV script that I've pretended has already attracted the attention of the media and I've implied is all set to make me rich and famous.

I'm typing fast and furiously on the computer to try to block out all uncomfortable thoughts from my mind. Thoughts about my unfair reaction to Martin's slight amendment to the truth about his job, and how this compares with my complete fabrication about my own. Thoughts about how there might indeed be a grain or two of truth in the sneaky feeling I've started getting about the unforgiving side of my nature.

I reacted, to Martin, with righteous indignation. "Why did you have to lie to me? There's nothing wrong with being a nurse!" Nothing wrong with being a cleaning lady, either, but this isn't me we're discussing here.

"I know," he said sadly. "I don't know why I did it. Except that I wanted to impress you."

"I'd have been more impressed by honesty," declared the Pretend Scriptwriter loftily.

"I *am* a nurse on a cardiac ward," he told me. "I just exaggerated a little . . ."

"What other lies have you told me?" I demanded unfairly. "I suppose you're really married with three kids . . ."

"No, of course not. This was the only thing I lied about. I've spent all week worrying about how to tell you."

"Well, OK. You've told me now."

"Are you pissed off with me? Do you not want to see me anymore?"

"I need time to think about it, Martin. I didn't have you marked down as someone who'd need to lie to impress."

"Fair enough," he said, sounding miserable. "Can I call you again in a couple of days?"

"If you like."

What the fuck was I doing? Playing some sort of power game? Like a cat, with a paw poised over the poor mouse, toying with it as it squirms on the ground, all bloodied and defeated?

I spend four days and a considerable amount of energy worrying about the fact that this guy hasn't called me since making very satisfactory love to me, and then as soon as he calls, throwing himself on my mercy, I grind his bollocks under my heel. Sometimes I think I need therapy.

The script is actually beginning to take shape. I've got ideas about where it's going; in fact, I'm getting ideas about it all the time, waking up in the middle of the night needing to look for a pen and paper to scribble down something, thinking of phrases while I'm shopping, while I'm cooking dinner, while I'm working. Not that there's very much work now, is there. All I've got left is one day a week at Dottie's, being more of a home help than a cleaner, and one day a week here, not in practice doing what I'm being paid for. I finally, out of desperation, asked at the playgroup today about the possibility of any vacancies there. Pat gave me a long look, as if she was assessing whether I could really be serious, and then asked curtly, "What experience have you got?"

"Four years," I replied, pointing to Ellie.

"But in a playgroup or nursery?"

"No, none."

"Done the course?"

"Sorry?"

"The PPA course for playgroup workers?"

"Didn't know there was one. But I'd be willing, naturally . . ." I added hurriedly.

"Any qualifications?" she demanded with a slight sigh.

I was beginning to get the distinct impression she didn't like me. And the even more distinct impression that I didn't want to work for her.

"Ten GCSEs," I said a bit sarcastically. "Three A levels. And a degree in media studies with sociology. A first. Will that help at all?"

Her expression didn't alter. "There's nothing at the moment," she said. "But I'll bear you in mind for next term, if anyone leaves."

Can't even get a job at a bloody playgroup. I'll have to do something. I save the work I've done today on the script and, while still on the computer, type out an ad for new cleaning clients. I describe myself as "experienced and trustworthy," only flinching slightly at the fact that I've been sacked by one of my employers and I'm cheating one of the others even by typing this ad. "References available" I type boldly, making a mental note to ask Louise and Dottie to write something nice about me. I add an hourly rate that is only slightly more than I've been charging so far, print it off, and put it in my bag. I'll put it in the post-office window, and perhaps phone the local paper with it.

Perhaps it's the only thing I'm good at, after all, I muse morosely, as I give Alex Chapman's flat its obligatory flick of a duster and hoover up the nonexistent dirt. What would my lecturers at university think if they could see me now? What would my mother think, come to that, if she knew I was advertising for more cleaning jobs? Was this what I studied so hard for?

But there are bills waiting to be paid, and we have to eat.

Ellie's finished her lunch-box snack in front of Alex Chapman's TV and is wandering around the flat, picking things up and putting them down.

"Leave that alone!" I snap at her as she investigates a duck-shaped white china soap dish in the bathroom. "If you break it . . ."

"I won't!" she answers me back, putting it down heavily.

I close my eyes and sigh. It was so much easier when she went to Fay's after playgroup.

"Look at your books," I suggest, trying to sound cheerful. "There are some new ones in the bag, from Louise's children."

"Don't want to," she returns, sitting down in the middle of the bathroom floor.

I hoover around her, tutting with exasperation.

"Ouch!" she says, glaring at me as the Hoover slightly nudges her bottom. She rubs herself, with an expression of exaggerated injury. I'd never have believed how a four-year-old can provoke a fight.

"I didn't hurt you," I say, playing right into her hands.

"Did! You *hoovered* me! It *hurt!*"

"Don't be silly, Ellie. You're making me cross now. Go in the living room and watch the TV."

I was never going to say that. When my child was born I made all these promises to myself, and one of them was that she'd never be stuck in front of a TV because I was too busy to provide her with a more worthwhile activity.

"Don't *want* to watch TV," she says in a whine that is rising dangerously toward a cry.

And the awful thing is, I actually feel so cross with her, I want to drag her into the lounge by the arm she's flinging out at me in a half-hearted attempt to smack me on the legs. I want to drag her in there and *force* her to sit in front of the TV. I actually have to turn off the Hoover and go out of the bathroom, walk away from her, to stop myself from doing it.

Calm down, calm down, I tell myself out loud as I stand at the kitchen sink, taking deep breaths. Why am I so upset with Ellie when she's just being a perfectly normal child, perfectly understandably being bored to tears by having to sit in a stranger's flat, not allowed to touch anything, while her mother inexplicably cleans it when it's already cleaner than our own flat has ever been in her entire life? I look at the clock. It's only ten minutes till I officially finish here.

"Come on, Ellie," I call.

She's crying to herself now, still sitting on the bathroom floor where I left her, still rubbing the imagined hurt on her bottom.

"Come on. Get your coat on. We're going to the park."

"The park!" she yells with delight, jumping to her feet, everything else instantly forgotten. "Can I go on the swings?"

"Yes, of course."

"Can I have an ice cream?"

There's only £1.50 in my purse. I don't get paid for today until I go to Louise's and collect the envelope from Alex's mother.

"I'll see," I say, and immediately wish I hadn't because Ellie obviously takes this as a yes.

We go to the post office on the way to the park. I hand over the ad and ask for it to be put in the window for two weeks.

"That'll be three pounds then, please," says the lady behind the counter.

I look at her in surprise. "Three pounds?"

"One pound fifty per week."

I count the money from my purse out onto the counter. "Just the one week for now, then."

I look from my empty purse to Ellie's little face. I know I should just tell her that I haven't got any money, she can't have any treats until I've been paid at Dottie's tomorrow. Ice creams don't grow on trees. She has to learn.

That's what I should do. That's what a good, sensible mother would do, and put up with the tantrum.

Instead, I get her back into the car and drive home.

"You said we were going to the park . . ." she begins to complain loudly as we pull up outside our flat.

"We are. We are, I promise. I just . . . forgot something. Stay in the car, Ellie—I'll be one minute."

When I park outside the post office again, she looks at

me with a suspicion bordering on accusation. "We've already been here!" she challenges me with a stare.

"I know. Forgot something. One minute!"

I feel a momentary sick pang of guilt as I hand Ellie's post office savings book over the counter, but I've been steeling myself for this feeling and I choke it back down with a huge swallow before I ask the cashier, "Can I withdraw forty pounds, please."

I take the four crisp tens from her hand without flinching.

Ellie can have her ice cream now.

And I can get some shopping.

Well, £40 isn't much, is it. I'll put it back when I'm out of debt, when I've got my new cleaning jobs. She won't ever know. And what makes me think she'd mind anyway, if she were old enough to understand? It's paying for her ice cream, her spaghetti, her Coco Pops, her orange juice. Any daughter, of any age, who had a bit of money in a post-office account, would say to her mother, "Take it, go on, if you need it, if you haven't got anything left in your purse, it's yours—all of it—just take it and spend it."

I would, wouldn't I, if my mother were to phone me up today and tell me she was destitute. Well, I would if I had any savings.

There's nearly £600 in Ellie's savings account.

Most of it has been presents from my mum and dad. They gave me £250 to put away for her, when she was born, and then every birthday, as well as giving her a toy or a game or whatever, they've given me another check—usually £50. But some of it has come from Daniel; and that's what I don't like thinking about.

Daniel has sent her money, on her birthdays, and at Christmas.

It's annoyed me at the time. I would have preferred it if he'd come to see her. I would have preferred it if he'd acted like a father, a proper father who showed some sign of missing his daughter, some sign of wanting a little bit of contact with her, even if it was only a couple of times a year.

I can't believe all his crap about not wanting to complicate her life. I think it's just too much trouble. He apparently only lives a half-hour's drive away. He pays me money every month, which salves his conscience, I suppose, and then on each of the two birthdays and two Christmases he hasn't seen her, he's actually made the effort to lift a pen, write a check, put it inside a card: "To my darling little Ellie, with all my love from Daddy"—and write underneath it: "Buy her something nice."

Just that.

"Buy her something nice."

Who's he talking to, do you think, when he says that?

Could it be me?

Could he be addressing the mother of his child, the woman he loved for seven long years before deciding he preferred some other bit of stuff?

No mention, you notice, of my name. No "Dear Beth," or even "Beth—how are you?"; just "Buy her something nice," as if he can't be bothered to remember who I am, any more than he can be bothered to buy her something nice himself.

So I haven't.

I haven't bought her anything out of his money. I don't want to search the shops for some cuddly bunny or some special doll, and give it to her and tell her it's from her daddy. I don't want to see her cuddling that bunny or taking that doll to bed with her, and attaching some special significance to it, as if *he*'d really bought it, bought it with her in mind, a loving gesture from a loving father.

Because he's not, is he?

He remembers her birthday—big deal. She was only born four years ago.

So I've paid his checks into her savings account and said nothing to her about it. It's her money—she'll have it when she's older.

Including the £40 I've just borrowed. It'll go back, every penny.

When we get home from the park, I sit Ellie down with her crayons and felt-tip pens and some sheets of paper.

"Do some nice pictures for Dottie," I suggest. "I can take them to show her tomorrow."

Ellie immediately starts to draw a huge black shape with four sticks for legs and a big red mouth. The mouth is smiling, so I don't recognize it straight away as that devil dog from hell, until she calls out, "How do you spell Tosser, Mummy?"

Perhaps it's just as well she didn't do the drawing at playgroup. Perfect Pat would probably have fainted on the spot.

"There's a man!" shouts Ellie a little later.

She got bored with her drawings and I left her in the living room watching the children's TV programs.

I rush back from the kitchen where I've been emptying the washing machine. I've got two towels and some knickers over one arm.

"Where?" I begin.

Ellie's stood up and she's pointing out of the front window. Someone's coming up to our door. Someone who looks like . . .

"Martin!" I mutter under my breath as the doorbell rings.

I'm frantically trying to remember whether I've brushed my hair today and whether I've eaten anything that's likely to be smeared round my mouth. Have I got time to run to the mirror in the bathroom before opening the door? What if I've got something stuck in my teeth?

The doorbell rings again. No time.

"Who is he?" asks Ellie, following me to the door.

"A friend," I tell her. "You don't know him."

"A *friend*?" she asks in a tone of such disbelief that I feel almost sorry for myself.

"Yes, I do have some."

Well, one, perhaps two.

I open the door and say, trying to make it sound as if I haven't seen him out of the window, "Oh, *Martin*! What a surprise!"

He smiles, steps forward, and produces a bunch of flowers from behind his back. "For you," he says, still smiling, and then he stops smiling and adds, "I couldn't wait any longer to see you. Do you mind?"

I shake my head, momentarily struck dumb with surprise. "They're lovely," I say, taking the flowers.

I hold the door open for him, dropping the towels and knickers from my arm. He bends down and picks them up.

Ellie, watching him shyly from behind my legs, steps forward at this point and informs him, "They're my mummy's knickers. They're big ones. Mine are little."

"Well," says Martin, grinning broadly, "I expect that's because you are only a little girl yet."

"I'm sorry . . ." I say, flustered, grabbing the knickers from him and rushing with them and the flowers to the kitchen, leaving Martin to close the front door after him and follow me. "Ellie—your program's still on the TV . . ."

As he follows me into the kitchen I stop, staring in horror. The floor's strewn with washing, the sink's full of dishes, and on the table . . .

"TOSSER," Martin reads out loud from Ellie's laboriously printed letters underneath the drawing of the black demon dog. He looks up at me curiously, not appearing to notice the mess all around him.

"It's a dog we know," I tell him vaguely, trying hurriedly to tidy up the table and make room to lay the flowers down. "Ellie drew it."

"Of course. Very artistic," he says with a smile, seeming to mean it. "She's sweet."

Something—I don't know whether it's the fact that he's being so nice about Ellie, or the surprise of him turning up like this, or the fact that he's brought me flowers, which has hardly ever happened to me before (Daniel used to say flowers should be left to bloom where they're supposed to be—outside)—something suddenly makes me feel ridiculously emotional. I have to turn away from him, pretending to be ever so interested in picking up damp clothes from the kitchen floor.

He squats down and picks up a sock and a tea towel and hands them to me.

"What's the matter?" he asks anxiously. "Have I said something . . . ?"

"No!" I shake my head, trying to swallow back this really stupid choking sort of feeling that's creeping up my throat. "No, of course not! You're being lovely, and the flowers are gorgeous, and you shouldn't be down on the floor helping me pick up these . . . socks . . . and things and I've been horrible to you and I'm sorry!" I wipe away a really ridiculous tear that seems for some reason to have leaked out of my eye.

"No, you haven't!" He smiles at me. "Of course you haven't been horrible! I—"

"Yes, I was!" I babble. "I was horrible about you saying you were a heart surgeon and it didn't really matter at all, and I'm much worse than you because I told you I was a scriptwriter and I'm not, I'm just trying to be! I'm trying to write a TV script when I'm supposed to be working, and I'm hardly even working because I've lost most of my work, and when I *do* work . . ." I stand up straight, wipe my problem eye again and take a deep breath. Might as well say bye bye now, Martin, 'cos you're going to finish with me when you hear the end of this. "I'm a cleaning lady."

Amazingly, he starts to laugh.

I stand there, arms full of sheets and towels and knickers and socks, sniffing back tears that seem to still be leaking for some reason, perhaps an eye infection, and wait for him to say, "Well, forget it then! A cleaning lady? Why should I waste my time with a cleaning lady, especially one who pretends to be a scriptwriter *and* gets all high and mighty about me pretending to be a heart surgeon? Give me back the flowers and I'll be on my way!"

But instead, he just laughs—a gentle, nice laugh, like he's laughing with me about a joke we're both sharing rather than laughing at me.

"Well, aren't we a right pair of fools!" he says.

He takes hold of the load of washing I'm holding and plonks it down on the table. Then he takes hold of me in his arms and sort of sways with me, like he's rocking me, with his cheek against mine, which is, embarrassingly, all wet and teary.

"We don't need to do that stuff anymore, do we?" he says

quietly, next to my ear. "We don't need to pretend, and try to impress each other anymore, do we? Not now." And he starts to kiss me.

Just as I'm getting into it, Ellie comes crashing through the door. "You!" she shouts accusingly, and Martin and I spring apart as if we've been shot.

I'm preparing my excuses for her.

No, of course the man wasn't kissing me. He was trying to get out something that was stuck between my teeth. He was trying to suck some poison out of my mouth that I'd swallowed accidentally. He was checking to see if I tasted of garlic. He was . . .

"You," she continues, turning to face us with a furious glare, "have put *wet washing* on top of my picture of Tosser!"

Oh.

Is that all!

Wednesday

———○◇◇◇○———

"And what did he say then?" gasps Dottie, holding both her sides to try to stop herself from laughing any more.

The picture of Tosser, only slightly crumpled by the damp washing, is lying next to her on the sofa. She keeps looking at it and shaking her head as if she can't really believe it.

"He was lovely," I sigh, smiling at the memory. "He moved all the washing again, picked up the picture, and promised Ellie he'd dry it off for her. He propped it up in front of the radiator, and then he straightened up all her paper and crayons and asked her if she'd be so kind as to draw a picture for him, too."

He actually said it like that. Would she be so kind. He had Ellie eating out of his hand. She'd drawn him three pictures by the time he went home.

"And?" prompted Dottie.

"And what?"

"Come on, girl, spill the beans! Are you seeing him again? Eh?"

"Of course," I tell her, smiling.

"Good for you!" she chortles in delight. "Bloody good luck to you, Beth. Give him one for me, eh!"

"Dottie!" I laugh, pretending to be shocked. "You dirty old woman!"

"Not so much of the 'old'!" she retorts. "I've still got me youth and me health, and there's no knowing what else I've still got, 'cos it's been a few years since anyone's tried to find out! But I've had a few bounces on the old bedsprings meself, you know."

What a lovely expression.

"I bet you have!" I grin at her. "I bet you'd still give some of them a run for their money, too!"

She chuckles appreciatively. "Oh, you've cheered me up today, Beth. I was down in the dumps before you came this morning."

"Were you? Are your legs hurting you?"

"No, no." She shakes her head dismissively. "No worse than usual." She sighs, a long deep sigh, and stares ahead of her as if she's trying to make up her mind whether to tell me or not. I wait. Tosser, dozing next to the gas fire, opens one eye and looks up at us, alerted by our silence. "It's Luke," she says at length, with another sigh.

I think for a minute, and then remember. "Luke. Your grandson in Australia? The one who wants to be an artist?"

"Yes, he's coming over."

"Oh! That's nice!" I search her face for some sign of agreement. "Isn't it?"

"Is it?" she throws back at me. "I don't know about that. What do I want with a boy his age turning up on my doorstep? How do they think I'm going to entertain him? Eh? He'll be used to going out all night to raves and love-ins and whatever else they get up to at those Australian universities. What's he want to come over here for?"

"To see you, perhaps," I suggest gently.

"Huh! What's he want to see me for? He'll be bored to tears by dinnertime the first day. No point even unpacking his bag. He'll be wanting to get the next flight back." She gives me a knowing look. "I'm no fool, Beth."

Oh, bugger. Has she guessed about me phoning Chicago?

"Of course you're not," I agree hastily.

"I know what they're up to."

"Do you?" I ask, puzzled. "Who? You know what who's up to?"

"My son and his wife. And my daughter. She's probably in on it, too. I can just imagine it—over the phone—nag, nag, nag. Do something about Mum. Like I can't do anything for myself, like I need them fussing—"

"What? What do you think they're up to, Dottie?" I interrupt before this goes on any further.

"They're making him come, of course. Luke. What twenty-one-year-old would want to come all this way, just to see his grandmother? He wouldn't have the money, for a start, what with never having done an honest day's work in his idle life. They'll have paid for his fare, to make him come. Can't you just hear it? Go and see your grandmother, make sure she's all right, so we don't have to worry about her."

"That's probably not very fair," I chide her. "I bet they do all worry about you, and I'm sure Luke does want to come . . ."

"Huh!" is all I get for a reply.

"So when's he coming, anyway?" I ask her.

"Tomorrow."

Well, that's a bit sudden, isn't it. No going back now—he's presumably on the plane already. Or how does it work? Will he have left Australia yesterday to get here tomorrow, or will he be leaving tomorrow to get here yesterday? I don't know, I can never work out things like that.

"They didn't give you much notice, then," I say to Dottie.

"Exactly. I'm not daft. They probably waited till he'd gotten his ticket and he was on the way to the airport before they phoned me. So I couldn't say no." She grunts and huffs a bit and fidgets in her chair. "Bloody nuisance, coming over here, wanting kangaroo steaks and Fosters lager."

"It'll be company for you, though," I say, laughing.

"Company? Probably spend all his time watching *Neighbours* and *Home and Away*."

I don't bother to point out that she herself never misses an episode of either.

"And I won't be able to understand a word he says," she adds with some satisfaction. "All that 'g'day' and 'fair tucker' nonsense."

"There you are!" I nudge her. "You're talking it like a native already!"

"Huh. Very funny."

She continues to look sulky and cross for most of the rest of the morning.

When I leave, I tell her, "I hope it goes well tomorrow, with your grandson."

"Hmph."

"Come on, Dottie—make him welcome. He's coming a long way to see you."

"I know," she relents. "All right, all right, I know. Might as well be nice to him—he'll only be here for a day or two. Soon as he's got over the jet lag, he'll be packing to go home. Mark my words!"

But I've got a sneaky feeling she's just putting up a front—protecting herself. She doesn't want to look forward to him coming in case she's disappointed. I hope to God she isn't.

* * *

I'm waiting outside the playgroup for Ellie when someone taps me on the shoulder.

"Hi, Beth. Haven't seen you for ages."

It's Simon.

"Oh . . . what are you doing here?"

Anyone would think it was me carrying on a secret affair behind his back, the way I'm stammering and stumbling like an idiot. What is it about knowing other
people's secrets, other people's guilt, that makes you feel
just as guilty yourself?

He looks at me rather strangely. "Same as you! Collecting the kid—oh, here they come! Prepare for trouble,
Jack!"

Jack's bashing his head rhythmically against the back
of his baby stroller and uttering a toneless "Baa Baa Back
Ship" over and over again. He looks at his father and
grins.

"Where's Fay?" I ask, suddenly concerned. My God!
Has she left him? Left the kids? Gone to live with Neil,
and no one's even told me?

"Brighton. You know, Beth—that midweek break with
her old schoolfriend, what's-her-name?"

He looks at me for inspiration. I shake my head
dumbly. Can hardly say that the name of the friend is
probably Neil.

"Didn't she tell you?" he asks in surprise. "She must
have! She's been excited about it for weeks!"

Mm. I bet she has.

"I . . . er . . . haven't seen much of Fay for a while," I
say vaguely. "Oh, hello, sweetheart, come and show
Mummy what you've been doing this morning!"

Thankfully we both get involved for a few minutes
with Ellie and Lauren, who both squeal like little pigs at

the sight of me and Simon waiting for them together (must be a welcome change from seeing me and Fay on opposite sides of the entrance hall, maintaining a stony silence and stony expressions).

"Why's your daddy here?" asks Ellie, looking at Lauren with undisguised jealousy.

"'Cos he's looking after me," says Lauren importantly.

Ellie scowls and gives me a look that implies this whole situation is my fault. "Why?" she persists. "Where's your mummy?"

"Gone on a holiday. With her friend."

Ellie considers this for a minute, then shrugs her shoulders and declares, "*My* mummy doesn't go on holidays. So *I* don't need a daddy."

Simon and I walk out to the parking lot together.

"Is everything all right?" he asks as I'm opening my car door. "Between you and Fay?"

"Of course!" I lie brightly. "Why shouldn't it be?"

"Well . . . I've taken time off work to look after the kids, and I expected to be having Ellie, too. I thought she always came home with Fay after playgroup. But Fay said you've made new arrangements?" He looks me straight in the eyes. "Have you two had a row?"

I feel uncomfortable under his clear gaze.

"Not really," I hedge. "I've . . . lost a couple of my cleaning jobs anyway, so I can fit Ellie in around the others."

"Sorry to hear that, Beth," he says kindly. "Are you managing all right? Can we help at all?"

I can't bear it.

I can't bear his kindness, his sympathy—this nice, kind guy who I've known all these years and who's always been so good to Fay and the children—and to me.

He might be a bit older than her, he might be a bit staid and a bit boring, according to Fay, but he's decent and caring and patient and honest and all those things that really matter at the end of the day, when the heat and the lust and the desperation go out of a relationship and you just want to sit down together and talk over a cup of tea.

I can't bear it that he's looking after the children while she's probably holed up in some sleazy hotel in Brighton with Neil, where they're shagging the life out of each other and thinking that they've just discovered the meaning of the universe.

And I can't bear it that he's being so nice and so concerned about me, when I know what she's up to but I'm never going to tell him.

"I'm fine," I say, turning away from him to fasten Ellie's seat belt in the back of the car. "I'm getting some new clients, and I've got other irons in the fire."

"Good," he says, looking a little puzzled. "Well, look—you know where we are if you need anything."

"Thanks, Simon," I say, managing to smile at him. "Have a nice week with the kids, and . . . give my love to Fay."

What made me say that?

I stare after him as he turns and wheels the buggy over to his own car, Lauren skipping along beside him waving to Ellie, and the words are echoing in my head: *Give my love to Fay*. Why? And what would she say if he did? And do I really mean it?

I suppose we just say stuff like that out of habit, don't we.

I dial ★69 when I get home, as I always do, not having an answering machine, and there's been a call from a number I don't recognize. I dial it back and a woman's voice answers. I'm hoping it might be a response to one of my ads—I've put one in the local paper now, as well as the post office.

"Hello. Beth Marston here. Did someone call me from that number this morning?"

"Oh, yes! Hello, Beth," says the woman. She sounds friendly, youngish. "I saw your ad in the paper this morning."

Yippee!! I cross my fingers in my lap. Only one set of fingers. More is supposed to cancel the luck.

"I've been looking for someone to do a bit of cleaning for me. I wondered if we could meet to discuss it."

"Of course!" I agree, trying hard not to sound too eager, too desperate. "Shall I come round to see you? Whereabouts are you?"

She describes an area a little way out of the town, on the other side. It'll probably only take me twenty to thirty minutes to drive there. I could cope with that, depending on the hours she wants. Best to see her first, impress her with my professionalism and expertise, and the references I'll be showing her, and discuss hours afterward.

"You'll have to come in the evening," she tells me. "I've called you from work—I work full time in London."

"That's fine, then," I say smoothly and professionally. "Friday night? Half past seven? Yes. See you then, Mrs. . . . ? Oh, sorry—*Miss* Waterstone. I look forward to meeting you on Friday."

I put down the phone, my pulse racing. This could be good, this could be very good. She lives in an upmarket area and she's obviously a career woman, a single career woman. Probably got pots of money and no time for cleaning. I might be able to talk her into two mornings a week.

But first I've got to organize a babysitter for Friday evening. Who the hell can I ask?

* * *

"Hello, Simon. It's Beth."

"Beth!" He sounds surprised, and just a little bit alarmed. "Is everything all right?"

"Yes, sorry. I'm sorry to bother you . . ."

"Don't be silly. You're not bothering me. What can I do for you?"

"Well—it's an enormous favor, actually, Simon. Would you mind having Ellie for a couple of hours on Friday night? I've got a new client to go and see, and . . ."

"Of course! You don't want to take her with you, do you, when you're meeting someone for the first time."

See what I mean? So understanding, so kind.

"Lauren will be pleased," he goes on. "She was telling me, after playgroup, that Ellie hasn't been around for a while."

"Yes, well—I've been busy, you know—one thing and another."

"Are you *sure* nothing's wrong between you and Fay?" he asks again.

Perceptive, too.

"No, no," I say, trying frantically to think how to change the subject. "And are you managing all right with the kids on your own this week, Simon?"

"No probs," he says lightly. "Jack doesn't seem to play me up as much as he does Fay. They need a father's touch occasionally. . . ." He trails off, and then adds, "Sorry, Beth. That was pretty crass."

"No, it wasn't. It's probably true. And Lauren and Jack are lucky that they've got you," I tell him.

And I hope they keep you.

God, Fay, what are you doing? What *are* you doing?

Friday

---◦◦◦◦◦---

It's nearly the end of March and just when you might have expected the weather to start acting as if spring were a possibility, it's got even colder, and the perpetual rain has turned to sleet. Ellie is chattering excitedly about snow as I help her button up her coat to go round to Simon's tonight.

"Well, I hope it *doesn't* snow," I tell her firmly. "Snow is a nuisance, Ellie. It makes it difficult to get out and about, and it's cold and horrible and . . ." I become aware that she's giving me a look of unconcealed disgust. I recognize that look from long ago, when I was a kid myself. It's saying: Listen to the boring old fart going on about nuisance and inconvenience and cold and stuff, when all I want is to get out there and have some FUN!

I force myself to smile, and add, "Well, I suppose it would be OK to have a bit of snow just for the weekend, so you could play in it . . ."

"Yes!!" she shouts as if I've already arranged it. "I'm going to tell Lauren! We can play in the snow, we can play in the snow!"

I wish I'd never said it now.

* * *

The street where *Miss* Waterstone lives is in upmarket suburbia. The houses are detached, 1960s, chalet-style. Georgian windows, double garages, wide plots with ornamental shrubs in the front gardens. The road is lined with pollarded trees. I bet it'll look lovely in the spring, if spring ever comes. I ring the doorbell, feeling strangely nervous. I can hear the radio playing inside the house, and someone talking on the phone.

"Anyway, got to go—someone at the door . . . yeah, see you later!"

Footsteps coming down the hall. Hall obviously not carpeted. The door opens and I'm greeted with a smile. Well, that's a good start, at least.

"Beth Marston? Hello; I'm Melanie Waterstone. Nice to meet you. Come in. Would you like a coffee or anything?"

She's only about my age. I wonder how she managed to become such a successful career woman and get a house like this, when I'm still living in a dump and cleaning for a living.

"Thank you," I say, following her into the kitchen. "A coffee would be great."

She shows me around the house. Talks about how the Georgian windows are such a pain in the neck to clean, and how the self-cleaning oven doesn't really self-clean, and how the deep-pile carpet tends to need extra suction to vacuum it, and I listen and nod and murmur sympathetic agreement. When we get to the master bedroom I try not to show my surprise. Somehow I'd presumed her to be single, but there are books and alarm clocks on either side of the double bed, and a pair of men's trousers slung casually over the back of the chair, and men's shaving gear in the en-suite bathroom. She doesn't mention her boyfriend until we're back in the kitchen, sitting at the round oak table drinking coffee.

"The reason I need your help," she tells me, as if the reason matters to me just so long as she does need it, "is that I work, sometimes, very long hours, Beth, and sometimes have to bring paperwork home, too. And my boyfriend works from home. I don't have time to do the housework, and I want him to be able to concentrate on his own work, and not have to feel he should be looking after the house just because he's here and I'm not."

I nod, impressed by this. I wish I had a boyfriend who worked from home. I'd bloody make him do the housework, I would! Then I think, briefly, of Oliver—but quickly dismiss it from my mind. No, it's ridiculous to assume that all men who work from home are raging uncontrollable lechers. This one will probably turn out to be meek and mild and will sit in silence while I clean around him, lifting his feet up for the Hoover.

I smile at Melanie. Now for the thousand-dollar question. "How many hours a week would you like me to do?"

"Well." She pauses, looking around the kitchen as if she's assessing the damage. "I think we'll start with one day a week, shall we? Can you do a Friday? So it's clean for the weekend?"

"Yes, but I can only do about three hours in the morning. I have to take my little girl to playgroup at nine, and pick her up at twelve thirty . . ."

"Hm. Probably won't be enough time, will it?" She looks at me, pondering this. "Well, let's start with Friday mornings, Beth, to do the basic cleaning, and then perhaps add another morning in, to do jobs like the windows and paintwork and so on when they need doing? What do you think?"

"Sounds good," I agree.

I'm feeling jubilant. I knew it. I knew I could probably

get two mornings a week out of her. She's just waiting for a few weeks to see if I'm any good before she makes it definite. Fair enough. I'll clean the place spotless. It's going to be a nice house to clean. Not too perfect, not too dirty. I'm looking forward to it.

"And what about the holidays?" she asks suddenly.

"Pardon?"

"The school holidays. When your little girl isn't at playgroup, will you still be able to come? Do you have someone to look after her?"

Making it quite clear she doesn't want some snotty brat coming to nose about in her house. I can see her point. Ellie would probably distract the nice boyfriend from his work.

"Yes," I lie breezily. "I have an arrangement . . ."

God knows what it is. But I'll work on it. And I'll have to hurry up. The Easter holiday isn't far away.

I drive back to Simon's in a good mood, singing along with the radio. Perhaps my luck's beginning to turn at last.

I tap on the front door with my car keys and wait for Simon to open it. I can hear Ellie and Lauren shrieking inside, and Jack crying. Poor Simon. I'll take Ellie straight home so he can get his two to bed and get a bit of peace.

But it isn't Simon who opens the door.

It's Fay.

"Oh," I say, stupidly, standing frozen on the doorstep.

"Come in," says Fay, walking away from me.

"I thought you were away."

"Just got back, half an hour ago. Simon's just gone out to get us takeout."

Of course. A midweek break would finish on a Friday, wouldn't it. Otherwise it turns into a weekend break.

"Well. I'll just get Ellie's coat on, and I'll . . ."

"Don't want to go! Don't want to go!" squeals Ellie, running up to me and dancing around my legs, wearing a straw hat and two nightdresses, tied around her waist with scarves.

Lauren crawls after her on the floor, giggling and pretending to be a baby.

"Beth," says Fay, turning to face me as the girls disappear into the living room. "Beth, please."

"Did you have a nice trip?" I ask her coldly.

"Yes, I would have told you, if . . ."

"If what?"

"If you were speaking to me!" she exclaims, suddenly sounding exasperated. "How long are you going to keep this up?"

Me? How long am *I* going to keep it up?!

I'm not the one having a secret affair, am I! I'm not the one deceiving everyone—husband, children, best friend—sneaking around the country having illicit midweek breaks.

"I'm sorry, Beth," she goes on, talking quickly now, but quietly, very close to my ear, so the children can't hear from the other room. "I hurt you, I know, and I'm very sorry. I didn't mean to. I've already explained—the only reason I held back from telling you about Neil was because I didn't want to ask you to lie for me. Perhaps that was a mistake. But surely our friendship is worth more than that?"

"Worth more than what? More than your affair with Neil?" I whisper back angrily.

She doesn't answer this and looks away, upset.

Well, this is the crux of the matter, really, isn't it.

"Who matters more to you?" I insist.

"I don't see that it's a question of choice," she replies. "If you're my friend, can't you accept the fact that I'm human? What I'm doing might not be right, but I'm just trying, the best I can, not to hurt people."

"Not doing very well, then, are you."

There's a silence.

The children have calmed down and put the TV on. Jack seems to have fallen asleep.

"So how long are you going to punish me?" Fay asks at length.

"I'm not punishing you," I retort. "I'm just waiting for you to say you're sorry."

"Beth, that's what I've just been doing. What more do you want me to say?"

"You're sorry for what? For having an affair? For cheating on Simon?"

She looks down at the floor again, shaking her head.

"Or just for ruining our friendship?" I persist.

I pick up Ellie's coat from the hooks by the door. "Come on, Ellie—time to go home. Quickly!"

Fay looks up at me again. I see the misery in her eyes and I flinch, turning away to wait for Ellie.

"You certainly know how to hurt someone back," she tells me softly. "I can't apologize any more than I have done, Beth. It's up to you, now. You have to decide whether to forgive me."

I seem to keep hearing this lately, about forgiving.

Bugger it.

I was in such a good mood ten minutes ago, and now I feel like shit.

Sod Fay.

Sod apologies, sod forgiveness, sod her and her sad looks and all her talk about friendship and hurting.

It's not *me* who's doing the hurting, is it.

* * *

I do *69 when I get home, and my mum has called. But before I have time to call her back, and while I'm still putting Ellie to bed, Martin phones. I tell him about the new cleaning job.

"Sounds good!" he says. "Well done. Start next Friday, then?"

"Yes, and I think she's going to increase it to two mornings after a while. I just need to make a good impression."

"Spray plenty of polish around. Always does the trick."

"Is that what you do to keep the wards clean?" I laugh.

"Well, we have to keep up a pretense . . ." He hesitates for a minute and then says, "I suppose you wouldn't fancy coming out tomorrow night? I'll be finishing a week of night shifts tonight and I'll be off duty till Monday morning. We could see a film or go out for a Chinese or something?"

"I wish I could. It sounds lovely."

It does, it really does. When did I last get taken out to the movies or a restaurant? Oh, some time in another life, I think.

"But I haven't got anyone to look after Ellie."

"Still not made it up with Fay?" he asks.

"No!" I snap. "And it isn't up to *me* to make it up!"

"All right, sorry I asked."

"No," I sigh. "No, I shouldn't have bitten your head off. But I've just seen her, and she seems to want to make me feel guilty for not falling at her feet and saying whatever she wants to do is fine by me."

"I thought that was what friends were supposed to say?" he puts in.

I just about stop myself from slamming the phone down. "Perhaps we should agree to disagree on that one,"

I say frostily. "How would you feel if she was *your* wife, having an affair with someone else?"

"OK," he says lightly. "OK, point taken. Let's change the subject, shall we?"

Yes, let's. I've had quite enough of the subject of bloody Fay, and quite enough of her and, apparently, everyone else, thinking she's right and I'm wrong.

"How about Sunday?" he asks. "Could I perhaps come over? Take you and Ellie out for a drive or something? Sunday shopping? Or whatever?"

"That's sweet of you!" I smile, cheering up. "We could . . . oh! I've just remembered! No, Sunday's no good. I'm doing a boot sale for Louise—she's one of my clients— *was* one of my clients."

"Well," he responds immediately. "Would you like some help?"

By the time I phone my mum back she's watching a very loud gardening program and doesn't want to spend long on the phone. I can hear someone yakking on about pruning, and putting down plenty of manure but watch out for that frost.

"Where have you been?" she shouts over the noise of the TV. "I tried you four times!"

"Out. At an interview," I say with deliberate exaggeration.

"Oh! At last! I hope it's a decent job!"

"Yes, I think so."

She's not really listening so I can get away with it.

"Good pay?" she asks.

"Excellent."

"Holidays? Benefits?"

"Mm. Excellent."

"Well, I hope you get the job. Where did you say it was again, dear?"

"I'll tell you all about it when I see you. I'll let you get back to your program . . ."

"All right. But look, Beth, I wanted to talk to you about your birthday. It's not far off."

"I know, Mum."

"It's your thirtieth."

"Yes, I know."

"And we were thinking it would be nice to go out to a restaurant."

Oh. Yes, that would be nice. What was I just saying about never going out for a meal?

"Lovely!" I say. "Yes, Mum, that'd be lovely. Just you and me?"

"Yes—and the others, of course."

The others are my brother Steve and my sister Jill, and their respective partners. My heart sinks a little. Of course I love Steve and Jill, and I don't see either of them often enough, but when we all get together the focus of conversation always seems to be Beth's life and what's wrong with it.

"And perhaps we could make it a Sunday lunch, and have the children come, too?" she adds.

Thank God. I won't have to find a babysitter. I make a mental note to teach Ellie a few table manners. Jill and her boyfriend haven't got any children but Steve's two boys are older and will probably sit still all through their meal, use the proper cutlery, and make polite conversation with the adults. If Ellie makes a collage on the table-cloth out of peas and tomato sauce and then crawls under the table and plays with people's feet because she's bored, it'll only lower everyone's opinion of my lifestyle even further.

"Sunday lunch would be great," I agree carefully.

"And, of course, if there's anyone you'd like to bring . . ." adds Mum coyly.

"I'll see," I say vaguely, wondering whether it's too soon in the game to inflict a family gathering on Martin.

"What?!" Mum almost shouts at me. She turns the TV down. Oh, I've got her attention now, have I? This is suddenly more interesting than the digging in of manure, is it? "What, is there a new man on the scene?" she demands excitedly. "Beth! You never said!"

"No, no, there isn't," I backtrack hastily. "Not really. No one in particular. I just said—well, I just meant I'd see whether anyone turns up. Anyone, like a friend, or . . ."

"Well, I'll need to know," she replies disappointedly. "I mean, I need to book the table, don't I. We can't just leave it that you'll bring someone along if someone happens to turn up on the day. I don't mind who you bring, Beth, of course I don't, but the restaurant will need to know how many . . ."

"Yes, of course. Don't worry, Mum. I won't bring anyone. Just book the restaurant for the family. Yes, it'll be lovely. I'll speak to you soon, Mum."

You know what? My mum's been on her own for about ten years—we lost my dad with cancer when he was only in his early fifties—but she's as happy as a clam. I think they had a good marriage. His dying like that was a terrible shock, and I thought she'd never get over it; but look at her now. She's got hundreds of friends, a part-time job in her village post office, a lovely house with the mortgage all paid off, she drives a nice little Peugeot and, at sixty-one, she looks younger than ever. Last year when she turned sixty I asked her if she was going to retire and she looked at me as if I were mad.

"What for?"

"Well, Mum, you surely don't *need* to work?"

Dad seems to have left her pretty comfortably off.

"Need to?" she retorted. "Beth, I *want* to work. You don't seem to have grasped this yet"—another dig at me and my employment status, you notice—"but work is as important to the human soul as love."

Oh well. I don't have either, really, do I?

And there's another phone call, just as I've finally got Ellie to sleep and I'm starting on the sink full of dishes. Three calls in one evening. I'm really in demand tonight.

"Beth, it's Louise." She sounds almost breathless with excitement. "It's good news!"

My mind whirls with possibilities. Please say it's all been a mistake—she and Ben aren't in difficulties after all, they haven't got to move, they've won the Lottery.

"We've sold the house."

"Oh."

Well, yes, I suppose it's good news, comparatively.

"Good for you," I say as warmly as possible, thinking sadly of Park Cottage and how Louise and the family are going to feel when they leave it for a poky little house somewhere in a shabby part of town.

"And we've found a house to rent," she adds.

"Oh! Good, that was quick work."

"Yes; the new people want to move in here as soon as possible—they've got a completed chain. But, Beth, guess where our new house is?"

I can't. I know they can't afford to pay much rent, which is why it has to be in a shabby area. But I can't tell her that—it'd be too rude.

"Where?" I ask, trying to make my voice sound bright. Why do I feel more depressed about this whole thing than she seems to? How can she bear it? How has she adapted so quickly to her whole life falling in ruins around her? I just know, if it were happening to me, I'd be wailing and wringing my hands, sulking, crying, blaming everyone and making everyone else miserable.

"Dudley Road, Beth! Just around the corner from you!" She laughs delightedly.

Like I said. The shabbiest part of town. I should have known!

Sunday

―――――――――◦◦◦◦◦―――――――――

It snowed yesterday, as predicted, but thank God it didn't actually settle, and this morning it's suddenly turned a lot warmer. Ellie's disappointed.

"I wanted to make a snowman," she says, grumpily, spooning milk over her Shreddies and getting most of it on the table.

"Never mind. It's much nicer for playing outside when it's warmer, Ellie. It'll soon be summer and you'll be able to ride your bike . . . Ellie! Stop that!"

She's purposely slopping the milk over the edge of the bowl now, and watching it form drips on the tabletop. I take the spoon out of her hand and she struggles to snatch it back, making grizzling noises.

"Stop playing with food!" I tell her crossly, thinking of the forthcoming family dinner. "You're a big girl now, not a baby. You should sit nicely at the table and not make a mess."

"Don't want to," she says, pouting at me.

"Well, in the future if you act like a baby at the table I'm going to treat you like one. I'll put a bib on you and sit you in a high chair," I threaten her firmly.

Haven't got a bib or a high chair of course, gave all that stuff away.

"You haven't got a high chair," says Ellie.

"I'll buy one."

"No, you won't," she says with a bit less conviction.

"Eat properly, please, then I won't have to," I say wearily, giving her back the spoon.

"Don't want any more," she responds, throwing down the spoon and turning to get off her chair.

"And when you're finished," I tell her, "you should ask to leave the table."

She gives me a look of complete bewilderment. "Why?"

"Because it's polite."

"What's polite mean?"

"It means . . ." Hmm. "It means saying the right things, doing the right things. Pleasing people."

She sits still for a minute, frowning, thinking hard about this. Good. Perhaps I'm getting through. I smile at her, thinking fondly of the good impression she's going to make when we go to the restaurant with the family. She can wear the red velour dress again, and white tights, and everyone will congratulate me on her behavior as she sits quietly on her chair waiting for permission to leave the table.

"I don't want to be polite," she announces, jumping down from her chair. "*You* aren't!"

Well, we'll have to work on it some more.

We're up very early, for a Sunday. We're going to do the boot sale today. Martin calls for us and we drive to Louise's house in his car because it's bigger than mine. Louise and Ben have already loaded up a van when we arrive.

"Borrowed it from one of the neighbors," says Louise, slamming the van doors shut.

We load the remaining black sacks full of clothes and books and toys into Martin's car.

"Pleased to meet you," say Louise and Ben when I introduce him.

They both give me a knowing smile.

"Good of you to help out, mate," says Ben, slapping Martin on the shoulder as if he's an old friend.

"Pleasure," says Martin, slapping Ben's arm.

Don't know why men always have to slap and thump each other when they're being friendly. I think it's some sort of primal thing. Apes do it, in the zoo.

Ben starts up the van, leaving Louise with the children. "See you at the field," he calls out to us as he drives off.

"Good luck," says Louise. "Thanks, Beth."

Almost as an afterthought, she adds, "Hey, would Ellie like to stay here and play with my lot?"

I look at her doubtfully. "Surely you've got enough to do? You don't want an extra . . ."

The new buyers are coming around today to measure for their furniture and stuff. She's got to tidy up and carry on with the packing.

"Don't be silly. The girls will look after her. They'll love having someone else to play with. She won't be any trouble, and she'd only be bored at the boot sale, wouldn't she?"

I look at Ellie. "Would you like to stay and play with Jodie? And Annie and Solomon?" I ask her.

Her eyes grow wide with awe. The famous Jodie and Annie and Solomon? The much-quoted perfect children who gave her all their toys and clothes and videos?

"Yes, please!" she squeaks shyly.

She gets out of Martin's car and holds my hand tightly as we walk to the front door of Park Cottage.

"I will be *very* good, Mummy," she whispers to me as I kiss her good-bye. "And *very* por-lite."

"Good girl." I smile.

She stands in the doorway, holding Louise's hand, as we drive away, and I see her looking behind her into Park Cottage, her eyes still wide and her little face excited but uncertain.

"A whole new world for her!" laughs Martin, following my gaze.

"Yes, but not for long. They move next week. And the children will be going to the same school as Ellie."

Strange life, isn't it.

We park Martin's car on the field, next to the van. Ben's already unloading boxes and hanging things over the van doors and laying things out on the table in front of the van.

"I've never done one of these before," he admits. "In fact, I've never even been to one before."

Wouldn't have needed to really.

"It's easy," I tell him, having been to quite a few of them over the years. "You just sell as cheap as necessary. People are only going to buy bargains, otherwise they won't bother. They'll knock your prices down really low. You have to let them, otherwise we'll be taking all this stuff home again."

"Fine," he says. "I just want to see the back of it all."

"That's what Louise said to me," I say, sadly, looking at some of the lovely things we're unpacking. China and glassware, ornaments, garden tools.

"We won't have room for any of it," says Ben, his voice sounding flat. "I don't want to look at it, really,

Beth. If I don't get rid of it all quickly, as quickly as possible, I'll probably start crying."

He says it calmly, matter-of-factly, but I look at his face and I think he means it. It's not surprising, is it? Some people would probably have had a breakdown, in the circumstances. I don't really know what to say to him. What do you say to someone who's got themselves so badly into debt that they've dragged their wife and children down from a lovely comfortable lifestyle into poverty? And been too afraid to even tell them, until it was too late?

"At least you still have each other," I tell him quietly, watching him laying out all his possessions to sell off cheaply, and wondering whether I know him well enough to try to console him, or whether I should just stay out of it.

"Yes," he says a bit shortly.

So perhaps appearances are deceptive. Louise and the children still seem OK, the family's still together and seems to be acting as a solid unit in the face of all this adversity. But what do I know? No one but Ben and Louise really know what it's doing to their relationship.

"The thing is," he says suddenly, putting down a box of china and turning to face me, "that's what everyone says, and it makes me feel kind of bad because I know it's true—yes, of course we still have each other, and the kids, and how can you compare what we're going through with something awful happening to one of the family, a death or a serious illness or something . . . ?" He trails off.

"I'm sorry," I say. I feel awkward, completely inadequate. I'll just get on with unloading the car and shut up.

"You shouldn't feel bad, mate," Martin puts in unexpectedly. "I don't see why you should feel guilty about mourning what you're losing. OK, they might be material possessions but they still mattered to you. You worked hard to get them. You must feel now like all that work and effort was wasted. No wonder you're gutted. Anyone would be."

Ben gives him a glance and a nod but doesn't say anything. We all drop the subject. Customers are starting to trickle onto the field and already a few are hanging around our "stall," picking things up, turning them over, putting them down again.

"How much for the big china pot?"

It used to stand in the porch. It had a cheese plant in it originally, but when it died they all used to shove umbrellas and shopping bags in it.

"What do you want for that set of encyclopedias?"

A whole set of *Children's Britannica*. I'd have had them for Ellie if I had the space for them.

"What about the Egyptian pictures, mate?"

Ben and Louise brought them back from a trip to Cairo. Two huge papyrus hand-paintings, depicting stories of ancient Egyptian kings. Framed in gold, they hung on either side of the fireplace in their living room. Too big to hang anywhere in a smaller house.

"How can he bear it?" I whisper to Martin.

"He can't. Look at his face."

I pour coffee out of the thermos flask, offer a packet of crackers. I don't know what else to do.

By midday we've sold over half of the stuff.

"Take the van back," I tell Ben eventually. "Whatever's over, we can get in Martin's car. Go back and help Louise."

"Are you sure?" The strain's showing in his eyes.

"Of course." I look at him carefully. "What do you want us to do with anything we don't sell?"

He shrugs. "Oxfam, I suppose, Beth." His voice is tired and defeated. "Thanks for all your help. Thanks, Martin."

They shake hands.

"Pleased to help," says Martin, gripping Ben's hand for a moment. "Good luck, mate."

"I'll see you next Saturday? At the party?" says Ben. He looks at me for confirmation.

"Oh!" I say, embarrassed. "I hadn't asked him yet . . . we haven't talked about it. I wasn't sure . . ."

Ben turns to Martin again. "Louise has asked a few friends and neighbors in, next Saturday night. It won't be anything wonderful—the house will be almost empty and everything'll be packed up. But Louise thought it'd be a good opportunity to get rid of my wine collection." He gives a snort. "She never did approve of it. Said I was a snob for keeping it hidden away instead of drinking it. Suppose she had a point."

"I'll be on a late shift," says Martin. "But I could come on after I finish. Are you sure?"

"Of course. Least we can do, after today."

"I've promised to help Louise with the food," I tell Martin. "So I'll be there early. I haven't decided what to do about Ellie, yet."

"Well, that's easy," says Ben at once. "She can stay overnight. We haven't got a spare bed anymore but two of the kids can share."

"She'd love that!" I say gratefully.

"They might as well get to know each other," says Ben. "They'll be neighbors in a week or so."

Like I say—funny old life.

After Ben's gone, Martin and I have quite a lot of time to chat, in between customers. It's nice to be on our own, without the distraction of Ellie, and really get to know each other—he's good fun to be with, and I'm enjoying

myself now that neither of us has to worry about keeping
up pretenses about brain surgery or scriptwriting.

"I *am* actually trying to write a script," I tell him. "But
I've only just started it. And I'm using someone else's
computer." Briefly I explain the circumstances. "Are you
shocked? Do you think I'm wicked?"

"Hardly wicked!" he laughs. "But why didn't you ask
the guy's permission? He probably would've agreed . . ."

"What! I couldn't. Anyway—I've never met him. I was
employed by his mother, who's a real old dragon. She'd
probably sack me even for *asking*. And besides, the whole
point is that the place doesn't need cleaning. So I've got
nothing else to do there."

"Weird," he agrees. "Weird to pay someone to clean a
place when it doesn't get dirty."

"I could tell you a few stories about the places I clean!"
I laugh, and over the next hour I keep him amused with
tales of Dottie and her evil dog and the Old Dears Next
Door, and Oliver the Lecher. I can laugh about that now,
now that I've got a new client lined up. I'm glad not to be
going there anymore, to be honest.

"So what are you going to do about Ellie, during the
playgroup holidays?" he asks at length. "You said your
new client made it clear she didn't want you to take her
round there."

"No."

Shit. I don't want to have to think about this. It's a
cloud on the horizon, a problem I can't decide how to
solve.

"I don't really want to take her to any of my cleaning
jobs," I admit. "It might be OK to take her to Dottie's, for
instance, in an emergency, but she'd get bored to tears if
she had to be at Alex Chapman's flat for very long, and
anyway I wouldn't be able to get on with my writing if
she was there."

"So you'll have to find someone else to mind her," he says levelly, "unless things are sorted out with Fay by then."

"Yes."

The mood's spoilt. I wish he wouldn't keep bringing up the subject of Fay.

"If you had someone to look after Ellie," he persists, "we could have an evening out occasionally."

"Yes," I say, a bit snappily. "But I haven't. Sorry."

"I didn't mean it to sound like that," he says quickly. "It isn't that I mind. I just think it'd do you good. Give you a break. I'd like to give you a break, Beth, that's all."

"I know. But it's difficult right now, isn't it."

What I want to say to him is that if he's as interested in me as he's implied he is, he'll just have to wait. He'll have to hang around, and bide his time, and not mind if the only evening out he can have with me is at my place, with Ellie asleep in her room. And if that's not good enough for him, it's tough shit. But, of course, I don't say anything.

We stay on the field till the sale's nearly over and everyone else starts packing up. There isn't much stuff left—it fits into two trash bags, which I'll take home with me and deliver to the Oxfam shop tomorrow.

When we get back to Park Cottage, Ellie's fallen asleep on the sofa in front of the TV. Louise has put a blanket over her and she's cuddling a toy tiger given to her by Jodie or Annie.

"She was absolutely exhausted," explains Louise.

"We've tired her out!" admits ten-year-old Jodie cheerfully.

Her younger brother and sister have both flopped down in front of the TV, too.

"You all look worn out!" laughs Martin.

"Can Ellie come and play with us again?" asks Annie. "I like having a little one to play with."

"Only so you can boss her about," sniffs Jodie.

"Well, *you* boss *everyone* about," declares Solomon. "I like Ellie. She does whatever we want!"

"I don't suppose that'll last long!" I tell him. "It's only because she's not used to playing with bigger children. She'll soon be answering you back when she gets to know you better!"

Solomon looks disappointed. As the youngest, with two big sisters, he's probably never been looked up to by anyone before.

"Ellie's going to come and stay on Saturday night," Ben tells the children. "If that's all right with you. When we have our friends round. But you'll all have to stay upstairs and behave yourselves!"

"Yes!" they shout in excitement.

Ellie wakes up, rubbing her eyes, looking around her in surprise. When she sees me, she slides off the sofa and comes to hold my hand. Her hair's all standing up on end and she's still half asleep, staring at the floor and swaying slightly.

"We'd better get you home," I tell her.

She holds out the toy tiger to Annie.

"It's all right," says Annie, planting a kiss on her head. "You can keep it."

"No, Annie—it's yours," I protest.

"I've still got loads of toys," she tells me with a smile. "And Mummy says we won't have much room for them in our new house. Ellie can keep it, really."

"They're nice kids," I tell Louise in the kitchen as I'm helping Ellie put her shoes and coat on.

"Yes, I hope the move isn't going to be too much of a shock for them. They've been spoilt, really . . ." She trails off, looking around her half-empty house. "I suppose we all have."

"Not spoilt. Just fortunate. You worked for it, though."

"Yes, and took it for granted."

"What are the new people like?" I ask.

"They seem nice. In their forties, probably. No children."

We're both silent, thinking about the family moving in, and the family moving out.

"And Martin's nice, too!" she tells me, suddenly changing the subject with enforced brightness. She gives me that knowing look again. "Full on, is it?"

"Ssh!" I smile, indicating Ellie. "Well, yes, he's nice. We'll have to see . . ."

"Martin *is* nice," puts in Ellie, finishing off fastening her shoes and standing up. "He calls me sweetie, and he says I'm very grown up."

"A real charmer, by the sound of it," laughs Louise. "Good for you, Beth! Is he coming on Saturday night?"

"He's coming later. When he's finished his shift. And are you sure it's all right to bring Ellie? You don't mind?"

"Of course not! And—listen, Beth—if you'd like me to keep her overnight—so you and Martin can have . . ." Her eyes sparkle mischievously. "Some time to yourselves—it'll be no trouble."

"Oh, Louise!" I find myself giving her a hug. "You're so sweet! But I couldn't dream of inflicting anything extra on you at the moment . . ."

"Look, I won't keep on saying this," she tells me firmly. "But you've been such a help to me, and such a friend, too. It's the least I can do, and Ellie really isn't any trouble. My kids have loved having her here. And after we've moved, I can have her whenever you want. It'll be so convenient."

"Then I'll have to repay the favor. I'll babysit for your three as well. Whenever you want."

"I might take you up on it," she says with a smile.

I go home feeling a lot more cheerful.

"What are you grinning about?" asks Martin, squeezing my hand as we get into the car.

"Louise. She's so nice. Considering all her own problems. She's just offered to have Ellie whenever I want. So we might be able to have an evening out after all!"

He smiles appreciation. "It doesn't solve the problem of your mornings at work, though, does it," he points out.

Isn't that just like a man? They can't enjoy good news without qualifying it with something negative. Tell them the weather's going to be hot, and they'll say their garden's going to suffer. Say you've got a pay raise, and they'll tell you how much more tax you're going to be paying. Show them a bargain you've bought from the sales, and they'll ask what was wrong with it and why was it reduced.

"No, but isn't it nice of her?" I persist, determined not to be discouraged. "It's . . . well, it's nice to have a friend again."

He nods, but frowns into the distance as he starts the engine. I feel his disapproval and guess it has to do with Fay. I don't like it. I reach out and touch his hand, as it rests on the steering wheel, and stroke it gently.

"She's going to keep Ellie on Saturday night after the party, for a start," I tell him very softly. "So you can stay the night at my place if you like. All night," I add, in a sultry whisper, watching his face.

He glances at me and catches his breath ever so slightly.

"That's good, then," he says. He looks in the mirror to check on Ellie, who's gone straight back to sleep in the backseat. "And what are we going to do, then? All night?"

I give him a list.

Men: they're easy to please, aren't they, really.

Wednesday

A strange young man answers the door this morning at Hillside Avenue. He's tall, thin, and has sandy-colored hair gelled into spikes. He's wearing frayed jeans and sneakers and a black T-shirt depicting a skull and cross-bones and the name of a heavy metal band.

"You must be Luke." I smile, holding out my hand. "I'm Beth."

"Come in," he says, ignoring my hand and leaving me to close the door behind me.

"Did you have a good journey?" I try, as I follow him down the hall. "How was the flight?"

"Long," he replies without turning round.

I feel like asking him if he's always this rude, but after all, I remind myself, I'm only the paid help.

Dottie's in the kitchen, washing up. She looks round at me brightly. "Morning, Beth! Lovely morning!"

Well, I wouldn't go so far as to say lovely. It's not raining, at least, or snowing, or sleeting.

"What are you doing?" I rebuke her gently. "Sit down—I can do that."

So could Luke. He's sitting in the living room with his

feet up on the coffee table, listening to his CD Walkman. I can hear the bass throb from here.

"Don't be silly," she replies, hobbling to get the tea towel off the hook. "I'm not so old and helpless yet that I can't do a bit of washing up for myself."

"You should still be taking it easy," I remind her.

"Easy, easy, I'm sick and tired of taking it bloody easy. What's the use of sitting around all day taking it easy—it won't change anything, Beth. Me legs won't get any worse or any better, will they. I might as well use them before they damn well shrivel up!" She gives a throaty chuckle and slams down a mug onto a tray. "Want a coffee?"

"*I'll* make it," I insist, filling the kettle and going to the cupboard for the coffee and sugar.

"Want a coffee, Luke?" Dottie calls into the lounge.

I look round the door and see him lift one earphone from his head momentarily to allow her voice to penetrate. "Good on yer," he replies without moving a muscle.

First impressions aren't always right, but I'm pretty sure I'm not going to like this young man. I think Dottie's assessment of him as idle is not far wide of the mark.

"How're you getting on with him?" I ask her quietly.

"Lovely!" she replies surprisingly. "He's a lovely boy, Beth."

"Is he?" I say, unable to help myself. "He doesn't look it."

"You mustn't go by appearances," she tells me sternly. "You shouldn't judge a book by the cover."

No. But when the first chapter isn't very good, it doesn't help.

"So you're enjoying having him here?"

"Oh, yes." Her eyes are twinkling. "It's so nice to have some company again. Someone around the house to chat to."

I can't imagine Luke going in for cozy chats. Perhaps appearances *are* deceptive.

"And Tosser loves him!"

Now, that I can believe. Probably recognizes a kindred spirit.

I clean the living room first, so I can get out of Luke's way quickly and he can get on with the business of sitting on his arse listening to his music. He sighs when I turn on the Hoover.

"Sorry," I say, not meaning it. "I won't be long."

He grunts.

"Could you just move your feet, please?" I ask him when I get to his end of the sofa.

He gives me a disparaging look and lifts his legs in the air. Tosser, lying by his side, growls at me warningly.

"Bad-tempered little tyke," I tell him cheerfully.

And not only the dog.

Actually, I've decided by mid-morning, Tosser's a ray of sunshine compared with Luke. I can't find anything to recommend the boy. Surly, sullen, lazy, rude—I don't know how he traveled halfway across the world without somebody giving him a smack. I can't understand how Dottie's apparently doting on him. Or perhaps I can.

"I didn't realize I was lonely," she confides in me. "I've got kind of used to it, you know? Living on your own, you just learn to fend for yourself, do things on your own—I even talk to meself sometimes. And I've always had Tosser for company." She pauses and looks across the room at Luke. I can't believe the fondness in her eyes. "But since the lad's arrived—well, it's given me such a boost, Beth. To have someone young in the house again, someone to make a fuss of and cook for . . ."

I thought the idea was for him to make a fuss of her.

But I keep quiet. Maybe looking after him makes her feel young again, in a way—like having one of her own kids back.

"For all your nagging," she says, grinning at me, "I could never be bothered to cook a proper meal for meself. Never seemed worth the effort. But now he's here, I'm doing chops, and pies, and roast potatoes and veg."

"And you're eating them yourself, too? Not just giving it all to him?"

"Of course," she says stoutly. "Got me appetite back, I have. I made an apple crumble yesterday. Want a bit?"

"No." I smile. "You and Luke will want it. I'm glad you're enjoying yourself, Dottie. But don't overdo it, will you? How long is he staying?"

She shrugs.

"Don't you know?" I persist.

Christ. He's not come for good, has he? I feel a flutter of anxiety. I can just imagine him getting used to this life, being waited on hand and foot, and deciding to stay put. And whatever she says now, it's going to wear thin after a while.

"Another couple of weeks," she says, not looking at me. "He's here for another couple of weeks."

I suppose she doesn't want to think about it. It's going to be hard for her when he goes. That's when she'll *really* feel lonely.

I get on with cleaning the kitchen, making up my mind that when the time comes, when Luke's on his way back again, I'll come round more often. I'll come and see her, with Ellie, and put up with Tosser attacking my legs, and make her some dinners and cakes and pies because she'll probably lose her appetite and her enthusiasm all over again. I feel sad, thinking about her enjoying this new lease on life only to have it taken away from her again in a few weeks. I should try to be nice to Luke. Even if he's not doing it intentionally, he's giving his gran some pleasure for a while.

When it's time to take Tosser for his walk, I ask Luke if he'd like to come with me. I have the idea in mind that perhaps he can hold the lead and have *his* arm wrenched out of its socket, and *his* ankles savaged.

"Nah," he says without looking up. "I don't do walking."

"Never learnt how to?" I ask sweetly, but he just gives me a blank stare.

Dottie, however, looks at me anxiously, obviously picking up on my tone, so I quickly give a false little laugh, to pretend I'm joking. She goes to ruffle his hair as if he were a little kid, but her hand sits awkwardly on the sticky spikes.

"What shopping do you need?" I ask Dottie.

She fusses around, producing a list and adding a few more items to it. "Sorry," she says, "but it's quite a lot."

I look at the list. It's more than I buy for a fortnight for me and Ellie. "I'd better take the car," I tell her. "I'll give Tosser a quick walk when I get back. I'd never be able to carry all this."

I look at Luke, who's nodding his head to the beat of his music, completely oblivious. "Hasn't he done any shopping for you?" I ask Dottie quietly.

"I don't like to ask him, really," she says. "He's only here for a little while. It's his holiday, isn't it?"

"It wouldn't hurt him to offer, though," I say through gritted teeth.

She goes out to the kitchen to get some shopping bags and her purse.

It's no good.

I can't.

I can't be nice to him.

I can't watch him sitting there with his feet up and his eyes closed while she runs around after him, and not even say anything to him. The nasty, spoilt, lazy little shit. I lean over him and take the earphones off his head. My face is about two inches away from his.

"What the—?" he starts.

"Listen!" I hiss, anger almost coming out of my ears. "Your gran is old, and crippled with arthritis. Get off your arse and come and help me with this shopping. Most of it's for you anyway."

Dottie comes back into the room just as I straighten up. To my surprise, he gets up and lumbers out to the front door, turning to give me a glare as he opens it.

"Luke's coming to help," I tell Dottie brightly.

"Oh, lovely," she says, almost rubbing her hands together with delight. "He's such a nice boy, isn't he," she whispers to me as we go out.

The nice boy gets into the passenger side of the car with a face like thunder, and slams the door shut. "Fucking shopping," he growls as I start up the engine. "I don't *do* fucking shopping."

"Well, you do now," I retort. "Never too late to learn a new skill."

"You're only the cleaning lady," he tells me scathingly.

"That's right," I agree. "But I'm also very fond of your gran and I'm one of the only friends she's got. So I don't intend to see her being abused."

"Abused?" he snorts. "Listen, lady, I've come all the way from Australia to see her, right? Twenty-four-hour flight, right? I don't know how you'd call that abuse."

"Why did you come?" I ask him bluntly, deciding not to trade insults about how lazy and ignorant he is. "You don't seem particularly fond of your gran."

"None of your fucking business."

"Probably not. But your gran's not stupid. She guessed, as soon as she heard you were coming, that it was your parents' idea—that they probably bribed you to come over."

"They didn't bribe me," he retorted.

Oh, so that got a reaction.

"They paid my fare. They wanted me to come."

"Nice. Free holiday, all home comforts . . ."

We're pulling into Tesco's parking lot.

"Listen, bitch," he says, suddenly losing it. "Shut the fuck up and just get on with what you're being paid to do! I'm doing you a favor here."

"No," I tell him calmly. "This isn't a favor, Luke. It's just what any civilized adult would do. You should have been doing your gran's shopping for her all week. And walking the dog. And doing some cooking for her. She's wearing herself out looking after you. It's a good thing you're only here for a couple of weeks!"

I should have done what he said—shut the fuck up. I've said more than I intended. I wonder for an instant whether he's going to hit me. But he just gives me a with-ering look and then shrugs contemptuously.

"Tell someone who gives a fuck. You'll be out of a job soon anyway," he says.

He's going to tell Dottie. He'll tell her I've insulted him, and he thinks she'll sack me. She won't, but I don't want him to tell her about this because she'll be upset, and she'll take his side, and I'll have to say I'm sorry.

"There's no point in upsetting your gran."

"Upsetting her? Who's upsetting her? You'll be out of a job because she won't be living here much longer." A light of realization glints in his eyes. "She hasn't told you yet, has she! Ha!" He laughs out loud. "She's coming back to Australia with me. That's the whole point of the exercise. I thought you had it all worked out? My parents sent me over here to talk her into it. We're moving her out to Sydney. We've booked her flight."

No. She'll never agree to it.

She hates the place.

She never has a good word to say about it, does she. She thinks the Australians are all mad. She wouldn't live there if they paid her.

The whole way around the supermarket, which we do in stony silence, I'm turning this over and over in my mind, trying to convince myself. But I'm getting nervous. The more I think about it, the more it seems to me that Dottie's quite capable of having had a change of heart since she met and apparently fell in love with her charming young grandson. What has he said to her? What has he been told to say to her, to make her change her mind? Not that she *shouldn't* go to Australia. She just shouldn't go if she doesn't want to.

I unpack the shopping and put it all in the cupboards without saying anything to Dottie.

"You all right?" she asks me once or twice. "You've gone quiet."

I'm quiet because I don't know how to broach the subject of Australia with her. I don't want to tell her that Luke and I had an argument, or that he's told me the real reason for his visit. I'm trying to decide how to bring it up casually in conversation.

I take Tosser for his walk and when I get back it's time to leave for playgroup.

"Dottie," I blurt out as I'm getting my coat on to go. "You know what you said about Luke only being here for a couple more weeks?"

She nods, looking at me a bit warily.

"Has he . . . talked to you? About going out there yourself?"

I know already, from her expression. It's true.

"I was going to tell you," she says, not meeting my eyes. "I just didn't know how. I thought I might phone you. I wouldn't find it so hard, you know, not being face to face." She pauses. "I'm sorry, Beth. I'm really sorry."

"Sorry? Why? Don't you really want to go?"

"Oh, yes!" Her eyes light up. "Yes, I want to go, now I've met Luke, and talked to him. I never met him when I went out there before, you see, Beth. He was away at university. I didn't give him a chance, really, before. Just assumed the worst of him, you know, because of not getting a proper job and all that. But I'm not too proud to admit it, I made a mistake. I can see why he'd want to be an artist, now. He's such a sensitive young man, you see. And now he's talked to me about how nice it'll be, to be with the family out there . . . instead of being on my own . . ." She trails off. "No, what I'm sorry about is you, dear. You're the only person I'll miss. Those two next door— poor old things—they won't really miss me, they'll probably think it's a good riddance, I've been more trouble to them than anything else just lately. And there's no one else, except for . . ." She nods in Tosser's direction and her eyes fill up with tears. She shakes her head, unable to go on.

The dog! How can she leave him? She loves the old devil, absolutely dotes on him.

I take hold of her hands and grip them. "Listen, Dottie. Are you sure? Absolutely sure? He hasn't talked you into this, has he? Bribed you? Persuaded you?"

She looks shocked. "Of course not, Beth! Bribed? Of course he wouldn't . . ."

"But you've never wanted to go to Australia! You always said you couldn't stand it out there . . . they were all mad . . . and how can you leave Tosser behind?"

She wipes her eyes and swallows hard. "I've got to be sensible, Beth. If I'm going to spend the rest of me days with the family, I need to go now. While I've still got me youth and me health. Before I get too old and decrepit to enjoy it. It nearly breaks me heart to leave old Tosser behind. But the only way I can live with meself is to give him a better chance himself."

"A better chance?"

"Yes." She raises her chin bravely. "Yes, I've got to think about what's best for him, too. He doesn't get his walks now, Beth, not the way he should. Living with me, with me legs being so bad . . ."

"But you love him. That's the important thing. He's happy with you."

As happy as a foul-tempered, mean, grizzly beast can be.

"He needs someone younger," she says firmly. "Someone who can take him out for some exercise, play with him, give him a bit more of a life."

"Well," I say doubtfully, not wanting to upset her, "I suppose you could advertise, or ask at the vet's."

"Advertise?!" she retorts in amazement. "What on earth are you thinking of, Beth! We're not talking about selling a bloody car, you know, or a three-piece suite! No, I'm not advertising him, you silly girl! I'm giving him to you!"

Oh, joy.

Oh fucking, fucking joy.

Friday

———◦◦◦◦◦———

I can't help remembering how just a few short weeks ago I was reflecting on my life and thinking how it wasn't really so bad. I might not exactly have had the most wonderful career prospects in the world, but I had a little job of sorts and it helped to get me through my regular financial nightmares. Now in that short space of time I've lost nearly all my clients, one by one. One's turned out to have worse financial nightmares than me, one's sacked me for refusing to shag him in a cupboard, and now one's not only defecting to Australia but wants to palm her hellhound off on me, too.

"Say no!" Louise exclaimed yesterday when I told her the story. "You can't possibly be considering it? You're mad! You hate that dog!"

"But how can I? If I refuse to take the dog, she won't go to Australia."

"Well? You don't want her to go, anyway. It'll solve the problem."

"She *needs* to go, Louise. I don't want her to. It's not just about losing another job—I'll really miss her. But *I* can't look after her, and she's getting to the stage where she's going to need someone to. She's too proud to admit it, but I know she realizes it now. And what's better for her—to swallow her pride, pretend she's changed her mind and can't wait to go and live in Australia, where at least she'll be with her family, or to be put into a home, with no one to visit her except me?"

"So wait till she's on the plane, then take the dog straight to the nearest animal shelter."

"I couldn't. I couldn't live with myself. Not while she's alive, at least."

"Say you can't afford to keep him!"

"That's the thing. She's making provision for it, out of the sale of her house."

"You're joking!"

"No, a regular payment, to cover all his expenses, pet insurance in case he gets sick, and on top of that, an allowance for me as a sort of thank you for having him."

"Bloody hell, Beth. Maybe it's not such a bad idea, then. In fact," she laughed, "I wish I knew an old lady with a horrible dog myself!"

"Don't speak too soon. I might ask you to take him for walks sometimes!"

Thing is, the payments won't start coming in until the house has been sold, will they. Dottie doesn't exactly have a fortune just lying there in a savings account waiting for me to start dipping into to buy tins of Chum and Chunky Meal or whatever it is he has to have. I've had to reassure her that I'll manage until such time as her solicitor hands over the first check.

"Till then, I'll just have to scrape along somehow," I told Louise philosophically. I hesitated. I hadn't told anyone this yet, but it'd been gnawing away inside me and, like confessing a sin, I needed to hear someone else's reaction before I'd know how bad I should be feeling. "I've been borrowing little bits," I told her carefully, "out of Ellie's savings."

She didn't respond straight away. "How little?" she asked eventually.

"Oh, just a couple of tens here and there. When I can't think how else to buy the next meal. You know."

Or maybe you don't know. I hope you don't. I hope you still haven't fallen *that* low, from your lofty heights of comfortable wealth where it used to be slumming it a bit if you ate in the same restaurant twice.

"Oh, be careful, Beth," was all she said. And she sighed, a huge, sad sigh. "It's such a shame," she added.

I know that. I know it's a bloody shame. I wish I hadn't told her now.

Well, I've still got my new job to go to, and I feel quite nervous in a funny sort of way after I've taken Ellie to playgroup and I head out on the main road toward Melanie Waterstone's house.

I'm thinking about how I'm going to make a good impression. How I'm going to work my guts out, cleaning everything in that house until you can see your face in it, so that Miss Melanie Waterstone comes home from work and fairly drops dead with astonishment at the amazing shine on everything. How her boyfriend, distracted from his working-at-home by the gleam coming from all the furniture, to say nothing of the sparks flying from the Hoover and the mop and the dusters as I fly around the house, driven by a fervor of cleanliness such as he's never witnessed before, will describe me to the homecoming Melanie as an absolute paragon who cannot possibly only be costing them such a paltry sum of money. How they'll decide, as they contemplate their shining, spotless home together with awestruck admiration, that they will, in the future, not be able to rest unless they employ me for at least three mornings a week, and they'll need to double or even triple my pay before anyone else gets in first and whisks me away to clean mansions for film stars in Beverly Hills.

With this firmly in mind, I ring the doorbell and wait for Melanie Waterstone's home-working boyfriend, whose work is so important that he mustn't be disturbed by nagging worries about contributing to the housework, to answer the door.

I hear his footsteps coming along the polished wood flooring.

He opens the door, holds the door wide for me, starts to smile, and the word *Hello* starts to form on his lips, but doesn't get any further.

It's Daniel.

I don't know how I get from the front door back to my car. The ground seems to have gone soft beneath my feet, and my legs don't feel real. I'm struggling with my key in the car door when he arrives behind me.

"Wait! Beth, wait!" He puts a hand on my shoulder. I shake it off, roughly. I can't look at him. "Don't just go," he says. "Please."

The only reason I *don't* just go is that I can't get the key in the fucking lock. My hand's shaking. I drop the key and stumble as I bend to pick it up. Without wanting to see it, I see his hand reach in front of me and pick up the key for me.

"Here."

I take it, still not looking at him.

"Don't drive off like this," he says. "You'll have an accident."

"Don't kid yourself," I try to say, but my voice comes out wobbly.

Why should he think I'd have an accident just because I happened to come face to face with him on some doorstep on the other side of town? Some doorstep belonging to some rich, clever, beautiful *Melanie* who just happens to be his girlfriend? Why should I care?

"The shock," he says. "It wasn't . . . exactly . . . what either of us expected."

"No, obviously."

My voice is coming under control now. And my hands are feeling less jittery. I try the key again, get the door open, and manage to throw myself into the driver's seat. I'm so busy trying to remember how to start the engine, which pedal does what, and how to put it into gear that I don't notice Daniel going around to the passenger side and opening the door. He slides into the seat beside me before I can say anything to stop him.

"You've left your front door open," I tell him, staring straight ahead.

"Beth . . ."

"Please. Don't make this any more embarrassing than it already is. Just let me drive away and pretend I've never been here. Give me that one small shred of dignity."

"There's no need to be embarrassed, for God's sake. We didn't realize . . . it was going to be you. Just a coincidence. Why . . . ?"

"Because you and *Melanie* are living *here.*" I wave my arm at his detached four-bedroomed, Georgian-windowed, double-garaged house. "And *I* came to clean for you. If you can't work out why I should find that embarrassing . . ."

"At least let's talk about it?"

"Get out of the car, Daniel. Please."

He's still looking at me. I can feel his eyes on me. Don't turn round, don't look at him, don't meet his eyes, don't turn round, don't look at him . . .

I turn round and look at him.

"I'm sorry," he says softly.

I can't reply.

I can't bear this.

I'm not going to cry.

"Don't cry," he says.

"I'm not fucking crying. I'm not!"

"I never meant for you to be put in this position. I never wanted you to have to go out cleaning . . ."

"Pay me some more money, then. It's easy enough."

"I wish it was. But it isn't. I haven't got any."

I look back at the four-bedroomed, Georgian-windowed, double-garaged . . . and just raise my eyebrows at him.

"It's Melanie's. Everything's hers. The house, the money, the car, the lot." He shrugs, spreading his hands in a gesture of helplessness. "I'm a kept man, Beth."

"Well, lucky old you."

Do I sound bitter? Well, wouldn't you?

"It isn't quite how it sounds. I do play my part."

"Oh, I bet you do." I close my eyes, trying not to remember just how well he used to play his part.

"I'm a writer," he says.

Oh, I see.

If I needed to hear one more thing to make me feel any worse, just to top it all off and make me want to go and drive off a bridge somewhere, this would be it. He's a writer, is he? So while I'm struggling to pay the bills and keep a roof over his daughter's head by cleaning for people living in houses like this, he's found someone with enough income and enough assets and enough fucking stupid *lust* for him to keep him in the style he's never been accustomed to while he fulfills the one ambition we both shared, the one dream we both dreamed together for all those years. He's doing it on her back. And he's doing it without me.

"Fuck off, Daniel!" I turn on him, the tears suddenly erupting and my control slipping away completely. "Fuck off out of my car! Go on! Get the fuck out!"

He opens the passenger door slowly and I push ineffectually at his back as he slides out.

"I wanted to ask how Ellie is?" he says as he turns to close the door.

"Mind your own fucking business!" I slam the door and drive off at a screech, not changing out of first gear for about a quarter of a mile.

He's still standing in the road, watching, as I turn the corner.

Bastard. Fucking, fucking bastard.

"Fucking bastard!" says Louise.

I've driven straight to Park Cottage and I'm sitting in her kitchen, crying into the cup of strong black coffee she's just made me.

The kitchen's almost completely bare. Louise is at home today, finishing the packing. They move on Monday. The bareness of the house just adds to my misery. I'm overwhelmed by it.

"It's not *fair*!" I wail for the twentieth time. "It's just not fair!"

"No," she says, handing me another tissue. "No, it bloody isn't." She sits down opposite me and stares at me across the table. "What are we going to do, Beth?" she asks me flatly. "Eh? Look at us. Here we are, two young attractive women . . ."

"Huh!"

"Young and attractive, *and* intelligent, and kind, and

caring, and . . ." She sighs. "And everything seems to have gone wrong for us both."

"At least you've got a husband," I point out, sniffing.

She grunts dismissively.

"And at least you've got a good job. I haven't even got my *new* client now, never mind the others I've lost."

"I've been thinking about that," she says carefully. "I can't promise anything, you know, but I might be able to make some enquiries."

"Enquiries? What about?"

"Well, the new family. The Patels, who're moving in here. They both work, and you never know. They might need a cleaner. I'll tell them about you. They're going to be here tomorrow night, at the party, to meet some of the neighbors. I'll introduce you."

I brighten a little bit, but only a little bit. "Well, that'd be *one* morning's work again, at least—if it comes off. And it would be nice to still come here."

"Yes," she says wistfully, looking around her bare kitchen.

"Sorry," I say, blowing my nose. "I've been feeling so sorry for myself—it's awful for you, you poor thing."

"It'll soon be over. I'll be OK once we've moved into the new place, I expect. And anyway, of course you're feeling sorry for yourself! It must have given you the shock of your life when *he* opened that door."

"I thought I was going to die. Honestly, half of my life flashed before me . . ."

"Half of it?"

"The half he was in."

She stirs her coffee and looks at me thoughtfully. "Are you still in love with him?"

"No!" I say hotly, too quickly.

She nods knowingly. "Bastard."

* * *

What's it all about, anyway—this business, this thing about being in love? I'm not at all sure about it anymore. I used to think it was quite straightforward. You meet someone, you fancy them, you spend your whole time eyeing them up and dreaming about them and, if you're lucky and they fancy you too, it leads to a relationship. Sometimes that's all that happens. But once in a while . . . every once in a while and, I admit it, I was a gullible little girl who listened to fairy stories and read Mills & Boon romances . . . every once in a lifetime, perhaps, you realize you not only fancy this person so much it hurts, but you also like everything about them. And the more you find out about them, the more you can't believe it because there doesn't seem to be anything wrong with them at all. They seem to be perfect. Not necessarily a perfect speci-men of humanity, because perhaps there isn't one, but—perfect for *you*.

That's what it was like with Daniel.

I couldn't believe my luck. Couldn't believe it when he said he felt the same way about me. I used to wake up and pinch myself. I'd always assumed I'd have to spend years and years searching for the perfect person, and in-stead I'd just sort of bumped into him at university. It was almost too easy. Almost too good to be true.

Now? I don't know. If Daniel stopped loving me, stopped just like that, almost overnight, because he met Melanie and decided he loved her instead, then how reli-able is love anyway?

Maybe that isn't love at all.

Maybe the only real love in the world is the love you feel for your child—the love that's so big and so scary be-cause you know you'd actually fight the world for them. You'd lie down in front of a bus for them. You want to kill anyone who hurts them, even if it's a kid at playgroup who kicks their shin under the table—you actually want to kill that kid. It's frightening.

Maybe being in love, feeling all that passion and all that perfection, isn't a reliable reason for living with someone at all if it can just be switched on and off like that. I think, now I'm older and wiser, that friendship's more important. You can have sex with anyone, you don't have to love them. But if I ever find a man I can have a close friendship with—a close, loving, and caring friendship like the one I *used* to have with Fay—then I might consider sharing my life again. *Might*.

If I've gotten over Daniel by then.

It's unsettled me so badly, seeing him like that, so unexpectedly, and in such a mortifying situation, that I still feel shaky when I go to pick up Ellie from playgroup. I must look awful, because one of the other mums asks me if I'm all right.

"You're very pale. Hope you're not coming down with this flu bug that's going round," she says, moving away from me a bit.

Fay is standing on the other side of the room, waiting for Lauren to collect her paintings. She's looking at me. I try not to look back. Next thing I know, she's come over to stand next to me. We don't do this now. We always wait on opposite sides of the room. It's become so normal, even the children have accepted it. But she's standing here now, next to me, just looking at me.

"Are you all right?" she says.

Just like that.

As if nothing had ever been wrong between us, as if we hadn't had the worst quarrel of our lives and spent several weeks not speaking to each other.

And suddenly, more than anything in the world, I want to talk to her. It was nice of Louise to listen, but it wasn't the same. She didn't know Daniel. She wasn't there with me when I met him, she didn't sit up with me all night in my room at university listening to me going on about how much I loved him. She wasn't there when he left me, didn't see me fold up and break down, wasn't the one holding me together and helping me through it. Fay was.

"I've just seen Daniel," I tell her. I take a huge gulp that nearly chokes me. "I just . . . he was just . . ."

Silently, she puts her arms round me. There's something so huge stuck in my throat I can hardly breathe.

"It'll pass," she says. "You'll be OK. We'll get through this, Beth."

"We?" I whisper.

"We," she replies firmly.

Saturday

———◇◦◦◦◇———

Martin phones this morning before he goes to work. "I tried you last night," he says. "Quite late. Were you asleep?"

"I was at Fay's."

"Fay's?" he asks in surprise.

"Mm. Went there for lunch, and . . ."

It sounds funny, now, but I went there for lunch and ended up staying the night.

We talked over lunch, and into the afternoon while the children played. Simon came home from work and, obviously relieved to see us together again, offered to go out and get takeout for us all. Fay opened a bottle of wine, and then another bottle of wine. We talked about Daniel, and how I didn't love him anymore but had merely been overcome by the shock of seeing him so unexpectedly. We then discussed the possibility that perhaps I *did* still love him but had been suppressing my feelings and seeing him had brought it all out into the open. We finally settled on the theory that I had *almost* stopped loving him and that, in time, I'd see this as good therapy because now I knew he'd only gone to live with Melanie because she was rich and could keep him in her posh house while he became a writer, I'd never be able to think of him as perfect again. We then discussed Melanie at great length and with great pleasure, deciding she was so unattractive and such a bitch that she could only get a man by paying for him. By the time we'd finished with her Simon had put the children to bed, including Ellie, and had gone upstairs to watch soccer on the TV in the bedroom.

"You won't be able to drive home now," Fay pointed out, slurring slightly. "You're much too drunk."

"I'll sober up in a minute. I'll slow down. I won't drink much more," I said, pouring myself out another large glass of wine.

"You'd better stay the night. You can sleep on the sofa."

"All right then."

Nothing seemed to matter. We were back together, friends again. She'd made me feel better about Daniel and Melanie, about losing my cleaning jobs, about everything. I was so happy I couldn't quite remember why we'd ever fallen out in the first place.

"Oh, yes," I announced suddenly. "I remember. Neil."

"Ssh!" warned Fay, pointing to the ceiling.

We could hear soccer-crowd noises from the TV in the room above us. I didn't think there was much chance of us being overheard, unless Simon was lying on the bedroom floor with a glass to his ear. But, nevertheless, I dropped my voice to a whisper.

"Tell me," I invited. "Tell me again, how you met him."

So I heard the whole yucky story again, about the doctor's waiting room and the moment when time stood still, and the recognition of a soul mate who'd been waiting for her all her life. But this time I tried not to make faces or pretend to vomit. I gave her the same courtesy of listening as she'd given me. And to my surprise, probably because by now I was almost paralytic from the wine, I found myself quite moved by the whole thing.

"I never wanted it to happen," she said. "I've been happy with Simon, you know—but something was always missing."

"What? What was missing? You said you were bored, but everyone gets bored."

"I know. It wasn't that. I didn't know what was missing, Beth, until I met Neil." She looked at me very pointedly. "What you had, with Daniel . . ."

I flinched, but she carried on quickly, "I used to envy you. I knew we didn't have that—Simon and I. It was never like that between us."

"So why did you marry him?"

"Because I *did* love him—*do* love him. I thought it would grow into . . . something more."

"Passion?"

"That, too, but—more than that. The feeling that he's the only person in the world—the right person for you, the one and only . . ."

"Fay," I said gently. "I'm not sure I believe in all that, anymore."

"That isn't fair," she said. "It isn't fair to say you don't believe in it now. You had it, Beth. It should have lasted forever and it didn't, but that's no reason to deny it. You know you had it, with Daniel. Everyone who knew you could see it. It was special."

I had to take a long swig of wine before I could answer. "So what are you saying? It's better to have loved and lost than never to have loved? All that crap?"

"I don't think it's crap. Not now I don't. Whatever happens, however this ends up with Neil and me, I won't regret it, Beth. I can't regret meeting him, because it's been the most fantastic thing that's ever happened to me. Even if it ends tomorrow and breaks my heart, I can't be sorry it happened."

"No." I finished off the wine. My head hurt and my throat was sore from talking so much. "No," I said huskily, staring at the empty wineglass. "No, you can't be sorry, can you?"

"Am I forgiven?" she asked me softly, her eyes welling up with tears.

"Nothing to forgive," I said brusquely. I tried to get to my feet to give her a hug, but the room swayed from side to side and I sat back down again abruptly. "Going to sleep now," I said, lying back against the cushions.

"I'll get you some blankets," said Fay, stumbling out of the room. She stopped beside me and just touched my arm, briefly, lightly. "Thank you," she said.

"Daft cow," I told her as I sank into unconsciousness.

"I'm glad," says Martin. "Glad you've made it up. What prompted it?"

I tell him about Daniel. I miss out the bit about not being sure whether I'm still in love with him.

"It was such an awful shock when he opened the door," I explain. "Him living in a house like that, and me just coming to clean it. I felt so . . . humiliated."

"You shouldn't feel humiliated!" Martin says angrily. "It's his fault you're in this position! If he hadn't left you on your own with Ellie . . . if he were paying you a proper amount of maintenance . . ."

"I know, I know," I say wearily.

I've run out of steam.

That, and I'm feeling a bit hungover.

"You really should consider taking him to the CSA," he goes on. "He must be able to afford—"

"Yes, well, that's my decision, isn't it!" I snap.

I've only known him for a few weeks and he thinks he can tell me how to organize my life. I don't like this. I don't want him telling me what to do. He doesn't know anything about me and Daniel.

"Yes, of course," he says coolly. There's an uncomfortable silence. "See you tonight, then?" he says.

"Yes." I try to sound a bit nicer, but I'm having difficulty. "Yes, see you later. Have a good day."

When I hang up, I realize I'm not too bothered whether he comes tonight or not.

I go to Louise's in the afternoon and help her make sandwiches and quiches while Ellie plays with the children in their empty bedrooms.

"I'm glad," she says, "that I've got something to do today. And the children have got Ellie to play with. I think we'd all be getting on each other's nerves, otherwise."

"Where's Ben?"

"Gone to watch soccer with one of his mates." She makes a face. "Men!"

"I don't suppose he knows quite how to handle it, either," I suggest gently.

"No, I'll be glad when we've moved out of this place, now. It used to feel lovely. It was the home I brought all my babies back to when they were born; where they all grew up. Full of happy memories. Now it feels . . . tainted."

"Later, though, when you look back, it'll feel nice again. Won't it?"

She shrugs, doesn't answer. "Shall we have a drink, Beth? While we're working?" She opens the first of the bottles of red wine out of Ben's wine cupboard.

"Here's to your move," I tell her, raising my glass and smiling at her. "And I hope you'll all be happy in Dudley Road."

"Thank you," she says, clinking her glass against mine. "And here's to a good party tonight."

The first guests start arriving about eight o'clock. I've been home quickly, after all the food was prepared, and had a shower and got changed, but Ellie insisted on staying at Park Cottage with her new friends. She's looking tired already—I don't think it'll be long before she crashes out.

"Play quietly like a good girl," I remind her when I look in on her.

She's sitting on Annie's bed, cuddling a teddy bear. "Goo-goo," she says.

"Don't be silly, Ellie," I warn her.

"She's the baby," explains Annie. "Jodie is our mummy and Solomon's our daddy."

Solomon, who's playing with his Superheroes on the carpet, looks up at me with a sigh of resignation. "I'm only being the daddy," he says, "if I can be out at work all day."

"You have to come home at *night*," says Annie. "Silly boy."

"Goo!" says Ellie.

I go back downstairs, smiling to myself, smiling at my memories. I always had to be the baby when I played with my older brother and sister. I think I spent half of my childhood crawling around with towels wrapped round me for nappies, sucking my thumb, and saying "Goo" and "Wah!" and "Mamma" like some sort of demented baby doll. It's a wonder I ever grew up into a normal child at all. In fact I sometimes wonder whether this was the root of half of my problems.

"I wish Ellie had a brother or sister," I say wistfully to Louise.

"Still time, isn't there!" she says reassuringly.

"Time isn't the issue. Not particularly wanting a man in my life, or to have another baby, is rather more of an issue."

"What about Martin?"

"Hmm. Well," I sigh, thinking about Martin. What about him indeed? "I do like him. I do fancy him, and everything. But . . . I don't know. I'm not sure I'm ready for him, or anyone else, to get stuck into my life and start taking it over, the way men do. Know what I mean?"

She nods agreement.

"He got on my nerves this morning, on the phone," I admit.

"Already!" she laughs. "You've only known him a few weeks!"

"Exactly. So what's the point of thinking long term, if he's pissing me off already?"

"You'll probably be fine with him when he arrives tonight. You've got all night together!" she reminds me.

"Hm."

By ten o'clock I've met most of Louise's friends and neighbors and I've drunk so much wine I've started to forget who's who. She's introduced me to the Patels, who are moving in here on Monday, and they seem very pleasant, and very interested in the possibility of a cleaning lady. I make a point of picking up empty glasses and dirty ashtrays every time I walk past them, to take out to the kitchen, to impress them with my tidiness and cleanliness.

"Calm down," mutters Louise when she catches me at it. "You'll be getting the Hoover out in a minute. It's not exactly normal behavior for a party guest, you know."

"If the Hoover needs to come out," I respond, slightly more loudly than I intend, "then I'm your man. Just because I'm off duty doesn't mean I can forget about hoovering, you know! It's in my blood!"

"You're drunk," she says cheerfully.

Yes, she's quite right—I am. In fact I think I'd better fetch myself something to eat and lay off the alcohol for a while, otherwise I'm going to be legless before Martin even gets here tonight.

I go out to the kitchen, find myself a paper plate, and start loading it generously with prawns, chicken, salad, bread, and slices of the quiches I made earlier. The plate, soggy with mayonnaise, sags dangerously, and a little of the mayonnaise runs over the edge and onto my fingers. I turn from the table, balancing the plate carefully in one hand as I raise my fingers to my mouth to lick the mayonnaise off them. And I look up, into the eyes of the most gorgeous man I've ever seen in my entire life. So gorgeous, I nearly drop the fucking plate.

We're talking George Clooney here, but much, much better. He's tall, broad, with the sort of dark good looks normally referred to as brooding, but the effect's lightened by the lazy laughter lines around his eyes. His hair's just the right length for running your fingers through—just long enough to look slightly and wickedly tousled. George Clooney on a good day, just out of bed and looking at you like he wants to go back.

Or Robbie Williams, just back from the gym and ready to get into the shower.

Or Brad Pitt, just *out* of the shower.

Or Russell Crowe . . . no, sorry, much better than any of them. *Much* better.

"Hello," he says, smiling at me.

The voice is like melted chocolate.

The smile is like the sun coming up over the desert.

My knees feel like jelly and my toes are curling up toward the ceiling.

"Jesus fucking Christ," I whisper to myself.

The mayonnaise is running down between my fingers and trickling onto my wrist. I lift my wrist to my mouth, not taking my eyes away from his eyes, and try to lick my wrist, but I seem to keep missing it.

"Here," he says. "Let me." He picks up a paper napkin from the table, takes hold of my hand, and wipes my wrist clean.

I'll never wash again, I swear to God.

"I'm Alex," he says, staring into my eyes.

His eyes are like pools of warm dark molasses. I want to drown in them. I don't really care what your name is. I just want to throw myself into your arms and kiss the face off you.

"Hi, Alex," I simper.

I know I sound like a purring kitten. What can I do? A couple of hours ago I was pretty sure I didn't want another man in my life in any shape or form. Now this guy walks into the room and looks at me, says hello, and wipes the mayonnaise off me and I want to marry him and have his babies.

"Oh, good, you've met!" cries Louise, barging into the kitchen, elbowing us apart, and picking up a bottle of wine from the table. She plants herself between us, grinning at me. "Beth, this is Alex!"

"I know." I glare at her pointedly. We can do our own introductions, thank you. I'll call you if I need you. Just close the kitchen door after you and leave me alone with him to throw myself at his neck and kiss the living daylights out of him.

"Alex, this is Beth!" she persists, turning to him and raising her eyebrows meaningfully.

"Yes, thank you, Louise . . ." I try to interrupt, but she's obviously overplaying the hostess role tonight.

"*Beth*, Alex!" she tells him again. Then turning back to me, "This is Alex! Alex *Chapman,* Beth!"

I see the realization dawn in his eyes just a fraction of a second before it hits my brain.

Alex Chapman.

This is Alex Chapman whose flat I clean every Tuesday morning. Alex Chapman the Single Young Executive whose apartment his mother, Louise's next-door neighbor, pays me good money to clean, even though he never makes it dirty, even though he never makes so much as a smear on a mirror, never drops a crumb on the carpet or leaves a single one of his lovely thick dark hairs in the plughole. Whose computer, in fact, I sit at every Tuesday writing my TV script when I'm supposed to be cleaning his home, because there's nothing to clean.

Well, thank you, God—thanks a bundle.

It hasn't really been my week, has it?

As if I hadn't suffered enough humiliation yesterday, coming face to face with my ex on the doorstep of a cleaning job, now I get to sink to another all-time low in the realms of self-esteem.

I don't remember volunteering for some mad, masochistic Japanese game show.

OK, here we go. Here's a laugh for the audience. Cover yourself in mayonnaise, get the most gorgeous hunk in the history of the universe to lick it off for you while you drool and wet your knickers over him, and guess what?! You've actually been scrubbing his floors for him! He's looking at you, imagining you sweeping under his bed and washing his toilet!

I put down the soggy plate of food. I lost my appetite

as soon as I looked into Alex Chapman's eyes anyway. I turn away from him, away from Louise, and head for the door.

"Wait!" He takes hold of my arm and pulls me back toward him.

I feel sadly like a lump of putty. He may be a cleanliness fetishist, but the touch of his hand on my arm still makes me want to shag the life out of him.

"Wait, Beth," he says.

All my life, if necessary.

"I've been wanting to meet you."

To find out what the hell I've been doing every Tuesday? Sitting in his apartment watching the clock while the place keeps itself spotlessly clean?

"I'm sorry," I tell him, afraid to look at him in case I find the urge to rip off his clothes completely irresistible. "I'm sorry if I don't do very much cleaning. If you don't think I'm worth the money."

"No, I don't think . . ."

But I'm on a roll now. It suddenly all spills out.

"But what am I supposed to do? How am I supposed to clean the flat when you never make it dirty? There's never anything to clean! I don't know how you manage it! Do you clean it the day before I come? It looks . . . it looks almost unlived-in!"

I take a breath and look up at him, and he smiles—a nice smile; not a teasing type of smile, but a laughing-along-at-the-joke one.

"That's just the thing," he says gently, speaking so close to my ear that his breath feels hot against my face and the hairs stand up on the back of my neck. "It *is* unlived-in."

"What? I don't understand. Your mother said . . ."

"Exactly," he says. There's a pause of about a hundredth of a second, during which his eyes meet mine and

I swear to God it feels like he's looking straight into my soul. "That's exactly the point. My mother thinks I live there. But I don't. I live somewhere else."

"Oh?" I breathe.

"Yes, my mother thinks my wife and I are separated. She'd make things awkward if she knew we'd decided to stay together. So it was easier to keep up the pretense. Saves upsetting anyone. You see?"

Oh, yes, I see.

Oh, shit.

Shit, shit, and fucking shit, he's married.

Perhaps it's just as well I didn't rip off his clothes after all, then.

Sunday

———◆◇◆◇◆———

What am I going to do about myself? Perhaps I need therapy. Perhaps I need to take some medication for my mood swings, or my hormones.

First I hate Daniel, then I become very angry and cry my eyes out when I meet him again.

First I fancy the pants off Creepy Oliver the Landscape Gardener, then I call him a wanker for wanting a shag in the wardrobe.

First I don't much like Martin, then I like him enough to have sex with him in my kitchen, now I think I find him irritating.

First I never want anything to do with another man as long as I live, now I collapse into a steaming mess as soon as someone looks into my eyes and cleans off my mayonnaise.

And he's married.

And actually, too, I've got a boyfriend, haven't I.

It's twelve-thirty in the morning of Sunday, March 30, and I'm dancing with Martin in the living room of Louise and Ben's beautiful house, their half-empty beautiful house—dancing to "Lady in Red," its soulful tune and soulful words going straight through me as Martin holds me close against him and I look over his shoulder, across the room, to where Alex Chapman is sitting on his own with a glass of wine and a cigarette. And he's looking back at me.

Now, what am I supposed to make of this?

He's definitely looking at me. Straight at me. Not at Martin, not at the carpet, not at the door behind us or the people dancing next to us.

Martin and I turn around the room, slowly, the way you do when you're slow-dancing to a slow number with a person you're going out with, who you're going to be sleeping with tonight, who you're presumably at least slightly fond of, and immediately I get within eye-contact range of Alex, so that I can look at him without having to twist my neck 180 degrees, which Martin might quite reasonably construe as slightly weird. I lock eyes with him, and I try to slow Martin down a bit in his slow-shuffle around the carpet so that I can hold the eye contact for as long as possible before Alex goes out of range again. And my nerves are stretched practically to shreds with wondering whether he's looking at me because he thinks he might have left a bit of mayonnaise somewhere, or because I'm dancing funny, or my skirt's tucked in my knickers, or whether there's any chance he might be able to see inside my head and figure out that I'm melting inside, absolutely melting away with white-hot lust throughout every 360-degree turn around our bit of carpet, just looking at him and thinking what it would feel like to be dancing like this with *him* instead of with Martin. And I don't care a fuck about his wife-who-his-mother-doesn't-like, and I don't care a fuck about . . . whoops. That was a close one, wasn't it?

I nearly said I didn't care a fuck about Martin, and I can't mean that, can I, when here I am, snuggled up close to him, and about to spend a night of passion with him, which is obviously very much to the forefront of his mind judging by the firmness of his loins against mine.

Of course I care about Martin, and to prove it I lay my head against his shoulder and cuddle in a bit closer.

But I still lock eyes with Alex next time around, and he's still looking back at me.

"Shall we go?" asks Martin as the slow number finishes. He's looking at me like I'm a cream cake sitting on his plate and he's been on a diet for a month.

"One more dance?" I suggest.

But the next number is "Achy Breaky Heart" and there's no way he's going to believe I want to smooch round the carpet to that.

I go upstairs to check on Ellie. She's sound asleep, her hair splayed out on the pillow like a picture of a fairy-tale princess, with Annie's teddy bear still in her arms. She sleeps with a smile on her face. I watch her for a few minutes, like mothers probably always do all over the world, thinking how perfect she is and how clever I've been to give birth to her and bring her up as such a perfect child. And when I turn to tiptoe away from the bedroom doorway, Alex is standing behind me in the dim light of the landing.

"Oh! You made me jump!" I whisper hoarsely.

"Sorry," he whispers back.

I stare at him.

It's ridiculous to feel short of breath just standing here in a perfectly normal way, in the dark, outside a bedroom door, talking in whispers to the most gorgeous man I've ever met. Ridiculous. Pull yourself together, girl.

"I've got to go," I whisper.

"Yes, I came to say good-bye."

Came *upstairs* to say good-bye? Followed me up to the bedrooms, to say good-bye in the dark, away from everyone else, away from Martin?

I can't think of anything to say to this.

"I need to talk to you," he says.

"Do you?"

I still don't know what to say. I mean, he might need to talk to me about my cleaning. About the lack of it, about the lack of need for it. He might need to tell me he doesn't want me to bother anymore, and there goes my last remaining client. But I don't want to think this is what he needs to talk to me about.

"Yes," he says.

He leans toward me. I feel the floor start to go wobbly. He's going to kiss me. Christ! I've got beads of perspiration breaking out in places where I didn't know it was possible to perspire. I'm working hard to try to control my breathing. As his face comes nearer, I close my eyes and turn my lips toward him.

"Good night, Beth," he whispers, planting a chaste kiss on my cheek. "I'll phone you."

And he goes back downstairs.

"You're quiet," says Martin as we drive home.

"Sorry. Got a bit of a headache."

Actually I feel hot and shaky like I've just gone down with the flu.

He rests a hand on my thigh and says, "Hope it's not too much of a headache . . . ?"

Well, what can I say? I've promised him a night to remember and I can hardly play the reluctant virgin now.

* * *

It seems strange having a man here again, in my bedroom, where I've slept alone since the day Daniel left. It's a different matter from having a quick drunken shag in the kitchen. I feel a bit awkward about it all now it's come to it. I don't want to go through the whole thing of going to the bathroom, getting undressed, and then him going to the bathroom, getting undressed . . . cleaning our teeth, brushing our hair, getting into bed . . . it all seems such a turn-off, so . . . premeditated. We stand just inside the bedroom door, and look at the bed, and look at each other. I don't feel like doing it at all, but I can't bring myself to refuse, not now, after all the buildup.

"Let's start like this," says Martin suddenly, and he pulls me toward him, takes my face in his hands, and kisses me, very slowly, very gently, and I wonder how he knew that it's just exactly what I needed, and I gradually feel myself relaxing, and we sit on the bed, and kiss a bit more, and by the time we're lying down I've changed my mind and I'm ready and willing.

"Headache gone?" he whispers.

"What headache?"

This time I don't think about Daniel when I come.

I think about Alex.

And as if that isn't bad enough, as if I don't feel mixed up and guilty enough about my conflicting emotions and the way I appear to have become a nymphomaniac inhabiting the body of a celibate nun at her first orgy, as if I don't feel bad enough in every possible way about Martin and how I ogle another man while I'm slow-dancing with him, and fantasize about the other man while he's making love to me—on top of all this, when we're lying here together after we've woken up in the morning and had sex again, more energetically, more spectacularly than last night and making me fantasize even more about Alex Chapman—Martin turns to me, does that thing again where he holds my face in his hands, and says, "I love you, Beth."

No!

No, don't say that, for God's sake!

Say you fancy me, say you want me, say you'd like to cover me with jam and cream and have me hanging backward off the table but don't, for God's sake, say you love me.

Not while I'm still not sure how I feel about you.

Not while I'm not even sure whether I really want you in my life, or whether you're going to end up irritating the shit out of me.

Not while I'm being unfaithful to you, in my mind, with someone I've only just clapped eyes on for the first time at the party.

"No," I tell him, trying not to sound panicky. "You don't. You don't have to say that."

"I'm not just saying it. I do." He pauses. "I know it's too soon for you to feel the same way. I know you're still wary of commitment. It's all right, Beth. I understand. I can wait."

Oh, no!

Oh, yuck, yuck, yuck!

I lie still, with my eyes closed, and wish I could, decently, just get up out of bed, have a shower, get dressed, and walk away from it all—from Martin and his love, and his commitment, and his understanding, and his waiting for me. I wish I could, decently, tell him I don't want him to wait for me. I don't want him to be so nice, and so understanding, and such a thoroughly decent guy, because he's going to drive me mad; he's going to try to control me, he's going to try and take over my life whether he means to or not, and he thinks he'll wait for me patiently to decide to love him back, but he won't. He'll keep on at me, badgering me with his niceness and his kindness and his love and his understanding, until I weaken and give in because it's easier than hurting him and rejecting him, and I'll convince myself that I do love him really, and we have great sex, and why should it matter that I think about someone else? And he'll move in with me, and perhaps we'll even get married, and perhaps we'll have a child together, and Ellie will get the little brother or sister I've wanted her to have, and eventually we'll have a good lifestyle, with dinner parties for friends, and holidays and weekends away, and it'll all be hunky-dory and wonderful, and it will all be a fucking lie.

Is that what happened to Fay and Simon? Is that how easy it is?

I suddenly feel like crying.

"What's the matter?" Martin says, softly, tracing his finger gently around my closed eyes.

"You're too nice," is all I can say.

And he chuckles happily and takes it as a compliment, and I have to lie there for a bit longer before I can decently get up. Because I haven't got the guts to add, "But I'm never going to love you."

He goes about lunchtime, and I go over to collect Ellie from Louise.

"Have a nice night?" she asks me with a grin.

"Yes, thanks."

I don't really feel like talking about it.

"And thanks for a great party. And for having Ellie."

"No, you helped with all the food . . ." She looks at me

with sudden concern. "Are you all right? Is everything OK—with Martin?"

"Yes, fine."

Why is everyone so concerned about Martin? If I decide not to keep on seeing him, am I going to feel like a complete shit because everyone else seems to like him?

And why am I thinking about the possibility of not seeing him, anyway?

I change the subject quickly. And the first subject that comes to my mind just happens to be: "It was interesting to meet Alex Chapman at last."

I feel myself go hot, just mentioning his name.

"Yes," says Louise.

She's busy doing a last load of washing before Ben disconnects the washing machine ready for moving. She doesn't seem to have noticed that the subject of our conversation has got me breathing funny.

"I thought you ought to meet him—after all this time you've been cleaning for him!"

I wait for her to make some comment. She must, surely, give me that knowing look we girls give each other when we're talking about someone we both know is a demi-god, a perfect male specimen, someone we're going to fantasize about when we're alone at night. She will, surely, shake her head and raise her eyebrows and laugh about how she's always fancied him and knew he'd make an impression on me as soon as I saw him.

"Nice bloke, isn't he," she says, slamming the washing-machine door shut.

Nice bloke?

I stare at the back of her head. Is she kidding? I mean, it's like saying the Sahara Desert is a bit warm, or the Pyramids are getting on a bit.

She looks at me. "Don't you think so?"

"Yes," I say, carefully, trying not to give myself away

too much. But I can't help it. I've got to know that it isn't just me. Am I going mad? Was I on drugs last night or something? "Good-looking, too," I add as casually as I can, without looking at her.

"What, Alex?" she says, sounding surprised.

She is. She's got to be kidding with me.

I look straight at her now. She's staring at me. "Alex, good looking?" she repeats. "I don't know. I've never thought about it. He's all right, I suppose. He's not really my type." She looks at me a bit more directly. "You fancy him!" she says, starting to smile. "You do, don't you!"

I turn away and go to call Ellie down from upstairs.

"Do you fancy him?" she persists, following me.

"He's OK," I say.

Was that cool enough? She'd never tell from the tone of my voice that my heart's leaping about like a mad thing inside me.

"Bloody hell," she says quietly, behind me. "I should have realized. I saw you. I saw you looking at each other, when you were dancing with Martin. I should have realized!"

"There was nothing," I say, with as much dignity as I can manage, "to realize."

This has got me worried.

If it isn't apparent—no, not just apparent but blatantly, totally obvious—to every other female in the world who's met him that Alex Chapman is the most gorgeous thing on the planet, then I must have something seriously wrong with me. I mean, OK, we all see good-looking men everyday, we all meet attractive men whose voices and smiles and charm and charisma turn us on and make us feel good. I admit to having got horny about kinky Oliver, but he had a good body—believe me, anyone would have fancied him; most women might even have been tempted by the wardrobe offer. It's not like I've led a sheltered life, not like I've just been let loose from a convent school in a remote part of Outer Mongolia and just seen a man for the first time since puberty.

So what's the matter with me?

What was so special about Alex Chapman last night?

Why him?

Why me?

And why now?

Why now, when I've got the lovely Martin all to myself and begging to be allowed to wait for me to start loving him?

Why now, when for the first time since Daniel left me, things aren't actually too bad on the nooky front? For the first time, the whole male population of the planet doesn't seem to have declared a unanimous verdict of no interest in my sexuality. My life has ceased to be the sexual desert it used to be, when I might have been forgiven for having lingering thoughts of an impure nature about passing strangers.

Now, I ought to be satisfied.

Oughtn't I?

I do my best to feel satisfied for the rest of the day. I cook, I clean, I play with Ellie. I do my washing, I do my ironing, I read Ellie stories. I think about Martin and remind myself about how nice he is. How sweet, how caring. How good it's been in bed with him. How he thinks he loves me. Yes, I should feel well satisfied. And then this evening, late this evening, after Ellie's in bed, the phone rings.

"Hi, Beth. It's Alex."

My heart hasn't done this pounding, thumping stuff since I was a teenager. Since I first met Daniel.

"Hello," I stammer, trying to make myself heard above the pounding.

"I . . . said I'd phone you."

"Yes, but I wasn't sure . . . if you really would."

There's a silence of about twelve hours. I can't think of a single thing except that he's on the other end of this phone line and I can hear him breathing.

"I wanted to talk to you," he says eventually. He sounds as shaky as I feel. Is he nervous? Am I making him nervous?

"Yes?" I say, trying to be encouraging.

"About . . . well, about Sarah."

Sarah? Sarah? Who the fucking bollocks is Sarah? Where did she come into it? Have I missed something?

"Sarah's my wife," he adds.

Oh. Lovely. During the course of the last twenty-four hours I've had a million fantasies, several of them about this phone call, and none of them, strangely enough, included him mentioning his wife within two minutes of starting to speak to me.

"She's . . . got her own business. She's a . . . well, she's got connections . . . she's, well, she knows people . . ."

He's lost me now.

"What sort of people?"

And why are we discussing her?

"People in business . . . who can help . . . other people. If people need . . . to be, well, introduced . . . to other people . . ."

She runs a bloody dating agency!

"Why are you telling me this?" I ask him, pain streaming out of my pores like blood from a wound. "Do you think I need her help? Or what?"

He sighs. There's another long silence.

"Look, forget it, Beth. I'm sorry, I probably shouldn't be saying anything at all. Just forget I said anything."

"I'm not lonely," I tell him, choked and stung. "I'm not alone and pathetic, you know. I've got a man already."

"I know. I saw you with him. At the party. You were dancing . . ."

Yes.

And watching you.

Watching you, watching me.

"What is this all about?" I say, almost in a whisper.

And I don't just mean the phone call.

"I don't know," he half-whispers back.

There's another silence.

I don't want him to hang up.

"Do you still need me? To clean the flat?" I ask him quickly. "I mean, now I know you don't really live there."

"It's OK. You keep it tidy for me."

Tidy? It's tidy already. I've seen funeral parlors less tidy than that flat.

"And your money," he says. "My mother will give your money to Mrs. Patel to give you. Apparently Mrs. Patel's going to ask you to carry on cleaning Park Cottage."

"Oh. Brilliant. They said they'd probably give me a ring about it."

"So that's OK then?"

"Of course. Fine."

I hesitate. That can't be it, the end of the conversation. He can't have just phoned me to talk about his wife's business and my cleaning money. Can he?

"So," I begin.

"Yes, so . . ."

"Are we . . ."

". . . going to . . ."

". . . see each other . . ."

". . . again, at all?"

Who said it first? Was it me, or him, or did we both say it at the same time? Or did the words just fall out of the sky, bouncing along the phone line between us—*Are we going to see each other again, at all?*

Are we?

Are we?

"Of course."

"Yes, of course."

"Later in the week?"

"Yes, that'd be good."

"Perhaps Friday?"

"Whenever. Whenever you like."

"Friday, then. But I'll phone you."

"Yes, OK."

"See you then."

"Yes, bye."

I don't want to hang up. But I do. And I stand there for a while staring at the phone as if it's become something strange and unfamiliar to me.

As strange and unfamiliar as the territory I'm going into.

I think I'm about to start seeing someone else's man.

And being unfaithful to mine.

Monday

Ellie and I have lunch at Fay's after playgroup. Everything's back to normal, like we never fell out, like we never stopped confiding our secrets to each other.

"I've met someone," I tell her while we're making toasted sandwiches together in the kitchen. "And I can't stop thinking about him."

"Who? Where?" she asks, buttering bread, not missing a beat.

"It's Alex Chapman. The one I clean for, in Oakleigh Court. He was at Louise's party."

She looks at me in surprise. "I thought you were there with Martin."

"I was. Well, he came later. But . . ." I hesitate.

She puts down the knife and turns to give me her full attention. "So what happened?"

"Nothing. We just talked. And looked . . . we looked at each other. Kind of like . . ."

Like we knew each other already.

Like we both knew something no one else in the room knew.

Like we knew there was more to come.

"You fancied him. And he fancied you back."

"I don't know," I say. "But he phoned me last night. It was a really weird conversation, about his wife, and my cleaning money. But I just can't stop thinking about him. It's crazy, isn't it. It's stupid."

"Why?"

"Because I'm seeing Martin. We're in a relationship. I don't want to spoil it. And anyway . . . he—Alex—he's married. He lives somewhere else with his wife. That's why his flat is never dirty. But his mother hired me to clean for him because she thinks he's separated and she doesn't know he's gone back to his wife."

Fay raises her eyebrows. "What kind of man is too scared to tell his mother something like that?"

"I know," I admit. "It's very odd. He said she'd be awkward about it. She's a miserable old bat, his mother. But I can't quite see why it's any of her business."

I hesitate, and then tell Fay, tell her very quickly so that it doesn't sound quite as momentous as it is, "We're going to see each other. On Friday."

"Are you?" says Fay, nodding slowly to herself. "I see."

"But—you know. Just probably to have a chat. I think it's a good idea, to meet up, get things straight. You know, the fact that we're both with other people so nothing's going to happen between us."

"Hmm," says Fay. She goes back to buttering the bread.

"Hmm, what?"

She doesn't reply.

"So what's he like?" she asks me after a minute. She turns again and looks me straight in the eyes. "Eh? What's he like?"

I feel my pulse quickening again. I have to look away. "Gorgeous. Just . . . gorgeous." I shake my head and shrug. "Just everything about him . . . not just the way he looks, everything. His voice . . . the way he stands . . . the way he breathes . . . the way he laughs . . . absolutely everything."

"Your voice has gone funny!" laughs Fay.

"So would yours," I tell her, "if you saw him." And then I remember. "Actually, Louise can't understand what I saw in him. Said he was OK but not really her type. Perhaps she's just got too much on her mind. . . ."

"Or perhaps it's just you," says Fay gently. "You and him. Chemistry."

I never was much good at chemistry at school.

Preferred biology.

On the way home I call in at 27 Dudley Road, where the removal van is still outside disgorging what's left of Louise and Ben's worldly goods into their new house.

"Here," I say, handing Louise a bunch of flowers and some cakes. "Welcome to your new home. Shall I come in and make a cup of tea?"

"That'd be lovely," she says, wiping the hair off her brow with the back of her hand. "Thanks, Beth—you're a gem."

The kitchen is even smaller than mine. Louise's microwave is perched at an awkward angle on the work surface because it won't fit anywhere. There are more boxes of crockery and cookware than there are cupboards, despite the boot sale. I rummage in one of the boxes and find the kettle.

"How has it gone so far?" I ask, unwrapping mugs and searching for tea bags and sugar.

"I feel exhausted," she admits, leaning against the kitchen door. "I don't know why, really."

"Stress. Hardly surprising. Culmination of everything."

"Yes." She sighs. "Beth, you wouldn't do me a favor, would you? Collect the kids from school in an hour's time? It'd give me and Ben a bit longer to try and get things straight here."

"Of course I will. And let me help you here, too, before I go. What needs doing first?"

"The children's rooms. I'd really like to have their beds made, their curtains up, a few of their things unpacked . . ." She trails off and looks at me, eyes big with appeal.

"Of course." I nod. "So they feel more at home when they get here."

We drink our tea, and then get to work upstairs, shaking out duvets, hanging curtains, fixing lampshades, and filling wardrobes and drawers with clothes, while Ellie sits on Jodie's bed sorting books and games into piles.

"Perhaps you should let them unpack some of their toys themselves," I suggest. "I think they might enjoy it. And it'll keep them occupied while you're doing things downstairs."

"Yes, you're right," says Louise, sitting back on her heels and looking around the girls' room.

They'll be sharing a room for the first time in their lives. It's not a big room, and there isn't much space between the two beds.

"It looks fine," I tell her gently. "They're going to love it, being in together."

"Do you think so? God, Beth, I just feel like we've let them down. We've let them all down so badly."

"Of course you haven't!" I put my arms around her and try to talk to her firmly. "Children don't look at things the same way we do. They're excited, aren't they, about moving to a new house. They won't care about it being smaller. They'll be more interested in the kids next door, and the park over the road, and the corner shop, and going out on their bikes . . ."

"Do you really think so?"

"Yes, I really do. Now why don't you have a sit-down for a while instead of working yourself into the ground, while I go and pick them up from school?"

"I want to get everything straight. I have to go back to work tomorrow . . ."

"OK. But take it easy."

Ellie's quiet while we drive back to the other side of town.

"Will Jodie and Annie and Solomon live in that new house for always?" she asks as we park the car outside the gate of their private school.

"Well, for now anyway. They won't be going back to Park Cottage. Someone else lives there now."

"And will Jodie and Annie always have both their beds in one bedroom like that?"

"Yes, lots of children do share their bedrooms with their brothers or sisters," I tell her.

She scowls out of the car window. "I wish *I* had another bed in *my* bedroom and a brother or a sister in it!" she says plaintively. "It's not *fair!*"

Jodie and Annie come out of school at a run when they see my car, and Ellie waving out of the window.

"Is Ellie coming to play?" says Annie excitedly, throwing her bag of books and her school hat into the back of the car.

"No," I tell her. "Your mum and dad are too busy unpacking, today, to have anyone extra to play."

"Oh, yes! I forgot about the new house!" says Annie, her face brightening.

"You've got both your beds in one room!" Ellie tells her enviously. "You can talk to each other *all night*."

"Throw things at each other, more like," declares Jodie.

Ellie looks at her in surprise. I don't think it's occurred to her that brothers and sisters sometimes get on each other's nerves.

"Where's Solomon?" I ask the girls. "Jodie, can you go back to the gate and look out for him? I don't want to miss him, and have him wandering up and down looking for your mum."

"Oh, all *right*, if I *have* to!" scowls Jodie. She gets out of the car, slams the door, and slouches over to the school gate.

Ellie looks even more surprised. The perfect Jodie isn't always perfect? Wow.

"She's so *moody*!" complains Annie. "I wish we didn't *have* to share the bedroom. She'll probably be horrible to me all the time."

I look at Ellie's face in the mirror. She looks like she's in shock.

"He's just coming," announces Jodie, turning to come back to the car. "He's seen me." She gets into the front seat, next to me, and puts on her seat belt, staring straight ahead. I notice her eyes look red.

"How was school today?" I ask her gently.

"All right," she says. Her lower lip wobbles and she turns away, looking out of the window.

"Hey!" shouts Solomon, crashing into the backseat next to Annie. "Are we going to the new house now? Have you seen it yet? Is it nice?"

"No!" Jodie turns on him, her eyes filling up with tears. "Of course it isn't nice, you idiot! It's miles and miles away and we can't come to this school anymore."

She subsides into silent misery, while the three children in the backseat lower their heads and look at one another with raised eyebrows.

I start the car and say to Jodie quietly as I pull away, "You'll make new friends at your new school."

"I won't!" she retorts.

"I know that's what you think, now. But you will—very quickly, because you're such a nice, friendly girl and everyone will like you. And I know you think you'll miss your friends here, but you can still see them. You can phone them and their parents can bring them round to play."

"They don't want to come and play," she says, tears gushing down her face now. "They say they don't want to come to the slums to play. They say they might catch something."

I take a deep breath. I know children can be the most appallingly cruel little monsters, but this still makes my head reel. "If they mean that, then they're not really very good friends, after all," I tell Jodie. "But they probably don't mean it. They're just teasing you, and it's spiteful teasing."

She sniffs and wipes her eyes with the back of her hand.

"What's the slums?" asks Solomon cheerfully.

"Shut up, stupid," says Jodie.

Ellie looks at her in amazement. "Shut up, stupid," she mimics.

I shake my head at her warningly in the mirror, but no one's taking any notice of her anyway.

"She's had a bit of tormenting from some of the kids at school," I tell Louise when she catches sight of Jodie's face. "Don't read too much into it—you know what kids can be like. She'll be fine. She's only got a couple more days there, and I bet they'll all be on the phone to her over the holiday."

Louise pulls her eldest daughter toward her and gives her a hug. "Come on, baby—don't take any notice of them," she tells her softly. "They're probably just jealous because you're moving, and going to a new school."

"I hate it," says Jodie. "I hate this house. I want to go back home . . ."

Louise looks at me over the top of Jodie's head.

"This *is* home, Jode. Come on, help me unpack the rest of your stuff. It'll feel like home in no time."

"Won't," scowls Jodie. "Won't ever!"

"Why doesn't Jodie like their new house?" asks Ellie on the way home. "Why is she crying? Why is she so cross?"

"Some children at school were being horrible to her today," I try to explain.

"Poor Jodie." She reflects for a minute, then adds, "She should tell them to shut up. Like she said to Solomon."

"Yes." I smile. "She probably should, shouldn't she. But it's rude, Ellie—so we try not to say it."

"*You* say rude things sometimes," she reminds me.

I would, if I could get my hands on some of those kids at that private school. All the money in the world doesn't necessarily make people nice to each other.

"Everything's fixed for Sunday," trills my mother happily into the phone. "The restaurant's booked for one o'clock. Now, don't forget—it's your birthday celebration."

"I know, Mum. It's the same date every year . . ."

"So you don't want to have to drive, do you?" She says this a bit coyly, a bit suggestively. The implication is that, as it's my thirtieth birthday, I might be contemplating the outrageous idea of having a drink or two with my meal and, as it's a very special occasion, she's prepared to go along with it. I feel about fourteen.

"So we're going to come and pick you up. Jill and Peter and I. We'll be around for you and Ellie at about half past twelve."

"That'll be lovely, Mum. Thanks."

"And we'll meet the others at the restaurant."

The others are my brother Steve and his family. The ones who'll be putting Ellie's table manners to shame. I make a mental note to work on her a bit more between now and then.

"OK."

I write "12:30" on my kitchen calendar next to Sunday's date, to remind me to get ready in time. Ellie is sitting at the kitchen table playing with her baked beans, making patterns of them across the mashed potatoes, so I take the opportunity to nag at her.

"Eat your dinner properly, Ellie. Don't play with food."

"I like playing with it," she says.

"I know, but it isn't polite. It makes a mess. People don't like looking at it."

"They don't have to look at it," she says reasonably, piling the potatoes up into a tower and spooning baked-bean juice over it.

"Food is supposed to be for eating. People in poor countries would be very upset if they saw you playing with it, when they'd like to eat it."

I hate this. I hate saying all this stuff my mother used to say to me when I was little. Children always play with food. I bet they even play with food in poor countries, to be quite honest. What harm does it do? Why do we say all this stuff to children about things that don't really matter? Why do I care about my brother's children looking down on Ellie on Sunday and thinking she's a Philistine? Why can't I just let her get on with being four years old? I doubt very much whether she'll still be making castles out of mashed potatoes and baked beans when she goes out on dates when she's eighteen.

"Just try not to make a mess," I say, sighing, turning to go. "And eat it before it gets cold."

"Shut up, stupid," says Ellie brightly.

I make the mistake of telling Martin about it.

"You shouldn't let her say things like that to you," he says seriously. "It's not funny. Don't let her think it's funny."

Heaven forbid.

"I know it's not funny. But she's picked it up from someone else, and she doesn't mean to be rude. Children mimic."

"Yes, well, they have to be told, don't they. If she mimics everything she hears other people say, she'll be in trouble when she goes to school."

"Martin!" I snap, throwing down the dishcloth and whirling around to face him. "Would you mind *not* telling me how to bring up my child!"

He stares at me across the kitchen.

I've been washing up the dinner things, and he's just leaning in the kitchen doorway, watching me. I know it's my own dishes, and he's only called in on his way to work, and there's no reason why he should soil his hands to help me, but it still rankles a bit that he's standing there watching me.

And it rankles even more that he's criticizing my daughter.

"I wouldn't dream of telling you—" he begins.

"But you did. You just did."

"Well, I'm sorry. I was only giving you my opinion."

"I don't want it. OK? If I want your opinion about Ellie, and how I bring her up, I'll ask for it. But I probably won't."

"So I should mind my own business?"

"If you like, yes. Yes, I think you should."

"Fine."

There's a stony silence. I bury myself up to my elbows in the dishwater and splash things around noisily.

"Perhaps I'd better go," he says crisply. "If that's how you feel." The wounded tone to his voice now is even more irritating than the bossiness a few minutes ago.

I stop splashing, heave a long sigh, and wipe my hands on the tea towel. "There's no need to be like that," I tell him.

He doesn't move. He doesn't say anything.

"Put the kettle on," I add, "if you're staying."

After a minute he comes to the sink with the kettle and leans across me to fill it up from the tap.

"Tea?" he asks.

"Thanks."

He stays leaning across me after he's turned off the tap, and turns to give me a quick peck on the lips.

I suppose it means he's sorry.

Or, more likely, that he thinks I'm a moody cow with PMS and he's being magnanimous enough to forgive me.

Either way, he thinks everything's fine now. One quick kiss and everything's better. If we had a proper kiss now, he'd think I'd changed my mind, backed down completely, and wanted him to make every future decision about Ellie on my behalf. If we had sex, he'd strut out of my flat thinking I'd signed my life over to him.

All it is, is a kiss.

All it is, is sex.

It doesn't change the fact that I've got alarm bells ringing in my head like the clangers of hell.

He's not taking charge of any aspect of my life, least of all my child, just because I've slept with him a few times. Who does he think he is?

But I drink my tea and keep quiet.

For now.

Wednesday

There are bags and cases packed all over the place in Dottie's bungalow. She really means it, then. I suppose I was kind of hoping she'd had time to change her mind.

"Some of this stuff will have to be shipped out," she says cheerfully, stepping over a box of books. "Luke is sorting it all out for me."

You don't say.

"When do you go?" I ask her, trying to disengage Tosser's molars from my shin without actually screaming out loud. I've got to get used to him, and he's got to get used to me, so we need to start deciding who's going to be boss.

"Next week. Next Saturday." She grins at me excitedly. "Can't come soon enough now. I don't know what took me so long, really, Beth, to make up my mind."

I thought she actually made up her mind almost as soon as Luke started talking her into it, but there you go.

Tosser sinks his fangs in a bit deeper and I weaken and let out a gasp.

"You all right?" Dottie says, staring at me. "He's only being friendly, aren't you, boy?"

Friendly, my arse. I rub my leg and snarl at him as Dottie turns away. We need to get this relationship onto a new footing, bastard dog, if you're coming to live with me. He growls and bares his teeth and I growl back. He flattens his ears and lowers his head, watching me.

War has been declared.

I spend most of the morning helping Dottie with her packing instead of cleaning. I feel sad and depressed, seeing all her things going into boxes. Some of it's going into storage, with her furniture, and I suppose it's unlikely ever to come out again in her lifetime. She doesn't seem bothered by this at all, she's so caught up in the excitement of moving to the other side of the world to live in the country she couldn't say a good word about just a few weeks ago.

"You're the second one," I tell her. "The second one of my clients whose homes I've helped to pack up."

I tell her about Louise and Ben, and their children, and their new house. She shrugs. "Life's about more than boxes of worldly goods," she says philosophically.

"I know that. But I still think it's sad."

"You won't, when you're my age. This sort of thing becomes irrelevant. What matters is yer health and yer strength, and having someone around you to love." She reaches out and tries to ruffle Luke's spiky hair. I have to concentrate hard on not vomiting.

I chat to her, while we're packing her china and her glassware, about Martin and my sudden doubts about him. "He says he loves me," I tell her gloomily.

"Good God, girl! You've only known him five minutes! He probably just wants to have his wicked way with you!"

"Oh, he's had that," I say dismissively.

"Not good?" she asks with a twinkle in her eye.

"Actually, yes!" I smile. "It was good. Very good. But that's not everything, is it."

"So what's up? Is he boring? Moody? Farts in bed?"

I laugh out loud. "No, no—he's very nice, really, Dottie. I think I'm just being too fussy, aren't I?"

"Fussy?" she exclaims. "Fussy?! Listen to me, young lady! You be as fussy as you damn well want! You don't have to carry on with anyone if you don't want to! You don't have to have a reason! You don't have to keep on seeing him just because . . . well, just to *reward* him for being nice to you and saying he loves you!"

That's it, isn't it. That's exactly what I'm doing. I feel like I owe it to him, like it's the least I can do, because he likes me and he's good to me and Ellie. How did Dottie get to be so wise? Will I be like that when I'm her age? Do I have to wait that long?

"And I've met someone else," I tell her suddenly, all in a rush, not looking at her.

I can feel her looking at me, though. Even though I'm concentrating very hard on wrapping these bone-china ornaments up in bubble wrap and corrugated cardboard and putting them gently into the packing cases, I know her wise old eyes are watching me, watching the flush rising in my cheeks and the pulse quickening in my neck and the breath coming a bit sharply in my throat, and I know there's no fooling her.

"Someone you've fallen for," she observes calmly.

"I can't say *that*. I've only just met him. It's just . . . strange. Scary, in a way. I don't know what to make of it."

"And what about him? Do you think he feels the same way?"

"He's married."

"That wasn't what I asked." She chuckles.

"Dottie . . . I don't know. I think—I get the impression—he might feel as confused as I do. But perhaps I'm just imagining it. Perhaps it's just wishful thinking?"

"Has he asked to see you again?"

I nod.

"Doesn't sound much like wishful thinking to me, then."

"I think we're just going to have a chat. On Friday. Just meet up and have a chat, talk about what's going on."

"Oh, yes?" she says. "You'll be telling me next you were only attracted to his mind."

That, among other things.

I couldn't relax in Alex Chapman's apartment yesterday.

I've always loved being there, always imagined that I'd like to live there myself if I were a Single Young Executive having dinners for one and glasses of chilled white wine on the patio.

But that was before I met him; when the flat was just an empty, clean flat that I quickly pretended to clean before getting on with the serious business of my writing. When I let myself in there yesterday, the whole place was changed forever—because although he doesn't live there, hasn't been in there for any length of time that would imprint his mark, his character, his soul upon the place—I still knew it was *his*. Perhaps he hasn't even furnished it. Perhaps his mother, or even his wife, has chosen some of the furniture, or the curtains, or the ornaments and pictures around the living room. But he must have walked through this door, turned on this light, picked up this phone, switched on this kettle. He must have picked up his mail from this carpet and sat in this armchair while he read it. He must have opened these wardrobe doors to take out clothes and pack them to take back home again.

He must have turned on the TV or radio to listen to the news. Which cup would he have used to drink his coffee? Which spoon? Would he take sugar or milk? I don't even know. I don't know the slightest thing about him, yet I'm beginning to obsess about his coffee cups, for fuck's sake.

Am I cracking up?

It took me longer than usual to do my cursory cleaning of the apartment, because I kept stopping to imagine him in this room or that room, doing this or that, looking like this or like that. I only ended up with about an hour to work on my script. Still thinking about Alex, wondering if he ever uses the computer himself, whether, for instance, he might turn it on quickly to check his e-mails while he's here collecting his mail and watering his plants and having a coffee . . . I logged on to the A: drive, got my disk out of my handbag and put it into the disk drive, opened the file of my potential masterpiece—and stared at it in horror.

Where was the work I'd saved the previous week?

If you've ever worked on a computer, especially on something creative, you'll know how I felt at that moment. I even forgot to fantasize about Alex Chapman's hand having held the mouse. My mouth went dry, my head felt faint. I couldn't have lost last week's work. Don't tell me that, please, please God—let it not be true. I'd written about two thousand words last week, two thousand words that I'd entrusted to a technology that I could never hope to understand; entrusted and then forgotten, confident that the technology would take care of it for me, keep it safe, and deliver it back to me on the screen by something akin to magic, next time I wanted it. I'd never be able to rewrite those two thousand words. I couldn't ever get the same words back from my brain, in the same order, with the same meaning, making the same story come together in the same way. Frantically, I took out the disk and put it back in again. Opened the file. There it was: everything I'd written up till last week, but not the last two thousand words. What had I done wrong? I never close down without saving my work. The program won't let you, anyway. Will it?

"Bloody hell!" I groaned out loud. "What have I done?"

I came out of the A: drive and clicked on MY DOCU-MENTS—and there on the screen was an icon for my script, with the same file name I'd given it on the A: drive. Holding my breath, I clicked on the icon and opened the file. Relief washed over me. The whole document, including last week's work, was there. I must have saved to the hard drive by mistake. I'd been in a rush when I closed down last week—I'd been running late and obviously wasn't concentrating.

Thank God for that.

I put the disk back in and resaved the whole document, before deleting it from the hard drive.

Not a good idea to leave my masterpiece on the computer's hard drive, especially as it's not my computer! But by then, what with the time I'd wasted fantasizing about Alex everywhere in the apartment, I hadn't really got enough time left to get into the business of writing, and I just abandoned the whole idea for once. I'll never get to be famous at this rate. See? He's not only invaded my thoughts and dreams and fantasies, he's stopping me becoming famous, too, and I only met him on Saturday.

"When do you want to take Tosser?" asks Dottie flatly, resting a hand on his head. He looks up at her lovingly and I wonder, not for the first time, whether he's suffering from a canine psychotic disorder.

"I suppose it'll have to be soon," I say, trying to

sound happy about it. "Do you want to keep him right up to the last minute, say good-bye to him just before you go?"

"No," she says firmly. "No, Beth, I want you to take him as soon as you're ready. I want to be able to go off to Australia knowing he's settled with you. It'd be a weight off my mind."

"Are you sure?"

I'm praying for a miracle here.

I'm praying that some long-lost relative's suddenly going to turn up on the doorstep, and Tosser's going to run to him or her with his tail wagging, barking joyfully, and everyone's going to agree he'd be better off with the L.L. relative than with me.

Or that Dottie's suddenly going to hear about a special service whereby beloved pets can be flown to Australia free of charge with all home comforts laid on, and reunited with their owners as soon as they walk through Customs.

"Yes, I'm sure," says Dottie, lifting her chin bravely. "It's for the best."

So much for the power of prayer.

The worst thing is that I haven't got much money left in my account. I won't get the money from Alex Chapman's mother, for yesterday's apparent cleaning, until I start at Park Cottage for the Patels, and they haven't phoned me yet to say when they want me to start. And I've got a red gas bill to pay.

"Here," says Dottie, going to her battered old brown leather purse. "Here's your money, Beth, and a bit extra—you'll be needing to get some food in ready for Tosser. Will that be enough to keep you going for now?"

Yes. It'll help toward the gas bill. But there won't be any left over for food for the hellhound.

I'll have to borrow a bit more from Ellie's savings.

I have lunch with Fay and we take the children to the park in the afternoon. It's a lovely sunny April day and the housebound mums are out in force, babies sitting up gurgling in strollers and toddlers running about on the grass with the urgency of young woodland creatures trying out their legs.

"We'll look back on days like this," says Fay wistfully, watching Ellie and Lauren racing each other toward the swings, "after they've started school."

"You'll still have Jack," I remind her.

Jack is toddling along beside us, helping to push his own stroller, seemingly contented for once. Perhaps by the time Lauren's gone to school he'll have grown into a nice little boy who can be good company for Fay.

"And you'll have got yourself a Proper Job," she says, even more wistfully.

"Don't count on it!" I sniff. "With my track record . . ."

"You will. And anyway, even if you go back to temping, you won't be around, will you."

We walk on, slowly, in silence. The girls have reached the swings and we can hear them squealing and giggling as they try to climb onto the seats, which are still too high for them.

"I missed you," says Fay. "When you weren't talking to me. I missed having you around during the day. I was lonely. I know I've got the kids, but . . ."

"We'll still see each other. When I'm back at work, we'll still have times together! I'll make sure of it."

She shakes her head. "It won't be that easy, Beth.

You'll be tired after you've been at work all day. You'll just want to collect Ellie and take her straight home."

"Weekends . . . holidays . . ."

"You'll be catching up on everything at home. And you'll want to spend time with Ellie." She sighs and shrugs. "It's inevitable. You'll make new friends at work. And I . . . won't."

"It's not inevitable!" I say crossly. Cross because I haven't thought about it before. Because I don't want to think about it now. Because she's making me feel guilty about something that hasn't even happened yet. Might never happen! "I haven't even started looking for a bloody job yet!"

"But you will. You know you will. You need the money. As soon as Ellie starts school—"

"And anyway," I interrupt, "it won't be that long, will it, before Jack's old enough to start playgroup, and then before you know it you'll have a bit more freedom yourself, too . . ."

"Maybe not," she says quietly.

"Maybe not what?"

"The freedom thing. I might not." She takes a deep breath. "I think I might be pregnant."

We help the girls up on to the swings and put Jack in a baby swing, then sit down on the bench.

"Fucking hell, Fay," I tell her. It's all I can think of to say. "Fucking hell."

"I know. I keep going into the pharmacy to buy a pregnancy test, but while I'm there waiting to buy it I convince myself that my period's just about to start and it's all just a false alarm."

"It might be, mightn't it? It still might be."

"I'm never this late. Never."

"Does he know? Have you told him?"

"He? Which one?"

"Oh. Fucking hell."

I suppose if I'm honest I'm a bit shocked about this. About two aspects of it. One is that she's still having sex with Simon. And that's absurd, really, isn't it? I mean, I seem to have accepted, now, despite my histrionics at the beginning of the whole thing, that she's having sex with this guy she's fallen madly in love with. I think I've even begun to sympathize a little bit, since meeting Alex Chapman and realizing it's perfectly possible to behave like a hyena in heat with a married man when you're in a relationship with someone else yourself. But I seem to have trouble accepting that she's going home from nights of illicit passion with Neil and jumping into her marital bed to do anything other than turn over and fall asleep.

"Simon *is* still my husband," she says piously. "I can't expect him to go completely without it."

No, I suppose not. And probably a good thing, too, come to think of it, or he might be forgiven for wondering how the baby got started.

If she is pregnant.

And that's the other thing I'm a bit shocked about.

How does an intelligent woman, who takes the Pill, risk getting pregnant by accident?

"Did you forget to take it?"

"No, I had an upset stomach. You remember—when the kids caught that bug that was going round the playgroup. I had a touch of it myself."

"Yes, but you know. You must know that puts you at risk for the Pill not being absorbed—that you're supposed to use something else for the rest of the month."

She must know. We talked about such things endlessly

when we were students. There wasn't a single aspect of sex or birth control that wasn't debated in depth, late into the night, during the course of the many and varied relationships we and our friends experimented with.

"I knew," she replied. "But knowing, and doing, are two different things aren't they. I kind of . . . presumed . . . it'd be OK."

"So there really is a risk. It's not just a missed period for some reason?"

"Beth, I really think I'm pregnant. I'm just putting off having it confirmed."

"And you really don't know whose it is?"

She smiles ruefully. "It's much more likely to be Neil's."

We look at each other silently for a minute. I can't imagine what she's thinking, what she's feeling. I just can't imagine.

"You know what?" she says, and I see a glitter of tears in her eyes.

I put my arms round her. "What?"

"I'm putting off having the test because I want it to be positive. And I want it to be Neil's. I want to have his baby."

What a mess. What a fucking mess. How do we women get ourselves into these states? Look at men. Look at the difference between our lives and theirs. They can spend their whole lives screwing around, if they want. As long as they don't die from AIDS or get some other terminally disastrous sexually transmitted disease, they never really need to give it a second's thought if they want to behave like complete bastards from puberty to old age. And yet it's us who seem to do all the suffering. It starts with periods from the age of about twelve (which always seems to me to be an unfair biological kick in the guts at an age when we ought still to be out playing in the park) and continues with regular monthly pain, inconvenience, mood swings, and assaults on our bodies—to say nothing of money thrown literally down the drain on sanitary products that aren't exactly top of the list of preferred retail therapy—through the indignities of pregnancy and the horrors of childbirth, the worry and exhaustion of motherhood, and finally culminating in nature's last little trick up its sleeve, a few years of hot flushes, sleeplessness, probably a bit of weight gain and depression for good measure, followed by loss of libido and slow decline into old age. Great. And we're the ones who tend to languish around, desperate for some man to come and have his few minutes of fun with us and leave us with all the problems.

What does Fay want with another baby?

Why would she want to have Neil's baby just because she's having *him*?

Why did she take that chance, risk having sex with him without using a condom when she knew it was possible she could get pregnant? These things aren't completely accidental, not in this day and age, not when there's still the last resort of the morning-after pill. Why didn't she even take that?

But I know the answer, know it with a certainty that's almost a primal instinct.

She wants his baby because she doesn't know whether she'll always have him.

The mess we get ourselves into doesn't always just happen to us. We often open the door and invite it in.

I dial *69 when I get home, in case Alex has phoned, but the number that comes up instead is Louise's. I call her back while I'm cooking Ellie's chicken nuggets and fries.

"Beth!" she yells into the phone, nearly making me drop the grill pan. "Where have you been?"

"With Fay. In the park. And back at her place. Why?"

"For God's sake! I've phoned you about twenty times! Have you seen Jodie?"

"Jodie?" I frown at the chicken nuggets sitting neatly on the grill pan. I seem to have missed something here. "Why should I have seen Jodie?"

"I don't know where she is!" Hysteria bubbles out of Louise in a series of gasping sobs. "Help me, Beth! She went out on her bike and she hasn't come back! What shall I do? Shall I call the police? She's been gone for ages! I've been out looking . . ."

The chicken nuggets roll off the grill pan onto the floor as I grab Ellie by the hand and run back out to the car.

"She's only ten!" Louise keeps saying as she paces up and down the living room.

Paces to the window, lifts the curtain, looks up and down the street, drops the curtain, paces back to the door again. "Only ten, for God's sake! What was I thinking about, letting her go out on her own?"

"She's old enough, Louise. You used to let her ride her bike around Park Farm. She's sensible. She won't have done anything silly . . ."

"So where is she?" she demands shrilly. "Why isn't she back? I told her to be back by five. I told her she wasn't to go out of this street. She doesn't know her way around here yet. For God's sake!" She looks at her watch for the hundredth time. "For God's sake!" she repeats, her voice wobbling.

Annie and Solomon sit, huddled closer together than usual on the sofa, silent and white-faced in the flickering light of the TV. I steer Louise out of their earshot.

"Do you think she might have tried to find her way back to the old house?"

"Tried that," she says curtly. "Tried that first. Called the Patels. And went round there. In case."

I nod. "What about friends from school?"

"Phoned all of them."

"OK."

I look at her in concern. She's shaking slightly. I don't want to talk about police yet. How soon do you do that? How soon does this stop being a worry, an anxiety, and start becoming a nightmare?

"You stay here," I tell her, trying to make her sit down with the children but getting my hand shaken off. "In case she suddenly turns up. I'm going to drive up and down every street systematically one more time. OK?"

She nods, still pacing, still lifting the curtains.

It's starting to get dark. I drive slowly, looking carefully on both sides of the road, my heart beating horribly right up in my throat.

"Please, God . . ." I pray silently, without knowing how to go on. Just: "Please, God," over and over.

And then, suddenly, there she is.

Three streets from home, she's sitting astride her bike under a lamppost, looking up and down the street as if she were lost.

She *is* lost.

She's ten years old and she's tried to be too clever, tried to find her way around her new neighborhood on her own, stayed out too long and got lost, that's all. Nothing sinister, nothing shocking or terrifying, just a little girl being disobedient and a bit adventurous.

But I'm crying with relief and her mother's having a nervous breakdown at home.

I screech to a halt, jump out of the car, and grab her by the arm, my relief turning to annoyance as soon as I start to speak.

"What on earth were you thinking of? Your mum's frantic with worry! Get in the car, now, quickly!"

I'm expecting the sullen face of grudging repentance, perhaps a little mortification, even a little gratitude for having been found.

I'm not expecting to be almost knocked over by a tight, desperate embrace.

"I was looking for you!" she splutters against my chest. "I couldn't find you. I couldn't find your street."

"Why?" I hold her away from me, looking with a new concern at her pinched and tired little face. "Why were you looking for my street, Jodie?"

"I wanted to see you. You, and Ellie. I wanted to come and talk to you."

"Mummy would have brought you, if you'd asked her. You've scared her to death."

"I didn't mean to. I didn't want Mummy to know. She hasn't got time to talk to me. I wanted to see *you*."

I put Jodie and her bike gently into the car, where Ellie's gawking at her from the backseat, the whole episode having reduced her to stupefied silence.

"Jodie," I tell her as we drive the short distance home. "You can come and see me and Ellie whenever you want. We'll show you the way, and you can come on your bike. It's not far. But you must tell Mummy. OK? That's got to be part of the deal, otherwise it's not allowed."

"OK," she says. "Sorry, Beth."

"No, say sorry to your mummy, not me."

I want to say a lot of stuff to her. Stuff about how much her mum loves her, and how she only seems like she hasn't got time for Jodie at the moment because she's so full of anxiety about her own life and its problems, and that if she knew Jodie wanted to talk to me, or anyone else, because she didn't think Louise had time for her, it would break her heart.

But instead I just take her back indoors to Louise, who's almost wailing with a mixture of relief and anger. The anger's going to take over, in a big way, as soon as the realization that she's safely home and nothing bad has happened to her has properly sunk in—and I take Ellie home before we can witness that happening. It's a family thing.

I hold Ellie closer, tighter, for longer than usual when I put her to bed tonight.

I close my eyes and try to imagine how I'd feel if anything were to happen to her, and my mind reels with horror, unable to contemplate it.

Nothing, nothing else in the world matters compared with this: not work, not money, not Daniel and his treachery, not Martin and his declaration of love, not even Alex Chapman, coming into my life to turn it all upside down and confusing.

I kiss the soft, smooth skin of Ellie's forehead and cheek as she lies down to sleep, and I can't even think of any words for the prayer I want to say, but it's there in my heart.

Any God worth having will know what I'm saying.

Thursday

❖━━━◦◦◦━━━❖

I didn't even think to check for phone calls again last night, so it's not until early this morning that I remember to dial *69, and a number, a local number, that I don't recognize has been left.

My heart gives a quick little jump and I tell it not to be so stupid. There are other people living in this town apart from Alex Chapman, you know. And even if it is him, so what? He said he was going to phone, didn't he, about tomorrow night, so what's the big deal?

I call the number back, telling my hand not to be so stupid for shaking while I'm dialing. Honestly, hands these days just won't stay under control properly.

But it isn't Alex Chapman who answers. It's Mrs. Patel from Park Cottage.

"Oh, Beth, how nice that you've phoned back!" she tells me brightly. "I thought I might have missed the chance of having you start this week."

"This week? Today? Would that be all right?" I ramble, desperate for the work, hoping I don't sound as desperate as I feel.

"Yes, of course, certainly. But I have to leave for work

by eight-fifteen. I don't suppose you'd be able to get here before then? I can give you a key for next time."

It's ten to eight. I phone Fay, getting her out of bed, throw some clothes on Ellie, who's too surprised and half-asleep to protest, and run her over to Fay's house with her breakfast cereal in a bowl on her lap.

"Sorry." I kiss her good-bye and wave my thanks at Fay, who's standing in the doorway in her dressing gown, yawning.

I wonder briefly if she's suffering from morning sickness and feel a momentary pang of guilt—but only momentary. No time for anything more.

It's strange going back to Park Cottage now it's someone else's house. The Patels are both doctors—Dr. Patel (Mr.) is a GP, who's already left for his morning surgery, and Dr. Patel (Mrs.) is a Senior House Officer in thoracic medicine at St. Joseph's Hospital. She tells me a bit about her job while she's putting on her coat and picking up all the bags and boxes of files and papers that she seems to need for treating people with sick chests.

"It's mostly old people with bronchitis and bronchopneumonia, and emphysema, and of course lung cancer," she says brightly.

"Oh." Lovely. "Don't you find it a bit . . . depressing?"

"No." She smiles, looking surprised. "It's just a job, you know, like anything else."

Not remotely like my job, really—although perhaps there are similarities between clearing out dirty sinks and clearing out dirty lungs, I don't know.

"Now, then," she says, looking quickly at her watch. "Will you be all right? You know where everything is, of course, and here's a key so you can let yourself in next time."

"Is there anything in particular you want me to do? Apart from the basics, hoovering, dusting, cleaning the kitchen and bathrooms?"

She looks even more surprised. "Well, I don't know," she says vaguely, her hand on the doorknob. "Whatever you think, really, Beth. Whatever you used to do when Louise was here. That'll be fine." She opens the door, starts to head for her car, and then turns back and adds, "Oh, I almost forgot. Your money's in the kitchen, by the kettle. And the money from the lady next door." She looks around her and continues in a lower voice, "Is it me, or is she a funny woman?"

"Yes." I laugh. "I think so, too. But I don't think she likes me very much."

"She seems to me to be the sort of person who doesn't like anyone very much."

"You're probably quite right, Dr. Patel."

"Oh, call me Rashma, for goodness sake! Look, I've got to run, Beth—if you have any problems today, leave me a note, or phone me tonight. OK?"

"Of course. Thanks, Rashma."

I think I'm going to like working for Rashma Patel. She's got the house looking nice already—not at all cluttered like it was when Louise and Ben were here, of course, but there are only the two of them. There aren't any children leaving toys and shoes and school things all over the place, or cats shedding hair everywhere and bringing in the occasional dead mouse. There are lots of books, most of them medical textbooks, but also loads of big books about the art of ancient Egypt and ancient Rome, Greek myths and legends, African civilizations, and the history of art. They've obviously only just been unpacked because they're stacked on the floor by the bookshelves, so when I've finished cleaning the living room I start arranging them on the shelves for her, and get so carried away looking at the Greek myths I almost forget to do upstairs.

If it wasn't for the fact that I'm still daydreaming about Greek and Roman gods, as I carry the Hoover upstairs, I might have heard her the first time. As it is, I'm in one of the back bedrooms when Mrs. Chapman shouts again, really loud, from her garden.

"Beth! Beth! Are you there?"

I nearly jump out of my skin.

I open the bedroom window and look out. It's pouring with rain, and Mrs. Chapman's getting washing off her line, throwing pegs into a bag and towels and sheets into a wicker laundry basket.

"Beth!" she hollers again, half turning back toward the house. She sees me looking out of the window and drops her voice a couple of hundred decibels. "Oh, there you are! Rashma's left some washing out, Beth. It's getting soaking wet."

"I'll come and get it in. Thanks."

I run back downstairs and pull on my jacket. I can't believe I didn't notice it start raining, but I also can't believe the awful Mrs. Chapman is actually being civilized and helpful. Or perhaps she just wants to make the point that I'm not paying attention to duty.

The rain's pelting down. I pull Rashma's wet washing off the line as quickly as I can but I'm still soaked through.

"Want a cup of coffee, Beth? I've just made one," calls Mrs. Chapman from her back door, having taken in all her own washing.

Now, this is getting seriously worrying. She's never been nice to me before. She's barely even spoken civilly to me before, and now I'm getting calls from the garden about the rain, and offers of cups of coffee, and all before half past ten!

I don't like to turn her down in case of offending her, but I feel uneasy about the whole thing. What if she tells Rashma I skive off work to have cozy chats over coffee? Perhaps this is a trap.

"I don't know if I ought to stop work . . ."

"Don't be silly. It's quicker than stopping to make your own coffee, isn't it?"

Well, put like that, I suppose so. I lock the back door of Park Cottage so she can't report back to Rashma that I'm lax with security, and go through the side gate, following Mrs. C into her kitchen.

"Well," she says, as she puts coffee and cookies in front of me on the kitchen table. "This is nice, isn't it?"

Is it? I'm not sure. I think it's a bit peculiar, actually, and quite surreal.

I stir my coffee, and nibble on a chocolate Hobnob, and wonder what the hell to talk about to this woman, who up till now seemed to regard me as a lower life-form and suddenly seems to want to act like my mother.

"So how are you getting on, Beth?" she asks as if she cares. "Plenty of work, eh? Plenty of nice cleaning jobs?"

She makes it sound like a little hobby I have. Something to do with myself, to keep me occupied while Ellie's at playgroup. A bit like voluntary work but with some payment thrown in.

"Well, not really," I admit. "It's a good thing Rashma wanted me to keep doing Park Cottage."

"Yes, must be nice for you."

We look at each other blankly over the coffee. This is awful, like one of those stilted conversations you have when the host at a party introduces you to someone and then goes off to get a drink and leaves you to it. *So, anyway, how long have you known John?*

In a minute perhaps she'll get to the point, whatever the point turns out to be. I can't believe she's invited me in here just to be friendly.

"And how are you getting on at my son's apartment?" she asks suddenly, flashing me a steely look and making me nearly choke on my coffee.

So this is it.

"Fine," I say cautiously. I put down my coffee cup and stare at the table, waiting.

"I hope he doesn't leave things in too much of a mess?" she says eventually.

I can feel her eyes on me, watching my reaction to this. I keep looking at the table. "No. No, it's fine."

What am I supposed to say?

Well, actually, no, he doesn't leave things in a mess at all. He doesn't make any mess because he doesn't live there, you see, he's living with his wife—yes, the wife you thought he'd separated from! Funny, that, isn't it! Ha! Yes, you pay me this money every week and I go to his apartment and sit around, amusing myself, using his computer, because there isn't any cleaning to be done, but nobody's bothered to tell you that!

I lower my head and frown into the dregs of my coffee. I feel as though I've been struck dumb. If I look up, she'll see guilt written all over my face.

"Would you like another coffee?" she asks in a charming tone.

I think she knows. She's got her suspicions, and all she has to do now is keep being nice to me and plying me with coffee and Hobnobs, and sooner or later I'll spill the beans.

"No, thank you." I push the empty cup aside and get to

my feet quickly, turning away before she can see my guilty face. "I really should get back next door and get on with my work."

"Very commendable." She smiles.

"Thank you very much," I mutter, trying to back out of the room without looking her in the eyes.

"My pleasure."

And I'm just about to make my escape when she adds, "We must make a habit of this, Beth. It's really quite silly, you working next door every week and us never having got to know each other."

"Yes," I say faintly.

"I insist that you make this a regular part of your routine. Let's say coffee at ten thirty?"

Let's. Coffee At Ten-Thirty.

"OK. If you . . ."

"I absolutely insist, Beth." She waves an arm at me graciously.

"See you next week, then."

I bolt out of the back door like a criminal on the run.

"Are you all right?" asks Louise.

We're sitting together in her living room, having a cup of tea before she goes to collect the children from their last day at their old school. She's just got back from work and I've just called in with Ellie, to see how things are with Jodie.

"I don't know. I had a really strange experience with Mrs. Chapman."

I recount my morning's experiences, beginning with a description of how Park Cottage looks under its new ownership, through to the rain and the washing and finally the inquisition over Coffee At Ten-Thirty.

Louise chuckles but I'm not amused.

"She's fishing for information about Oakleigh Court. She's going to keep feeding me coffee and cookies until I drop my guard and tell her something I shouldn't."

"Why should you worry? It's his problem, isn't it, if he can't even tell his mother about his domestic arrangements?"

"But it's my problem, too. If she finds out, she won't pay me anymore, and I won't be able to use his computer either. I think I'd rather not go to Park Cottage."

"You're joking, aren't you? Give up a good client like Rashma Patel, for what?"

I give her a sideways look. If she doesn't see "for what," then it's hard for me to explain to her.

The fact is that I don't want to do or say anything to risk upsetting Alex. If I keep having coffee with Mrs. C, it's going to get more and more difficult to fend off her questions. If I make excuses not to have coffee with her, I'm going to arouse her suspicions anyway. I know Louise is going to think I'm mad. I even think I quite possibly *am* mad. But I think I've made up my mind already that I'm not going back to Park Cottage.

"So how was Jodie last night?"

"Very contrite. I read her the riot act."

"I bet you did. Poor you, what a scare." I'm not sure how much to say. "She's going through it a bit, isn't she? About the move, and the change of school."

"I know. And I know I haven't given her the time she needs, to talk about it. I will, I will, but there's always something else pressing. I have to go to work, you know!" She says this in a slightly high-pitched voice, almost hysterically defensive. "I need the money now, more than ever. It's not as if I have any choice . . ."

"I know that. So do the kids. Nobody's trying to say . . ."

"I still love my kids. I still do what I can . . ."

"Of course you do! Louise, everyone knows that."

But her face has set hard.

"Better get over to the school now to pick them up."

"OK."

She lets us out of the front door and goes to her car, barely looking at me as she says good-bye, and I settle Ellie into my own car, wondering what I've said.

But of course, I haven't said anything. It's what's going on inside Louise's head that's upsetting her.

I've spent all the money Dottie gave me, which was supposed to be for stocking up on dog food ready for the arrival of the hellhound. I spent it on the gas bill and I've run out of milk, bread, butter and eggs, and soap, toilet rolls and cereals, to say nothing of getting any meat or vegetables—so the cleaning money from yesterday and today isn't going to go very far. And any day now, Luke's going to bring that bastard dog round to eat its way through my house, and probably my legs into the bargain, and I won't have so much as a tin of Chum in the place. There's nothing else for it, is there? I go to the post office and draw a bit more money out of Ellie's account, just enough to make up the difference between what the supermarket bill's going to be and what I had in my purse, and to stock up on some tins of Value Meaty Chunks ready for Tosser. He'll probably turn his nose up at them, having been used to a superior brand, but he'll have to eat it or go hungry. I also invest in an economy-size bag of Super Value Dog Biscuit Meal (Promotes Healthy Teeth). I'd really prefer something that promotes blunt teeth. Perhaps I can give him something to chew on that'll wear them down. Like a live grenade.

I know this is getting to be a habit—drawing out Ellie's money. But it's only when it's absolutely necessary, and it's only going to be very temporary. Once Dottie's house has been sold and I start getting the regular payments for having the dog, I could end up having money to spare if I play my cards right and only buy him the supermarket brands. It's really just a question of a short-term reallocation of funds. I might even pay it back with interest. So I don't feel bad about it now, not at all. In fact I don't even check the balance of the account. I think it's better not to, otherwise I might start worrying about it going down, and start panicking about paying the money back in, when in fact it's only going to be, as I say, a short-term loan with interest.

I talk about it a bit to Martin when he comes round later. I don't know why—I should know better, after the way he interfered the other night when I told him about Ellie being cheeky. It's none of his business. Anyone would think it was preying on my mind.

"So how much have you borrowed out of her account?" he asks.

"Not a lot," I say evasively. "Just little bits. Occasionally. Never very much."

"But all those little bits—they add up, don't they."

"Not to very much, though." I'm backtracking quickly now. Backtracking so fast I'm practically tripping over myself. "I've only done it once or twice. Hardly even a pound or two," I lie.

"You shouldn't have, though. You shouldn't touch her money, really."

"But it's only a short-term loan. I'll be paying it back in no time."

"Still, it's not a good idea, is it. It's Ellie's money. It should be earning interest for her."

I'm annoyed, now—annoyed with myself for telling him, as much as anything. "It is going to earn interest for her. I'll be paying it back with interest. What do you think—I'd cheat my own child out of her interest? I'll pay it back with *twice* the interest."

We've been sitting together on the sofa, watching the TV, his arm round me, my head on his shoulder, but I'm through with that. I'm on my feet now, moving around the room twitchily, straightening cushions and rearranging things unnecessarily on the shelf unit.

"You don't seem to realize," I tell him, "how difficult it is for me, at times."

"I do," he says. "Actually, I do."

"So what do you expect me to do? If I get a job, a proper job, before Ellie starts school, I'll have to pay someone to look after her. It wouldn't be fair to ask Fay to have her all day everyday . . ."

"I know. Beth, for Christ's sake, what are you getting aggressive with me about? I respect what you're doing. I admire you for managing the way you do—the fact that you prefer to be with Ellie until she starts school."

I sit back down on the sofa, on the edge, a bit stiffly, not looking at him. "So what am I supposed to do when there's nothing left in the bank?"

"Get some more money out of her father. You know where he lives now."

I have this sudden brief mental picture of Daniel, as he appeared on the doorstep of Melanie Waterstone's house. My heart constricts with an unexpected pain, that sharp stab of indigestion again, that always catches me out.

"Out of the question," I say curtly. "He's being supported by . . . that woman."

There's a silence. I want to change the subject, but feel too cross now to think about anything pleasant to talk about. I pick up the remote control and change channels twice, looking for something interesting.

"You should have told me," says Martin quietly.

"Told you what?"

"That you were having money problems."

"Martin, I'm always having money problems. It's my normal state. I'm used to it. If I started whining to you about it you'd be sick of listening to me within a week."

"I wouldn't. That's not fair. I'll always listen to you."

"So what would you have said? If I'd told you I didn't have the money for the gas bill, apart from advising me to ask Daniel for the money and not to borrow it from Ellie's account, what would you have come up with? Buying a Lottery ticket? Selling the furniture? Gambling?"

"Borrowing it from me," he says.

I look at him quickly to see if he's joking.

I mean, he's a nurse—they're not renowned for their high salaries, are they? And he has his own rent and everything to pay, his bills, his car, his food, and so on; I don't think he's exactly well off himself.

"I wouldn't dream of it," I tell him when I see he's serious.

"Well, you should. I'm upset, to be honest, Beth, that you haven't asked me to help. I thought we were pretty close by now . . ." He pauses, looks at me for confirmation but I just wait for him to carry on. "And I thought it would have been the most natural thing in the world for you to turn to me if you were in trouble."

I don't know what to say to this.

Don't know, because as far as I'm concerned it isn't natural at all. Just because we're lovers, just because we're having a relationship, doesn't mean I have to start *relying* on him. It doesn't mean my finances have anything to do with him, or his finances have anything to do with me.

"But I wouldn't . . . I wouldn't even ask *Fay* to help me out," I tell him. "Unless it was a matter of life or death."

There's a serious implication in what I'm saying here. I'm not aware of it until the words are out of my mouth and I see the reaction in his eyes—a sudden flinch, as if my words were arrows aimed straight at him.

"Not *even* Fay," he repeats slowly.

I shake my head.

"And certainly not me."

Sorry. I just shake my head again.

"I see," he says.

Well, that certainly cleared the air, didn't it?

We sit in an awkward sort of bristly, half-polite state for a little while longer pretending to watch the TV, him at one end of the sofa and me at the other. I know what he's doing. He wants to leave, because I've hurt him and offended him, and he wants to sort of creep off and lick his wounds on his own. But he doesn't want me to think that's what he's doing, so he's staying just long enough to make it look like he's being mature and decent about the whole thing, that it's all settled down and blown over and oh, guess what—he's just remembered he's got to leave early tonight.

I ask him if he wants a coffee but he says, "No, thank you," very politely and goes back to watching the very interesting documentary about the life cycle of Amazonian frogs.

I ask him if we should perhaps switch channels again and he says it's up to me.

I wonder about asking him if he wants a quick shag but perhaps it's not a good idea.

And just as he starts looking at his watch and putting his face into the right position for surprised exclamation that time has flown and he needs to get going, the phone rings, and it's Alex.

"Hi!" I say, and my legs go weak at the sound of his voice. "Hi, Fay!"

"Fay?" says Alex. "Who's Fay?"

"Listen, Fay—can I give you a call back later?" My hand's sweating holding the phone. Does my voice sound as shaky as it feels?

"You're not alone?" says Alex.

"That's right. We'll have a chat later. OK?"

"If it's difficult I'll call you tomorrow."

"No problem. Speak to you later. Bye now!"

I put down the phone and take a couple of deep breaths before I turn back to Martin. He's on his feet, putting on his jacket. "You didn't have to do that on my account," he says, in a tight, strained voice. "You could have talked to Fay. I was just going anyway."

"You don't have to go yet. It's not even ten o'clock."

I feel like shit now. I feel like shit because I've not only hurt his feelings, although I didn't mean to, for God's sake—he shouldn't be so touchy—but now, despite what I'm saying, I really can't wait for him to go so I can get straight back on the phone to Alex. I want it so much I've got my fists clenched behind my back.

"I've got things I need to do tonight," lies Martin, who's off home to sulk and feel sorry for himself about me wanting to borrow money from him even less than I want to borrow it from my best friend.

"Well, if you insist."

I don't think I sound very convincing. But I don't think I can be doing this. I'd like to be honest and just tell him to piss off and come back when he's got over it. But, as I say, I feel like shit.

And then, just to make it worse—

"Can I see you tomorrow?" he asks as he's leaving.

I gape at him, mouth open like a goldfish.

Tomorrow? Not tomorrow!

"I thought we might go out for a drink or something," he says. "Fay would have Ellie for the evening, wouldn't she?"

"Oh," I say, goldfish-like. "Tomorrow?" I'm playing for time now. "Tomorrow's Friday, isn't it?"

"Yes—is that a problem?"

"I think Fay's doing something . . ."

"Oh, well. Not to worry, then. Shall I just come over, instead?"

"Oh! No—what I mean is, I think Fay's *arranging* something—you know, for me and her. To go out together. That's probably what she phoned about, in fact! I promised to go out with her tomorrow."

"Would you like me to look after Ellie, then?"

I can't bear this. I've hurt his feelings so much that he's going home early, I'm lying to him and I'm about to see someone else behind his back, and he's offering to *babysit* for me.

"It's all right. She's staying over with Lauren. Simon doesn't mind."

He nods, looking sad but brave. "Perhaps Saturday, then?"

"Yes!" I say brightly. "I'll phone you."

He gives me a quick, husbandly sort of kiss and leaves.

And I feel, now, like the biggest piece of shit in the whole universe.

But it doesn't stop me getting straight on the phone to Alex the minute Martin's car's out of sight down the road. And this time I sit down first, and close my eyes so that I can concentrate on his voice better, and picture how he looks while he's talking, and get hold of a cushion so that I can squeeze it tight and imagine it's him I'm holding in my arms. And long after we've made the arrangements for tomorrow night and hung up I lie on the sofa, still holding the phone, my eyes still closed, thinking about how it's going to feel to see him again.

And about how the hell I approach Fay with this one.

Friday

———◆◦◆◦◆———

"Can I ask you something?"

I've never felt the need to approach Fay like this before, in this polite, apprehensive way, as if I think she'd say no.

That's because I think she might.

And I don't blame her.

She looks at me strangely. "Of course you can ask me anything you want, you daft cow. Why are you looking so shifty about it?"

"Because I feel embarrassed asking you."

She looks at me more closely, frowning now, waiting. "Go ahead."

"Would you have Ellie for me tonight, and . . ."

"You know I would, but . . . I'm going out."

"You're seeing Neil?"

She nods. "It's our regular night now. Simon thinks I meet a crowd of friends."

She gives me a quick, appraising look. Can she talk about this, she's thinking. Am I OK with it? Am I going to disapprove?

Am I in any position to disapprove, now?

"Shall I ask Simon to have Ellie stay over?" she offers. "He won't mind."

"Yes, please, Fay. That'd be great. But the other thing is . . ." I hesitate again.

She gives me a sudden, knowing smile. "Oh, yes. That's right. You're seeing *him*, aren't you."

"Yes."

A flutter of excitement at the thought of it, even now, even while I'm negotiating a delicate test of my restored friendship with Fay.

I'm unsure how to go on, but she beats me to it. "You want me to pretend we're going out together? That's what you've told Martin?"

I can't meet her eyes. "I know what you must think. After the fuss I made about you, and Neil . . ."

She laughs. "Oh, come on, Beth—that's ancient history. And I'm hardly likely to raise moral objections, am I, when I'm going out with Neil myself tonight."

"Thanks, Fay. I . . . feel really bad about it. But I've just got to see him—this once—and get things straight in my head."

"I don't know why you should feel guilty. You're not married. You're not committed to anyone. You can see whoever you like. *His* marriage is his own problem."

"But Martin seems to be so serious about this relationship already. I don't want to hurt his feelings."

"But you will," says Fay with a shrug. "You will, sooner or later."

"Why do you say that?"

"Because you're not in love with him."

She hasn't done the pregnancy test yet. She's bought the kit, now, and it's in her bathroom cupboard. She shows it to me. We both stand there, in her bathroom, looking at it.

"Go on, then," I say.

"No, I can't. I just can't."

"You need to know."

"I think I know already."

"But you need to confirm it. Come on, do it now, while I'm here."

"No, I think I want to be on my own."

"All right, then. Later. Give me a ring. Yeah?"

"OK."

She puts the box back in the cabinet.

I don't think she's going to do it later.

I have a mental picture of her, large and happily pregnant with (presumably) Neil's child, going about her life, looking after Simon's kids and looking after Simon, knowing that she's living out the biggest lie any woman can ever tell.

Darling, wonderful news, I'm pregnant again!

Darling! Wonderful! I'm so happy! A little brother or sister for Lauren and Jack! Another few years of sleepless nights and dirty nappies! Another lifetime sentence of care and anxiety! Another eighteen years of financial burden!

And darling, you'll never believe the best bit.

You're not even the father.

"What if he finds out?"

"He won't," she says, quickly, sharply. Snaps the lid down firmly on any further discussion.

"If he suspects? If the baby looks nothing like him?" I persist.

"Babies often don't look like their fathers. They can be genetic throwbacks."

"You'd deny it? You'd keep on denying it, over and over again, all the rest of your life, every time it comes up?"

"Absolutely," she says, her mouth firm, her eyes hard as steel.

She's probably thought about nothing else since her period was one day late. Who am I to wonder? Who am I to cast doubt on her certainty?

Jesus, life can be a bitch.

Since my promising new client turned out to be Daniel's girlfriend, I now have something of a hiatus in my weekly agenda on a Friday. The ad in the post office doesn't seem to have brought forth a flood of eager enquiries. How can that be? In a town with a population of at least a hundred thousand people, one person responds to my ad, and it has to be her. I think I must be cursed.

We pick up the girls from playgroup, and Fay says she needs to get home to do some housework. Perhaps she's going to do the pregnancy test. Or perhaps she's going to spend all afternoon getting ready for her evening with Neil.

I feel twitchy and unsettled. I don't want to go home to do housework. I don't know what's the matter with me. Probably I'm feeling guilty and anxious about upsetting Martin last night.

"Why can't I go and play with Lauren?" whines Ellie, kicking her feet against the car seat on the way home.

"You're going round there this evening. For a sleep-over," I add for good measure.

That should satisfy her.

"I want to go *now*," she retorts.

Kids these days get their own way too much. It isn't good for them. They need firm boundaries.

"Well, you can't. We're going home, and you're going to help me with the housework like a big girl."

"I'm *not*! I *hate* housework! I hate *you*!" She kicks the back of my seat, hard, making me jump and crunch the gears as I approach a roundabout.

"Ellie, don't kick! That could have been very, very dangerous—you must *not* do that while I'm driving! That's very naughty and you've made me very cross!"

She starts to cry, noisily, giving the occasional soft little prod to the back of my seat, which is her way of trying to be defiant without quite having the courage to do so.

I mustn't give in to this.

It's emotional blackmail.

If I'm not careful she'll have me feeling like Attila the Hun, and I'll be pulling over, apologizing for telling her off and offering to take her round to play with Lauren every time she clicks her fingers.

This is how children get to be nasty spoilt little brats, grow up to be juvenile delinquents, go off the rails, end up in young offenders' institutes, and die nasty premature deaths from heroin overdoses.

"I'm not taking any notice of you," I tell her calmly.

"I hate you!" she sobs.

Did I ever tell my mother I hated her when I was Ellie's age? I suppose I wouldn't remember, now, but it does seem unlikely that she would have let me get away with it. How did Ellie learn to say things like that? I've never told her I hated anyone. Where has she heard it? It can only be the television, can't it.

That's it. She's not watching any more television.

"You're not watching any television today," I tell her, my voice wobbling a bit with a mixture of feeling cross with her and feeling upset that she hates me.

There. That'll shut her up.

"Don't care!" she shouts at the back of my head. "I hate you!"

* * *

We're not going to Fay's.

I don't care how much she screams, she's not getting her own way.

I'm not having her turn into a heroin addict.

When we pull up at Louise's house, Ellie gives a hiccup of surprise and stops yelling.

"Why are we here?" she asks in a hoarse voice.

Because you've tried my patience so badly and upset me so much with all your screaming about hating me, I couldn't bear the thought of taking you home yet.

"Because I want to talk to Louise," I offer lamely.

I've wimped out. OK, so I haven't brought her to play with Lauren, but . . .

"Can I play with Jodie and Annie and Solomon?" The voice is rising with excitement. What about all that hatred, eh? Suddenly forgotten? Oh, the inconsistencies of childhood!

"If they're home. If it's convenient. And if you start behaving nicely." And oh, the inconsistencies of parenthood, hiding behind a facade of sense and reason!

I'm giving in to her, and she knows it. I'm pretending I'm not, and she's playing along with it.

"Yes, Mummy." Butter wouldn't melt in the mouth. "I will be good, Mummy!"

Climbs out of the car, eyes red, face puffy from the crying tantrum, straightens her hair and her socks like a teenager on a date, smiles at me sweetly and offers me her hand to hold (wet with wiped-up tears and snot), and I smile back with the benevolent patience of the all-forgiving mother.

Another scene behind us, and so we move on—I pretending, she learning to act.

This is how we teach our children the subtleties of life.

* * *

It's the first day of the Easter holiday for Louise's kids—their last holiday before they start at the local primary school.

Annie and Solomon are playing a noisy and raucous game upstairs in Solomon's bedroom. Jodie's lying on the floor in front of the TV, with her legs in the air, looking at her feet.

"I hate my toes," she says in response to my greeting.

"What's wrong with them? They look normal," I tell her.

"They're fat, and sausagey. And my legs are disgusting. How can I get my legs thinner, Beth?"

"Jodie, your legs are lovely. They're not fat. Who's told you your toes and your legs are fat?"

"No one. They just are. I try to do these exercises I saw in *Kiss*"—she points to a lurid pink-covered preteen magazine lying on the sofa—"and it says you can get thin legs and firm up your bum if you practice them regularly."

Ellie's rooted to the spot, thumb in mouth, staring at Jodie in serious amazement, and I don't blame her.

"You do *not* need to do any of that, Jodie!" I tell her quite sternly. "You get quite enough exercise with all your running around, playing sports, riding your bike, swimming and—"

"But I think I need to cut out butter and cheese . . ."

"Does Mummy know you've got all these ideas in your head?"

"She just tells me off and says I have to eat what she gives me." She brings her legs down to the floor with a thump and looks round at Ellie. "Do you want to watch TV with me?" she asks Ellie with great gentleness, holding out her arms to her.

Ellie goes to her and sits down, half on her lap, leaning against her and still sucking her thumb, and Jodie strokes her hair and kisses the top of her head, and I suddenly feel such a strange urge to cry that I have to leave the room and find Louise in the kitchen. She's still sorting out the cupboards and packing things away out of boxes. She's taken most of her annual holiday so that she can be here with the kids for the Easter break and while they settle into their new school.

The au pair had to go.

"I don't know what I'm going to do about the six weeks in the summer," she says now, leaning against the kitchen worktop and pushing her hair out of her eyes. She looks so tired and defeated, I just put my arms round her and hold her.

I was going to talk to her about Jodie and her legs, but I can't add to her worries.

And then I suddenly find myself saying it.

It's been in my mind, of course, buzzing away there in the background, all the time, sort of waiting in the wings, daring me to push it out onto the stage. And now it's heard its cue, there's no holding it back.

"I'll look after them," says my voice, coming out of my throat without my permission, without engaging my brain. "I haven't got a job, have I. There's only Tuesdays left now."

I think about Tuesdays. I think about working in Alex Chapman's flat, fantasizing about him while I'm supposed to be doing his unnecessary hoovering, working on my script while I'm supposed to be doing his unnecessary dusting, and I suddenly feel hot with shame for taking his money. Now that I've met him; now that I . . . like him . . . I don't know if I can go on doing it. I don't know if I can keep up the dishonesty much longer.

"And I'm not even sure about Tuesdays," I add, half to myself. "So I might as well look after your kids, as well as Ellie. It'll keep her amused."

Louise looks at me with eyes that want to cry but can't even work up the energy. "But I can't pay you," she whispers.

"It doesn't matter. Some day, you might be able to return the favor."

"I can't. It's too much. I can't let you . . ."

"It's what friends do," I tell her, and I mean it, I really mean it. "It's what friends are all about."

I'm thinking about Fay now, and how she's looked after Ellie for me for all this time without taking any payment. She might not be able to go on doing it if she's really going to have another baby. Even if I had any cleaning jobs left, I could be stuck for a babysitter.

I feel a shiver of anxiety.

I need to make some money.

I need to start listening to my mother, start looking at ads and Web sites and employment agencies. I need a job lined up for September, after Ellie starts school and Louise's children go back. But before that, I need some way of earning from home—and I need it desperately quickly. What have I been doing? What have I been thinking about, shilly-shallying around with a little bit of cleaning here and there and a promise of some dog-fostering payments? It just isn't enough. Any fool can see it isn't enough.

Any fool can see why I've been spending Ellie's savings.

And it's Friday night now, and I'm going out with Alex Chapman. I've taken Ellie to stay the night with Lauren, and I've spent an hour arguing with the inside of my wardrobe about what suits me, what makes me look fat, what makes me look tarty and desperate, what makes me look too casual and what makes me look too serious. I hate this. I hate everything about it—the adrenalin rush that makes you start getting ready two hours earlier than you need to; that makes you run a nice warm scented bath to relax in, but then makes you unable to sit and relax in it because you're too nervous and twitchy; that makes you mess up your mascara and have to do it all over again, hand shaking like you're an inexperienced fourteen-year-old on her first date . . .

That's what I feel like.

Christ!

That's *just* what I feel like. Is there never any respite? Never any relief from the onslaught of our hormones? Is this going to go on for the rest of my life? Every time I go to meet a new man, even when I'm fifty, even when I'm sixty or seventy or eighty, am I going to be carried back in time to this gawky, trembling, socially inept teenager still lurking within my soul, never having grown up, never having gained any confidence or maturity or poise in all the intervening years that will stand me in any stead when faced with this most petrifying, disabling situation in life—a date with someone important?

And why is it important anyway?

As I drive into town to meet Alex I keep lecturing myself. There's nothing particularly important about this. It's just an unimportant little meeting with someone completely unimportant, to discuss a few unimportant little things. I check my mascara in the rearview mirror for the twenty-fifth time and wonder again about my hair. Probably should have used less mousse. And is that a *spot* by my nose? Should I pull over and check?

I make it, somehow, to the parking lot next to the wine bar, and sit in the car for ten minutes trying to pluck up the courage to get out of the car and walk inside. Just as I finally take a deep breath and open the car door, having a last check in the mirror as I slide out of the seat, a voice in my ear says, "I thought you were going to sit there all night."

"Alex!"

I feel myself going hot. I stumble to my feet, catching the heel of my too-high shoes in the hem of my too-long too-wide trousers, and flush even hotter as he takes my arm to steady me.

And he's smiling at me. I don't think I can cope with the way he's smiling at me.

"I was sitting at that table in the window." He nods toward the wine bar. "I saw you arrive."

Ten minutes and forty mirror checks ago.

"I thought perhaps you were worried about coming in on your own."

What, me? Veteran of hundreds of student pub crawls, survivor of dozens of impromptu flat-share parties, regular customer of late-night Accident & Emergency sessions with serial groups of friends in various states of alcohol-induced injury—me, suddenly reduced to a status of pitiful shrinking timorous femininity at the thought of walking into a licensed establishment without the supportive arm of a man to lean on?

"I was," I simper. "Just a bit."

He smiles again. He doesn't believe me, but it doesn't matter. He offers me his hand, and I hold it, feeling a thrill like an electric shock shooting up my arm.

This is crazy.

It's crazy, and it's unimportant.

Unimportant that he stares into my eyes like he's going to hypnotize me while he's asking what I want to drink.

Unimportant that he brushes my hand with his when

he passes me the glass, and both our hands shake, and the wine slops over the bar in a pool of bright crimson shock.

Unimportant that we both start to speak together, and we both stop, and stare at each other, and try to start again, and get so flummoxed we have to go and sit down at his table in the window and sip our wine and frown at the table as if we don't really want to talk to each other at all.

It really doesn't mean a thing.

I don't know what I'm getting so worked up about.

"There are some things," he says at length, "that I need to tell you."

Did I imagine it or did he take a deep breath before he said that? I take one myself, now. I'm trying hard to pull myself together.

"OK," I say. "OK, what are the things?"

"When you come to clean my flat—"

I knew it. I knew it, knew it, knew it.

"Yes," I interrupt him. There's no point in him going any further. "Yes, I know. There isn't really anything for me to do. The flat's clean already. I'm sorry. It's dishonest of me to keep taking your money when it doesn't need cleaning."

He puts out a hand, rests it on mine, shakes his head to stop me.

His hand feels like it's burning my flesh. I'll probably have a scorch mark when he takes it away. But I don't want him to take it away. Impulsively, I put my other hand over his, resting it there, resisting the urge to stroke, to pet, to pat, just resting it, and then suddenly he brings his other hand across the table, too, and we're both gripping each other's hands, not saying anything, just sitting there gripping as if we're both drowning and there's nothing else to hold on to.

And actually that's just what it feels like.

"I don't care about the money, or the cleaning, for God's sake," he says. "Stop the cleaning. It doesn't matter. What I have to tell you is—I know about your writing. The script. You left it on the hard drive the other week. I saw it when I checked my e-mails."

I stop gripping and use one hand to cover as much of the embarrassment on my face as possible. "I'm sorry." My voice sounds feeble and silly. "I'm so sorry—I should never have . . . I had no business using your computer, and without even asking, while you were *paying* me! And not even doing any cleaning . . ."

Should I offer now to pay for the electricity? Offer to pay back all the wages he's been giving me? How the hell can I afford to do that? And why's he smiling at me?

"Don't be sorry. I really owe *you* an apology." He pauses, looking at me very seriously now. "I read it."

"The script?"

Anyone who's ever had any aspirations as a writer will understand my next question. Despite everything, despite being indisputably at fault in this whole situation, I just have to know.

"What did you think of it?"

"I think it's brilliant. I think it's clever, and funny, and I think when it's finished it ought to be read by a publisher."

I can't keep the smile off my face.

"And so does Sarah," he adds.

There goes the smile.

Sarah! Fucking Sarah!

Why does she keep coming into it?

What sort of a man takes a girl out for a drink, looks into her eyes as if he's never seen anyone in his whole life that he wants so much, stammers and shakes when he talks to her, touches her with hands that burn her flesh, grips her like he's a drowning man, and then calmly discusses his wife?

"What's it got to do with her?" I can't keep the moody tone out of my voice. "Why did you show it to your wife?"

He starts to laugh, very softly. He takes my hands again across the table, but gently this time, holding my fingers as if they were silk and might crease.

"I've given you the wrong impression," he says. "Sarah and I might still be married—but only in name. Only on paper."

"But you said . . ."

"I think I told you we've stayed together. We have. When we decided to separate, I got myself the flat in Oakleigh Court."

"But you didn't move in? Why?"

He shrugs. "She wanted me to give it another go. So I agreed to go back."

"But you still had to pay for your own flat! And why did your mother think you were living there?"

"She'd cause trouble if she found out I'd backed down and gone back to Sarah. It was easier to avoid telling her."

"You're frightened of your mother?" I ask him.

It's certainly true she's scary. But, for God's sake—he's her son!

"No, it's just . . ." He sighs and fiddles with his wine-glass, and then, finally, meets my eyes and blurts it out. "She helped me through a really rough time when Sarah and I split up. I had a . . . kind of breakdown. So she blames Sarah."

Mother's loyalty. I suppose mine would be the same if I said I was going back to Daniel. She refers to him as The Pig.

"So you still haven't plucked up the courage to tell her you've got back together?"

"I know it sounds pathetic." He shrugs. "But I was protecting myself, too. I didn't know how long it would last. Sometimes I think Sarah only wanted me back to fix the boiler and mend her car."

He's still looking straight at me.

"I don't think she loves me at all," he says quietly.

"She sounds pretty selfish," I say indignantly. The cow! The unbelievably ungrateful cow—how can she not love him!? How can she not appreciate her unbelievable fucking luck, living with him, being married to him?! "I can't imagine why you've gone along with it!" I continue hotly. "I can't see what's in it for you . . ."

"Can't you?" he says simply.

"You're still in love with her? You're hoping it might change, it might be better this time?"

"I was," he corrects me.

"And now?" I hold my breath. It hurts, somewhere in the middle of my chest.

"Suddenly," he says, and I'm letting the breath go, little by little, as he watches me across the top of his wineglass, "suddenly I seem to be over her."

I ask, having to raise my voice above the furious noise of a symphony being played at high volume by a full orchestra complete with drums and harps inside my head, "So what's it got to do with Sarah—my script?"

"She's an agent." He smiles at me. "A literary agent. She specializes in TV and film work. And she's seriously interested."

Saturday

<hr>

"And . . . ?" says Fay.

We're having a coffee in Tesco's coffee shop. Simon offered to keep the kids for a couple more hours this morning while we both do our shopping.

"And what?"

"Come on, for God's sake, what happened? You and Alex? Did you or didn't you?"

"Fay! I'm telling you about my *script*! This Sarah, his . . ." (I hate to say it) ". . . his *wife*, she's a literary agent, and she's interested, she thinks it shows potential, she thinks it's funny and bright."

"I know, I know, it's great, but did you kiss him?"

"Honestly, can't you think about anything else?"

"You did, didn't you!" she squeals, almost dropping her coffee cup. "Did you . . ." She looks at me, narrowing her eyes, and I have to look away. I fiddle with my purse, pretending to be looking for my shopping list.

"You slept with him, didn't you!" she says excitedly, in such a loud stage-whisper that two elderly women at the next table look round with their eyebrows raised so far into their perms that their glasses fall down their noses. "You did, didn't you?"

"I didn't *mean* to," I start defensively, but I can't help it. I can't help myself. The smile is spreading across my face like a rash. Just thinking about it, I want to jump up from the table, climb onto my chair, dance and throw my arms around, punch the air, shout aloud at the top of my voice, "Yes! I slept with him! It was wonderful! It was absolutely fucking wonderful and I want to do it again! I want to keep on doing it for the rest of my life!"

And I think I'm in love.

"I think I'm in love," I tell her, still grinning like a demented Cheshire cat. "I know it's stupid . . ."

"No," she says, smiling back. "Why should it be stupid?"

"I hardly know him."

But I feel as if I do.

"We've only just met."

But it seems like we've always known each other.

"It must just be . . . a physical thing."

But it feels much more. So much, much more I can hardly contain it. Hardly contain myself.

"Don't try," says Fay. "Don't try to analyze it, rationalize it—it won't work. Just enjoy it. Bloody good luck to you, Beth—just enjoy it, and go with the flow." She sounds sad.

"Is this how you felt—when you met Neil?"

She nods.

"And I was so dismissive," I admit. "I thought it was all bollocks. I remember saying that to you."

"Perhaps you were right. Who knows?"

"What's the matter?"

She shakes her head. "Nothing. I'm just saying: live for today, enjoy it, make the most of it. But it may not last forever."

"Is something wrong? Between you and Neil?"

"Perhaps."

I reach out for her hand. I feel a quiver of fear around my heart. I don't want her to be hurt. But how can she not be? How can she not be hurt—one day, if not now, if not yet?

"Tell me," I say gently.

"Nothing to tell, yet," she responds a bit brusquely.

"Have you done the pregnancy test?"

She shakes her head.

"Fay—why? Why are you putting it off?"

"Neil," she whispers hoarsely, looking down at the table. "He doesn't want . . ." She swallows and rubs her eyes. She can't finish the sentence.

But she doesn't have to.

Ellie plays with her toys downstairs while I make the bed.

It takes me a long time to do it.

Every shake of the pillows, every smoothing out of every crease in the sheet, reminds me of Alex. The bedroom still smells of him. I don't want to open the windows and lose the memory.

It reminds me of the first time I ever had sex—the way I felt, afterward, that I'd never be the same, that I was in some way changed forever, that everyone looking at me could see that I was now this different person. But this second new me, this experienced and adult version—having brought all my previous sexual experiences, all my huge and devastated love for Daniel, all the crushes and infatuations and flings and one-night stands of my teenage years, all my fantasies about Nasty Oliver and all my warm and grateful feelings for Martin into this bed with me last night, and having, in one wild and passionate night of unbelievable love, reduced the lot of them to the ashes of the past—this new me is something different again, something so amazing and confident and happy and *sure* that I find myself standing up taller, walking straighter, looking myself in the eye in the mirror and liking what I see. I feel alive, vibrant, brave, poised on the edge of something marvellous.

And is it going to last?

I think about Fay and I shake my head at myself in the mirror. I'm not going to wonder. I'm not going to spoil it by wondering that.

And what am I going to do about Martin?

The brave new me looks back at me accusingly out of the mirror and I avoid my own eyes.

Don't want to have to face up to this one, then?

Not as brave as you think you are?

I phone him later this afternoon. "Come round for dinner," I say.

Can he hear the new vibrancy and confidence in my voice? Do I sound, immediately, like someone who's spent the night in bed with a wonderful new lover? Can he tell?

"I'll cook something special," I tell him quickly, desperate to make up to him for what I know I'm going to have to do.

Like ordering the condemned man his last favorite meal.

"Lovely," he says. "I'll bring a video."

We may not get that far.

Louise phones me a little later. She sounds worried. "It's Jodie," she says. "I don't know what's the matter with her."

"What? Is she ill?"

"I don't know. She won't eat. Oh—I don't just mean the normal way kids won't eat, fussy stuff about not liking this and not wanting anything at the minute—it's not liking *anything* and not wanting anything at *any* time."

"How long has it been going on?"

"Only a couple of days. But all she's doing is lying around, on her bed or on the floor, rolling around . . ."

"Has she said anything to you about her legs?"

"Her legs? What on earth have her legs got to do with it?"

"I just wondered." I'm reluctant to tell Louise that her daughter has confided something in me rather than her. "You know how some girls get obsessive about their weight, their body shape . . ."

"Beth, she's ten years old!"

"Yes, exactly."

It's not her fault, but Louise has been so caught up with her own problems, she hasn't noticed something significant about her own child.

"She's growing up, Louise. She's on the verge of puberty."

"At *ten*!"

"It's not unusual."

There's a silence while this sinks in. I half expect the phone to be slammed down. I think I'd be upset if it were me—indignant, defensive, feeling inadequate as a mother because someone else had pointed out something so important to me that I should have realized for myself.

But instead, she says, quietly, "Do you really think that's what's wrong with her?"

"She's been a bit moody, hasn't she."

"Well, yes, but I thought it was all because of the move. The girls at the old school being bitchy. I was hoping it'd all settle down when she makes new friends at the new school."

"I'm sure it will, Louise. You're right, I'm sure—she'd have been fine if it wasn't for all the upheaval of the move. But talk to her about her legs anyway."

"Her *legs*, for Christ's sake?! Her legs are lovely."

"Just keep telling her that! For the next thirty years, if necessary!"

She laughs ruefully. "Poor kid, having to grow up. And poor us, Beth, having daughters to get through it all. Were we this much trouble to our own mums?"

"I think I still am," I admit. "Mine tells me all the time how much she worries about me."

Martin arrives at eight o'clock on the dot, with a bottle of red wine and a copy of *Sleepless in Seattle*. "It's romantic," he tells me unnecessarily, putting it on top of the VCR ready for later.

I've seen it before, but it doesn't matter.

"I haven't gotten very far with the dinner yet," I apologize. "I've only just got Ellie to sleep."

"It's OK. I'll give you a hand." He starts cutting up chicken for stir-frying while I root around in the cupboard for rice. "Did you have a nice time last night?"

I drop the rice, spilling half of it all over the floor. My hands are shaking as I try to sweep it up.

A nice time last night? Images of Alex flash through my mind like a series of electric shocks. Alex leaning toward me in the wine bar, touching my cheek, touching my lips, whispering my name. Alex and I getting into my car to come home together, leaving his at the wine bar to pick up in the morning, not looking at each other as we fasten our seat belts, as I put the key in the ignition, until he suddenly reaches over, his arm round my neck, and finally kisses me for the first time, sparks seeming to fly from our lips, heat engulfing my body, excitement and urgency making me groan out loud. Alex and I falling through the front door of my flat, falling into my bedroom in our haste to get to the bed, tearing off each other's clothes and falling at each other like mad ravenous beasts, having sex that left me raw, sore, and gasping for breath. And the second time, slower, gentler, the room seeming to whirl as my head spun with the pure sensuous pleasure of it. Did I have a nice time?

Oh, yes, of course. I was supposed to be going out with Fay last night.

"Lovely," I say, hoarsely, picking up rice, keeping my face averted from him and my eyes on the floor.

"Did you go somewhere nice?"

Oh, just to the moon and back. Halfway to heaven.

"The . . . er . . . just to the wine bar."

At least this isn't a lie.

This is awful. How do people do it all the time? Does it get easier, if the deception goes on for months, or years, if an affair goes on all your life—does it become so easy to lie and cheat that it doesn't even bother them?

Well, I'm not going on with it. I'm going to tell him. Tonight.

After dinner.

I don't love him. He's very sweet, very kind, but he's already beginning to get on my nerves, and . . . I have to see Alex. Even if it doesn't last, even if nothing comes of it, I've got to see him, now, as often as I can. I'd have seen him tonight if it wasn't for Martin. I'm even wondering whether I can get Martin out of the flat early enough to phone Alex and ask him round here later. My body starts to feel warm again at the thought of it.

I'm just serving up the dinner when the phone rings. Martin takes over while I answer it.

"Beth," says a very familiar voice. Too familiar. Too bloody familiar by far. "Hi. It's Daniel."

"Daniel!"

It's only been a week since I bumped into him on the doorstep of his house. It's hard to believe that so much has happened in between—that my life has been turned around, turned upside down, shaken and stirred until I don't recognize it anymore.

Hard to believe this is really Daniel on the phone, and I don't feel a thing, like I've had an injection of anesthetic to my mind and soul.

"This is unusual," I tell him, amazed at the calmness of my voice.

Unusual? Fucking unusual! He's been gone over eighteen months and this is the first time he's ever phoned! Have I taken a home-study course in understatements or what?

"I know," he says, and I realize his voice sounds strained—strained with something serious or something he's going to find hard to talk about.

"What's wrong?" I ask immediately.

He doesn't beat about the bush. We knew each other for too long, prior to the eighteen months of complete estrangement, to monkey about with formalities and niceties.

"I wanted to pay some more money into Ellie's account," he says.

Forgive me for not being able to respond to that one. I mean, for being struck totally dumb in response.

He wants to pay more money? He just phones up like this, out of the blue, after eighteen months of not giving me enough to buy her a decent breakfast everyday never mind dinner and tea, never mind shoes and coats and playgroup fees, never mind ice creams and swimming and ponytail bobbles and all those little things that make up a childhood—suddenly now he wants to pay more, after telling me only last week he couldn't afford to?

"Why?" I ask ungraciously. "What's changed? What's happened, since last week, last week when you told me you had no money, everything was *hers*?"

"*I* have," he says. "*I*'ve changed. I've got a job."

"But I thought you were writing a book?"

"I was. I am. But I've got a job, too, now."

There's a silence. It's none of my business. He doesn't have to explain to me. But he goes on, and I let him, because I want to hear it.

"It upset me, meeting you like that last week."

Oh, good.

"I know I haven't been much of a father to Ellie."

He's obviously done the understatement course, too.

"I thought it was for the best—staying away, not seeing her, not interfering . . ."

"I don't want you to interfere," I put in quickly.

"I know. I understand. But I should be paying more. I'm not being fair. You're having to go out cleaning . . ."

"Yes, it hasn't been easy."

Twist the knife.

". . . while I sit at home, playing at being a writer."

"Playing?"

"Time I faced facts, Beth. Most people who write novels never get them published, do they? I'm kidding myself. It's a hobby. I should have a job, too."

"So you . . . haven't had any interest from an agent?" I ask innocently.

"Not yet. No."

"What a pity."

No. No, I'm not telling him about Sarah and the TV script. You think I should? You think I'm mad? No—it's still only a possibility, isn't it. A vague hint of interest from a person I don't know, whose existence I've only just heard about, through a source I've only just met. I know it sounds good—well, it certainly looks better than his own prospects—and I could use it now to really twist his bollocks. I could screw him up the arse with it, couldn't I, and get a lot of satisfaction out of it. But if the whole Sarah thing turns out to be false hope on my part, I'll end up with egg on my face. Better to wait, and just enjoy this moment privately inside my own head, inside my own heart—enjoy the restorative effect it has on my self-esteem after he ground it into the dust and spat on it.

"What a pity," I repeat sadly, smiling to myself.

"Well, you never know," he says bravely. "Something could still turn up . . ."

"But in the meantime you've got a job. Doing what?"

"Just a bit of office work at the moment. Waiting for the right thing to come up, you know."

"I see. Working for . . . ?"

Pause. "Several companies so far."

He's a temp!

A fucking temp!

Oh, the sweet, sweet fucking irony of it!

Thank you, God, thank you so much, thank you so, so much! I couldn't have wished for a better, more fitting career for him.

The angel of revenge has pooped right on his head.

"Well, that's very nice," I tell him, grinning from ear to ear.

Can he hear me grinning? I hope he can.

"Yes, but the thing is," he returns to his subject as if he's suddenly remembered why he phoned. "The thing is, Beth, I got my first week's pay today, and I intend to start straight away. I'm going to make up for lost time. I'm paying as much as I can over to Ellie. I want to start being a decent father again."

Hm.

"OK," I say warily.

"So I went to pay some money into her savings account."

"You can't. Can you?"

"Yes, I can. I still have access to it. We still have joint control."

Shit, shit, shit. I should have taken his name off the account. What else have I forgotten? What else can he still get into, that he's got no business getting into? I need to check. I need to check quickly, before he starts meddling in everything, in things I don't want him meddling in. Shit, I don't want him meddling in *any*thing. I don't want him prying into . . .

"Ellie's account," he says slowly, deliberately, pausing to see if he's got my full attention. Which he has. Suddenly, horribly, he has. "Ellie's account is nearly empty."

He hasn't rung up to accuse, he says firmly, calmly, loudly. He hasn't rung up to criticize or to rebuke or to start an argument.

He has to say it loudly because I'm yelling into the phone at the other end.

How dare he? I'm yelling. How dare he start throwing his weight around now, about empty accounts, now after eighteen months of hardly any money and lolling around at home writing rubbish novels that don't get published while I scrub people's toilets and get sexually harassed in their wardrobes?

He's not throwing his weight around, he tells me in his firm, loud voice. And he's already admitted the lack of money and the lolling around writing novels, and what's all this about wardrobes?

Mind your own business, I scream back at him. If I want to have sex in wardrobes I will, and anywhere else come to think of it. What does he expect me to do—behave like a nun just because he walked out on me? Doesn't he think any other man will ever find me attractive? Doesn't he realize men are falling over themselves to go to bed with me? Does he really think I'm going to sit around for the rest of my life pining over him when there are lots of other fish in the sea—better looking fish, nicer fish, and much better in bed . . .

"Beth!"

I stop shouting, having completely lost my train of thought anyway, and having discovered I'm dribbling down my chin.

"Beth, what on earth are we arguing about?" says Daniel. "Why on earth are you telling me you're shagging *fish*?!"

And suddenly, heart-wrenchingly, he sounds like the old Daniel. He's laughing and half-teasing and I want to laugh with him but I can't because I ache too much, ache for what's gone—gone for good, and glimpsed just momentarily in that laugh, that tease, that tone of voice. I don't love him anymore and I don't want him back. But it still makes me ache for what we had.

"I don't know," I admit. "I've lost the plot."

"Don't get angry. Don't get on the defensive, about the money. I just wanted to know if it's right. If you knew—that it's nearly all gone."

"Yes," I say, in a small, small voice that I'd like to make even smaller. "Yes, I knew."

"Only it could have been a mistake. With the account, you know. Or it could have been fraud. Theft. I had to find out."

"Yes, of course. I understand."

"Beth, I'm so sorry. I knew things were bad, but if I'd known . . . you should have told me. If I'd known things were so bad that you'd had to take money out of Ellie's savings . . ."

"It's all right. It was only a loan. I'm going to pay it back."

"No, I will. I'll make it all up, and more. I'll pay money into the account every week, and I'll send you much more money every month—proper money, like I should have been doing. And maybe one day . . ."

Oh, I don't know. I don't know about this . . .

"Maybe one day I'll start to see Ellie again?"

"I'm not sure."

"No, I understand."

There's a long, long pause now.

I feel like something that's been coiled up inside of me, with one end in my head and the other end in my feet, something that's been twisted and knotted and pulled tight and tugged from either end, until it's frayed and torn and about to rip into pieces, has suddenly been loosened. If I stand here for a while, with the phone in my hand like this, just breathing quietly, perhaps it will unravel and drop away from me completely.

"I'm glad you called," I say eventually, to my own surprise.

"Yes, so am I."

I can't exactly say: No hard feelings! Let's shake hands and let bygones be bygones!

I can't exactly say: Good luck, hope all goes well with your temping and your novels and, oh, give my love to Melanie!

Not yet.

But when he says, "Take care—maybe I'll call again?" I agree, and I put down the phone feeling calm and even smiling a little.

I'd forgotten about Martin.

Completely forgotten about him, sitting quietly behind me at the kitchen table while I swore and shouted and talked about going to bed with fish.

And now, as I turn back to him and almost jump with surprise at the sight of him there, he looks up at me moodily, his brows drawn together, his mouth turned down with disapproval.

"I *told* you," he says. "I told you, you shouldn't have been borrowing Ellie's money. You should have asked me for some. Didn't I tell you . . ."

"Martin," I say calmly, still smiling, "get stuffed."

We never actually get to eat the chicken stir-fry.

Sunday

It was quite a reasonable parting.

I told him I couldn't put up with him trying to interfere and take over my life, and I couldn't cope with him loving me and wanting to wait for me to love him back.

He told me he was beginning to find it difficult that I didn't love him and wouldn't take his advice or his money.

I told him I wasn't ready to be anyone's codependent.

He told me he didn't like being used as a sex object.

I laughed and said some men would think they'd died and gone to heaven.

He didn't laugh. He looked sad and hurt and said he hoped I'd be happy and hoped I'd eventually learn to trust another man, that not all men were like Daniel and not all men would let me down.

I didn't tell him I'd become passionately involved with someone I was eyeing up over his shoulder when we were carpet-dancing at the party last week. It seemed superfluous to the conversation somehow.

Instead I smiled gently, like I was dealing with a

slightly confused invalid, and tried to edge him toward the door, wondering if it was too late to phone Alex.

He asked if a good-bye kiss was out of the question.

I resisted the urge to look at my watch.

We kissed briefly and he left, looking brave and promising not to bother me as long as I occasionally kept in touch.

"All achieved with the minimum of upset," I tell Louise with some satisfaction.

She's come round to talk about Jodie's legs.

Jodie's outside with Annie, Solomon, and Ellie, trying to teach them how to dance to the latest *Atomic Kitten* hit. I can see Ellie out of the window, gazing at Jodie with openmouthed adoration. She's trying so hard to copy her movements, she keeps falling over.

"You think he'll be all right?" she cautions me.

"Martin? Yes, of course—I was very gentle with him. I didn't mention Alex."

"But he'll take it hard, Beth. He was crazy about you. It was so obvious."

"Was it?"

Don't. Don't make me feel guilty, now. It's too late. I don't want to have to think about him taking it hard.

"He seemed all right," I say, less confidently. "He even said he'd been finding it hard—putting up with me being . . . you know. Too independent."

"I suppose he'd hoped he'd change you."

"Well, in that case, I'm glad I'm out of it. That's something even Daniel never tried to do."

"No, you're right, of course. And it's good that you and Daniel are communicating."

I think about the way we laughed about shagging fish,

and I find myself smiling. "Who'd have thought it?" I muse. "Only last week I saw him and went to pieces."

"But now you're different."

"Does it show?" I ask. "I've got this suspicion that I look different. That everyone can tell, by looking at me . . ."

"You look like a kid who's just arrived at the biggest and best party she's ever been to."

I smile happily.

Louise squeezes my arm. "You know I'm pleased for you," she says.

"But?"

"But . . . parties like that don't last forever."

"Maybe not. I don't want to think about that."

"Of course not. But I don't want you to be the kid who cries herself sick when it's time to go home. Just enjoy it while it lasts."

Funny. That's what Fay said, too.

We're showing Jodie some magazines with pictures of film stars with nice, normal, shapely legs, and other ones with pictures of anorexic-looking models with legs like twigs. Don't those twig legs look horrible? See how much nicer these proper female-shape legs look?

Jodie stares at the pictures for a while and shakes her head. The twig legs look better. The other legs are too fat.

"They should go on a diet," she declares.

None of the superstars in the magazine can be more than a size 10.

"They're not fat," I tell her gently. "They've got nice figures."

"Yuck," she says. "Disgusting."

"Do you think your mum looks disgusting?" I ask her. "Or me? Do I look disgusting?"

"No," she says, squirming with a little embarrassment at this. "But that's different. You're *old*."

"You say the nicest things." I smile at her.

It's my thirtieth birthday on Tuesday.

And, of course, we're going out to lunch today—me (the birthday girl), Ellie, my mum, and my family.

After Louise and the children have gone, I get myself and Ellie changed and ready. Ellie's wearing the red velour dress again and she keeps looking at herself in the mirror and smiling.

"Do I look nice?" she asks me.

"You look beautiful, darling," I tell her, breathing in to zip up a skirt that's got a bit tight for me.

"Are my legs fat?"

I let all the breath go at once, nearly breaking the zipper as my stomach suddenly expands.

"Ellie!" I'm horrified. I go hot and cold with fear. I'll have to stop her playing with Jodie if this is going to happen. "Of course they're not fat! You mustn't listen to Jodie . . ."

She frowns. "I want fat legs. I like those fat sort of legs, like sausages. Like Jack's got."

I sigh with relief. "Jack's legs are chubby because he's only just started walking," I tell her, lifting her onto my lap for a cuddle. "They're baby legs. Yours are proper little-girl legs. You need them for running around and playing games."

"And dancing?" she says eagerly, putting her arms 'round my neck. "Dancing like the 'Tomic Kitten?"

"Yes."

Don't grow up. Please, don't grow up. I wish you could be four years old forever.

"Come on," I say softly against her ear. "They'll be here in a minute. Let's brush your hair and get your shoes on. And remember—be polite, Ellie. Please!"

* * *

The restaurant's busy but, unlike the pubs I occasionally went to with Daniel for Sunday lunch when Ellie was a baby, where they catered for children almost to the exclusion of any paying adults—with swings, slides, and bouncy castles in the garden; ice-cream machines where the cigarette and condom machines should have been; and Mr. Men menus on the tables—unlike those riotous establishments where you felt in the minority if you sat still for more than five minutes and didn't shout across the pub that you wanted another Coke and a wee-wee, this place is somehow busy yet calm. Full yet sedate. Obviously expensive. My mother's smiling graciously at all the other diners as we walk to our table, as if we were local dignitaries and they should be delighted at their luck, having us eat with them.

Soon change that, then.

I sit Ellie between me and Mum, and hope my brother's boys are going to be at the other end of the table. No such luck: they rush to sit immediately opposite us, grinning at her as they sit down, and my heart sinks as I see her eyes light up. Whatever they do, she'll try to copy them, so I just hope they're going to behave.

"Lovely restaurant, Mum," says my sister appreciatively.

They all look at me, the birthday girl, for confirmation.

"Lovely," I agree.

The background music is something slow and dreary about love and strangers. Music to slit your wrists by.

"What does everyone want to drink?" asks Mum brightly.

"Coke, please," say Steve's two boys in stereo.

"Coke, please," echoes Ellie immediately.

Everyone except me laughs and Jill says how grown-up she's getting.

Don't encourage her, she'll be asking for a Bacardi Breezer next.

The appetizers are ordered, as are the main courses and the wine. So far, so good, although I'm a little nervous about the fact that Ellie wants soup (because James and Thomas are having soup) and scampi (ditto). I'm nervous about the scampi because she's never eaten it before, and I'm nervous about the soup because . . . well, have you ever seen a four-year-old with a bowl of soup and a clean white tablecloth? But at least she's being quiet and sitting still, completely engrossed with watching everything her cousins are doing, so I try to relax and get into the family conversation.

"So how are *you*?" asks Steve eventually, after we've discussed the legal profession in some depth and heard all the latest news from Jill's hospital.

"Oh—fine, fine," I say, waving my hand dismissively. "But that's enough about me . . ."

"You haven't told us anything yet!" laughs Jill.

"Not a lot to tell. Oh, look—here come the appetizers!"

A few minutes while everyone gets the correct dish in front of them and looks appreciatively at what everyone else has got before getting started. A few minutes of silent munching (and slurping in the case of the bowls of soup), and then, "So come on, then, Beth. What's the latest? Mum says you mentioned a new job? And you were hinting about a new man?"

Was I? Oh, shit, so I was.

"The new job," I say, fiddling with my asparagus. "Well . . ."

"When do you start, dear?" asks my mother.

It's unbelievable, isn't it? I'm sure I only told her I was going for an interview. In her mind she's got me taken on for the job—whatever it is. I should, now, just be done with all the pretense and the shame and stand up (figuratively speaking; I don't want the whole restaurant watching) and announce that the job in question was cleaning the house of my ex-boyfriend's mistress. That not only did I not want the job, but I also left the premises in tears having had a nervous breakdown on the doorstep.

"I didn't take the job," I say with a shrug.

"Oh, dear," says Steve. "Salary not high enough?"

Are you joking? I'd have been happy with £4 an hour.

"Well—I decided to concentrate on other things."

I take a mouthful of asparagus. It seems to have gone very quiet on our table, apart from the sound of soup being slurped by the two boys opposite me. I turn to look at Ellie. She's stirring the soup enthusiastically. So far only a minimal amount has gone over the tablecloth.

"Eat it up," I whisper to her.

"Can't," she whispers back.

"Why not?"

"Can't eat it. It doesn't eat. It drinks."

Silly me.

"Drink it up, then."

She sighs, still stirring it, looking less enthusiastic. "Can I have some bread?"

I pass her the basket of dainty little bread rolls shaped like miniature loaves. She looks at them, entranced, and takes one. She puts it, whole, straight into the middle of the bowl of soup, which slops over the edges according to the principle of Archimedes. Thomas and James snicker and nudge each other. She looks up at them and grins.

"Don't laugh at her," I warn them in a quiet but deadly voice. "It encourages her."

I turn to Ellie again. "Now," I say very firmly. "Try to drink some of your soup, like this, with your spoon." I demonstrate. "Or if you can't, I'll feed you."

She doesn't like this. "Not a baby!"

"So—feed yourself. Please."

I turn back to the silent, expectant faces around me.

"What other things," asks Jill, "are you concentrating on, Beth?"

If I had any guts, I'd say Being a Mother. Bringing Up My Child in a Secure and Stable Environment. Practicing Safe Parenthood.

But I admit it. When I'm outnumbered by my family, I become gutless.

"Writing," I say, without much conviction. "I'm writing a TV script."

"*Really!*"

"Wow!"

"Amazing!"

"Well *done*, Beth!"

"Always knew you could do it . . ."

"It's . . . still in the early stages yet."

"Of course!" says my sister-in-law excitedly. "But you've had some interest?"

"Well . . ." I wasn't going to tell them this. I wasn't going to tell any of them any of this. "Well, yes, some interest from an agent."

"Amazing!"

"Wonderful!"

"Congratulations, Beth!"

My brother raises his glass. "Here's to you, Beth—to the success you deserve, and to a happy thirtieth birthday!"

The rest of the family raise their glasses. I cower with embarrassment.

"Success!"

"Happy birthday!"

"Happy thirtieth!"

"Success to you, Beth!"

They all drink, put down their glasses, and there's a satisfied sigh around the table.

"Happy birthday to you!" sings a little voice next to me.

I look round at Ellie, just in time to see her pick up her glass of Coke and tip it into her soup.

The remains of the appetizers have been cleared away and a fresh white cloth spread over Ellie's part of the table. She sits, looking sulkily at the table, while Thomas and James giggle and raise their Coke glasses at each other, pretending to tip them over.

"All right, boys," says their mother sharply. "It's not funny. You're both old enough to know better."

"So's Ellie," I point out, giving her a meaningful look.

She glares at me, her lower lip wobbling.

OK, OK, don't cry, for God's sake.

I pick up her serviette and try to give her messy face a wipe, but she pushes my hand away crossly and folds her arms tightly across her chest.

"Look, Ellie, darling," says my mother gaily, trying to distract her by folding her serviette into a flower shape.

Ellie pushes the flower across the table.

"Best to ignore her, Mum," I say behind the back of Ellie's head.

The main course is being brought up now. I watch the plates of children's portions of scampi and fries being placed in front of Thomas and James. They smile in happy anticipation and start looking for vinegar and tomato sauce. Ellie looks at her own plate with a mixture of surprise and distrust.

"It's just like fish fingers," I tell her encouragingly.

"Not!" retorts James.

"Try a little bit," I tell her. "And if you don't like it, just eat the fries." I put some tomato sauce, from a little glass dish, onto the side of her plate.

She stares at it. "I want it all over," she says. "I want it out of the bottle."

"They don't have bottles in here. And it's polite to put it on the side of the plate."

She stabs a fry with her fork and starts to dip it in the tomato sauce.

"So, Beth!" says Steve. "What's this about a new man, then?"

"No." I smile. "I don't know where you got that from. I haven't got a man."

No way are they going to hear about Alex.

"Martin," says Ellie, through a mouthful of fries.

"Martin?" asks Jill, looking at me with raised eyebrows.

"I like Martin," says Ellie. "He calls me Sweetie."

"Martin's just a friend," I say, panicking desperately. "Ellie, get on with your dinner, please."

"So how long has he been . . . just a friend, then?" asks Steve, with a chuckle.

"You should have brought him along for lunch!" exclaims Mum. "I told you, Beth, you could have brought your new man . . ."

"I haven't *got* a new man!" I say, more loudly than I intend, wanting to be done with this whole conversation.

A woman on the next table turns right around in her chair to look at me and it's as much as I can do not to tell her to mind her own fucking business.

I glance at Ellie, and then lean closer to Jill, sitting on my other side, and whisper very quietly to her, "Ellie doesn't know I've just finished with Martin. For Christ's sake, can't you drop the subject?"

"Oh!" says Jill, nodding sagely. "I see." She smiles and cuts into her steak.

"What?" demands Steve from across the table.

"What's all the whispering about down there?" calls my mother.

"Nothing!" says Jill. "Beth wants to change the subject."

"Tell us later, eh, Beth?" says Jill's boyfriend Peter, with a broad wink.

"Maybe," I say half-heartedly.

Can this get any worse? Are families always like this?

And Ellie chooses this very moment to spit out her scampi, pick it up, and throw it across the table at Thomas, hitting him right in the eye.

"He did ask for it," Steve tries to soothe me later, over coffee.

We've retreated to the restaurant's bar area, where, thank God, the children are sitting quietly together, looking at a miniature computer game that Thomas has been allowed to bring with him. The row over the scampi was diffused with some immediate adult intervention, some separation of Thomas and James to one end of the table and Ellie to the other, and some chocolate ice cream all round.

"Thomas was making faces at her," admits my sister-in-law. "And she's only little, Beth. I think she's been very good, considering."

"Do you?"

I look at Ellie now—lying in a chair, sucking her thumb, which she only does when she's very tired—with soup, tomato sauce, and ice cream stains on the little red velour dress and something not very appetizing sticking to her hair, and I think—yes, she hasn't been too bad. Considering their ages, Thomas and James have behaved worse than she has. This makes me feel relieved and reassured. I'm not such a terrible mother, then. Perhaps my family will see this, and realize that it's been worthwhile, me staying at home and not having a career, devoting myself to motherhood and household drudgery. And writing a TV script.

I smile to myself.

"So," says Jill, catching my eye and smiling back at me. "What do you want for your birthday, then, Beth?"

"Yes, come on, darling—what would you like?" joins in Mum. "It's a special birthday, and we haven't bought you anything yet. We wanted to get you something you really, really want."

"Or we could just give you the money," adds Steve, who probably doesn't want the hassle of buying anything.

The money's very tempting. If they all give me some money, I could . . .

"But only if you spend it on yourself!" Mum puts in. "We can't have you spending birthday-present money on groceries, can we? Or things for the flat, or clothes for Ellie!"

Money to spend on myself? I think, briefly, of the open-toe shoes I wanted from Faith—but they've got new stock in since then. I think about a new dress, or some new jeans. Or a suit, in case I ever get a job. Or even a proper haircut.

And then I think of the thing I really, really want. And when I start thinking about it, I suddenly want it so badly I feel shivery with excitement.

"Actually," I say, and I can hear the excitement in my

own voice, and I know all the others can hear it, too, because they all turn to me with this look on their faces—a *pleased* look, and I know they're pleased to think they might be able to give me something I really, really want. And I know that, despite everything, despite my feeling that they all look down on me and my life, that they all go on at me about getting a job and getting a man and getting my act together—they all love me really. They all love me and they all love Ellie, and they only keep on at me because they want us to be happy, because that's what families do.

"Actually," I say again, now I know I've got everyone's attention, "there is something. But it's something very expensive, so what you could do—if you really want to give me a special present—is perhaps chip in together for a deposit . . ."

"Jesus, Beth!" jokes Steve. "We're not buying you a house!"

"No," I laugh. "Not quite as big as that. What I'd really love more than anything is my own computer."

They look at one another in silence for a few minutes. I hold my breath. Have I offended everyone? Is it too much to ask for—too much for anyone to have the nerve to want for their birthday, thirtieth or otherwise?

"Only the deposit!" I say in a small voice. "I'd pay the rest off over easy terms . . ."

Steve speaks first. "Between us all," he says, "I don't think a computer is out of the question, do you, Jill?"

"You can get some very good deals nowadays," says Peter. "I've seen ads where the printer and even a scanner are thrown into the price."

"I think it would be an investment, really," says Mum, smiling at me. "If Beth produces this masterpiece . . ."

"Mum!" I protest. "It may not even be accepted."

"Think positive!" she declares. She looks all round the family. "So can I leave it to you to get the best deal? I'll just write out the check?"

"Just the deposit," I whisper.

"It's your thirtieth birthday," she tells me firmly, "and we're your family."

"We'll get you your computer," says Jill. "It's really nice to be able to get you something you want."

"Something that'll really help you," says Steve.

I have to look down at my coffee so they don't see my eyes getting watery.

I'll never be annoyed and sarcastic about my family, ever again. I promise.

Tuesday

―――◆◇◆◇◆◇◆◇◆―――

So here we are then. Today's the day.

Thirty years ago today, at about this time in the morning, my mum was on her way to the hospital to give birth to her third and final child. And I, the child in question, was squirming about inside her on my way out to my big adventure: Life in the Outside World.

"Happy Birthday, Mummy!" sings Ellie, jumping on my bed and smothering me with warm wet kisses. She considers me carefully, head on one side, narrowing her eyes in concentration. "*How* old did you say you are?"

"Thirty."

"*Thirty*!" she exclaims, shaking her head in wonder. How amazing that someone of such advanced years can still stand up.

I haven't, yet, of course—not this morning.

"Are you getting up, Mummy? Old Mummy?" She giggles, starting to bounce on the bed.

"Well," I joke, yawning and snuggling back under the covers. "No, I don't think I will. As it's my birthday—as I'm so *old*—I think I'll just stay in bed all day!"

Her face drops. "But who's going to make my breakfast?"

Nice to be valued.

I sigh and sit up again, pretending to push her off the bed, and stretch my poor old legs out onto the floor. Yes, I can do it. I can still stand up. Here goes the next decade, then!

Ellie brings a battered cardboard basket out of her bedroom. I recognize it as the vague gray shape that was smuggled out of playgroup last week in a Safeway's carrier bag. It's been cut and pasted from a Cornflakes box and has five paper flowers, suspended from pieces of wire, stuck into its center and wobbling merrily over its edges.

"This is your present," she informs me solemnly. "I made it."

"Oh, Ellie—it's beautiful!" I take the basket gingerly by the handle, trying not to shake the wobbling flowers too much in case they come unstuck. "You must have worked very hard to make this!"

"Not really." She shrugs. "I got bored and Pat finished it."

The brutal honesty of children! Well, thanks, Playgroup Pat, for the present. I put it on display on top of the TV. At least Ellie thought about my birthday—at least she asked Pat if she could make me a present, even if she didn't finish it.

"Everyone had to make one," Ellie informs me, as if determined to shatter all my illusions.

So—not even a birthday basket, then—just the playgroup project for the day. Never mind, at least she made the decision to use it as my birthday present.

"It's got writing on it," she points out.

So it has.

"Happy ester."

* * *

I'm not going to work today. I'm not going to Alex Chapman's flat anymore, not to pretend to clean it, anyway. He says I can go there any time I like to use his computer because he wants me to work on my script so that his (*I hate to say it*) wife can read it and get it sent to a publisher. I still can't take this in. I still can't believe it's all part of the same dream—the dream about this amazing, gorgeous, lovely man who wants me as much as I want him. I'm going to wake up any day now and find out it's just God playing tricks on me.

So you thought you've met this wonderful man and you thought your writing's been recognized by this literary agent and you're going to become famous and happy all at the same time and all your problems and worries are going to be over? Ha! Fooled you! Just a dream! Go back to sleep!

The doorbell rings at about nine o'clock while we're still having our breakfast. Postman loaded down with lots of lovely presents and cards for me? I look out of the front window as I go to the door and my heart sinks.

It's Luke, with the Monster Hound snarling and salivating at the end of his leash.

He hands the leash to me and goes to unload a dog basket, several blankets, and a couple of bags of toys and dishes out of a battered white van standing at the curb.

"I thought you must have forgotten," I say faintly, trying to sound enthusiastic while performing an elaborate dance display on the doorstep with Tosser, who's apparently decided the best line of attack is to tie my ankles up tightly with his leash.

"Thought you were coming to get him," retorted Luke.

I don't want to argue about it. What's the point? It's my birthday and I've got probably the worst present I can possibly imagine. Isn't that bad enough? Luke slams the door of the van and climbs back into the driver's seat. "See ya," he calls as he drives off, without looking back at me or the dog.

The dog basket and all Tosser's worldly goods are sitting forlornly on the pavement. Tosser looks at me with surprise in his evil red eyes and for a minute I almost feel sorry for him, being dumped like a piece of unwanted baggage. Then he uses the opportunity of my ankles being tied up to have an introductory gnaw at my leg, and I instinctively shout in pain and smack him across the nose. The surprise in his eyes turns to absolute amazement. He whimpers very softly and sits down by my feet, looking for all the world as if he's sorry.

Well, well, well.

Do we have a reformed character here, or did I smack him harder than I intended?

"Good boy," I say, without very much conviction. "That's much better. Shall we try to be friends, now?"

He wags his tail.

Fucking hell! Doctor Dolittle, eat your heart out!!

"Who are you talking to, Mummy?" calls Ellie, emerging from the kitchen. "Oh! *Tosser!*"

She runs up and encircles him in her arms, almost knocking him over. I struggle to stay upright myself, my legs still being entangled in his leash.

"Oh, Mummy!" She looks at me with pure joy in her eyes. "Is he ours now? Is he really, really ours, to keep? For always?"

Oh, happy day!

We find a space in the kitchen, next to the boiler, for the dog basket and line it with two of the blankets. Ellie fills one of his bowls with water and gives him a couple of dog biscuits "for breakfast." Tosser, his tail between his legs, prowls around from room to room for ten minutes or so, looking at me with anxiety whenever he passes, closely followed by Ellie who keeps telling him how much she loves him.

"Let him settle down now," I tell her eventually.

"Can't we take him out for a walk?"

"Yes, later. But he really needs to be left quietly for a while, to get used to his new home. Think how strange he must be feeling—he must be missing Dottie and wondering why he's been left here with us."

"Poor Tosser!" says Ellie, looking at him sadly. She sits down on the floor next to him. "I'll just talk to him quietly," she tells me.

"Fine."

While she's talking to him quietly, the postman calls with—perhaps not loads of lovely presents for me, but several nice cards anyway. One, from Martin, promises to love me forever and I try to make out the date on the postmark to see whether he actually posted it before I told him it was over. By contrast, the card from Alex just says, "See you tonight xxx"—but this is enough to make my blood almost boil in my veins with excitement.

Just as I decide I ought to be getting dressed, there's another ring at the bell and this time it's a delivery van.

"Computer, Miss?" says the driver. "Where do you want it?"

"Oh!" I clap my hand to my mouth in surprise. "I didn't know it was coming!"

"What is it, Mummy?" asks Ellie, watching intently as cardboard boxes are carried in and stacked on the kitchen table. "Is it toys?"

"No!" I retort with unreasonable irritation. "Haven't you got enough toys, Ellie? This is *my* birthday present!"

Instantly bored, she goes back to her conversation with Tosser.

I'm going to unpack the boxes and start trying to connect everything up. It'll just have to live on the kitchen table for now, and we'll have to eat on trays on our laps. I can't believe I've really got my own computer at last! I must phone Mum, and Steve, and Jill, and thank them as soon as I've got dressed . . .

But there's another ring at the bell almost as soon as the delivery van's driven off.

"Hi, Beth," says Jodie a bit shyly when I open the door. "Is it all right if I come and play with Ellie?"

Ellie flies out of the door to greet her, hopping excitedly from one foot to the other. "We've got Tosser! We've got him forever! He's come to live with us! But," she lowers her voice a fraction, "he's got to sit quietly and get used to us 'cos he's missing Dottie."

Tosser has followed Ellie out to the front door and stands behind her, looking warily at Jodie, whose eyes are large with surprise and delight.

"Jodie," I caution her, "does Mummy know you're here?"

"I left her a note. Can I bring my bike around the back?"

"Yes, yes, bring the bike around. But why did you leave her a note? Why didn't you tell her?"

"She was cleaning the bathroom."

She disappears with her bike and I'm left frowning at the front doorstep. This doesn't sound right. I'm going to phone Louise.

I try dialing her number but it's busy so I head for my bedroom with the idea of getting dressed first, and then trying again. But believe it or not, there's another ring at the doorbell just as I'm getting out of my dressing gown.

"You're still in your 'jamas!" exclaims Fay when I open the door.

"It's been like Piccadilly Circus here this morning. Come in. Want some coffee?"

"Please."

"Where are the kids?" I ask her as I put the kettle on.

"At my mum's."

She sits down at the kitchen table, leaning on one of the computer boxes, not even seeming to notice it. Tosser runs up to her and sniffs her feet, and she doesn't seem to notice that either.

"Hello, Fay," says Ellie, and Fay just smiles at her vaguely. "This is my friend Jodie," says Ellie importantly. "And this is Tosser!"

Fay just nods. She sits there, leaning on the box, and keeps on nodding, looking down at the floor.

"Go and play in your bedroom," I tell Ellie sharply. "With Jodie."

The kitchen door swings shut behind them. Tosser sighs and tries out the new position of his basket, turning round four or five times in it before sitting down and looking around him mournfully.

"What is it?" I ask Fay quietly, sitting down next to her at the table.

"I did the test," she says. "I'm pregnant."

I take hold of her hands in mine. They're as cold as ice. I rub them, watching her face. A tear rolls down her nose and she doesn't bother to wipe it away.

"I thought it was what you wanted?" I say softly.

She nods, unable to speak.

"So what happened? Did you tell Neil?"

Nods again. More tears well up in her eyes and her face begins to crumple. I get up and put my arms around her, holding her face against me, holding her tight, rocking her, murmuring to her. *It's all right, shush, shush, it's all right. It'll be all right.*

But it won't.

I can't make it all right for her.

Everything's gone wrong for her, and I can't help. I want to cry myself, cry out loud at the unfairness of it all. Why did she have to meet him? Why did she have to fall in love with him, have an affair with him, get pregnant with his child—only to have him reject her? Because that's obviously what's happened. He's rejected her because he doesn't want to know about the baby. His baby.

"He said he didn't want complications," says Fay shakily after she's blown her nose and had a couple of mouthfuls of hot coffee.

Complications! This is a *child* we're talking about, not a mortgage or an endowment scheme or a hire-purchase agreement. A child, conceived by him with the woman he says he loves!

"Are you sure he doesn't just need more time to think about it?" I try, swallowing back my anger. "Perhaps the shock . . ."

She shakes her head. "He says . . . he thinks it's best"—she swallows and shakes her head again—"To call it a day."

Call it a day.

Run away.

He didn't want *complications*—he just wanted an affair, a bit of excitement, a sexual relationship. He doesn't want to mess up his life with the threat of a baby, which might or might not be his, might or might not encroach on his time or become his responsibility, either now or at some time in the future.

"I told him," she says. "I told him I won't ask him for anything—won't expect anything from him, but . . . but . . ."

But he's a coward. He's scared of commitment, scared of responsibility, he's had enough and he wants out.

"Perhaps it's for the best," I start to say.

"No!" she says, on a sort of strangled wail. "No, it's not for the best, Beth!"

So there's nothing I can say.

"I knew, I suppose," she admits at length as I pour out the second cup of coffee. Her eyes are red from crying and she looks tired enough to drop. I bet she hasn't slept all night. "I suppose that's why I hoped I was pregnant."

I just nod. I knew it.

"I think I knew it was coming. I knew he was going to finish it."

"Sooner or later," I say, softly, stroking her hands, "something had to happen. It couldn't have gone on like that forever."

The party had to be over.

And the child who was so excited at the beginning of the party has ended up crying herself sick.

It's lunchtime when Louise turns up at the flat with the other two children. I'm still in my pajamas and Fay and I have started on a bottle of wine.

"Oh my God! I'm so sorry! I was going to phone you about Jodie but it was busy, and then . . ."

"It's all right, Beth," says Louise. She gives me a kiss and hands me a bunch of flowers. "Happy birthday. Are you all right?"

"Yes, but . . ." I pull the kitchen door closed and whisper, "It's Fay. A crisis. I'm really sorry. Jodie . . ."

"I knew she was here. She left a note."

"She told me. But I thought it was a bit strange."

"We had an argument this morning. She wouldn't eat

any breakfast, again, and was going on about being fat and . . . well, I suppose I've got so worried about her, I just snapped and shouted at her. Then when I came downstairs later, she'd gone and there was this note in the kitchen saying she was going to live with you and Ellie!"

"*Live* with me?!"

At this, dead on cue, Jodie comes out of Ellie's bedroom, leading Ellie by the hand, and looking very sheepishly at her mother.

"They've got a dog," she tells Louise in a sulky tone.

"His name's Tosser!" says Ellie. "Tosser!" she calls.

The dog, having slept off his anxieties and apparently waking in a much more confident mood, pushes the kitchen door open with his nose and bounds out, nearly knocking her over. Ellie and Jodie both start to giggle. This sets off Annie and Solomon, who have both been hiding a bit shyly behind their mum, and before we know it all the kids are falling about laughing and the dog's jumping around going mad with excitement.

"It's nice to see you laughing," Louise tells Jodie. "You're always so sad nowadays."

Jodie shrugs. "I can't help it."

"I know," says Louise. "I know it's been a horrible time for you, Jode—but it hasn't been much fun for me, either."

Jodie hangs her head, watching the dog loping around the room, sniffing into corners, investigating strange smells.

"I didn't mean it," she says eventually in a very small voice. "About leaving home."

"I know you didn't. Beth wouldn't have you, anyway!" jokes Louise.

"But you can come whenever you like, Jodie," I remind her. "It's really nice for me to have someone so grown up round here to play with Ellie."

She looks at me gratefully. "And play with Tosser?"

"Yes, of course. That would be especially helpful."

At which Tosser, having found the spot he likes best, just behind the sofa, promptly squats and defecates profusely on the carpet, to squeals of excited and exaggerated disgust from the children.

Well, I'm glad he's cheered somebody up, anyway.

"I forgot it was your birthday," says Fay sorrowfully.

I've cleaned up after the dog, accompanied by a lot of laughter and some help from Louise, and now the three of us are sitting at the kitchen table again, facing one another across the computer boxes, and while the children are absorbed in the TV we're well into the second bottle of wine.

"It's OK. I wouldn't have expected . . ."

"No, it's not OK. What sort of a friend forgets a thirtieth birthday?"

"Fay, for God's sake—we'll celebrate it another time. When things are . . . better."

"They won't be," she responds, helping herself to another glass of wine. "Things won't ever be better."

I don't know what to say to this. It's not just like getting over another love affair, another break-up, another broken heart. She's having a baby. It's not exactly something you can eventually forget.

"Should you be having another drink?" I suddenly remember.

"No!" She pushes the glass aside. "No, I shouldn't."

There's a silence. Louise looks at me with raised eyebrows. I don't think it's my place to enlighten her.

"I'm pregnant," Fay tells her. And then, as if it's only just hit her, "My God! I'm pregnant. I'm having another baby! Fucking hell. I'm going to have to tell Simon."

* * *

And so the mess spreads, and becomes someone else's
mess, too. It becomes Simon's mess by default, even
though Simon isn't expecting it, doesn't know anything
about it, and might not even mind it. He might think it's
wonderful—who knows?

Other people's mess doesn't even always look like the
mess it is, does it?

Tuesday Night

I've only just changed out of my pajamas by the time Alex comes round this evening. It's been that kind of a day. I couldn't ask Fay, in the circumstances, to look after Ellie tonight so she's gone home with Louise. She was beside herself with excitement.

"Can I sleep in the same room as Jodie and Annie? Can we have a Night-night Feast?"

"What's a Night-night Feast?" Jodie wanted to know, trying not to sound too interested in case anyone thought she was still just a little kid herself.

"You get into bed and then you have Coca-Cola and chips and stuff," explained Ellie importantly.

"It's called a Midnight Feast," Annie told her kindly.

"Yeah, we used to have them when we were little," said Jodie. "But I expect we could have one specially for you—couldn't we, Mum?"

Louise looked at me with her eyebrows raised in surprise and relief. Jodie was asking for food—and junk food at that. Perhaps the Midnight Feast would be the turning point for her.

"It's a *Night-night* Feast," insisted Ellie, looking at me worriedly. "I'm not allowed to have a Midnight Feast."

"Oh—probably 'cos you're too little," said Annie, smiling. "I remember when *I* wasn't allowed to stay up till midnight . . ."

"You're not now," said Louise firmly. "A Night-night Feast is an excellent idea, Ellie. We'll sort out some food and drink when we get home."

"Take some chips and things with you," I told her. "There are some chocolate cookies in the fridge."

The children made a dive for the kitchen. I could hear Ellie telling the others in anxious tones that she's only allowed to have the cookies if she cleans her teeth afterward, and I was slightly shocked that she'd not only listened to all my naggings in the past, but was repeating them like a mantra.

"I think I've made her neurotic," I told Louise a bit guiltily.

"Rubbish. Kids always cling to Mum's rules when they go away from home. Makes them feel secure. Enjoy it while it lasts!" She pulled a rueful face. "She won't be listening to you anymore by the time she's ten!"

"Jodie's going to be fine," I told her gently.

"Yes, I think perhaps she'll pull through."

"Can we take Tosser home with us, too?" called Solomon. "He could stay the night, too, and have a feast!"

"No, I don't think so," I told him quickly. "Poor Tosser's had enough excitement for one day. He'd better get used to his new home before he gets taken anywhere else."

Actually he seems to have got used to the place amazingly quickly. Apart from the one poo on the carpet, he's asked to go outside whenever necessary and has found his way unaided to his food, water, and bed. He's followed me about, without any further incidence of ankle-savaging, and has even looked at me once or twice as if he quite likes me. It's weird. Perhaps he's lulling me into a false sense of security and he's planning to go for my throat during the night. I think I'll lock him in the kitchen.

And now it's half past seven and I've finally managed to have a bath and get myself dressed with only four or five changes of heart about which skirt looks the sexiest, which top the most flattering, which underwear's the easiest to get off when the moment arrives, which perfume's the sultriest, and how much makeup makes me look attractive without being tarty.

"Hi," says Alex in his melted-chocolate voice when I open the door. "Happy birthday, honey. God, you look gorgeous!"

I've never been spoken to like this in my life. Daniel used to think he was being romantic if he turned the TV off before we had sex.

And here's Alex, taking me into his arms before he's even closed the front door behind him, and kissing me with such passion that things are already heating up and I can see it was a waste of time getting dressed at all, except that it's so nice being undressed again . . . especially by someone who notices the clothes as he takes them off. It's a whole new experience.

"Was that my birthday present?" I ask him eventually, afterward, as we're lying on the carpet surrounded by castoff clothes.

(The front door's shut by now by the way.)

"Well, that depends whether you want this or not," he teases, rolling over and taking something out of the pocket of his jacket, which is hanging over the armchair. He passes me a little box—the sort you get small but very expensive gifts in.

I sit up on the floor and look at the little box for a minute without wanting to open it.

Now, this is embarrassing.

This is very embarrassing.

When all's said and done, no matter how gorgeous and wonderful he is (and he is!), I've only known him for . . . well, less time than it takes most people to go to Spain or Greece or Turkey, have a holiday romance, finish with them, and fly back to Gatwick.

I've known him for less time than it takes for the contents of most people's fridges to go moldy.

Less time than it takes to catch most infectious diseases.

He shouldn't be buying me small but expensive gifts in little boxes.

It makes it all seem very serious.

"I didn't know what to do," he says, watching my face as I sit here looking at the little box and not wanting to open it. "I didn't want you to think I was coming on too strong—too serious. But it's your birthday! I couldn't just buy you flowers, or chocolates, or a bottle of wine! I wanted it to be a bit special."

I look up at him. Shall I open the box now?

"It wasn't horribly expensive," he says with a smile.

It's a silver bracelet, plain but delicate. It's lovely. I put it on, turn it around on my wrist, and I can't keep the pleasure out of my voice as I tell him, "Perfect! Thank you— I was worried . . ."

"That I'd go over the top? Try to buy your affection with gold and diamonds?" He smiles again. "Perhaps next year."

Before my head stops spinning with the significance of this remark, he's leaning over to kiss me again and I'm just beginning to wonder whether he's up (literally) for a rerun, when he suddenly jumps up with a shout, "What the *fuck*!"

He's hopping on one foot, holding his ankle, and Tosser, having been dealt an instinctive and well-aimed kick, is sloping back out to the kitchen with his tail between his legs.

"I thought I'd shut him out," I apologize, investigating his ankle for tooth marks.

"It's all right." Alex is laughing now. "It wasn't so much the pain as the shock. Frightened the shit out of me—you didn't tell me he was here!"

"I seem to have forgotten about him," I admit. "Had other things on my mind . . ."

Amazingly, Alex is rubbing Tosser's head affectionately now and they're beginning to look like old friends. I could very quickly get jealous.

"I think he might go for the jugular later," I warn him.

"Nah, I think he's a good old boy, really," chuckles Alex, rolling the vicious little sod onto his back and rubbing his stomach. "He's probably had a frustrating life these last few years, living on his own with that old dear. That's all that was wrong with him."

"But Dottie's lovely!" I protest. "She'd hate to hear herself described like that!"

"She might be lovely." He shrugs. "But I bet she wasn't fit enough to exercise him and play with him like this. And I bet it was pretty quiet and boring most of the time at her place."

He's got a point, I suppose. Tosser's probably seen more of life in one day in my flat than he used to see in a year with Dottie—at least until Luke turned up.

"Shame she didn't keep a cat instead," says Alex.

Knowing my luck, it would've used my legs as scratching posts.

Before we go out, Alex helps me unpack the cardboard boxes and connect up the various bits of the computer. This plug goes in the back here, and connects the keyboard to the terminal. This wire plugs in here to connect the monitor, this one is for the mouse. This is where the printer connects to the computer and this is in case you get a scanner. These wires go down here and connect up the speakers—here and here. And the whole lot plugs in here. Got it?

Run it past me one more time.

OK, switch on here—this light comes on. OK? Double-click on the corner of the screen there—no, not there—there! Bring up the drop-down menu and right-click on the icon. . . . Yes, I know you've been using my computer but this is Windows 2000—I'm trying to show you the subtle differences.

Let's leave it now, and go out.

You don't want me to show you . . . ?

No, I don't want you to show me. I know from experience that when a man tries to show a woman anything technical, whether it's mending a puncture or changing a CD, it inevitably, eventually, leads to a nasty argument.

And if I haven't known you for as long as it takes to catch most infectious diseases, I'm sure as hell not ready to start having nasty arguments with you!

Let's go out.

We go to a Thai restaurant and over the appetizer we talk about his wife.

I don't want to talk about her, but it happens like this.

"It's great that you've got your own computer now," he says.

"Yes, I'm going to write everyday now. Get into a routine. Every evening after Ellie's in bed, I can spend a couple of hours on it."

He nods agreement.

"The only thing is," I add, taking a sip of my wine, "that I really need to earn some money, too. Now I haven't got any cleaning jobs, I thought perhaps I could advertise to do some home typing. Word processing. Perhaps," I joke, "there might be other authors out there who want someone to type up their manuscripts for them!"

"That's true—there might be," he says quite seriously. "Although I think most writers these days work on computers themselves. But Sarah could make enquiries for you, about anyone who might need any home typing. She's got a lot of contacts—friends in publishing companies and so on."

"Sarah?" I say, staring at my plate.

What I really want to say is: Fucking Sarah again?

I don't want Fucking Sarah to get me a job, thank you very much. Why does she have to butt in every time we start a conversation?

"What have you told her about me?" I ask abruptly.

"About you?" he asks in a surprised tone.

"Yes, me. What have you told her, apart from the fact that I've written part of a TV script on your computer? Does she know we're out together tonight, for instance? Does she know we're . . ." I hesitate here.

We're what? What are we? This is the crux of the matter, you see. Are we "lovers" or are we "having an affair"? "Having an affair" implies that one or both participants are doing something illicit. Is this illicit or isn't it? Is he married, or isn't he?

"Does she know we're seeing each other?" I substitute.

Strange modern expression meaning sleeping together.

"Well . . . I haven't exactly given her the whole picture!" He laughs nervously, picking up his fork again and tucking in with exaggerated enthusiasm to his appetizer.

"So how much of the picture have you given her?" I insist quietly.

He takes a long while chewing and swallowing some beansprouts that really didn't look very difficult to digest.

"She knows you used to clean my flat," he says eventually, still rooting around with his fork for the next mouthful. "And she knows about you using the computer . . ."

"Yes."

"But I haven't . . ." He looks up at me now and shakes his head. "No, Beth, I haven't told her yet that we're seeing each other . . . in this way."

"Yet?"

"I will. When an opportunity presents itself."

"So what does she think's going on? What does she think you're doing tonight? Out with your mates, I suppose?"

I don't mean to sound like this. I don't want to sound challenging, be difficult, pick a fight. I wouldn't have minded so much if her name didn't keep coming up, and always in this context of doing me a favor.

Should I be grateful to her? For reading my script, for trying to find me a job? For letting me shag her husband?

"No," he says. "I haven't told her any lies. She knows I'm with you tonight. But . . ." He looks uncomfortable. "But she thinks it's just to talk about your writing, and to discuss her trying to find you some typing work."

We eat the rest of our appetizers without saying very much.

This isn't going the way it should, is it? And it's my own fault—I know, I know. What did I expect? Did I think he was going to go rushing home to his wife—even if she *is* a wife "on paper only"—and tell her all the details of how we had sex twice in my bed on the first night we went out, and how we rolled naked on the carpet tonight with the dog chewing his ankles?

"Don't be angry with me," says Alex eventually. "Please. I'm sorry. Be patient with me, Beth, if you can. I need time, to tell her . . . to explain that it's really over this time."

"You told me she doesn't love you anyway."

"I don't think she has for years. But she's decided she still wants the marriage."

"Then surely she has to accept that you might meet someone else?"

"It'll be a shock. She still thinks I'm desperately grateful to her for having me back."

"And you're not? You don't still love her?"

You have to remember that I'm in a terribly weak position here. The weakness of my position is directly related to the severity of my feelings for this man. I've never felt so desperate about someone so quickly, never fallen so suddenly into a state of shaking, quivering, *unease*. I don't even know if it's a happy state—it's almost too frightening, too catastrophic, to be enjoyable.

I'm so frightened he's going to get up and walk back out of my life any minute now, as quickly and suddenly as he walked into it, that I've been reduced to this pathetic, whining, pleading mess.

You don't still love her, do you? Tell me you don't! And even if you tell me you don't, I won't believe you! How can I be sure? How can I trust you? How do I know you're not lying to me?

How does anyone ever know?

"I finished with Martin," I remind him pointedly, "because of meeting you."

"I know. But you hadn't been seeing him for very long . . ."

"He said he loved me! He wanted to marry me!"

OK, that's a bit of an exaggeration, but he was probably heading in that direction.

"I don't blame him," says Alex.

"Aren't you jealous?"

I want him to be jealous.

"I had sex with him all over the place. In the kitchen, the first time—against the sink! And one night . . ."

"Beth, don't let's do this to each other. Let's not try to score points. Neither of us are teenagers. We've both had other relationships." He pauses. "Mine just happens to have been a marriage. It's been a long time. I don't love her anymore, but I did. For ages."

I suddenly think about Daniel. How it felt to be with the same person, the person I knew best in the whole world, the person I'd been with from one Christmas to the next, from one summer holiday to the next, from one birthday to the next, and the next, and the next, until there wasn't even any question of it not going on forever. Or so I thought.

"OK," I say. "Yes, I know."

"I can't just cast it off—cast her off—like you finish with someone you've . . ." He smiles at me again. "Had a lot of sex with in the kitchen."

"OK."

I feel a bit ashamed now.

So he needs time to tell her it's over. So what? We haven't exactly had a lot of time yet, have we? And didn't he say that thing earlier about buying me gold or diamonds next year?

So perhaps he's not lying to me. Perhaps he really means it. Perhaps I can trust him.

Perhaps he's not going to let me down, like Daniel did.
Like Neil did to Fay.
Perhaps I can start trying to relax and enjoy this?

"I won't mention Sarah anymore," he says as he finishes
his dinner.
You just did, though.

Good Friday

———————◇◆◇◆◇———————

I'm getting used to the computer. In the evenings, after Ellie's in bed, I've been doing a bit of work on my script. But I've also been writing myself a résumé, and I've been on the Internet to find out about possible job opportunities. I've made myself a list of companies to start approaching.

My mum's proud of me.

"That's right, Beth," she says. "Get your résumé out to as many companies as you can. Flood the market! Sell yourself!"

I don't like to tell her that "the market" isn't like that these days. People aren't just sitting in their offices drumming their fingers on their desks waiting for a letter from me, selling myself, to pop through the post with its accompanying résumé, which upon reading they'll be so impressed they'll be straight on the phone offering me shares in the company and a six-figure salary.

"There's still no desperate rush," I remind her instead. "It's nearly five months till Ellie starts school."

"Never too soon to start making enquiries," she responds predictably.

I don't want to argue with her anymore, especially not now she's provided probably the lion's share of the computer. It's easier to spend a few hours a week preparing the résumé and the list of names and sending out the occasional letter to keep her happy.

Meanwhile the problem of my current lack of earnings has become acute. I went to the post office yesterday and put in another ad. Not for cleaning jobs this time but for:

WORD PROCESSING: Fast, professional, reliable service. Manuscripts, dissertations, résumés, all types of documents. Reasonable rates.

I haven't decided yet what the reasonable rates are going to be. I've had one response already, from a lady doing an Open University degree who wants a couple of essays typed. Should be easy.

"What do I charge her?" I asked Alex last night. "I've got no idea."

"I'll ask around," he said. "I'll . . . I'll find out."

He's going to ask Sarah, I suppose.

At least he hasn't mentioned the idea of her finding me work, anymore. There's no way I could cope with taking on work from his wife. It would feel completely wrong; it's bad enough knowing that she holds the key to my future in her hands by offering to consider my script. If it wasn't such an obvious case of chopping off my nose to spite my face, I'd tell Alex I didn't want her having anything to do with it.

"When she finds out we're having an affair," I've already told him, "she'll dump me as a potential client."

"She's harder headed than that. She's a shrewd businesswoman. If she thinks you're worth anything, she won't risk you going to another agency."

So she hasn't got any emotions? Just a hard head?

"If she's not going to care, why don't you tell her now?"

"I didn't say she wouldn't care. Just that it wouldn't stop her being your agent."

Funny, we weren't going to talk about Sarah anymore, but she seems to be coming into almost every conversation we have.

When I was in the post office I checked the balance of Ellie's account, and sure enough, Daniel's kept his word. He's paid in £100. I felt a wave of relief washing over me. It's like things have finally turned a corner. A little while ago everything seemed hopeless: I was borrowing money from Ellie without a clue as to how I was going to pay it back, I was losing cleaning clients faster than I could clean, and had no idea where the next day's daily bread was coming from. That first hundred pounds going back into her account makes me feel like anything's possible now. If Daniel keeps this up, before long I'll be back to where I was, financially, before I started borrowing Ellie's money, and if he's true to his promise of paying me more money every month, then things could really start to get easier. The Open University woman will be so pleased with the way I type her essays (I'm going to do them slowly and carefully, spell-check them three times and use some interesting artistic touches with different fonts and styles to make the headings and subheadings stand out)—that she'll recommend me to all her friends and I'll be so swamped with work I'll have to start turning people away.

You need it by next week? Sorry, I've got a four-month waiting list. I'm taking orders for next year now.

And then I'll start getting responses from all the companies I'm sending out my résumé to. They'll all want me to start work immediately but they're so keen to have me, they'll agree to wait till September. I'll have to disappoint one or two of them because I won't be able to go for all the interviews—too busy with the home typing—and at the end of the day I'll be able to choose the company that offers me the best salary and perks, with all the school holidays off and, of course, part-time hours to fit in with Ellie's schooling. I might even insist on a company car . . .

"Wake up, Mummy! Can we take Tosser for his walk? Can we go to the park? Can Jodie and Annie and Solomon come, too? Can we go to Lauren's house for lunch?"

I'm not asleep, Ellie.

Just dreaming.

The sun's out and so are the Good Friday crowds. The park's full of families enjoying their bank holiday together. New babies are propped up in strollers with hoods down and bonnets off, experiencing the sunshine on their heads for the first time. I look at them and think about Fay. Who will her baby resemble? If it's Neil how's she going to feel, looking at her child everyday for the rest of her life and seeing his eyes looking back at her? How will she be able to bear it? What's she going to tell the child? How the hell will it all turn out?

Look at these kids running along ahead of me with the dog.

Jodie, holding Tosser's lead, marching on in front with her sturdy, non-fat, non-thin legs, taking charge, bossing the younger ones around as usual—followed dutifully by Solomon (shoelaces undone, mud up his legs, stopping every five minutes to pick up stones, kick empty cans, jump on twigs, thrash imaginary alien invaders with his space saber or execute a complex and highly skilled maneuver in his imaginary robot car). Both followed with desperate urgency by Ellie, trotting along a couple of paces behind, calling out to them—Wait for me, wait for me!

And Annie, dawdling along, bringing up the rear, pretending she doesn't want to walk with them, doesn't want to take orders from her bossy big sister, but her body language telling a different story: wanting someone to turn around and see she's getting left behind. Wanting one of the others to ask her what's the matter. Someone to listen to her instead of Jodie.

Wait for me, don't leave me behind! Don't leave me out, don't forget me, don't let me be the one with no friends, the one no one wants to play with, the one in the corner of the playground with their thumb in their mouth pretending not to care! Don't let me grow up to be the girl no one asks out, the one waiting at home by the phone that never rings, the one who says she prefers her own company anyway and gets so used to it that it finally becomes true.

How are they all going to turn out? When Jodie gets through her prepubescent worries, when Annie finds her feet in the family and her place in the world, and when Solomon stops being a space cowboy and starts being a real boy? When Ellie grows up and goes to school?

Why am I feeling so morose and so unsettled?

Good Friday was always a mournful day when I was a kid. We weren't allowed to go out with our friends. We weren't a particularly Christian family but there were certain tenets of the faith to which my mother stuck like glue—most of them to do with not offending the neighbors. Apparently it might offend the neighbors if we played pop music, laughed or shouted too loud in the garden, or hung around in the street outside the house on

Sundays, because Sundays were supposed to be quiet and *respectable*. This had the effect of making Sunday a thoroughly miserable day for the whole family, and Good Friday was ten times worse. I realized at a very early age that hot cross buns were a kind of peace offering to make us behave properly on Good Friday—*Be quiet or no hot cross buns!*—and that Easter eggs were the splendid reward for adhering to the Sunday Rules all year round.

Old habits are hard to break. Childhood rules stick with you, however much you like to think you've broken away. I still find Sundays depressing, and I still don't like Good Friday.

"Are you having hot cross buns for tea today, Beth?" asks Jodie.

Of course I am, Jodie. I've been good enough, haven't I?!

In fact I decide to take two packs of hot cross buns with me to Fay's at lunchtime. I phone her about lunch. Will Simon be there? Will it be OK? Should I come or not?

She's very evasive on the phone.

Is he there now? Is it difficult for her to talk? Just say yes or no. Has she told him about the baby yet?

"What baby?" puts in Ellie, listening while she plays with Tosser in the kitchen.

Simon's not there, apparently, and yes, we should come to lunch. I feel uneasy about her tone of voice.

"What baby?" insists Ellie again as we go out to the car.

"Jack. I was talking about Jack."

"Jack's not a baby anymore!"

"I forgot."

She shakes her head, pity apparently overcoming her curiosity. Poor Mummy's cracking up. Must be her age.

* * *

Simon isn't home.

Lauren and Jack aren't dressed. Lauren's still in her pajamas and Jack's wearing a vest and a pair of training pants.

Fay's sitting in an armchair by the window, staring at the garden, with a cup of very cold coffee by her side.

"Are you all right?" I ask her.

She looks at me blankly and doesn't answer.

"Done a wee-wee!" shouts Jack.

"Can we have something to eat now?" says Lauren, looking worried.

"Hot cross buns!" sings Ellie. "One a penny, one a penny, one a penny!"

I steer the girls out of the living room, put some dry warm clothes on Jack, and send Lauren (with Ellie to help) into her bedroom to choose some clothes for herself while I make lunch.

Fay has never been like this. The children have always been spotlessly, immaculately washed, dressed, brushed and fed, no matter what was going on in her life. When she's been ill, when she was suffering terrible morning sickness with Jack, even when she was in labor, Lauren was still looked after first and foremost. Fay was always a coper. She coped when everyone else around her was collapsing. Me, for instance.

This scares me.

Where's Simon?

I put hot cross buns on plates for the children, pour out drinks of orange juice, and sit them at the kitchen table. Lauren and Jack fall on the food as if they haven't eaten all day. I don't actually think they *have*.

I take a fresh cup of coffee in to Fay and kneel down on the floor next to her chair, holding her hand. "What is it?"

She covers her face and shakes her head.

"Tell me, Fay. Where's Simon?"

"Gone," she says. "He's gone."

Gone? Gone where? It's Good Friday. Simon's fanatical about being with the family at weekends and holidays. He can't have gone further than Do It All.

"When will he be back?"

I think she might be having a breakdown.

I wonder if I should phone Simon on his mobile, see how long he's going to be.

"He won't," says Fay quietly. "He won't be back. He's gone."

In the kitchen, I can hear Ellie and Lauren trying to outdo each other with their singing.

Hot cross buns, hot cross buns!

One in your belly, two in your belly!

Hot cross bums! Hot cross bums!

One is smelly, two is smelly!

Hot cross mums! Hot cross mums!

Each fresh burst of creative talent is accompanied by squeals of raucous laughter. Jack, who can only relate to the humor of the version about "bums," repeats this over and over, shouting it out and banging the table.

"Hot coss bums! Hot coss bums"—which evokes fresh gales of laughter from the girls.

In a minute I'll have to go and settle them down, or it'll end in tears.

Fay isn't even crying. She just sits, staring into space, twisting her fingers together in her lap.

"You had a row?" I prompt.

She sighs, a huge, deep sigh, and nods. Yes, a row.

"So, don't worry. He'll be back, you know he will."

He will, won't he? Good old dependable Simon. He'll have gone off to cool down. He's not the type to lose his temper. He'll go away, stew over whatever it is they've rowed about.

"Was it . . . about the baby?"

"Yes, I told him last night."

"So, was he . . . not happy? I suppose it was a surprise? Bit of a shock?"

She looks at me properly for the first time, as if she's just noticed I'm here. "He was pleased," she says. "Surprised, but pleased. Excited. He was really excited, Beth."

"That's good, then, isn't it?"

She shakes her head. But now she's started to talk, she carries on until it all comes out. I just kneel there, holding her hand, listening, while the singing and the laughing goes on in the kitchen.

"He asked me how long I've known, why I hadn't said anything. I said I didn't want to tell him until I was sure . . ."

Hot cross bums! Hot cross bums!

"And he said it was wonderful news, and I wasn't to worry about anything, although it wasn't planned we'd manage, we'd get by and he'd help me with the other two kids and he'd look after me if I felt ill like I did with Jack . . ."

One a penny, one in your belly . . .

"And he came over and gave me a hug, and told me how happy he was, and . . . Beth, it was just seeing his face, so . . . caring and concerned, and so pleased and proud and everything . . ."

Give them to your daughters, give them to your sons!

"I just started to cry. I couldn't help it, I just couldn't stand seeing him so happy, and being so lovely and thinking it was his child and everything was fine, and I started to cry and I just couldn't stop . . ."

One old smelly, two old smelly . . .

"And he asked me what was wrong, why was I crying,

was I worried about having another baby? Was I worried about money, because he'd take on more work, I wasn't to worry, and the more he said, the more I cried, until I was almost hysterical and he was getting really worried, trying to calm me down and asking, 'What is it? What's wrong? What's wrong?' And then he suddenly stopped, and stared at me, and it was like a light came on in his mind and he knew. He went, 'It's not mine, is it? It's not my baby.'"

"What did you say?" I whisper, my voice hoarse.

"I don't know. I don't think I said anything. I was still crying, just crying and not even caring what he thought, or that he knew. I felt like I was past caring . . ."

Hot cross tums! Hot cross tums! In your belly, in your belly . . .

"And he walked away, across the room, and turned his back on me, then he just said, 'Who is he?' And I think I said, 'It's finished.' Or 'It's over.' And . . ."

There's a sudden, unnatural silence from the kitchen. I try not to notice. They can't be killing each other: they'd make some noise about it.

"And?" I prompt.

"And he said so were we. We're finished too, he said. He went upstairs, and I went after him—I was still crying, I could hardly see, or speak, or walk I was in such a state. I followed him upstairs and he was getting stuff out of the wardrobes and packing a bag . . ."

"He'll be back, Fay—I'm sure he will."

"I begged him. I was begging him, telling him I was sorry, it was all a mistake, it didn't mean anything, I still love him . . ." She turns to look at me now, shaking her head, her face creased with frowns. "But it was Neil I was crying for. I said all that to Simon, but it was Neil . . ."

"You're upset. You're confused. You don't know what you want."

"And he picked up his bag and . . . went. He just went, and slammed the door, and I don't know where he's gone." She shudders, and her eyes suddenly fill with tears. "I didn't mean for this to happen!" she says, in a thin wail, shaking her head and beginning to rock herself back and forth. "I didn't mean to tell him! I didn't want him to go! I didn't want . . ."

Mummy! Mummy! Jack's thrown his drink all over the floor! Mummy, Jack's climbing on the table! MUMMY!

It takes a while to clean up the kitchen.

The children are quiet now that their hysteria has subsided, and somewhat subdued by the sight of their mother curled up on the sofa sniffing softly into a wad of tissues.

"Mummy's not very well," I tell them gently. I cover her with a blanket and tell her to close her eyes. She's told me she didn't sleep all night and I'm hoping she'll be so exhausted she'll doze off.

"Has she got a cold?" asks Ellie. "Or a tummy ache?"

"She was sick," Lauren informs her. "This morning, in the toilet."

"She needs you to be very grown up and very helpful," I tell Lauren, before she can go into detail as only a four-year-old can, "while she's not feeling well. Can you do that, Lauren?"

She looks doubtful. "I can, but I don't know about Jack."

"I know. Jack's only little. But if you're both good children it will really help Mummy to feel better."

"Where's Daddy?"

It was only a matter of time, wasn't it. I don't know what Fay would have wanted me to tell them. "He's just had to go to work for a while," I prevaricate.

She seems to accept this without any surprise whatsoever. I close my eyes and inside my head I'm praying: *Please, Simon, come back, if only for the kids. Never mind you and Fay, you can sort it out later, or even if you don't, come back now for the kids and work something out that's acceptable for them. Please don't just stay away, now, without even saying good-bye to them, without even telling them where you are—just come back, please, please, come back tonight, or tomorrow, please!*

"What's the matter, Mummy?" asks Ellie.

"Nothing, darling," I tell her quickly.

I look at their anxious faces, all looking back at me, waiting for direction, waiting for me to take control of a situation they're not comfortable with. Mummy's not well. The world is thrown off its axis. Who's going to look after us?

"How about," I say to Lauren and Jack, putting my arms around them both and steering them toward their bedrooms, "we get your pajamas, and some of your things, and you come back and stay with me and Ellie tonight?"

When we've packed their bags I take Fay a cup of tea. "I'm going to take the children back to play with Ellie," I tell her.

"Thank you," she says flatly, sounding completely uninterested.

"Would you like to come too? You can have my bedroom, and sleep all day and all night if you want, and I'll look after you . . ."

"No." She turns over to face me. "No, I'll stay here," she says in the same flat voice. "I want . . . to be here."

In case he comes back.

"Let me make you something to eat, then."

"No."

"Fay, you must eat. You've got to . . ."

"I'm not hungry."

"You've got to think about the baby. Let me just make you a sandwich. Please."

She shrugs.

I go out to the kitchen and make her two rounds of sandwiches. My hands are shaking as I butter the bread. I don't know if I'm doing the right thing. Am I helping her by looking after the children, or should I be staying with her? Should I leave the children with her so that she has to make an effort? But I'm scared that she won't.

"I'll phone you later," I tell her firmly, putting the sandwiches down beside her. "And if you need me, I'll come straight back. Try to go to sleep."

"All right."

If she's still like this tomorrow, if Simon's not back, I'm going to call the doctor.

I try to call her later, when the children are in their pajamas and watching TV. There's no reply. Is she asleep? Should I go round there and check on her? Has she gone out? Perhaps Simon's come back, or phoned her, and she's gone to meet him somewhere?

My heart thumping, sick with anxiety, I call Simon's mobile, and there's no reply from that either.

What a mess.

What a bloody, fucking mess.

Saturday

———◦◇◦———

"What did you think? I'd kill myself?"

Fay answers the phone at seven o'clock in the morning. It's the third time I've tried to phone since quarter past six when I couldn't stand it any longer, lying awake staring at the clock, imagining everything imaginable (and unimaginable) that might have happened to her. I'm beside myself. When she finally answers, I feel faint and sick with relief.

"I didn't know what to think. You were in a state. I shouldn't have left you . . ."

"Yes, you should. It was what I needed. I couldn't cope with the kids. I needed to sleep but I didn't want to. Once I did, I must have slept like the dead."

She sounds better. Calmer, quieter. I don't want to ask.

"I haven't heard from him," she says.

"Have you tried his mobile?"

I don't tell her that I already have.

"Turned off."

"I'm sure he'll be back today."

She doesn't answer. I feel useless, utterly and completely useless.

* * *

Jack wakes up early and starts shouting, waking up the girls. I've gotten out of the habit of having a toddler around, especially a noisy and lively one like Jack.

"He gets on my nerves," says Ellie with heartfelt irritation as she eats her breakfast.

"He can't help it," Lauren defends him, to my surprise. "He's only little."

I'm just thinking how nice it is that siblings will stick together when they're in an unfamiliar situation, when Jack responds by throwing his spoon at Lauren, making her cry.

But he can't help it. He's only little.

"When are we going home?" asks Lauren.

Normally I can't tear her away from Ellie but today they don't even seem to want to settle down to playing together. It's like they're waiting for something to happen.

"Well, I've spoken to Mummy," I tell her in my false, bright, adult-in-control-of-the-situation voice, "and she's feeling quite a lot better now."

I want the children home now.

Are you sure? Are you sure you can cope?

Yes. Thanks for everything, Beth, but I think I'll feel better if I try to get on as if everything's normal.

Even though it isn't.

"But Daddy might not be home for a while, yet," I add. I don't want Lauren going bouncing into the house expecting to see him, calling out to him, her face dropping when she sees he's still not there. "So you need to help Mummy as much as you can."

"I thought you said she was better?"

"Yes, but she's still . . . quite tired."

* * *

I drive them home toward lunchtime.

"Still no word?" I ask Fay quietly.

She shakes her head. She looks pale, but more composed, more in control.

"Is there anything else I can do?" I ask her, still feeling helpless. "Perhaps you should ask your mum and dad to come over?"

"No, not yet. If . . ." She hesitates, and then, taking a deep breath, goes on, "If he doesn't come back, I'll have to tell them. God knows how. I feel . . . so ashamed, Beth."

"Ashamed? But it's not your fault . . ." I stop, and we stare at each other.

"It is, isn't it, you see?" she says calmly. "It's all my fault. And all for what? A bit of excitement."

"No. No, you couldn't help it. Remember how you felt, when you met Neil? How it felt like it was meant to be, like you'd always known each other?"

"I seem to remember you telling me it was a load of bollocks," she says with a sour, twisted smile.

"I wasn't being fair. I didn't know . . . didn't understand how these things can happen. Don't be so hard on yourself. You didn't mean for it to happen."

"No, I didn't. But look where it got me. I think you were right all along. A load of bollocks."

A load of bollocks.

I keep thinking about it, turning it over and over in my mind, as I'm driving home. All that emotion, all that excitement and life-changing, life-threatening feeling for someone—all she went through, the deceit, the lies, the risk to our friendship and to her marriage, to say nothing of finishing up pregnant and deserted—dismissed, in the end, as rubbish, nonsense, a load of bollocks.

No! It had to be worth more than that, didn't it? Remember her saying that even if it ended, she'd have no regrets, because she couldn't ever regret having met him? Surely she can't have changed her mind?

Can she?

I hear the phone ringing as I get Ellie out of the car, but it's stopped by the time I open the front door. I punch in *69 and it's Alex's number. Just hearing the number, I start to feel breathless and almost dizzy with excitement. I'm supposed to be seeing him tonight. Perhaps he can't wait.

But it's a girl's voice answering the phone.

I can't think what to say.

"Hello? I . . . er . . . Beth Marston here. Did someone call me from this number?"

"Yes, hello, Beth. It's Sarah. Sarah Chapman."

She's calling me about my script, she says.

She says she thinks it's great.

It shows amazing potential.

I listen, and nod, stupidly, as if she can see me, and I stare at my reflection in the mirror in the hall, and I mutter things like *Oh, thank you!* and *Do you really think so?* and *Oh, that's kind of you!* until they begin to stick in my throat and I can't say them anymore, and all I can think of is: this is Alex's wife.

I'm having this conversation with Alex's wife, and she doesn't even know. She doesn't even know that I've been screwing him, we've been shagging each other at every possible opportunity, and we're looking forward to doing it again tonight. Even while she's telling me how she can't wait for me to complete the next part of my masterpiece, how she's looking forward to working with me, how she hopes we're going to enjoy a very successful partnership . . . even while I'm listening to her saying these things to me, which should be the most exciting things anyone's ever said to me in my life, the things I dreamed of hearing a literary agent say to me all those years ago when Daniel and I used to dream our dreams together back in college when we were young and bright and eager and our vision was clear and our ambitions pure . . . even now, I'm imagining myself in bed with her husband and she's got no idea, no idea at all that when she thinks he's talking to me about my writing abilities he's actually kissing me and taking off my clothes and sucking my nipples and . . .

". . . and Alex and I were talking about you yesterday."

I snap back to reality with an unpleasant start. She and Alex were talking about me?

"We were saying how amazing it was that there you were, cleaning his flat for him, and all the time we were completely unaware that this amazing work was unfolding almost before his very eyes, this amazing talent . . ."

"Oh, please, Sarah!"

I feel embarrassed now. The only talent of mine that Alex is interested in has nothing to do with scriptwriting.

"No, I mean it. I'm really very glad that you happened to be working for Alex, and you happened to use his computer."

She wouldn't be glad, if she knew what I was doing for Alex the other night.

"And as I said to Alex yesterday—we should think ourselves very lucky. I told him: Beth Marston could quite possibly be the best thing to happen to us for a long time."

* * *

Ellie and I are going to say good-bye to Dottie today. She and Luke are leaving for the airport early this evening. I offered to drive them to Heathrow, but Luke said he'd already booked a taxi.

"My parents have paid for it," he told me, quite brusquely, making me feel unwanted.

We've purposely left Tosser at home. No point in making things any more painful than they have to be.

"How's Tosser?" she asks, nevertheless, as soon as we're through the front door.

"He's settled in really well," I reassure her, unable to keep the amazement out of my voice.

She tries not to look offended.

"But I expect he's probably just a bit quiet at the moment because he's missing you," I add quickly, watching her satisfied nod.

"Tosser's my best friend in the whole world," Ellie tells her in her Poor-Little-Orphan-with-Nobody-to-Love-Me voice. "He licks my toes."

"Ah, well," says Dottie with a smile. "He only does that to his *best* friends."

"Why are you going to 'Stralia? I don't want you to go. Tosser doesn't want you to go."

Dottie gives her a huge hug and takes her by the hand out to the kitchen. "I'm going to miss you, and your mummy, and old Tosser, but I'm going to live with my family so I'm happy about that," she tells Ellie. "Now, why don't I cut you a nice piece of my special Good-bye and Happy Easter Cake?"

She takes the lid off a cake tin and reveals a chocolate sponge, iced and decorated with chocolate buttons and a bright yellow Easter chicken. Ellie's face turns red with excitement and pleasure.

"OH!" she exclaims. "Oooh!"

She looks as though she's never seen a homemade cake before. Actually, I don't think she ever has.

"Dottie!" I chide her gently. "How have you managed to find the time to do that, with everything else . . ."

"Everything else has been done for days now. I've been kicking around here, all my stuff packed or sold, not knowing what to do with myself. I'll be glad when we're on our way now."

I suppose I can understand that.

"Piece of cake, Luke?" she calls into the lounge.

"Yer, right," comes the unenthusiastic response.

I resist the urge to take the whole cake and ram it, custard-pie style, into his miserable little face. No, the cake looks much too good for that.

Dottie and I sit in the kitchen with our cups of tea and our plates of chocolate cake. Ellie, who's been given the yellow Easter chick that she's holding lovingly in a sticky, chocolatey hand, has already finished eating and has gone to watch TV in the living room with Luke. I hope she asks him lots of awkward questions about whatever he's watching.

"So what have you been up to?" asks Dottie eventually. "How's that new man of yours?"

"Martin? I finished with him."

She nods wisely. "Not surprised. You didn't really want him, did you."

"I suppose I couldn't have. I thought I did. But I only really finished with him because of Alex."

"Mr. Gorgeous Hunk? The best thing in the universe?"

"Don't make fun, Dottie." Unexpectedly, ridiculously, my eyes fill up with tears.

She puts down her plate, grabs my hand with both her old fleshy ones, and looks at me with concern. "Hey, what's all this? I was only teasing, you daft thing! What's up with you?"

"Nothing. I don't know. It's just . . . been a bit of an emotional weekend."

I tell her about Fay.

She listens, shaking her head and tut-tutting sympathetically.

"Will her husband come back, d'you think?"

"Yes, I'm sure he will, because of the children. He's such a good family man it's just inconceivable that he'd walk out on them and stay away. He'll be back when he's calmed down and got over the shock. But I don't know whether he'll stay. I don't know what's going to happen. And now, she's saying—"

"That she's sorry? That she wishes it hadn't happened?"

"How did you know?"

"Nothing like consequences for making you have regrets!" She smiles. "Bet she wouldn't be feeling sorry if she hadn't got found out!"

"Dottie!"

"Come on, Beth! Your friend's only human. She's not the first or the last person in the world to have an affair. It goes on all the time, all over the world, all through history, and we still think when it happens to us that we're unique. Not that I don't feel sorry for the poor girl," she adds. "Love's a pail of shit, isn't it!"

"I don't think she even knows who she loves, now," I tell her, frowning again at my own confusion, at Fay's confusion. "Neil, or Simon."

"Or both of them, or neither of them. Who can blame her? Who really has any answers to any of it? Pail of shit!" she chuckles. "Tell you what, Beth, it's a relief when you get to my age and you start getting immune to it all. The only thing that gets *my* pulse racing these days is a plate of cod and fries and a glass of Guinness!"

"Lucky you," I tell her with feeling. "Right now, I think I'd swap places with you." Except I don't like Guinness.

"So what's wrong with Mr. Wonderful?" she asks me gently, getting up to pour another cup of strong dark tea out of her big brown china teapot.

"Nothing," I say, folding my arms tightly across my chest as if to protect myself. "Nothing. He's . . . just that. Wonderful. But . . ."

"He's married?"

I have to wait a few seconds before answering.

A few seconds, during which the world keeps turning round, and all the clocks in the world keep ticking away, and all those babies out there keep on being born and all those people everywhere keep on dying. And everyone's life goes on, and nothing really changes, but somewhere in the back of my mind, in the recesses of my heart, I know something, even though I don't want to admit it yet.

"He's *kind* of married."

"He still lives with her?"

"Yes, but they separated and . . . she had him back. But . . ."

"He says it's over? They don't love each other? They're only together for convenience?"

I nod.

"And he's going to tell her about you . . . when the time's right . . . and he's going to leave her . . ."

"When the time's right." I nod again.

"And you believe him?" she asks, even more gently.

"I think he means it," I say, looking down at my feet, wondering whether this pain in my chest is the beginnings of a heart attack. How would I know? When should I scream and call for an ambulance?

"I'm sure he does," says Dottie matter-of-factly. "Here. Drink your tea."

"How am I going to manage, Dottie?" I ask her, sipping my tea and swallowing it hot, gasping as I feel it all the way down past the pain in my heart. "How am I going to cope without talking to you? What am I going to do without you?"

"You daft moo!" she laughs. "What you bloody crying about? I'm only going to Australia! I'm not dead yet! They've got phones in Australia, you know—they're getting civilized over there now! I'll phone you up, you silly cow, I'll phone you every week! Do you think I'm going to spend all the rest of me life wondering what's going on back here? I want to know how Tosser's getting on, for one thing. I want to know what these two old dears next door are up to. I want to hear about Ellie starting school, and what happens about your poor friend and her husband, and her baby." She stops and gives me a very pointed, very old-fashioned look. "And I want to know what happens to you, too."

"Nothing, probably, Dottie," I say moodily, wiping away a tear.

"Don't talk daft. Nothing? Is that what you call it? Agents falling over themselves to sell your writing . . ."

"Not quite!" I manage to smile.

"They will be. And men falling over themselves for you, too."

"Hardly!"

"It looks that way from where I'm standing, Beth, believe me! And sooner or later . . ."

"What?"

"Sooner or later, dear," she says, and her voice wobbles a bit as she reaches over and pats my hand. "Sooner or later, Beth, dear, there'll be a Mr. Wonderful who doesn't belong to someone else."

* * *

That's the thing I knew.

I knew it; perhaps I knew it all along but I didn't want to.

I still don't want to, but now I know that I know it, it's kind of hard to go on.

Tonight is the night we're going to face it. Both of us.

I've asked Louise to have Ellie, and I wait till we're in bed together. Afterward.

"I don't want to go on doing this," I tell him softly, tracing his lips with my fingers. "I don't want to go on having an affair . . . with a married man."

"Oh, Beth, I've told you. You know how it is. We're not *really* married."

"Shush." My fingers come to rest against his mouth, holding it still. "You're married," I say. "The details aren't relevant."

He looks surprised, almost hurt. "Are you asking me to leave her?"

"No, I'm not asking anything of you. I can't. I can't make rules for you or give you ultimatums. I can only do that for myself."

He's silent, holding me, but looking at the top of my head as if he can't bear to look into my eyes.

"And what are they?" he asks eventually. "The rules? The ultimatums—for yourself?"

"Not to cause any more mess," I whisper.

It wasn't meant to be a whisper. When I thought about what I was going to say to him, I planned to say it firmly and strongly, like I was convinced it was right. Like there would be no hesitation, no turning back. Instead, it comes out as this pathetic and puny little sigh that any fool can tell I haven't got my heart in.

"I don't want to go on," I persist, trying again to make my voice come out with a bit more conviction, "unless it feels right."

"And it doesn't?" he asks me sadly. "This doesn't feel right?"

"No."

I don't know what else to say to him. I don't want to make a big scene. I also don't want my heart broken.

"Can't I see you again?" he says, sitting up on the edge of the bed, facing away from me.

"Yes, when you're free—really free, Alex. However long that takes. If I meet you again next month, or next year, or in ten years' time, and you're not with her any-more . . ."

"You might not wait. You might meet someone else!"

"Yes, I might."

And you might never leave her.

"Was it because of me?" Fay asks me sadly. "Because of how things have ended up with Neil? With Simon?"

"Partly."

Partly because of Neil, partly because of Simon.

How can I explain it?

Partly because of Sarah, who talks about me to her husband and thinks he's only seeing me to discuss my writing.

Partly because of Dottie, who's over eighty and knows that nothing's new in the world, nothing's new about any-one's affairs, anyone's love or lust or pain or suffering, and can laugh and shrug and say she'd rather have cod and fries.

Partly because of Louise and Ben, and how they've

stayed together, with their children, despite everything that's happened to screw up their lives.

Partly because of Daniel, who hurt me so much I didn't think I'd ever recover, and I'm only just beginning to be able to talk to him now like he's not a psychopathic monster but a fallible human being who just happened to fuck it all up.

Partly because of Ellie.

Partly because of my mum, and my sister, and my brother, who want to see me make something of myself, not because they think my life's crap or that they're better than me because they've got careers while I've been going out cleaning, but because they happen to care about me.

It's because of all those people.

But mostly it's because of me.

That's all. Because of me, and who I am, what I want to be and what I don't want to become.

I hope Alex can understand. But, if he can't, I suppose one day I'll get over it, and I'll still be myself, and I won't have fucked up.

Monday

◆─◆◆◆─◆

Mondays are chicken sandwiches. Cheese and onion chips, Jaffa cakes, and an individual carton of orange juice. Ellie's lunch box is ready and her little yellow school bag is hanging on the chair where she's sitting doing up her school shoes.

"Come on, Ellie," I remind her gently as I finish my coffee and look at myself briefly in the mirror. No time for makeup. Is there ever? At least the reflection looking back at me is half-decent. A new blouse, a new jacket—a smart new hairstyle. A new job in an office. A new life.

Ellie's been at school for five weeks now and it's going well. She's in Mrs. Williams's class and sits next to Lauren on the Red Table. She wears a round cardboard badge, colored red, with "r—e—d" on the badge in her own writing. It seems unfair on the kids on the Yellow Table—more letters to learn.

"My numbers book!" she shouts, jumping off the chair and tearing into her bedroom. "Where's my numbers book?"

"In your bag," I tell her, trying not to get impatient, trying not to initiate the process that will lead to frayed tempers and a bad start to her day (and a bad whole day for me, sitting in the office agonizing about being a terrible mother, long after she's recovered and enjoying herself at school).

"OK," she says, collecting her bag and smiling at me. "Let's go, Mummy!"

Sometimes, on ordinary school days like this, now that we're both used to the routine, I look at her and feel a flutter of something like fear in my heart. Only a few weeks ago she was my baby, but now she belongs to an outside world I can't even share. She's growing up. She's becoming a person I will gradually know less and less about until the day she leaves home.

"Tell me everything!" I say to her sometimes in the afternoons when I pick her up from Fay's after work. "Tell me everything about your day at school!"

She looks at me and laughs, probably wondering why I have to be so fierce about it, so determined, so anxious not to miss out on a single thing.

I turn off the car radio so I can listen properly.

"What did you do first? And what after that? And who did you play with at playtime? And what did Mrs. Williams say about your drawing? And how many pages of your book have you read now? And what did you do after lunch? And what was the story about?"

Don't keep anything from me. Don't leave me out of your life! She doesn't mind this interrogation. She likes to share it all with me—the lessons, the stories, the games, the little dramas of life in the reception class. Who was naughty, who fell over, who was sick, whose mummy is having another baby . . .

* * *

"When is Fay's baby coming?" she asks me suddenly this morning, in the middle of a long complicated story about why Samantha isn't allowed to sit next to Nadia anymore.

"Around Christmas time."

She smiles. "She'll be like Mary, then. In the Baby Jesus story."

Well. Perhaps not quite.

It's Simon who answers the door when we get to Fay's house.

"I'll take the girls to school today," he says, holding the door open for Ellie. "Fay's still asleep. She had a bad night with Jack."

Jack normally sleeps better now but he's got a bad cough that's keeping him awake at the moment.

"Poor Fay. Are you sure it's OK, Simon? I could take them . . ."

"No, don't be silly. Your new job . . . !" He shakes his head almost crossly. He's different these days, yet in a funny way even more like himself than ever. More serious, more responsible, even more caring. But somehow a bit more distant. "I've phoned work—it's no problem," he says. "I'll go in a little later. I want to make sure she's all right. Maybe Jack should see the doctor."

I'd like to give him a hug and tell him how much we all appreciate him—me, Ellie, Fay, Lauren, Jack. How glad we all are that he came back. I've never said those things to him but I suppose Fay must have.

Has he forgiven her?

She says she doesn't know. She says sometimes she sees something in his eyes, a cold, sad, bitter look that he blinks away when he notices her watching him. She says he talks about the baby as if there isn't any doubt it's his—as if they planned all along to have a third child.

"We never mention Neil," she says, her eyes going watery.

"Better than endless recriminations. Better than always rowing about it."

"But it's like he never existed. Like it was a fantasy."

Perhaps it was.

Perhaps love always is a fantasy, and that's all it deserves to be. It's the villain in too many stories, too many people's lives, messing up too many happy endings, to be anything else. It probably should never be taken seriously. Look what it does to us! It's a pain in the neck. We're better off without it. Do I sound like I'm trying to convince myself?

I'm keeping myself busy. That's the best thing.

I work for a public relations company. It's quite a junior position but I like the work and the people are friendly, and they've told me they'll be very flexible about odd days off for Nativity plays, non-teacher days, and sudden vomiting illnesses. If I stay there I might get a pay raise after six months and if Kate in the next office leaves I might even apply for her job. Who knows? I could own the company before I'm forty. No harm hoping. We all need ambitions.

My screenplay's finished and it's being considered by a publisher. Sarah Chapman keeps telling me how hopeful she is. She tells me that, and she tells me other things, too. It was surprising how easy she was to talk to, how easily we became friendly, once I stopped seeing Alex.

"A while ago," she told me when we met over drinks some time back, to discuss my work, "I had a suspicion my husband was seeing another woman."

We were in the wine bar where I'd met Alex, the first night we had sex. I felt my face go hot, followed swiftly by the rest of my body.

"And?" I prompted weakly. "Was he?"

"I don't know," she admitted, toying with her glass. "If he was, I'm pretty sure it's over now. Not that it matters." I didn't dare to ask why it didn't matter, but she carried on, "We're . . . in a silly sort of situation, really. Married, but not really married. Separated, but still together. We need to sort it out. It isn't fair on either of us."

"So . . . ?"

"So, we're discussing it. We both need to be free, properly free. We're sorting it out."

She might have wondered why I found it hard to concentrate for the rest of the evening. But ever since then, if the subject comes up (and it does, quite frequently) of her and Alex and their relationship, she raises her eyes, shakes her head, sighs and mutters about difficulties and financial situations and problems of finding other accommodation and how long it takes to "sort things out," until eventually she shrugs and changes the subject.

I think they're letting it drift on. I suppose it's easier to just drift on like that, when the alternative is facing a lot of hassle. And the longer it goes on, the easier it is just to accept the situation.

Especially if neither of them is involved with anyone else.

When I think about neither of them being involved with anyone else, I cry a little bit into my pillow, and then hit the pillow and call myself names for crying. Then I hit the pillow again and call it bastard, pig, fucking bastard, and ask it why it doesn't sort its life out, leave her and come back to me. And then I grab the pillow and hug it and squeeze it and tell it I didn't mean it, I still love it and will wait for it forever . . . and then I cry all over it again.

Still not being entirely rational, then.

Today, at work, I cope on my own, without losing my cool, with a notoriously difficult client and my boss actually pats me on the shoulder and tells me I'm doing very well. I feel myself grinning all the way to the sandwich bar where I buy my lunch. I sit for a while in the autumn sunshine on a bench by the river and watch the swans and the boats and contemplate how my life has changed since the beginning of the year. I feel almost happy. Almost. I dare to ask myself, quietly, just very quietly in the depths of my soul, whether I'd be able to deal with it now if Alex never comes back to me. Could I be happy on my own? Could I eventually settle for that? Me and Ellie and the dog forever?

A new me—a self-confident, self-assured, self-contained me—could I do it? Could I look the world in the eye and say: Fuck you, I don't need you, I don't need any man to make me happy?

I hold up my head and feel the breeze and imagine myself saying it. It feels good, but still like an act, a cover-up—something I can't quite manage—yet—to carry off properly.

Ask my pillow.

Ellie's chattering excitedly in the car about a boy who shut his finger in the toilet door and got taken to the hospital.

"He was screaming!" she tells me with great pleasure. "And his finger was all squashed and red and it might fall off!"

"I don't think so," I try to reassure her.

But she looks disappointed at this and insists, "Everyone said it might fall off!"

"Well, OK, it might," I concede, "but probably not. Still, it wasn't very nice for poor Thomas."

"Thomas is horrible," retorts Ellie. "He runs around the classroom and won't sit down."

Lucky he only got a squashed finger, then.

We're still talking about Thomas and his finger and his lack of discipline when we get home. While I'm feeding Tosser we discuss the latest page of the adventures of Robert Red Coat and Binita Blue Coat, and while we eat our tea we get on to the subject of the classroom autumn collage for which Ellie has to provide leaves, pinecones, or acorns, all of which, she informs me, we can find when we take Tosser for his walk in the park and which MUST be conveyed to school in a small plastic bag measuring twenty centimeters by thirty centimeters, bearing a white label with Ellie's name on it.

"But I don't mind," I point out reasonably, "if the leaves and pinecones don't get returned afterward."

"But they have to have my name on it. Mrs. Williams says so."

As I'm washing up, and contemplating the goddess-like status now afforded to Mrs. Williams, who has the power to make thirty-odd parents scour the park for leaves, scour the supermarket for the right size of plastic bag and stick a label on it even though none of us want the bloody thing back, the phone rings and I answer it absent-mindedly, acorns being uppermost in my mind.

"Hello, Beth. It's Sarah."

My heart gives a jump and acorns are forgotten. Is it the script? A decision from the publisher? Already? Surely not—not this soon.

"It's not about the script," she preempts me. "Not yet."

"No . . . I thought it was a bit soon. So what . . . ?"

There's a silence of perhaps ten seconds before my life changes forever.

"I know, Beth. About you and Alex. He's told me."

She's calm.

She's not upset.

She knew there was someone, she tells me, and she did sometimes wonder . . .

"You guessed it was me?" I ask her weakly.

"Well, you know how you pick up on things. When you see someone everyday, you see changes . . . notice little things they say . . ."

"But we're not seeing each other anymore," I say all in a rush. "I stopped—I finished it—when I realized he was still with you."

"I know. Thank you," she says.

Thank you? Fucking thank you?! She's thanking me for kicking her husband out of bed? Can this conversation get any weirder?

"I'm sorry," I tell her, having no idea what else to say.

"You don't have to be. I won't try to hold on to him. I knew it was only a matter of time. It's not as though things have been awful between us—there aren't any fights or arguments. But there isn't anything else, either. We've been a—kind of a habit for each other. Like a security blanket. It's been easier to stay together than to split up. Do you know what I mean?"

Not really, but I mumble something that I hope sounds sort of understanding.

"We've been talking for ages about sorting it out—separating properly. In the end I forced the issue. I said, 'Look, this is ridiculous. Are you ever going to get around to telling me? Have you got someone else, or haven't you? Are you going to leave, or aren't you?' He's already got his flat, as you know. We'll get on with the financial stuff now. And divorce, I suppose, eventually."

I hear her sigh.

"I'm sure you'll meet someone new, yourself . . ." I'm trying, desperately, to make it all feel better.

"I don't really care whether I do or not," she replies sadly. "I think my career is more important to me now. Don't worry, Beth. This won't affect our business relationship—needless to say . . ."

Six months. It's taken him six bloody months to make up his mind.

I don't know how I should be feeling about this.

Perhaps I should be thinking—well, if it takes you this long to decide whether you want me or not, whether you'd rather stay in a security-blanket marriage with someone who prefers her career and only hangs on to you because it's too much trouble to get a divorce—if you couldn't even be bothered to make a decision until she asked you outright whether you'd prefer to stay or leave—well, fuck you then! Now you haven't got me *or* her! See how you like being in your Single Young Executive apartment all on your own for the rest of your life, because *I* don't give a shit.

Except, of course, that I do.

"Men are so bloody lazy, Beth," sighs Sarah as if she can read my mind. "They'd never do anything unless they're driven to it."

And—even then—perhaps they still don't. After all, he's not here now, is he?

I stay sitting like this after I put down the phone—staring at the floor, staring at my feet.

I look at the clock. Half past seven.

I look at it again. Quarter to eight.

"Mummy! Tosser hasn't had his walk!" shouts Ellie from the kitchen.

I put his leash on, put my coat on, help Ellie into hers, pick up my key and a plastic bag.

"Is it the right size?" begins Ellie anxiously.

"It's too dark now for leaves and acorns. This is the poop-scoop bag. We're not going as far as the park."

We set off down the road, Tosser pulling on his lead, wanting a run.

"Why are you quiet?" asks Ellie.

"I'm thinking."

I'm not, really, because I'm numb. I'm afraid to think. I don't want to start wondering: What if . . . ? What if not . . . ?

I'm trembling inside with the weight of what I'm not allowing myself to think about.

It's ten past eight when we've completed a quick circuit of the streets and reached home again.

"Come on, Ellie—bedtime—it's late already," I tell her.

She starts whining. She's tired; it's my fault.

"I'll get you a drink of milk and a cookie while you get into your 'jamas," I offer. "If you're quick."

I read her a story while she drinks her milk and nibbles her cookie, slowly, turning it around, licking the edges, devouring it crumb by crumb to make it last longer. By the time she's cleaned her teeth and brushed her hair she's half asleep on her feet. School does a good job of tiring her out.

I close her bedroom door and go back into the living room.

What now?

I can't watch the TV, can't read, can't even bring myself to phone Fay or Louise or my mum or my sister. Perhaps I'll just go to bed, bury my head under the pillow that's taken so much battering and so much tear-soaking, close my eyes and go to sleep—and not wake up until I know the answer. I need to know the answer, for God's sake! For fuck's sake! I need to know the answer to the only question that matters now. How long have I got to wait? Hours? Days? Weeks? Months? The longer I wait, the longer it goes on, does it mean it's less likely to be yes, more likely to be no, or does it just mean I've still got to wait? Can I stand it? Will I go mad?

The doorbell rings at the precise moment that I decide I'll probably go mad.

"Hello," he says.

He's standing on the doorstep, half-hidden by a bouquet of roses almost as big as himself, trying to look at me through the stems, trying not to get his face scratched by the thorns.

And maybe I am going mad, after all, because all I can do is laugh.

We stand there, with the front door open and Tosser sniffing suspiciously around our feet, and we both laugh as if this is the funniest happening in the history of the world, and a squadron of about two hundred moths comes pouring into the light and they buzz around our heads, making us duck and wave our arms about ridiculously, and he's nearly dropping the bloody roses and still we're both laughing and I think actually I'm crying, too, and then he notices me crying and says, "Don't!"

He comes into the hall, pushing the front door shut behind him, dumping the flowers on the floor, and takes both my hands in his, looks at me, and says, "I'm sorry, Beth."

Just that—I'm sorry.

"Six months," I say, sniffing. "Six bloody months, Alex!"

"I know. I know, I know, I'm sorry! I'm a stupid bastard and I don't deserve . . ."

"Oh, shut up! Just shut up and kiss me, will you! Don't you think I've waited long enough?!"

It must be past nine o'clock and I could have sworn Ellie was sound asleep so what's she doing now, standing in her bedroom doorway in her pajamas, holding her teddy bear and rubbing her eyes and saying, "YUCK! You're KISSING!"

"Back to bed, now," I tell her gently, leading her back to her room while Alex takes the roses into the kitchen to find a vase or two, or several very large bowls, to put them in.

And as I cover her up with the duvet she gives me a tired little smile and says, "Tell me the story again, Mummy."

"Not tonight, Ellie. Another time."

"But Mummy! I've forgotten how it ended!"

"Happily, Ellie. It ended happily. That's all you need to know."

And can it really? Can it really all end happily ever after, or does that only happen in children's stories? Can I really believe we're going to make it, when all the odds seem to be stacked against anybody's relationship with anybody making it these days? When everyone's lives seem to be in a mess, and no one seems to want to clean up after themselves. Who can say how long it'll be before we fuck it all up?

I think I'm just going to have to close my eyes, jump straight in, and start swimming like hell.

Here I go. Wish me luck . . .

READY OR NOT

Rosie Peacock feels like her life is over. She works all day with plenty of hot, young doctors . . . but they're men who describe her as "comfortable as an old armchair." *Comfortable?* That's almost as bad as . . . well, "armchair." She wants to be (cue fireworks) interesting! Exciting! Alluring! Fascinating, even! OK—time for a new Rosie.

HERE SHE COMES

Now the girl who has always done the sensible thing— please see: dependable wife, mother, friend, and agreeable-to-the-point-of-being-a-doormat—is about to embark on a crazy, unpredictable, fabulously sexy ride that will surprise everyone, especially herself. Rosie's life is *far* from over. In fact, it's only just begun!

**Please turn the page for an exciting sneak peek of
Sheila Norton's
WILL SHE OR WON'T SHE?
coming next month in trade paperback!**

CHAPTER 1

The Old Armchair
Bites Back

It was purely a coincidence that on the same day I went to the Body and Soul lecture, P.J. told me I looked like an old armchair. And the trouble with pure coincidences is that no matter how much you rationalize and tell yourself there's nothing sinister about them and certainly nothing meaningful or spiritual about them, you can't help building them up into a big deal.

I wasn't feeling great about myself, to be totally honest, even before subjecting myself to Body and Soul. I only went along because of Sara's nagging. Sara does that to people. She doesn't call it nagging, of course – she calls it caring about people, and to be fair that's probably what it is, but in the course of her caring she manages to get them to do things they don't really want to do at all. Body and Soul was a good example. Who in their right mind, working in a hospital as we do and surrounded all day every day by the sick, wounded and mortally miserable of this world, would want to spend even half an hour of their spare time listening to a lecture with a title like that? Fun and Games, or even Peace and Quiet might perhaps have attracted a more enthusiastic cross section of the staff, and if I'd been responsible for promoting the monthly Occupational Health lecture (which thank God I wasn't – I had more than enough on my plate already), I'd have seriously contemplated calling it Kinky Sex and Threesomes to trick people into attending, and only giving out the leaflets about bodies and souls when the doors were locked.

"*Body and Soul* – Help for a Healthy Lifestyle." Sara had read out to me enthusiastically a few days earlier. "There you go, Rosie!"

"Where?" I responded sourly. "Where do I go?"

"To the Occupational Health Department. For their talk, Friday lunchtime. It sounds just exactly what you need!"

I wasn't offended. I'd spent most of the past few weeks (or maybe the past few months . . . or was it beginning to run into years?) complaining about my life, so she couldn't be blamed for suggesting that I needed something. Anything. Even an Occupational Health talk in my lunch break.

"I don't. I don't need anything. I'm fine, thank you."

"You're not."

She looked at me with this look she gives people who aren't fine. It's a look that's hard to describe, but it would break the heart of anyone in the throes of a personal tragedy and would probably make a baby animal roll over and lie on its back with its tongue hanging out.

"You keep on saying," she reminded me in her gentle, caring Mother Teresa voice, "about your life being crap."

"Yes, well, that's because it is. I don't need a half-hour lecture to tell me about it."

"But it says here" – she jabbed at the computer screen, pointing out the words of the e-mail as if they were messages from heaven rather than mistyped, badly spelled communications from Occupational Health – "it says *Change Your Life*. It says *Help for a Healthy Lifestyle*."

"Yuck. I don't do healthy. I don't do lifestyles."

"You haven't tried, Rosie." She looked at me accusingly, as if I was hurting her. "You've never really tried, have you, if you're honest?"

I have so!

I bloody have!

I've tried eating fruit, I have! I've tried cutting out chips and chocolate, and walking to the pub instead of taking the car!

"Piss off," I said.

"Well, I don't see what harm it could do," responded Sara, walking away from me with a sigh that would have had any weaker person running after her, feeling like shit, begging for forgiveness, wanting only to be given a copy of the e-mail and details of where to go for the lecture.

"Give me a copy of the e-mail, then," I said when I caught up with her. "Where do we have to go?"

At this point, before we go any deeper into Body and Soul, I suppose I should tell you about P.J. and how the whole armchair scenario came about.

P.J. had been working at the hospital for more than a year at this time, which was a reasonable length of time as medical contracts go, so we knew each other well enough to trade the odd insult or two. We could have a joke, we could have a laugh. We'd got past the stage of polite deference. But there still should have been a line beyond which it wasn't acceptable to go, and I'll tell you what that line was – or should have been, if it was there: a line of *understanding*. Understanding a person's feelings and what might hurt them. What might make them feel small, or insecure, or lie awake at night worrying about themselves.

The thing about P.J. was that he had two serious social problems. One, he was young, and two, he was male. He couldn't help it. He didn't mean anything by it. It just had the effect of making his mouth open without his permission, allowing a stream of total crap to emerge and devastate all around him. He was also a surgeon, and believe me, having worked with dozens, possibly hundreds, of them over the years I can tell you that this is another serious social disadvantage. They get used to telling people the brutal truth with no holds barred.

I'm afraid this is going to hurt you quite a lot.
We're going to have to take your leg off.
If we don't operate you're going to die.

"The nice thing about you," said P.J. on the day I amazed the Occupational Health Department of East Dean General Hospital by going to their lunchtime lecture and actually listening to it, "is that you make me feel comfortable."

He settled himself into the seat next to me with a self-satisfied grin as if he'd just paid me the greatest compliment he could imagine.

"Comfortable." I tried to smile but felt the muscles in my face resisting the effort. "*Comfortable*? It makes me sound like an old armchair!"

"That's it exactly!" he agreed with far too much enthusiasm. "A comfortable, cozy old armchair where I can relax after a hard day. That's how you feel, to me."

I was sitting, at the time, on not exactly a comfortable, cozy old armchair but the green vinyl bench seat that served for comfort in the outpatient staff coffee room, drinking something pink and disgusting that was supposed to make you lose weight without hunger pangs. It was only eleven o'clock and I was already hungry, so not only was it disgusting, it wasn't working and it was making me bad tempered. Or perhaps it was the hunger making me bad tempered.

"Thanks a *lot*!" I snapped, shaking off the hand he immediately laid on my arm and the apology he immediately tried to force on me. A *laughing* apology, which to my mind wasn't any nicer than the original insult.

"Come on, Rosie! I didn't mean . . ."

I took the glass with the dregs of the pink shit to the sink and rinsed it out briskly, running the tap too fast and getting sprayed with water in the process. I could hear him behind me, still sniggering.

"I was trying to be nice!"

"Well, you need to try harder," I responded, flouncing out of the room – a bit theatrically, I suppose, in retrospect, but how would *you* have felt? The last thing I wanted, at the age of forty-four, was to discover I was perceived as *comfortable*. It sounds so middle-aged! It sounds like women's institutes and jam making, knitting patterns and cocoa. It's got a smell of fear about it; the fear of growing older that I'd been trying to ignore ever since I turned forty. I didn't want to be comfortable! I wanted to be interesting, and exciting, and alluring, and even fascinating. Nobody thinks of comfortable old armchairs as fascinating, do they?

Oh, God. Forty-four and my life was over.

* * *

"**I**'m sure he didn't mean it like that," Becky tried to soothe me when I got back to my post and told her about it.

All very well for her to talk – all thirty-two years and 112 pounds of her.

"He's just being a normal thoughtless male."

Men could be excused anything in Becky's book, as long as they were good-looking and charming. Charming to *her*, that is – which most of them were, of course, what with her short skirts, her long dark hair and two-inch-long fluttering eyelashes. It wasn't even, quite honestly, as if P.J. was particularly good-looking; he was on the skinny side with big brown eyes that made him look a bit like a frightened rabbit. But at least he didn't look like an armchair.

Becky and Sara were my two colleagues on the out-patient reception desk. Unlike doctors, our job necessitated us being sweet, welcoming and diplomatic to people all the time, every day, no matter how rude they were to us or how we felt ourselves. It didn't mean we had to be sweet and diplomatic to each other, of course, and sometimes having a gripe and a bicker among ourselves was the only way to relieve the strain of being constantly nice. Trouble was, we had to bicker quietly so the patients couldn't hear.

"It'd be nice if you took *my* side for once!" I hissed at her, dumping a pile of patients' records on the desk in front of her, making her move her hands out of the way with a startled jump.

"Side?" she muttered. "Who's talking about taking sides? Since when have you and P.J. been at war?"

"Since now. Since he called me an old armchair."

Wars have been fought over less serious things, if you ask me. P.J. had better watch out.

"Well, anyway," interjected Sara, who'd been half listening to our exchange while dealing with the problems of a pregnant woman who'd somehow turned up at the surgical clinic instead of the natal clinic, "perhaps you'll feel better about yourself after we've been to the talk."

"Talk? What talk?" I asked her tetchily.

"You know. The Occupational Health one. At lunchtime. *Body and Soul*."

"Oh, great. That's all I need. Insults and boredom, all in one day."

"You said you'd come . . ." she reminded me, looking at me over the top of her glasses.

"Yeah, OK, OK, I'll come."

Anything for a laugh. It couldn't make me feel any worse than I felt after being called an old armchair, could it?

Well, yes, as it happened, it could.

Sara and I were a bit late getting to the talk so we sneaked into seats in the back row and tried to hide behind the people in front. The Occupational Health nurse, who was tall and muscular and looked as though she went to the gym twice a day and spent her spare time climbing mountains, was writing on the whiteboard at the front of the lecture room. The board was divided into two halves and BODY was written in big capitals at the top of the left hand side, and SOUL on the right hand side. Underneath BODY were two words so far: SIZE and WEIGHT. Should I get up and go now, or would that immediately attract so much attention to my *Size* and *Weight* that it would be better to crawl out on all fours?

Someone near the front put her hand up and called out: "Fitness!" and Mountaineering Woman nodded enthusiastically and wrote FITNESS on the board under SIZE and WEIGHT. I slouched farther down in my chair. It appeared this was a class participation exercise.

"For the benefit of those who've just joined us," she said in a booming cheery voice, obviously developed during the course of years yodelling across mountain ranges – putting paid to any hope I still had of crawling out of the room, "what we're doing here is, we're sharing suggestions of words that talk to us about our Body Image."

There was an expectant silence in the room. I gradually became aware of the fact that everyone was looking around at Sara and me. That, in fact, Mountaineering Woman was staring straight at us herself.

"So!" she boomed. "Any suggestions, you two at the back?"

How unfair is that? Just because someone arrives late at the lecture, probably already stressed out because they've had trouble getting away from the line of patients waiting to abuse them at the reception desk, why pick on them like that and show them up in front of the whole class? I glanced sideways at Sara, who was smiling back at Teacher with a look of pleasant, interested cooperation and obviously no intention whatsoever of contributing. Sara turned to me and raised her eyebrows.

"Rosie?" she asked out loud.

Well, thanks, friend! With the spotlight now fully and solely concentrated on me, I said the first thing that came into my head – which, perhaps not surprisingly, was:

"Armchair!"

"*Armchair?*" repeated Yodelling Woman, rubbing her head as if for inspiration. "The word *armchair* speaks to you about your body image?"

"Yes."

"How very interesting . . ." she lied, turning to write it on the board nevertheless. "Can you . . . er, explain . . . ?"

"An old armchair," I told her, feeling my voice rising with indignation as I recalled the insult again, "is something comfortable to collapse on."

A titter went around the room. Did I say something funny?

"*Comfortable*," repeated Teacher, writing that on the board too. Must have been short of suggestions before we came in. She turned to look back at me. "So you feel comfortable about your body?"

"No!" Are you joking? Does anybody? "No," I repeated sadly, and the tittering died away and more heads turned to look around at me. Who was this madwoman, anyway, who came in late and started ranting about armchairs? "What I feel is . . . old. Old and battered and not . . . not very exciting."

The heads all turned back to the front again, probably embarrassed now. There were a few coughs and then one or two more hands went up, one or two more suggestions were called out – sensible suggestions, about diet and dental hygiene, and the prevention of constipation. Nothing else about items of furniture. But I noticed Mountaineeress looking at me once or twice and I could almost have thought she was smiling.

"What we're looking at here," she announced finally, having filled the left hand half of the whiteboard with what (apart from ARMCHAIR) looked like the jumbled up chapter headings of a Family Medical Encyclopedia, "is the sum of your insecurities about your physical selves."

There was a murmur of protest from some of the ranks.

Insecurities? retorted the surprised expression of a particularly beautiful young nurse in the front row who quite obviously didn't have any.

Insecurities? muttered a burly porter sitting just in front of me who didn't seem too sure what it meant.

Insecurities, I thought with a nod of agreement. She's hit the nail on the head. Every single word on that board made me feel insecure, even the date at the top. I sat up a bit straighter and began to take more interest. Perhaps the mountain air had sharpened her brain after all.

"Now, perhaps that gives you a clue," she called out with a fresh burst of enthusiasm, "to what I'm looking for, for the right hand side?"

She tapped the blank half of the whiteboard with her pen and looked around the room expectantly. Silence. Everyone had become too insecure to speak. She looked at me. I was trying to duck behind the porter's head but he kept moving.

"Rosie?" she prompted.

Trust Sara to announce my name to the world. That was it, now – I was marked for life.

I shrugged.

"Not sure what you mean by *soul*," I admitted.

"Soul, mind, heart, call it what you will. I'm talking about the *you* inside your body. Your personality. Your spirit. Give me a word that sums up your own image of yourself . . . *inside*."

Jesus, God, this was like being stripped naked and put on display in a shop window. I could feel myself cringing. Why me? Hadn't I already been punished for being late? Ask someone else, please, Teacher – let someone else go first . . .

"Kind. Fair," called out a low-grade manager from personnel with a nervous tic that resembled an attack of the hiccups.

I stared at her. How did she get the guts to go first, when that was all she could come up with? *Kind? Fair?* What sort of a self-image was that? I'd rather die than admit to having such a mealy-mouthed, pathetic, nondescript self-image. I'd rather think of myself as . . .

"Dynamic! Creative! Charismatic!"

Where the fuck did *that* come from? I felt myself blush scarlet as the tittering started up again all around me. Sara was nudging me.

"Well done!" she said, pointing to the Mountaineering Woman who was writing my words on the board with pleased, decisive strokes.

"Good," she announced. "Anyone else?"

As the right hand side of the board gradually filled up with the equivalent of a psychiatric report on a patient with a multiple personality disorder, I sat in stunned silence, seeing only those three words:

Dynamic – Creative – Charismatic.

I listened, genuinely interested, as Mountaineering Woman explained her theory of *Help for a Healthy Lifestyle*. It didn't matter, she explained, how much attention you paid to the left hand side of the board, if you didn't get the right hand side sorted out at the same time. Think what your own self-image was telling you. If you thought of yourself as slim and fit on the left hand side, but the stuff on the right was all negative, perhaps you were too obsessed with your physical appearance and should go to the gym less and make a few more friends at the pub. If your physical self-image was bad but you were happy in yourself, maybe all you needed was a good diet.

"All a bit obvious, really," whispered Sara, looking disappointed.

I lingered behind at the end of the lecture.

"Are you all right, Rosie?" asked Mountaineeress as she passed me on the way out of the room.

"Yes. Thanks."

I hesitated.

"Can I ask you something?"

"Of course!" She smiled.

Must have done her self-image a power of good.

"What would you say," I asked, quietly, in case anyone was listening, "to someone whose body image was an armchair and whose soul image was Creative, Dynamic and Charismatic?"

"Get out of the armchair," she said at once, looking at me so directly that I suddenly felt as if I were in church, talking to the vicar. "And get creative, Rosie! Get dynamic! Be charismatic!"

Well, I probably would if I knew how, wouldn't I?

"**W**ould you call me dynamic?" I asked Barry while we were getting in each other's way in the kitchen that evening.

We always got in each other's way if we were both in the kitchen at the same time. Or anywhere else at the same time, come to that. Right then I was trying to peel things and chop things for a stir-fry. He was trying to fill up the kettle to make a coffee, and seemed to have to do a lot of elbowing me, dripping water over my hands and knocking cupboard doors against me in the process.

"Mm," he said, sitting down at the kitchen table with the newspapers to wait for the kettle to boil.

Couldn't do anything else while the kettle was boiling, of course, being a man.

"What do you mean, *Mm*? That's not an answer. I want an answer. Am I dynamic, or charismatic?" I paused, waiting for him to show some sign of listening, and then went on regardless: "Or would you think of me more in terms of being . . ."

He raised his eyes slowly from the paper. Possibly listening, possibly wondering whether the kettle was boiling.

". . . comfortable? Like an old armchair?"

He stared at me blankly.

"Well?" I demanded, waving a half peeled carrot at him. "Well?"

There was a resigned look about him, the look of someone who knows he's got absolutely no chance of saying the right thing, that he's a doomed man and he might just as well give up now.

"What's brought all this on?" he asked, trying to buy some time.

I sighed and turned back to chopping the carrots. I didn't want to tell him that a guy at work, ten years my junior, had called me an old armchair. He'd find it far too difficult not to laugh out loud, and far too tempting to use it as ammunition in future arguments.

So what if I'm lazy and selfish and bad-tempered – at least I don't look like an old armchair!

"I don't want to get middle-aged," I said instead, crossly, throwing bits of carrot into a pan.

"What are you talking about, you silly girl?"

A little healing wave of warmth began to creep back into my old, cold, frightened bones. Perhaps I was worrying unnecessarily. At least Barry didn't see me as an old armchair. It's true he didn't ever really look at me at all anymore, but maybe if he did, if he made the effort and really thought about it, he wouldn't just see me as Rosie, plain, dumpy, mousy-haired, boring old Rosie, but someone dynamic and charismatic that he fell in love with all those years ago.

"Of *course* you're middle-aged!" he went on calmly, returning to his paper. "We all are, aren't we? You have to face it sooner or later, Rosie, old girl!"

* * *

*O*ld girl! Bloody old girl!

I stomped around the kitchen, throwing vegetables into the pan with increasing venom, watching them spit in the hot oil and wanting to spit back at them. I elbowed Barry back, hard, when he got in my way again getting the milk out of the fridge.

"What's up with you?" he asked aggressively. "Bad day at work?"

What's up with me! How could he have forgotten already, after only about three and a half minutes, that he'd just called me middle-aged *and* old within the space of two sentences? Could he really not see that he'd just insulted me, done irreparable damage to my self-esteem and then just carried on reading a news report about high winds and storms in western France?

"*S*o how long has this been going on, then?" I demanded eventually, halfway through the meal which we'd eaten up till then in silence.

"What?" He looked at me warily. "How long has what been going on? And what's the matter?"

"How long have I been an *old girl*? How long have you thought of me as old, and boring, and . . ."

"Oh, I see." He nodded with satisfaction, proud of himself for working out what the problem was. "For God's sake, Rosie – you *ask* me what I think, and when I tell you, you don't like it."

Of course I don't, you idiot. You're supposed to lie.

"I didn't say you were boring," he added, looking at me as if he was considering it. "But what's the point of pretending? We're middle-aged, both of us."

"Well, I don't want to be," I retorted, childishly.

"What about me?"

Just like a man. Turn the conversation around to himself when he's not getting any attention.

"What do you mean, what about you?"

"Well, you can't tell me you don't think of *me* as middle-aged."

Fortunately I had a mouthful of dinner. I slowed down my chewing and swallowing so I had time to think of a response. Here was the difference between us, you see: I was far more considerate of his feelings. I didn't want to stick in the knife and twist it, the way he did. But there was no getting away from the fact that he'd hit the nail on the head. Of course I thought of *him* as middle-aged! Barry had been middle-aged since he was about twenty-five! He pottered about in his greenhouse muttering to himself. He talked about the 60s as the Good Old Days. He moaned about teenagers and pop music and people not talking properly. Sometimes I felt like I was still living with my father.

I finished my mouthful. I had to say something.

"Well, if I'm middle-aged then you must be, too," I allowed resentfully.

He smiled and got back to his dinner, quite happy with this.

"I'm not putting up with it!" I told him, throwing my fork down. "I don't want to be middle-aged and I *don't* want to be comfortable!"

"So what are you going to do?" he asked with a sigh, looking at me as if I were a rather wearing pupil in one of his remedial classes.

What indeed?

What do you do about an old armchair? Buy new cushions for it? Cover it in red velvet? Have it resprung and reupholstered?

"I'm going to reinvent myself," I declared, with a lot

more confidence than I felt and ignoring the fact that it sounded absolutely ridiculous. "I'm going to become a new person. I'm going to become dynamic, creative, and charismatic."

"Well, bloody good for you," said Barry mildly, getting up to put his plate in the dishwasher. "Is there any of that pudding left over from yesterday?"

I'd better say at this point that I realize you must wonder why I was overreacting to this whole armchair and middle-age thing in such a Prima Donna fashion. *Why the big deal?* you must be asking yourself. *What's so terrible about going through life as a comfortable armchair, when there are people in the world who don't know where their next crust's coming from and haven't got a pot to piss in?* Well, I take your point. But in fairness to me, you should perhaps understand that, Barry aside, everything about my life was very youthful. For a start, I had three very youthful children, one and a half of whom were still living at home. Emma, the eldest, had already flown the family coop and settled in a far more interesting tree – a house share in London, the sharees being her boyfriend, Tom, and an assortment of other bright young things. The half-flown fledgling was our second daughter, Natasha – in her first year at Leicester University and making brief but colorful weekend appearances in the house from time to time, followed by longer stays during the vacations when she reclaimed her bedroom, her stereo system and rights of ownership over the dog. This ownership had been in fierce dispute since she left for university, when Stuart, our youngest, decided that as he was expected to feed, walk, and entertain him while Natasha was away, Biggles would henceforth be known as his dog. Biggles, by the way, was also very youthful, having been born out of wedlock to a cocker spaniel mother and a large brown shaggy father of indiscriminate breed only a few months before the departure for university.

When the kids had all been little helpless creatures, crying in strollers and throwing up on rugs, I used to have a vision of the days ahead when they'd all be grown up, charming, sensible people who'd take their cups out to the kitchen, offer to put the trash out, and have conversations. You know, proper family conversations about serious, interesting things. Politics, religion, and whose turn it was to put out the trash. Instead, at this point in my life, Stuart and a succession of his friends spent their time racing in one door of the house and out of another, dropping school bags and football bags as they went, the conversation never really progressing much beyond:

Where are you going?
Out.
When will you be back?
Dunno.
What about your homework?
Ain't got any.

Their youth, energy, and verbal penury wore me out. I watched them, and felt my life ebbing away. I spoke to them, and heard my words echoing in an abyss of wasted breath.

And then I went to work and was confronted by the young and lovely Becky, and the younger-than-me, lovelier-than-me Sara, and about a hundred attractive young men and women in white coats who didn't look old enough to be medical students never mind fully fledged doctors.

All right, I admit it. I had a problem.

Got the picture? See where I was coming from?

I didn't want to be the old battered armchair in a life full of beautiful modern furnishings.

I wasn't going to sit back and accept it; I was going to fight back!

At some point in the future I was going to look back on this day and think – that was the turning point: the day of the Body and Soul lecture.

I loaded the dishwasher, went to bed and dreamed that the Mountaineering Woman was chasing me around the hospital car park and everyone was laughing at me.

But I'd show them! You see if I didn't!